STARR FAITHFULL & SOME UNKNOWN PERSON

Add to the fascinating lost souls of the flapper era, Starr Faithfull. Add to the page-turning chronicles of unsolved mysteries ingeniously solved, *Some Unknown Person*.

"SPELLBINDING . . . Scoppettone weaves fact and fiction together as she retells the story of Starr's eventful life."

—*Library Journal*

"STUNNING . . . This factual-fictional story of the girl John O'Hara wrote about in *Butterfield 8* is a stunning, sophisticated book."

—*UPI*

"ENTERTAINING—an interesting idea presented in an interesting way."

—*The New York Times Book Review*

"SANDRA SCOPPETTONE has unraveled the Starr Faithfull enigma in a convincing and marvelously ironic finale."

—Sumner Locke-Elliott

Some Unknown Person

by Sandra Scoppettone

BANTAM BOOKS · LONDON · TORONTO · NEW YORK

For Linda,
with love

This low-priced Bantam Book
has been completely reset in a type face
designed for easy reading, and was printed
from new plates. It contains the complete
text of the original hard-cover edition.
NOT ONE WORD HAS BEEN OMITTED.

SOME UNKNOWN PERSON
*A Bantam Book / published by arrangement with
G. P. Putnam's Sons*

PRINTING HISTORY
Putnam's edition published August 1977
Bantam edition / June 1978

ISBN 0-553-11731-9

Published simultaneously in the United States and Canada

*Bantam Books are published by Bantam Books, Inc. Its trade-
mark, consisting of the words "Bantam Books" and the por-
trayal of a bantam, is registered in the United States Patent
Office and in other countries. Marca Registrada. Bantam
Books, Inc., 666 Fifth Avenue, New York, New York 10019.*

PRINTED IN THE UNITED STATES OF AMERICA

Acknowledgments

Special thanks to: John Anderson, Alice Smith Constable, Inge Coogan, Winifred Fix, Ernest Leogrande, Marijane Meaker, Susan Ramunni and Marcelle Walsh.

On June 8, 1931, Daniel Moriarty, a beachcomber, discovered on an early morning search for salable drift the body of a young woman. The place was Long Beach, New York. The woman was Starr Faithfull. She was twenty-five years old, had been a resident of 12 St. Luke's Place in New York City and was the daughter of Helen and Frank W. Wyman. When they divorced years before, Helen remarried Stanley E. Faithfull. Starr had one sister, Elisabeth Tucker Faithfull, who was five years her junior.

Besides having an unusual and poetic name, Starr was exceptionally beautiful. She was also alcoholic, a pill and ether addict, and had been seduced by Andrew J. Peters, a prominent and respectable forty-five-year-old man, when she was eleven. The relationship lasted nine years. These were the ingredients that went into the selling of hundreds of thousands of newspapers that hot and uneventful summer of 1931.

Elvin N. Edwards, District Attorney of Nassau County where the body had been found, grabbed onto the case of Starr Faithfull like a man on a mission. The autopsy said death was by drowning. Starr was a champion swimmer. There was no alcohol in her system. There was enough Veronal to induce sleep, not death. Both Edwards and Stanley Faithfull insisted Starr had been murdered.

Even after suicide letters were produced—pronounced forged by one professional, genuine by another—Edwards

1

tenaciously held to his murder theory. In the June 30th *New York Daily News*, under a headline which read STARR'S SUICIDE NOTES FOUND GENUINE, Mr. Edwards proclaimed: "But the case is not closed. We will continue to work on the theory that she met her fate through the hands of some unknown person."

In 1977 the case is still on the books: UNSOLVED.

One

August 6, 1977
Orange, New Jersey

The end. It had to be. Finally. Seventy-two. He wasn't going to make seventy-three. Thank Christ! He hated life. There was nothing after death, he was sure of that. That was one of the few things he knew. She had known that, too. What was it she had said in her letter? He couldn't remember. He had to remember. Why?

Orlando heard the door open. Who was it? If only he could turn his head. Steps. He shifted his eyes to the left. Now they were in his line of vision. A man. A woman. White. Doctor and nurse?

"He's awake," she said.

"Good morning," the doctor said.

He couldn't answer. Didn't they know he couldn't? What were they saying now?

"Can you hear me, Mr. Antolini?" said the doctor.

He heard.

"What's the pulse rate?"

Pulse rate. Respiration. Heart beat. What difference did it make? He was dying. Surely they knew that. If *he* knew, they must know. What was it she had said in her letter? It was about afterlife. Something about fifty million priests.

3

His eyes looked straight ahead. Up. White. Walls green. Ceiling white. He closed his eyes. They were still talking. He could feel the tears welling up. Spilling over. Running down.

"He's crying," she said.

He's crying, he thought. Someone wiped at his temples, ears.

"Can you hear me? Open your eyes and blink once if you can hear."

If he could have laughed he would have. He kept his eyes shut. They felt too heavy to open. Now his eyes were like every other part of his body. Unmovable. Was he dead? No. He could still hear them.

"It's total," said the doctor.

"But the eyes," she said.

"Yes. Strange."

Strange. That was him, all right. He tried to think of the words people had used to describe him. Depressed. Moody. High-strung. Witty. Handsome. Intelligent. Talented. Failure. Selfish. Chump. Chump. That word kicked at him, unlike the others. He felt it in his stomach. Chump. A stupid word. *Don't be a chump.* He opened his eyes. Ceiling. He shifted them to the left. To the right. He listened. Silence, except for a hum. He was alone. He had always been alone. Wife, parents, daughter, friends . . . still alone.

He closed his eyes. Tired. He needed sleep. If he slept he might not wake up. Fear. But wasn't that what he wanted? There would be no getting better. He hadn't really gotten better after the first stroke and this one was a thousand times worse. It was a matter of time now. Hours? Days? Weeks? Not years . . . never years. That would be too cruel. Death would be a relief. But what if there *was* an afterlife? What then? He hadn't meant to . . . surely that would be understood. Understood? By whom? Was he crazy? There was no afterlife. What had she said in her letter? Something about fifty million priests. Afterlife . . . dirty trick. Yes. That was part of it. If there was an afterlife it would be a dirty trick. She had said that in her letter. But wasn't it all a dirty trick? Everything. All of it. Trick. Priests. Chump.

January 26, 1906
Evanston, Illinois

Frank Wyman sat staring at his knees. His arms hung down at his sides and his chin rested on the knot of his tie. He sniffed. The hospital smell even permeated this closed-off waiting room. How long had he been waiting? He reached into his hip pocket and pulled out the gold watch his parents had given him at graduation. He read the inscription as he did almost every time. *F.W.W. Harvard 1900.* That's all. Not who it was from. Not love. Never love. It was two minutes before nine. He snapped the watch shut and returned it to his pocket. He had been waiting for seven hours.

Why did women always go into labor in the middle of the night? Frank stood up, stretched his large body, adjusted his glasses and blew his nose. Not that he really knew anything about women and labor. This was his first child. Naturally, he hoped he would have a son. He ran a finger around the inside of his collar and thought about that. Was it true? Did he want a son? Men always wanted sons, didn't they? He stared out the window. He could see The Loop, could see his office building. It made him sad. Homesick. Boston was so much nicer. Well, they wouldn't stay in Illinois forever. Massachusetts was his home and he intended to go back. He knew Helen didn't like Evanston. She was anonymous here and Helen liked being known. She liked being socially prominent. Here her family background was meaningless. She was discontent. But perhaps now, with a baby, she would be more fulfilled.

A baby. Helen's baby. He had gotten into the habit of thinking of the coming child as Helen's. Now, sitting here, it slowly dawned on him that the baby was his, too. Of course, he wouldn't have too much to do with it. He wouldn't be expected to change it. Or feed it. He smiled. Well, he couldn't very well do that, could he? Damn. Frank could feel the color rising up the back of his neck. Wasn't that the limit? There he was all by himself and he was blushing. It never failed.

He walked back to the hard wooden chair and sat down, stretching his legs out in front of him. So what about this baby? It was almost impossible to think about it in the abstract. Maybe after he saw it. After all, what was there to think about something that didn't exist yet? He felt uncomfortable. Itchy. As though someone were watching him steal an apple from the greengrocer's, something he had done only once and not because he couldn't pay but because he wanted to be like the other boys. Why was he feeling that now? In the back of his mind he knew. He was lying to himself. It wasn't because the baby didn't exist yet that he couldn't think of it as his. It was because—he really didn't want it. Oh, Jesus. If anyone knew. Certainly Helen had accused him of that many times during her pregnancy but he had always denied it. And often convinced her. He was sweating now. He wished he could take off his jacket.

Frank stood up, ran a hand through his thick black hair and walked to the window again. The truth was he was too damn young. He couldn't help it. That's what he felt. It didn't matter that millions of other twenty-four-year-old men had children—*he* was too young. He had been too young to get married less than two years ago and he was too young now to be a father.

"Mr. Wyman?"

He whirled around, feeling caught with that damned apple.

"You have a daughter. Congratulations," the nurse said, smiling.

"A daughter?"

"That's right. Five pounds, six ounces."

"Five pounds, six ounces," he repeated. "Thank you."

She stared at him a moment and just before she turned he remembered to smile.

* * *

Helen was feeling very weak. And very proud. She had finally accomplished something, seen something through to its natural conclusion. She hadn't been sure she would be able to do it. But she had. If she hadn't felt so nauseated, she would have yelled that right out to Frank as he came through the door. I did it, she would have shouted.

He took her hand and kissed her cheek.

She smiled.

"You're very pale," he said.

She closed her eyes. Is that all he could say? Didn't he care? Didn't he understand? She'd never believed he wanted the baby anyway. Was this some kind of proof?

"Of course," he went on, "your skin is exceptionally fair."

Was he crazy talking about her skin when somewhere down the hall was a five-pound six-ounce baby who belonged to them? A baby girl. Oh, dear. Was that it? He was angry because she hadn't given him a son. After all, they hadn't even thought of girls' names. Not that Frank had really participated in thinking of names. She had tried out all sorts of names with Wyman. He either said nothing or grunted. Finally, she had settled on Andrew, the name of her second cousin who had been in the Massachusetts house of representatives and senate. Andrew J. Peters was going places and it wouldn't hurt to name a baby after him. You never knew.

But she couldn't name a girl Andrew. A girl. She didn't mind that. Girls were nice. Easier than boys, they said. But Frank. She looked at his somber face, the brown eyes revealing nothing.

"Are you angry?"

"Angry? About what?"

"The baby. A girl."

"Of course not."

He wouldn't say if he were. It had been pointless to ask him.

"I'm sorry," she said.

"Nonsense," he said.

She looked at him sitting stiffly next to her bed. She supposed they must think of a name. She wanted her child to be special and the name was very important. Andrew had been perfect. Although the name was rather common, the man was not. He was very special. A rising star. Star. If you wanted your child to be a star why not just say so? Star. She smiled.

"Frank?"

"Yes?"

"I want to name her Starr . . . with two r's. S-t-a-r-r. Starr."

"Whatever you like," he said.

"Yes," she said. "Starr."

February 14, 1906
Jamaica Plains, Boston, Mass.

A letter to Andrew J. Peters from his mother.

DEAR HEART,

As you can see by the date it is Saint Valentine's Day, a day of lavender, lace and love. A day, my darling son, when you should be with one who loves you: me, of course! However, I am understanding and know that only the demands of your career would take you away from me on this day of true hearts. I shall survive, as always, even though the absence of your grand countenance leaves me empty and wanting.

Aside from missing you these last weeks, I have been very busy. I headed the committee for the February Dance at The Somerset and, as you know, the women I have to deal with on these committees are brainless incompetents. So your poor mother was left with the complete responsibility. Naturally, it was a great success and though the President could not attend he sent me a personal note (I have saved it to show you) and signed it "Teddy." What do you think of that, dear boy?

Your father is in good health and good spirits. I suppose it has something to do with the new business merger.

Your sisters are their usual petulant selves. You, my darling Rew, have never given me a moment's worry, but Mary and Catherine are forever complaining and fussing about something.

Here is some family news. Your second cousin Helen McGregor Pierce Wyman has had a child. She and her husband, Frank (we decided he looked as though he would not add up to much—remember?) moved to Evanston shortly after they were married (a dreary wedding, but we had a number of laughs over his side of the family). At any rate, guess, my love, what they have named their daughter? Starr. Have you ever heard of anything more ridiculous? Starr. I almost laughed aloud when I heard. Well, what can you expect from someone like young Helen. She has never seemed completely right to me, if you know what I mean. I despair of ever understanding that part of the family!

Oh, dear Rew, how lonely it must be for you to stay in a dreary hotel and how tedious all those political meetings themselves. Of course, I suppose you get used to it all and that it's a necessary price to pay for holding political office. And don't misunderstand, my love. I shall be as thrilled to see you in the National Congress as I have been to watch your splendid performance in the state legislature. And, after all—dare I say it?—those posts are all stepping stones toward the highest office of all! Just the thought of you in the White House makes me tingle all over. Of course, I probably will not live to see it.

But enough of this morbidity! If your current meetings are necessary to your career, so be it. And I have no doubt you'll go to the Congress. Thank God I have a wonderful son to make my dreams come true. What would I do if I had *three* silly girls? I think I should take my life. Now do not scold me for saying that. And do not misunderstand. I have not had any bad thoughts for a long time. I promised you I would never do that again and I will not.

I suppose I must bring this letter to a close. I am seeing Harriet James at One and it is nearly Eleven now. Do take care of yourself, Rew. It has been so cold and I know how you are about mufflers and gloves and such—try to remember, dearest heart. If anything happened to you then I *would* end this arid existence. I live only for you, Andrew. Know that I love you with all my being and especially miss you on this day of days. Soon.

Your loving mother,
MARY

October 5, 1906
Newark, New Jersey

"What does wop mean, Papa?" Silvio asked.

Silence fell over the Antolinis as all heads turned toward the man at the head of the table. He removed his pince-nez, holding it between forefinger and thumb and, with his other hand, ran a finger down his nose, then touched each side of his trim mustache. His gaze settled on his five-year-old son.

"Why do you ask?"

The set of his father's jaw terrified Silvio. Perhaps he shouldn't have asked. But Papa said always to ask when you didn't understand. He looked at Mama. She was watching him, waiting for his answer. They were all waiting except for Orlando in the high chair who was still spooning food into his mouth. But what did he know? He was only two. This was his birthday party. Silvio looked at Nina, the oldest, then Connie. They were both waiting. Even four-year-old Toni was watching him.

"I am waiting, Silvio."

He had to answer. There was nothing to fear. He hadn't done anything. Still, sometimes you couldn't tell with Papa.

"A boy said it."

"A boy. What boy?" He returned the pince-nez to the bridge of his aquiline nose.

Orlando banged his plate and let out an absurd giggle. The girls hid their amusement behind their hands.

"Stai zitta!" Orlando Sr. roared. He was not above lapsing into Italian although he demanded that everyone else, except for his wife, speak English in his home. Orlando Jr. didn't understand much in either language but he comprehended his father now. He shoved a spoon in his mouth and looked wide-eyed at him.

"What boy, Silvio?"

"A boy on the street."

"His name?"

"I don't know." He began sliding down in his chair, knowing this answer would displease his father.

"You do not know? Is it your habit to engage in conversations with strangers?"

Silvio stared at him.

"Answer me!"

What could he say? Engage in conversations? What did that mean? Silvio felt like crying. He had to say something. "He was just a boy, Papa. He told me I was a wop."

Antonia looked away from her husband. She knew how this slur would affect him. He was a proud man with a fine education and a successful law firm. A member of the Roman aristocracy, a soldier in the Italian Cavalry. To be called a wop was almost more than he could endure.

She looked back at him. The muscles in his cheek danced as he looked coldly at his oldest son. This was rare. He adored the boy. Silvio, a brilliant child, was beginning to show great facility on the piano and this endeared him even more to his music-loving father.

"Mama," Orlando said.

"Shhhh," she said. No one must talk when Papa was speaking or thinking. Not even a two-year-old. Especially not this two-year-old. Antonia didn't know why, she couldn't put her finger on it, but she knew that her husband did not really like his namesake. His dislike was subtle but clear to a mother's eyes.

She listened now as Orlando Sr. explained the word "wop" to Silvio. Nina had also been called this once and had come to her mother for an explanation. Antonia had not bothered to inform Orlando of the incident. Just as she did not bother to inform him of the baptism of each of her children in the Catholic Church. He was an atheist who expected his wife and his children to be atheists as well. There were some things he was better off not knowing.

"Pa-pa," Orlando squealed.

"Antonia! Is it impossible for you to keep that boy quiet?"

"Orlando, per favore, it is his birthday."

"Fa!" He threw down his napkin, pushed back his heavy carved chair and stalked from the room.

Orlando Jr. began to cry and Antonia lifted him from his high chair. She kissed his sweet black hair, his dimpled cheeks.

"Shhhh," she whispered. "Don't cry, bambino. Shhhh."

December 2, 1906
Darien, Connecticut

In the small room on the third floor of the Butterfield house, Stanley E. Faithfull changed from his wedding clothes into his traveling suit. It was over. He was married.

He sat on the edge of the bed running his hand up and down the rounded brass bedpost. It was cold. As cold as he imagined Margaret's body would be. He was sure she would be frigid. After all, she was a spinster until he came along and made things right for her. She was thirty-four years old and a woman didn't get to that age unmarried unless something was wrong. He was thirty-four also but he had stayed unmarried by design. A man should be established in business before he married and began a family. True, most men were on their way sooner than he but he'd had a lot of bad breaks. And, of course, no chance for an education. Sometimes he wondered if things would have been different had his family remained in England. He was nine when they came from London to Decorah, Iowa, in 1873.

As he started to button his shoes he remembered those first painful years and how he struggled to lose the English accent that made his life hell. By the time the family had moved to Sioux Falls two years later he was completely accepted by his peers as an American from Decorah.

He had been happy in Sioux Falls for the five years they'd lived there. He managed to make two friends, something he didn't do easily, and to pass from one grade to the next. He would have graduated but, once again, his father, failing at one more business, moved the family to Minneapolis. His father insisted then he leave school and help out at home. His sister, Evalina, was not well and doctor bills, plus his father's penchant for failure, made young Stanley's assistance essential. Within a week after he'd quit school, Evalina died.

Grieving for her, he packed a satchel and set out for Los Angeles the night after the funeral.

Stanley stood up and looked at himself in the mirror. He was definitely losing his hair. There was no doubt that his hairline had receded at least half an inch in the last two or three years. He poked at the temples, trying to fluff it out just the tiniest bit. That way, his ears wouldn't be quite so prominent. He sighed. When his hair was gone, with those ears and that tiny mouth, he was going to look ridiculous. Well, at least his eyes were good. Knock wood. Maybe he should grow a mustache. Just a small one. He'd think about it. Stanley picked up the stiff collar from the dresser and attached it to his shirt. Yes, he'd come a long way.

After six months in Los Angeles, working at various odd and dirty jobs, he saved enough money to go east. Eventually, he wound up in Boston. Having always looked older than his years, he lied about his age and experience and got a job as Assistant Bookkeeper with Phipps & Tarbell, grain jobbers. He excelled at mathematics so learning to keep books was easy for him.

In 1900, after eight years with Phipps & Tarbell and two years with the American Cereal Co., Stanley decided it was time to start his own grain-jobbing business. Why work for other people? Even though the specter of his father loomed large, he opened his office in the Chamber of Commerce building. It was not as easy as he thought and within a year he closed his doors.

Now he was back with the American Cereal Co. He hated his job but he didn't plan to stay there forever. Stanley had lots of plans.

"Darn," he whispered to the mirror as he pulled open the bow tie for the second time.

There was nothing wrong with wanting nice things. Here he was, his life most likely half over, and all he had was an apartment in Jamaica Plains and a respectable job. He smiled. And now Margaret. It wasn't as though he were marrying her for her money alone. He liked her. Besides, she didn't have *that* much money. Just enough to elevate him to a station in life where he could begin to use his ingenuity and maybe get a break. The two most important things in life were contacts and money, and Margaret had them both. That's why his father had failed over and over. He'd had neither. With Margaret, Stanley just might have a chance.

"Ah," he murmured, getting the tie right. He reached for his gray jacket.

There was a knock at the door.

"Yes?"

"It's me, Stanley."

"Come in."

Margaret's youngest brother, Brooks, stood smiling in the doorway. "She's all ready."

"I'll be down in a moment."

Brooks took a step farther into the room and closed the door, shutting out the sounds of people and music from below.

"Can I ask you something, Stanley? I mean, we are brothers-in-law now."

Stanley felt suddenly awkward. What could this Harvard sophomore possibly want of him?

"I hope you won't think it's presumptuous of me or anything."

"What is it?" He noticed that Brooks was tilting to one side and realized the young man was drunk.

"Do you really love Margaret?"

"That *is* presumptuous and . . ."

"I mean, God, she's my sister and everything but God, she's so damn ugly!"

Stanley crossed to the door and opened it. Pieces of "Love's Old Sweet Song" crept up the stairs. "I think you'd better join the others," he said.

"Oh, come on, Stan, don't be an old sourpuss." He flung an arm around Stanley's shoulder.

If there was one thing Stanley couldn't stand it was a person who couldn't handle his liquor. He shook off the young man's arm. "I think you'd better go downstairs, Brooks. We have nothing further to say to one another." Although the room was cool Stanley began to sweat.

"Okay, okay." Brooks stepped out into the hall but held the door open. "I got just one thing to say, Stan . . . you're a brave man and I thank you for not letting my sister stay an old maid. But, God in heaven, I don't know how you're gonna do it."

Stanley pushed the door shut and listened as Brooks laughed to himself going down the stairs.

Now Stanley was soaked with sweat. He had tried to convince himself that there were secret reasons why Margaret Butterfield hadn't married until the age of thirty-four. Even frigidity was more palatable than the obvious reason. But now Brooks had bared the truth. Stanley leaned on the nightstand. The marble felt good to his sweating hands.

How *was* he going to do it? Margaret Butterfield was one of the ugliest women he'd ever seen. Maybe *the* ugliest. Naturally, it would be dark. But would he be able to blot out her face from his memory? He closed his eyes. There she was. The crooked eyes and off-center nose. The huge thick lips with the dark hair above the upper one. What would happen if he saw that face in the dark? Would he be able to perform? He must get another mental image. Who? Laura. Margaret's younger, married sister was as beautiful as Margaret was ugly. He would set Laura's features firmly in his mind and when the time came he would pretend Margaret was Laura. It was the only way. He felt better.

Quickly, he checked his part, making sure it was exactly in the middle of his head. Then he brushed imaginary lint from his jacket. Once more he closed his eyes and saw Laura. I can do it, he told himself, shutting the door behind him. Then as Laura's features dissolved into Margaret's he held tight to the bannister for fear he would faint as he went down the stairs to meet his bride.

If it were suicide do you think I would be devoting so much energy to it?
—Elvin Edwards, *New York Times,* 30 June 1931

June 5, 1931
New York, New York

When Starr opened her eyes it was dark. But it was always dark in her cubbyhole of a room. There were no windows. No door. Just curtains to give her some privacy. She could have shared Tucker's room but it was so small. Anyway, Starr liked the idea of being close to the front door and not having to go through any other room to get to her own. Besides, how much time did she really spend in it?

Amazingly, she did not have a hangover. She stretched her long arms over her head. Well, old girl, she said to herself, today's the day. It made her feel wonderful.

There was the sound of a key in the front door. She remembered. Stanley had gone to Boston yesterday and must have returned by the night boat. She heard his voice as he went into his bedroom.

"Good morning, Helen dear."

That goddamned ass, she thought. Oh, well, it really didn't matter anymore. "Isn't that right, Peter?" she asked her seventeen-year-old cat who was curled up under her arm. She answered for him. "Nothing matters anymore. It's all up. I'm free."

As she swung her legs over the side of the bed it registered that this was the last time she would ever do that. She smiled. This was the happiest day of her life. And the last.

Two

August 6, 1977
Orange, New Jersey

He woke up. Fear. Where? He wanted to lift his head and could not and then he remembered. He was paralyzed. Hospital. His assumption was that it was Orange Memorial. Where else would he be taken? That's where you went to die, didn't you? That's where Fran had died. Of course, he never saw her there. He had never come to the hospital. How could he? He'd had his first stroke by then and couldn't be expected to go traipsing all over. Some people didn't understand but he knew she did and that's what counted. She'd never expected him to visit her. Of course, they spoke every day on the phone. The first two times she was in, they spoke. The third time—the last time—there was no more speaking.

He could still remember that last time when the ambulance came to take her back to the hospital. His sister Toni was there. She had been staying with them, helping. What could he do with his right arm useless, his right foot dragging? The right side of his face unmovable . . . almost. The doctor said it was only a minor stroke. What did he know? Always telling him about people who learned to write with their toes or some damn thing.

The attendants had gone right upstairs. When they

17

brought her down you could hardly see her on the litter she had gotten so small. He started crying. Usually, she yelled at him when he cried. "Oh, cut that out." "C'mon, you make me sick." But not that day. That day she looked up at him out of great sunken brown eyes and said: "I won't be coming back, you know." That was all. Nothing else. Not goodbye or I love you or anything. Just that. And then they'd taken her away. He never did see her again.

When she went out that door his last chance to tell went with her. After she died he thought about telling Cathy. But how could you tell a daughter something like that? How could you explain?

June 23, 1910
Boston, Massachusetts

Andrew stood in the cloister of Trinity Church. He looked toward the library then shifted his gaze to the parish house. After a moment he turned to look at the back of the church. Even from the back it was spectacular. The stained-glass windows were brilliant in all their colors.

He had wanted to walk to the church. He liked walking through Copley Square. But his mother had said it would look terrible and that he must ride with her. While waiting in the small room behind the altar with John Richardson, his best man, they'd received word that everything would be delayed at least half an hour. Andrew hadn't been surprised. Martha was never on time for anything. He would have to break her of that. Punctuality was terribly important to him.

"Look, Andy," John said, "I can take a walk if you want to be alone."

That was the marvelous thing about John. He always knew what Andrew was thinking or feeling. There was nothing like having a really good friend.

"No," he said. "I'll take the walk. I want to."

And now he stood on the grass, pleased to be alone. He thought of how often he longed for time to himself. It had been much worse since he'd become a Congressman. There was always some affair to attend, some person to see. Oh, how he hated politics. The only time he had to himself was spent in sleep. And he cherished that moment: getting into bed, knowing he wouldn't be disturbed, knowing he wouldn't be required to do anything for four or five hours.

But that was over wasn't it? Now he would be getting into bed with another person. Where in hell would he ever be able to be himself? If only he could have remained a bachelor. But it wasn't good for a politician to be a bachelor. The people didn't trust you then. He had to marry. He'd put it off long enough. Thirty-eight was a bit late as it was.

Martha Phillips was a perfect choice. She came from a good family, had money and was damned attractive. She would give him the things he needed for his career. A picture of stability, encouragement, sons. Martha was young. Ten years younger than he. It was she who had pushed the marriage plans. He probably would have kept putting them off.

The sun was in his eyes. He turned and sat on the stone bench, his back to the church, rubbing the brightness from his eyes. Sarah, Sylvia—Sybil! Yes, that was it. Sybil! He smiled. She had run her fingers over his eyebrows.

"I never seen such bushy eyebrows in my whole life," she'd said.

Laughing, thinking about her whole long life, he said: "And you've been around a long time, haven't you, Sybil?"

"I'm eighteen," she said, indignant.

"Eighteen?" He was suspicious.

"Well, almost."

"More like sixteen, isn't it?" It better be.

"Well what difference does it make. You like me don't you, Andrew?"

"I like you."

She shifted her naked weight in his naked lap and ran her long fingers up and down his neck. "Then I don't see what you care about how old I am. You gonna choose me next time?"

"I'll think about it," he teased.

Playfully, she tugged at his ear. "You better."

"Why?"

"Well, if you don't then you might not get what you pay for. I'm the best in the house," she said proudly.

"Is that so?"

"That's so. Nobody else's gonna suck you the way I do."

"Tell me about it."

She smiled knowingly. Too old for her years. The thought almost spoiled it for him. He pushed it away.

"You want me to tell you or show you again?"

"Tell me first," he said.

"Well . . . first I'm gonna run my fingers all up and down your body. I'm gonna touch you real light on your belly and inside your thighs."

Andrew spread his legs slightly.

Sybil was encouraged by his movement. "Then I'm gonna . . . real slow like . . . I'm gonna touch you all light on those big fat balls of yours."

He shifted her slightly as his slowly swelling penis begged for room. "Go on," he whispered.

"Well, then I'm gonna get down on my knees and I'm gonna take my tongue," she ran her tongue over full purplish lips, "and I'm gonna run the end of it round your big shiny head."

He pulled her back so that his penis was wedged between her buttocks and his stomach.

"Then I'm gonna open my mouth and . . ."

"Andrew?"

He whirled around on the bench. It was John.

"We're ready," John said.

Andrew nodded vigorously, his mind splintering in a dozen directions. What was wrong with him? Didn't he have a shred of decency in his body?

When he stood his heart was thudding, his legs shaky. He took several long deep breaths to steady himself. Then he touched his silk tie, adjusted the stiff collar and entered the church to be married.

* * *

The reception was held at the Somerset Club on Beacon Street. Andrew stood by himself watching Martha dance once again with her father. The orchestra was playing "Shine On Harvest Moon," the big hit from *The Fol-*

lies of 1908. He had taken his mother to see it as a cheer-up. A weekend in New York with him did wonders for her when she'd let herself sink into one of those terrible depressions. He felt someone touch his sleeve.

"Congratulations, Andrew."

The woman was smiling, her long face pale under an egret-plumed hat. He knew he should know her.

"Do I look so different? I suppose motherhood does that." She glanced down at the child at her side.

He followed her gaze. The small face looking up at him was extraordinary. Never had he seen such large brown eyes, such thick black lashes. And the mouth. A perfect pink cupid's bow. Plush brown curls surrounded an almost heart-shaped face. He looked away, back to the mother, able now to place her.

"You just look more mature, Helen," he said, taking her hand smoothly.

"Oh, you do remember," she said with pleasure.

"Naturally. And how's your husband?"

"Frank is fine. He's around here somewhere."

Frank. Of course. And the child? Wasn't there something odd about the child's name? Hadn't he heard that somewhere?

"It's been so long since we've seen each other," Helen went on. "Certainly before Starr was born."

Oh my God, yes. Starr. He tried not to smile.

"That would make it over four years ago," she continued.

"We last saw each other at *your* wedding," he said. "So this is little Starr." He reached down and scooped her up in his arms.

"How stupid of me not to remember," said Helen. "Of course, my wedding. And now it's your wedding."

"So this is little Starr," he said again.

"Say hello to cousin Andrew, Starr."

The child looked at the man who held her.

"Starr, say hello," Helen insisted. "She's usually not shy at all. I don't know what's the matter with her."

"That's all right," he said.

"Starr, do say hello to your cousin Andrew, dear. It's his wedding day."

Andrew was about to repeat that it was all right when the little girl began to smile. Slowly, she reached out a tiny hand and with thumb and forefinger grabbed a thatch of his eyebrow.

"Starr!" Helen said, horrified.

"Hello, cousin Andrew," said Starr still holding onto his eyebrow.

"Hello, cousin Starr," he answered.

September 15, 1910
Newark, New Jersey

Orlando sat on the bottom step in front of his large house digging idly in the lawn with a small twig. He had to be careful not to get dirty. For some reason Mama had made him wear his cream-colored coat and matching hat that came down over his head like a bowl. Usually he liked wearing this outfit. It made him feel good. But not today.

He tried sticking the twig into the top of his highbutton shoe but there wasn't enough space between the tight shoe and the black stocking and he gave up. As he pushed the twig back in the earth it cracked in two. Orlando stood up, looking down the street toward Clinton Avenue. One of the security guards was opening the huge iron gate to let in a horse and buggy.

It must be Dr. Mazzeferro. He came to the house every day lately to see Silvio. He'd been in his bed for a long time. Everyone was sad about it, especially Papa. Silvio was supposed to play the piano in New York City soon and now he might not be able to.

"Whoa, Rosy." Dr. Mazzeferro stopped in front of the Antolini house. He climbed down, tied the reins to the iron horse post and lifted his black leather bag from the floor of the carriage. "Good morning, Orlando."

"Good morning, Doctor."

"Are you a good boy today?"

"Yes, sir."

"Bene, bene."

Orlando watched him climb the gray wooden steps, cross the porch and turn the bell. In a few seconds, Dolce, the maid, came to the door.

"Hello, Rosy." Orlando reached up and patted her

side. "Did you know that Silvio's sick in bed? Yes. He's very sick." The thing he hated most about Silvio's sickness was that everybody whispered all the time. He didn't miss his brother as a playmate. Even though Silvio was only nine years old, all he ever did was practice the piano. He was a prodigy. Orlando didn't know exactly what that was. He only knew it was something very good. His sister, Nina, was special too. She was going to be an opera singer. In another year, when she was seventeen, Papa was going to let her audition for the Metropolitan Opera Company in New York City.

Orlando wished he could get a sugar cube or carrot to give Rosy but Mama had firmly told him to stay outside. She'd also said not to leave the front of the house. Otherwise, he would have gone down the street to find his friend Warren. Warren's house was only three doors away. Maybe if he ran there very fast, Mama would never know! As he was contemplating the risks in this adventure the front door opened and Nina came out on the porch.

"Orlando. Come here please."

He turned, irritated at the interruption of his plan.

"Orlando, did you hear me?"

He pretended he did not.

"Orlando?"

There was a second of silence and then the rustle of her long skirt as she came down the stairs. He listened carefully and just as she neared him he darted away toward Warren's.

"Orlando, please," she cried.

He was giggling to himself as he jumped behind the hedge. If she wanted him, she could catch him.

"Orlando?"

He huddled closer to the hedge and listened for the sound of her shoes coming down the walk. The only thing he heard was the sound of his own breathing. Why wasn't she coming after him?

"Orlando? Papa will be mad."

Those four words struck his middle. Papa? Did Papa want him? His legs turned wobbly and his stomach went to mush. Slowly, unsteadily, he rose, his eyes just above the hedge.

Nina saw him at once. "Quickly, Orlando."

Whether it was the new tone in her voice, or the way she stood there, so unlike her usual perfect posture, almost drooping, he realized this was no time for a game.

"What, what is it?" He ran toward her. Now he could see that her eyes were all red.

She put her hand on his shoulder and squeezed gently. As though she had spoken, he suddenly knew though he couldn't name it or say it, even to himself.

Nina put her arm around him and they turned and walked toward the house. The sound of their shoes on the wood hung in the air like cracks of a horsewhip. Crossing the porch he stumbled once and Nina caught him. Then she opened the door and gently pushed him inside. Behind him he heard the door click shut. It was the loudest sound he'd ever heard.

*   *   *

It was a Saturday, three weeks after Silvio's funeral. Orlando was climbing into his play knickers when his father opened the door.

"Put on the blue suit and come to the living room." He left.

The boy stared at the door a moment, then began changing. This was the first time his father had spoken to him since Silvio died. And not just his father. No one was speaking. Except for Dolce. He hadn't even seen Mama. She was in her bed. And Nina hardly ever came out of her room.

The day after Silvio died, Papa had called them all into the main living room. The one which had the piano.

"There will be no more music," he'd said.

"But Papa," Nina said, "how will I practice?"

"You will not." He closed the piano with finality.

"How will I try out for the opera?"

"You will not. There will be no more music in this house."

Nina screamed and cried and Papa sent her to her room where she'd stayed most of the time since. Connie stayed with her trying to console her. Orlando listened to them through the wall.

"It isn't fair," Nina cried. "Silvio wasn't the only genius in the house."

"Don't cry, dearest," Concettina said. "Maybe Papa will change his mind."

"Never. He doesn't love me. He doesn't love any of us. He only loved him. Well, I'm glad he's dead."

Orlando put his head under the pillow then, afraid to hear anything more.

Now as he dressed in his good clothes he wondered if it was true his father didn't love anyone but Silvio. Mama always said Papa loved him. Still, when he was around Papa it didn't feel good. Not the way it did with Connie or Mama.

Leaving his room, he wished he could stop in and see Mama before he went downstairs. But the door to her room looked dark and heavy and there was no sound from inside.

Orlando Sr. sat in his chair in the smaller of the two living rooms. The doors of the main living room remained shut. Orlando stood a few feet away from his father and waited. Finally, his father said:

"You are ready."

Orlando nodded as the man rose slowly from his chair.

"Come then."

Orlando Sr. walked to the hall where he took his hat from the rack and his cane from the stand. The boy followed.

Out on the street, heading toward Clinton Avenue, Orlando Jr. asked where they were going. There was no answer. As he hurried along, trying desperately to keep up with the strides of his father, he was filled with apprehension. He reached for the man's hand and felt it flinch as though it had been wounded. Then it sought his and engulfed it. Orlando tried to concentrate on the mystery of where they were going. It was the first time he had ever gone anywhere with Papa alone and he knew he should feel proud and excited. But something spoiled it. He prayed he wouldn't throw up.

When they boarded the ferry Orlando realized they must be going to New York. Silvio had told him about the ferry which he and Papa took every Saturday when they went to the city. Of course! Since Silvio couldn't go to New York Papa was going to take *him*. He wasn't afraid anymore. He knew exactly what they were going to do.

Silvio had told him everything. First they would take a
walk on Fifth Avenue and look in the stores. Then they
would go to a grand restaurant and have lunch. After
lunch they would go to the opera. And after that for pastry and tea. Then home.

Standing on a chair so he could look out at the water,
Orlando thought that he had never been happier.

On the way home he sat with his eyes on his shoes,
his body slumped. He hurt and he wanted to cry but knew
he must not. It had been such a terrible day. Papa hadn't
spoken to him once. When they walked on Fifth Avenue
and he'd asked questions about what he saw in the stores,
his father remained silent. In the restaurant Papa stared
straight ahead and ordered fish for him. Silvio had loved
fish. Orlando wanted beef. At the Opera Papa did nothing
when he said he couldn't see over the big man ahead. So
he sat there, staring at the back of the chair, trying to blot
out the sound of the singers shrieking in a language he
didn't understand. It wasn't even Italian. How could Silvio
have liked it? It went on forever. At the tea shop, when
the cannoli his father ordered for him appeared, he was
positive he would throw up. Only fear of his father's rage
kept him from it. He choked down the sticky sweet pastry
and sipped the bitter tea. Silvio had not liked sugar in his
tea and Orlando Sr. moved the sugar bowl out of the boy's
path when he reached for it.

They got off the trolley at the corner of Clinton and
Van Ness. As the guards opened the gates, he heard his
father speak pleasantly.

"Good evening, boys. Nice weather, yes?"

"Very nice, Mr. Antolini."

"Hello, Sonny, have a good time with Papa?"

Orlando could not find words.

"Answer," his father said. "Where are your manners?"

"Fine, thank you." He struggled to control his nausea.

When they got inside the house, the boy wondered
whether he should thank his father? The problem was immediately solved as Orlando Sr. went promptly up the
stairs. Orlando Jr. waited until he heard his father's door
close, then ran up the stairs himself to his own room. He
lay across his bed and cried. When he was finished crying
he found he no longer felt sick to his stomach. Slowly, he

undressed. His brother, he decided, must have been loony. How could he have liked those times with Papa? And he thought of all the Saturdays he had watched the two of them go off down the street, wishing he were going instead of Silvio. Well, at least it was over.

But it was not. Each Saturday, for one year, Orlando Sr. told the boy to dress in his good suit. And each Saturday the two of them went to New York, never a word exchanged. By the time the year of silent Saturdays was over the mention of fish or cannoli sent the boy's stomach lurching and opera had become a torture.

Later, as a man, he could never remember why he hated fish or how he had come to despise the opera. If anyone pressed him for an explanation, he skillfully changed the subject. Left to his own devices, he simply didn't think about it. There was nothing to think about. Nothing to remember. It was just the way it was. Some people liked fish; some people hated it. Some people liked opera; some people hated it. He hated both because he did. That was all.

Her instability brought trouble to everyone who ever had anything to do with her.
—Anonymous, *New York Times*, June 13, 1931

June 5, 1931
New York, New York

She wondered if she'd dreamed that today was the day. Of course, she'd known it was going to be soon but why today? Why was she so sure? Well, what difference did it make?

She listened to the tapping of Congo's feet, his heavy breathing and whimpering as he greeted Stanley. A sudden sharp bark.

"Hush, Congo, stop that," Stanley said.

That impossible fool, Starr thought.

She ran a hand through her marcelled hair thinking that she needed a new permanent. It made her laugh. A new permanent for death. A permanent death. Was there any other kind?

She reached for her cigarettes. Would this be her last

pack? No, it was half empty. Surely she'd go through another pack before . . . before, before, before. For a moment it frightened her. But just for a moment. In the next breath, the next exhalation of smoke, it cheered her, revived sagging spirits.

Still there was one problem. She knew when but how, the perfect how, had not been solved. But it didn't worry her. She felt it would come to her during the course of the day. Again she was high. Within seconds her mood shifted, plummeting, as snatches of the night before entered her consciousness.

Three

August 6, 1977
Orange, New Jersey

Now what was this? Door opening? Who?

He waited until he felt the presence leaning over him, then opened his eyes.

"Hello, Daddy."

Daddy. Daughter. Child. His child. His and Fran's.

"Can you hear me?"

His eyes, slightly hooded, fastened on her face.

She was pretty. She looked like him. Like the way he used to look. Dark hair and eyes, small straight nose. She had his dimples, too.

"Daddy? I have to assume that you can hear me. I don't want you to worry about anything. Toni is taking good care of Michelle."

Michelle, his dog. The tears started. He could feel them burning behind his lids. What would Cathy do if he cried? He remembered the last time.

She had come to see him with Joan. Nice girl. Then what? He tried to speak . . . did speak . . . said: "Michelle is so old. She'll die soon." And suddenly Cathy was out of her chair, down the front stairs, into her car. Gone. Was it what he said about Michelle? Or the tears that came with it? He didn't understand. Then days later came her letter.

29

He had read it over and over and over. *I must fight my negativism, learned at your knee, every day of my life. I don't blame you but it is difficult for me to be around you. If only you would make some effort to help yourself you would have from me all the sympathy in the world.*

Tears were running down his cheeks.

"Don't cry."

The sound of her voice was gentle. He didn't detect the usual contempt. Now she was wiping his tears. They came faster. Out of nowhere he remembered a line from another letter. *The half hour before I die, I imagine, will be quite blissful.* The thought nauseated him. If only he could forget that terrible day but he'd never forgotten. Not for one day . . . not for one day in forty-six years.

June 18, 1911
Newark, New Jersey

Sometimes Antonia wished she had been born a man. Then she was immediately sorry and asked God's forgiveness. It was wrong to wish for something like that. She should be grateful for what she was, what she had.

Antonia looked at herself in the mirror, brushing her long hair, strands of gray crowding out the black. Her mother had been gray by forty-five but she was not yet forty. Inside she felt so young, sometimes childlike, and yet she must behave like an old woman. Why could she never go anywhere, do anything? Those thoughts led her back to her sinful wish. It had occurred to her more than once that God had punished her by taking her first-born son in exchange for some of her sins. But God was merciful and even as Silvio lay dying, a new baby was forming inside her. A boy. The second Silvio. She wondered if she would ever get used to calling him by her first son's name. She hated the choice but it was what her husband wanted. What could she do?

What could she do? It seemed she was always thinking that. Only when it came to God did she have the force, will, initiative to do what she wanted. Only then could she defy her husband. That was the one place she drew the line, separating mortal authority from divine. Today she would do it again.

Antonia began to twist and wind the long hair, ready-ing it for the bun she wore. She stared into her blue eyes. Not one of her six children had her eyes. Of course, it was too early to tell what the baby's would be. He was only two weeks old. She stuck hairpins into the sides of the bun. Probably his eyes would be brown, too. The genes of the Antolini family seemed to dominate the Fuerentinis's. This did not surprise Orlando. He thought it fitting, hat-ing her family as he did, feeling it was beneath him.

She expertly planted the tortoise-shell comb in the center of her bun. Why had he married her? There had been other girls more suitable. She knew that. Wasn't that why her father had been so set against their union?

She smiled, thinking of the second time she ever saw Orlando. It was afternoon and the Cavalry was due to march through her small town on their way to Naples. She, her mother and sister waited on their balcony to watch the parade. Unknown to her mother and sister, she was anxious to see the handsome officer with whom she had danced twice the night before at the Mayor's party. She knew his name but that was all. She also knew he was special but she didn't know why. And she knew, too, that he liked her. She felt it even though they hadn't ex-changed a word.

It was hot on the balcony and she fanned herself vig-orously. The air was still, the village quiet. In the dis-tance, faintly, was the sound of horse's hooves. As they came nearer, Antonia's excitement grew and she held her fan against her face, peeking over, afraid to look too di-rectly, afraid if she did they would all disappear. Soon the first white horse came in sight. Then flashes of red, glints of green and gold.

They came single file and soon Antonia was able to see that Corporal Antolini was fifth in line. As he ap-proached she saw he was looking up at the balcony. Again with her fan she covered her face, eyes exposed. Did he know where she lived? Was he looking for her? Oh, how straight his back was. How proper, severe and handsome he looked. Just before reaching the balcony he raised his right hand to his peaked cap, touching the brim, head lifted slightly, eyes almost meeting hers. And then it hap-pened. The white horse rose on his hind legs, whinnied, came down on his front legs, shooting out the back ones and in one swift buck threw the rider over his head into the dirt. After the initial shocked silence, the sound of laughter rose and flooded the street like rushing water. Antonia horrified by what had happened and by the swelling laughter in which her mother and sister joined, fled to her room. She could not bear to see him lying covered in dust or to have him see her.

The villagers talked about the *thrown officer* for days. When, after a week, he came calling at her house her father had heard much about the young man. He had heard, among other things, that he was quite a fellow with the ladies. However, he pérmitted Antolini to see his daughter, properly chaperoned, of course. Antonia never understood why her father allowed the courtship, only to deny her hand when Orlando requested it.

She and her sister Yolanda listened outside the library door as Orlando pressed his suit.

"I cannot accept no for an answer, sir," Orlando said, raising his voice.

"You will have to." Fuerentini raised his.

"I refuse."

"And I refuse to give my dearest daughter to someone of your reputation."

"To what reputation do you refer, if I may ask, sir?"

"Go away, boy."

"I insist that you tell me to what you refer."

"You insist on nothing. You are a flea in my ear. Now go away before I lose my temper."

"Sir, you have accused me of something. I have a right to know what it is."

"Ahh, what a pest you are, Antolini. You are a demon with the women. Everyone says this."

"But, sir, I want to *marry* your daughter. What does my past reputation with single ladies have to do with that?"

"It has everything to do with it. You will never be satisfied with one good woman."

"Forgive me, sir, for contradicting you, but I will *only* be satisfied when Antonia is my wife. It is a matter of life and death."

"And whose life and death would that be?"

"Mine, sir."

"How is that?"

"If you do not give me your daughter's hand in marriage I shall kill myself."

Both girls clapped their hands over their mouths in fear.

"Yes, yes, of course you will," said Fuerentini.

"I cannot live without Antonia. I would rather be dead than without her by my side."

"I am sorry to hear that because my decision remains firm. Good day."

Orlando slammed out of the house and Antonia took to her bed. In less than six hours the news came back that he had indeed shot himself and lay that very moment wavering between life and death.

Weeks later, Fuerentini, impressed by Orlando's act, sent word to the young man, who had recovered, to come and see him. He believed now, he said, that Orlando really did love his daughter and if he would give up the army he could have her hand in marriage. Orlando agreed and they were married within three months.

That was all so long ago, Antonia thought, and I was so young. But I am still young. Again, she felt angry. Thirty-nine was not old. It was certainly not old enough to be confined to her house with occasional rides in the car or walks to the store. She didn't even have a friend. Once she had complained of this to Orlando and he had said that his sister was her friend. His sister. Alberta. Bertie. Some friend. She came in Antonia's house like a kind of madwoman, changing this, criticizing that. She was always angry, barking orders, pushing, shoving. Bertie was no friend. She could never go to her, talk, confide, perhaps cry. Even an exchange of a recipe was like a battle. Bertie screamed the ingredients, jabbed her shoulder for emphasis, pounded the table to underscore. Antonia remembered the joys and frivolities she had shared with Yolanda. She missed the laughter only another woman could evoke. Now her laughter came from her children, which was lovely, but very different. The truth was, with all her children and her husband, she was lonely. But what could she do?

She removed her slippers and slid her small foot into her finest leather shoe and began buttoning. In a few minutes she would get the baby, meet her daughters downstairs and together they would walk to the end of the street and into Blessed Sacrament Church. Nina would be Godmother and Father Paul would have a man there to be Godfather. He knew and understood her situation. He had been through this with her five times before.

As usual on a Saturday, Orlando Sr. and Jr. were in New York. Sadness swept over her when she thought of her small son tagging along with his father. He had come to her months ago, begged her to get his father to stop taking him on these agonizing trips. But what could she do? She tried to explain, tried to tell the boy that his father didn't mean to hurt. Still, the child wept and pleaded and she said she would try. But when she broached the subject with her husband he silenced her with a look before she had completed a sentence.

Now, once again, they were on their weekly outing which made it easy for her to have her child baptized. She knew none of the children would ever let their father know. All of them understood how outraged Papa would be.

She finished with her shoes, checked the mirror once again. She looked lovely, nearly pretty. And her silk dress with the ruffles at the hem made her feel almost happy. But of course, baptism was a happy occasion. As she left her room her spirits began to climb. Soon little Silvio would be protected, saved, and if anything should happen to him he would go straight to heaven like his brother before him. Soon Father Paul would hand the baby over to—what was his name? Brononi? Bordoni? Oh, how much nicer if she could have had a relative or at least someone she knew for the baby's Godfather. But this was better than nothing. After all, she thought, opening the door to the baby's room, what could she do?

April 5, 1914
Malden, Massachusetts

When Starr returned to school after a long weekend, her two best friends, Mary Gray and Evelyn Henry, were waiting on the steps for her. She could hardly wait to jump from the Model T Frank drove. Most of the girls' fathers drove Packards or Cadillacs and one girl's *mother* drove a Baker Electric! But today she didn't care that her father's car wasn't as luxurious as some of the others. To-day she had important news.

She stepped down on the running board, waving to her friends. Her back to the car, she said: "Bye, Father."

"Goodbye. Study hard."

As she ran toward the girls the chugging sound of the Ford receded behind her. "Guess what? Guess what?" she called.

"What?" they said in unison.

"I have a surprise. I got a pussycat. My mother gave him to me." She reached the girls on the steps.

"How come?" Mary asked.

"Just because."

"Just because what?" asked Evelyn.

"Oh, I don't know. Just because she loves me."

"Is it a boy cat or a girl cat?"

"Is it a cat or a kitten?"

"Well," said Starr, adjusting the skirt of her dress, "he's a boy kitten and he's black and white and half his nose is black and half is pink."

"Oh, I wouldn't like that," said Mary.

"Why not?"

"It would be scary."

"It's not," Starr said.

"I like a kitten's nose to be all one color. Either all black or all pink. Only cows have two-colored noses. I would never love a kitten with half and half."

"Oh, Mary," Evelyn said, "you're just jealous. Go on, Starr, tell more."

"I am not," Mary said, sticking out her bottom lip and bringing her red eyebrows close together.

"Are too," Evelyn said.

"Not."

"Are."

"Not."

"I'm going inside," Starr said, standing up.

"Me, too." Evelyn stood also.

Mary said nothing and stayed where she was.

Starr and Evelyn began walking toward the front door of the dormitory. Then they looked at each other, stopped, turned and looked at Mary. The little girl, round and short, made them smile. They walked back to her.

"Are you coming?" Starr asked.

Mary shrugged her shoulders.

"Oh, come on, Mary," Evelyn said, tugging at her sleeve.

"Everyone hates me," Mary said.

Starr said: "Who hates you? We don't."

Mary stood up, her fat little body teetering on the step. Evelyn grabbed one arm and Starr the other. They started once again toward the door.

"Starr," Mary said, "what will you name your kitten?"

"Peter. I named him Peter."

"I thought Peter was a rabbit's name," Evelyn said. She opened the heavy oak door.

"It doesn't have to be," Mary said.

"I know."

Starr began to giggle.

"What's so funny?"

"Well, he's a cat, he has a rabbit's name and he looks like a cow."

They all began to laugh.

"A cat a rabbit a cow," Evelyn chanted.

"A cat a rabbit a cow," Mary echoed.

Then all three together. "A cat a rabbit a cow."

Hand in hand they started up the stairs singing their litany. To Starr life was perfect. There was nothing that could have made her happier than having a sweet cowlike kitten at home, and two dear friends at school. Perfect.

July 10, 1915
Lancaster, Pennsylvania

The Chautauqua was in town. To fourteen-year-old Frances Hess that meant a glorious, exciting and inspiring night. If, of course, it was anything like the one last year. That was a night! There was a Hawaiian man who sang about the beaches in Waikiki and a magician who made a rabbit come out of a hat. And the White Hussars. Who would ever forget them?

Frances leaned against the filing cabinet remembering. She could still see their white uniforms with the gold braid and the white kid boots. And they had satin-lined white capes and white fur hats with small gold tassles hanging off the sides. Beautiful. The Hussars had been the first on the program. They sang "The Boys of the Old Brigade." Never in her life had she heard such . . .

"Frances! What are you doing?"

"What, Papa?"

"I said, what are you doing?"

"I'm filing."

"You ain't filing anymore than I'm filing. You're dreaming, like always." Joe Hess clamped his teeth around his ever-present cigar.

"I'm sorry, Papa." Quickly, she opened a file drawer and began to look through the D's.

"What are you dreaming about?"

"Nothing." She knew if she told him it was the Chautauqua he probably wouldn't let her go. He wasn't mean but sometimes he had funny ideas about discipline.

"Well . . . don't," he said and left the office.

She wished she didn't have to work for Papa in the cigar factory. At least she didn't have to work in the factory itself the way her two sisters had. Now Catherine was married and at home. But Dorothy, who was eighteen, still worked in the factory putting the gold bands around the cigars. And she hated it. She thought she should be the one in the office, not Frances.

Frances didn't know why Papa had given her the office job and she felt sorry for Dorothy who said all she wanted was to be a lady and that it was impossible to be a lady working in the factory.

"Dotty, do you hate me?" Frances once asked.

"Why, for heaven's sake, how could you ask such a thing?"

"Well, because I'm in the office and you're in the factory?"

"It's not your fault, is it?"

"No."

"Of course not. Besides, I don't hate anyone, Fran, and neither should you. It's not right. There's no excuse for hating."

She felt terrible then because she'd hated plenty of people in her life. Sometimes she even hated Papa! She hated him for making her leave school at the end of sixth grade. That happened two years ago but she still hated him for it. She had loved school. She loved learning about the world, where different countries were, what different people were like, what they wore, what they ate. And history. She loved thinking about George Washington, Paul Revere, Benjamin Franklin, all of them. She had never liked numbers much but none of the girls did. Her favorite subject was reading. She read everything she could get her hands on. Right this minute she had *Pollyanna* hidden in her desk. Not that there was anything wrong with *Pollyanna*. But Papa thought *all* books were bad. He said they gave you *ideas*. The terrible fight over her having to leave school was more about ideas than anything else.

He announced at dinner one night that she must leave school. It wasn't a complete surprise because her sisters had been forced to leave when they were her age. Still, she burst into tears.

"Now don't go crying, Frances. It won't do you no good," Joe said.

"But why, Papa?" asked Catherine, the smallest of the sisters but the most outspoken. "We don't need the money, do we?"

"It ain't got nothing to do with money."

"Well, what then?"

"Catherine, you just mind your own."

"It *is* my own," Catherine protested. "Frances is my *own* baby sister and she loves school."

"That's just the trouble."

"What is?" asked Dorothy.

Frances was crying silently and her mother patted her hand.

"She loves it. She loves them books. All the time her head's in one of them books and books gives you ideas. I don't want her having ideas." He pushed his plate away and took out a cigar.

"Why not?" Catherine asked.

"Because."

"Because why?"

"Because is all," he said, angrily. "Now leave it be. I say she ain't going back to school and she ain't."

"Oh, Papa," said Catherine, "when I get married you'll have one less mouth to feed."

"I said it had nothing to do with money."

"That's what you *say*."

"You calling your Papa a liar, girl?"

"No."

Mrs. Hess tucked a loose strand of hair back up and looked down the length of the table at her husband. He was lighting his cigar and she wrinkled up her nose in anticipation of the smell. "Joseph, what would it hurt to let the child go to school for another year?"

He looked surprised. "What's that, Minnie? Did I hear right? I thought we'd talked this all over."

"Yes, but Frances seems to want it so much."

"I'll be a son of a gun!"

"Joseph!"

"Well, for dang sake, Minnie, I thought this thing was settled. I didn't expect you to go stabbing me in the back like this in front of my girls."

"I'm not stabbing you, Joe, I just thought . . ."

"You see . . . that's what I'm talking about! She *thought* . . . and where does thoughts come from? They come from *ideas*. And where does ideas come from? They come from books. And where do you get books? In school. That settles it. No school."

As far as Frances knew her mother never read books.

Joe got up from the table. "I don't want to hear no more about it. If you was a boy, Frances, you could keep going. But you ain't now and ain't never going to be a boy, so you don't need no school."

"You mean it's all right for *boys* to have *ideas?* Is that it, Papa?" Catherine asked.

"That's right." He pushed in his chair. "You girls don't need no ideas. What for? Frances will go work at the factory and then she'll get married and have babies and you don't need no ideas for that. Minnie don't have no ideas. Do you, Minnie?"

"No, Joseph."

"You see. And you're happy, ain't you, Minnie?"

"Yes, Joseph."

"You see. So let this be the end of it then."

"I don't want my little sister working in the factory," Catherine screamed out. "I'm getting married next month and I know Dorothy will be getting out soon and I don't want my baby sister in that dirty factory all alone."

"It ain't dirty and she wouldn't be alone. Anyway, you ain't got to worry. She's gonna work in the office with me."

"In the office?"

"I'll learn her what to do. Hester Sterns is getting married and Mr. Bayrik says I got to hire someone new. So I'm hiring Frances."

At first Frances didn't feel too bad. Working in the office was very different from working in the factory. It made her feel quite grown up. She guessed she was lucky that Papa was manager of Bayrik Cigars and could put her in the office just like that. But within a week, she mourned the loss of her school life. Office work was boring.

Boring, Frances thought, as she filed the last letter under D. She walked to her desk and got the E and F letters. The clock said two-fifteen. Five hours and fifteen minutes until the Chautauqua. She felt in her pocket for the ticket she'd bought the day before. Still there. She took it out and looked at it: *Redpath Chautauqua Admit One Child 25 cents.*

She opened the E file. Her eyes wandered away from it to the wall where one of the signs hung that Mr. Bayrik had scattered throughout the factory. *What this country really needs is a good five-cent cigar!* Papa told her it was something the Vice President had said. It seemed stupid to Frances who thought cigars were smelly and dirty.

Her thoughts drifted back to last year's Chautauqua. There had been three separate orchestras, a full-blooded Indian, a yodeler, acrobats, some Tango dancers and, Frances's favorite thing, two opera singers. A lot of the kids put their fingers in their ears and made faces when the singers came on, but Frances loved the sound and envied the beautiful ladies. She loved to sing and could easily carry a tune but she was no opera singer!

The highlight of the show was her second favorite thing. Last year it was a man called Harry "Gatling Gun" Fogelman. They called him "Gatling Gun" because he talked so fast. He was an inspiration. For the last year Frances had tried to start every day just the way "Gatling Gun" did. He'd said: "A negative thought is a poison as deadly as arsenic. Every morning when I wake up I think positive thoughts and say, 'Fogelman, get out and get to it.'"

"Gatling Gun" said if you did that you would be rich and famous and, above all, happy. He said that nobody had to be poor and miserable. All you had to do was get rid of your negative thoughts, replace them with positive ones and before you knew it you'd be a millionaire. For a year Frances had begun each day by saying: "Hess, get out and get to it." She still wasn't a millionaire but she wasn't discouraged. Frances was no quitter.

This year, if "Gatling Gun" was the orator she was going to try and get close and touch him. People said it was lucky to touch the orator. Then when she got to be a millionaire, she would go off to New York or Chicago or somewhere far away from Papa and go to school. She would definitely go to school when she became a millionaire. Feeling very happy about that positive thought and knowing the Chautauqua was only hours away, Frances began filing the F letters.

If I were a man I would join the Foreign Legion and forget my past.
—From a letter by Starr Faithfull

June 5, 1931
New York, New York

Starr put on her slippers. Who *were* those two men? Never mind. What difference did it make now? It was over and done with, a thing of the past. She remembered her underpants. So what? What was the point of wearing underpants anyway? She decided never to wear them again. That made her giggle. *Never* again!

She was hungry. Very hungry. And today she would jolly well eat. No watching her weight today.

The thing she hated most about this apartment was that she had to go through Stanley and Helen's bedroom to get to the kitchen. She could hear them whispering now. A romantic reunion? After only one night? They were sickening.

She reached for her silk robe, cleared her throat and coughed to signal them. Pushing through her curtain she walked into their room.

Stanley was seated on the bed fully clothed, Helen under the covers.

"Good morning, Bamby," he said.

"Sleep well, dear?"

"Morning. Fine."

"Starr had such fun last night, didn't you, dear?"

"Mmmm." In the small kitchen she put on the kettle. "Who wants coffee?" Why not be pleasant this last time? Let them remember her as kind and generous. What a bloody laugh!

Four

August 6, 1977
Orange, New Jersey

Cathy was gone. His little girl. No, that was a lie. She was no longer his little girl or anyone's little girl. She was forty-one. A woman. He remembered before she was born. They had tried for a child for six years. Then it happened. He had been frightened.

"I want you to get rid of it."

"I don't believe you said that."

"I don't want a baby."

"But all this time . . . all the things we've tried, the examinations, tests. . . ."

"I don't care."

"You mean you want me to have an abortion?"

"Whatever it takes."

Fran started to cry. "I won't. I just won't. You always get your way but not this time."

"What if I say that I'll leave you if you have it?"

Silence. Then: "I don't care."

He knew she meant it. How could he explain to her? What if they had a girl? He would go mad with worry. Any crazy thing could happen . . . he knew. He wasn't sure he could live with the worry.

43

And, of course, the baby had been a girl. He'd had his first breakdown a year after she was born.

April 6, 1917
Newark, New Jersey

"Yes, Miss Tilden?" Orlando Antolini looked up from the papers on his desk at his attractive secretary.

"President Wilson has declared war with Germany. I thought you'd want to know, sir."

"Thank you."

The declaration of war was no surprise, simply a finality to something which had been brewing for quite a while. Others, of course, would see it as a beginning. But to him war was a finality. How many lives would be lost? He was grateful that he was too old and his sons too young. He took his watch from his vest pocket. Almost time for lunch.

Orlando stacked the pages of the brief he was working on, put them in a folder and rose. Taking his hat from the rack and his walking stick from the holder he eyed the large, plush office as he did many times a day, thinking how very glad he was to be a lawyer in America. Though he would have been successful had he stayed in Italy, he would not have experienced the same sense of accomplishment. There a lawyer from the Antolini family would automatically get clients. Here, where no one knew what it was to be an Antolini, they came to him because he was one of the best, and honest. In his twenty-two years of practice here he had steadily built his reputation. And as always he had refused the politicians' offers. If he'd taken a judgeship he would be beholden to this one, to that one. There would be favors required, a matter of looking the other way now and then, a bribe perhaps. Wasn't there a saying that every man had his price? Who was he to refute that? Perhaps one day there would be a price so dear he would not have the strength of character to say no. As a lawyer he answered to no one other than himself.

There was also the matter of his private life. As a judge he might be subject to closer scrutiny. This way no one was interested in what he did with his leisure time, except perhaps for Antonia, but then what she didn't know—

and even if she did, what could she do about it? No, private practice was best for him. Everything was safe this way.

Out on the street he walked briskly, back straight, head erect, as always. There seemed to be more hubbub today than usual. News of war had agitated people. He quickened his pace.

When he arrived at Benita's street, before he turned the corner, he checked to make sure there was no one nearby who knew him. Even though it was a bit risky for her apartment to be so near his office, he enjoyed having it within walking distance. He never liked relying on the timetables of others, buses, trolleys, trains, even jitneys.

On signal, four taps of his walking stick against the glass panel of the door, Benita opened up.

"Ah hello, my darling. I thought you might visit today."

Orlando, as though seeing her for the first time, sucked in his breath in pleasure and touched her cheek with his gloved fingers. She took his hat, coat, gloves, walking stick. She brushed his cheek with her lips and led him to a green velvet arm chair. His chair. The ottoman, also green velvet, supported his feet. She strode from the room to the kitchen where he heard the new ice box, which he'd recently given her, open and close. Soon she was back in the room with a bottle of champagne and two glasses.

"What are we celebrating?" he asked.

"Just your being here." She handed him the bottle. "I haven't seen you for over a week."

"I know, I know. Forgive me. I have an important, all-consuming case."

She smiled. "I understand."

The cork popped and Benita held out the glasses as he poured. She sat on the ottoman. They touched glasses.

"Saluté," he said.

"Saluté."

They sipped.

"So you thought I would visit today?"

She nodded. "The declaration of war."

"Yes," he said. "A terrible thing, war."

"Yes."

They drank in silence, looking at one another, smiling gently. Orlando never tired of, nor completely absorbed, her beauty. She was tall, thin, but curvaceous. Her breasts were more than ample, nipples pink, large. He could just see a touch of them now, peeking from under her negligee. Benita's face, framed by thick brown hair, dipping and curling, was an almost perfect oval, a small cleft in the chin. Her eyes were large, gray, trenchant, adorned by long black lashes, evenly spaced on either side of a straight, delicate nose. The lips were bountiful with the feel of silk. And her unblemished skin had the texture of velvet, like the chair. He touched the back of her hand to confirm it once again.

She refilled their glasses.

"You look tired, Orlando."

"The case."

She nodded, understanding. "You need to relax more." Beginning their ritual, she leaned over, undid his stiff collar and removed his tie. Slowly, she unbuttoned his shirt.

By the time they finished their third glass of champagne, Orlando was naked in the chair, his erection complete. Benita stood, the negligee slipping down over shoulders, sliding past hips and gathering in a beige mass around her feet. With grace, she stepped out of the circle of material and neatly placed herself between his knees and the ottoman. He lowered his legs, pushing them between her ankles. She leaned over, grabbed both arms of the chair and gently lowered herself onto his penis. She groaned, swiveling once to ensure his penetration. Still holding the arms of the chair, she leaned forward so that her breasts caressed his face, then moving slightly to the left, her nipple neatly slipped into his open, waiting mouth.

In a few minutes, she pulled back, her hard nipple sliding over his chin. She pushed her pelvis forward, her hands behind her on the chair arms, and rhythmically began to rise and fall on his large, stiff penis. He reached up for her breasts, fingers gently kneading her nipples. Benita threw back her head and rode him with a quickening pace. She was the first to climax, moaning as she revolved round and round, pushing down as though she wished him to fill her forever. He soon followed, with equal, deep enjoyment.

They squeezed into the chair together, her head rest-

ing on his shoulder, his arm encircling her. He was relaxed, content. He gazed around the room, taking in the
various pieces of furniture, vases, lamps and other decora-
tive pieces, all of which he had paid for. Everything was
in excellent taste, all chosen by Benita.

Excellent was the perfect word for her. Her taste, her
looks, her mind, her lovemaking, even her cooking. No
man could ask for a more perfect mistress. She was fifteen
years younger than he and they had been together three
years. They met in his office. He had handled her divorce. All through the case he had been completely dis-
creet, not a look or smile out of place. When the divorce
was final he invited her to lunch, to celebrate. They drank
two bottles of champagne, he escorted her home and without an explanatory word or a single question they went
immediately to the large featherbed, lay down and began
easily and gracefully to undress each other. It had been
like that ever since.

Sometimes he worried that she would grow tired of
him, find someone else, younger, richer. There was no
question of a permanent union between them. Neither
ever entertained the idea. To him she was a mistress, a
divorcee, unmarriageable. And she liked life this way. The
only extra she asked for was the occasional stock in her
name, something for the future. He was happy to give
this. By now her portfolio was quite handsome and she
enjoyed a nice sense of security. She also enjoyed Orlando,
both emotionally and sexually. She had no intention of
looking elsewhere and assured him of that whenever he
showed signs of insecurity. Today, however, he needed no
reassurance. Today, he felt powerful and completely
wanted. Perhaps, he thought, it was because he was safe
from war, therefore indestructible.

"Are you hungry?" she asked.

"I am," he said, just realizing it.

She extricated herself and took him by the hand,
leading him to the small alcove in the kitchen where a
table was set for two.

He smiled. "You were very sure, weren't you?"

She said nothing but motioned for him to sit down.
He had long ago accepted doing everything with her naked. Even now he wished he could be sitting in a robe,
but Benita preferred it this way and he accommodated

her. He never wanted to appear stiff or formal with her. He never wanted to seem old. His body was still firm, the skin tight, muscles evident. He could afford to give in to her fetish even if it did make him slightly uncomfortable.

Benita set before him a platter of cold meats and cheeses. On another plate were olives, black and green, hot peppers, anchovies, capers and caponata. In a straw basket was a loaf of Italian bread.

"A feast," he said.

"Mangé," she said.

He laughed, as always, when she used Italian words, thoroughly enjoying the effort made by Benita O'Brien.

When they had finished their lunch and he had smoked a gold-tipped Turkish cigarette, he led her into the bedroom. This time he was the initiator, aggressor. He made long, slow love to her, using every part of himself, exploring every part of her. Afterwards, as they lay in each other's arms, he decided that declarations of war were definitely good for his libido.

Later that night, lying awake beside Antonia, he thought of Benita. Usually, he tried to avoid this. He felt it wasn't proper or fair. There were bound to be comparisons and, in the area of sex, Antonia would surely suffer. Not that it was entirely Antonia's fault. He could not approach his wife the way he could his mistress. He suspected, had he asked Antonia to mount him the way Benita did (and he could barely *imagine* asking this of his wife), she would have gone white with insult and horror. Nor was it conceivable that she would understand the desire to use his mouth, his tongue. Not that he would wish to do this to Antonia, mother of his children. He blushed at the thought. But perhaps it would be nice, during their weekly sex, to have her use her mouth on him. Quickly, he moved farther away from her, as if to lessen the chance that she might read his thoughts. He had decided long ago, with the first of his mistresses in America, that he was definitely oversexed. He needed more than one weekly orgasm with his wife. And he needed interesting and fresh kinds of sexual stimulation. This kept him terribly busy, juggling schedules, covering his tracks, but he had to have it. Antonia and, he guessed, most decent women, did not *need* sex. They indulged in it for procreation and to satisfy their duty to their husbands. He knew this was true with Antonia. As obviously as if she stated it, he knew that during the act of sex her paramount feeling was endurance. But that was the way things were arranged in this life. Another excellent reason for him not to believe in God.

Closing his eyes, forcing Benita from his thoughts, he once again thanked his luck, his stars, anything that was not God, for freedom from war for himself and his children. Tomorrow, for insurance, he would give one hundred dollars to a charitable cause.

January 16, 1918
Malden, Massachusetts

All the girls noticed Starr had been acting differently for the last couple of months but it was even more pronounced after Christmas vacation. She never joined them in the parlor for sewing or took walks to town or played games anymore. She just stayed in her room.

Evelyn Henry, particularly, found Starr's change puzzling and hurtful and was determined to find out what had caused it. She told Mary Gray about her plans.

"I'm just going to come right out and ask her."

"Do you think you should?"

"Well, how else are we going to find out what's going on? Don't you even care?"

"Of course I do. You always think you're the only one who cares about anything."

"I do not."

"You do."

"I do . . . Mary, please. This is important."

"I know." And she believed that, even though her eleven-year-old philosophy was that everyone should mind their own business.

Evelyn, on the other hand, believed friends should help each other and was fond of quoting Lord Byron to that effect: "Friendship is Love without his wings." In fact, both she and Starr wrote those words on all of their copy books.

It occurred to Evelyn, as she stood nervously outside Starr's door, that maybe her best friend just wasn't her best friend anymore. Maybe Starr didn't care for her the way she cared for Starr! That thought had been hovering around the edges of her consciousness for days. Of course, she was not as remarkable as her friend. Evelyn knew that. For one thing, Starr was beautiful. For another, her demeanor, her behavior, was special. She seemed like at least an eighth-form girl, even though she belonged to the sixth. And she always had such good ideas about things to do. Like Evol, a game Starr had invented. Evol was love spelled backwards. They played it out beyond the school where the old chicken coops were. They called it Evol so no one would know what they were talking about. The chicken coop was their house. Starr was the husband because she was taller, and Evelyn was the wife. Mary was the child. Starr would come home from work and kiss Evelyn before she'd sit down to read the *Boston Globe* while Evelyn prepared the dinner. After dinner both parents played with little Mary for a while, then Evelyn put Mary to bed. Mary was sick of playing the child she said, because they played the best part while she had to pretend she was asleep! The best part was when they lay down on the old gray blanket Evelyn had brought from home and hugged and kissed.

The last time they'd played Evol was near the end of October. When Evelyn suggested sometime in November that they play, Starr practically snapped off her head. She said it was a dumb game and she was sorry she'd ever played it and she had no intention of ever playing it again. That had been the beginning of Starr's change. Little by little she wouldn't do this or wouldn't do that. Evelyn could barely remember the last time they had one of their "Haveyouever" sessions.

These took place late at night, completely in the dark, with just the Big Three—Starr, Evelyn, Mary—playing. They had begun playing when they were about eight, asking things like: "Haveyouever eaten mushrooms?" or "Haveyouever been to the Copley-Plaza Hotel?" Over the years the questions changed to things like: "Haveyouever kissed a boy?" and even "Haveyouever seen a boy's bare behind?"

But right before Christmas vacation, when Mary suggested a "Haveyouever" session, Starr almost went through the roof. She said it was a baby's game and if they wanted to go on being babies forever they could but she didn't want any part of it. And since they'd come back from vacation Starr had barely spoken to them.

Now Evelyn was determined to get some answers. Until Starr Wyman explained why she was acting so strange, Evelyn swore she would not leave her room—even if she had to stay all night!

The knock on the door beat like a tattoo on Starr's heart. She considered ignoring it but the knocking grew louder and more persistent. Then she heard Evelyn's voice.

"I know you're in there, Starr. Please tell me I can come in."

Starr felt pleasure at hearing Evelyn, as well as dread. She knew she would be difficult to discourage. Continuing to read her book, she told Evelyn to enter.

Starr didn't look up as she came in but she sensed her sitting down on the straight chair across the room. The only sound was Starr turning a page.

"What are you reading?"

"A novel."

"What novel?"

"*Summer.*"

"Who wrote it?"

"Edith Wharton."

"Oh."

More silence.

Evelyn fussed in her chair and tapped the toes of her shoes together. "Is it good?"

"Very."

"What's it about?"

"Oh, what do you care?" Starr let the book fall on her stomach.

"I . . . I was just trying to make conversation."

"What for?"

Evelyn pressed her lips together.

"What do you want?" Starr asked.

"I want . . . I want to know what's wrong?"

"I don't know what you mean."

"Yes, you do, Starr." Evelyn rose and walked to the

end of the bed where she sat gingerly, her shoulder resting against the polished brass.

Almost involuntarily, Starr slid farther back on the bed.

"You've been acting funny," Evelyn said.

"I have not." She felt a rush of heat through her body. What did Evelyn know?

"You have. Ever since . . . ever since . . ."

"Ever since what?" she broke in. Did Evelyn know about November 3rd?

"Well, I don't know exactly but it's been for awhile."

Relief. "I don't know what you mean."

"For instance," Evelyn said, looping her arm around one of the shiny posts, "you never want to do *anything* anymore."

"What's anything?" She needed to get her inner breath.

"Just anything. All you want to do is stay in your room by yourself."

"I like to read, unlike other people I could mention."

"I like to read too, Starr, if that's who you mean . . . you know very well that I read a lot. But that's not *all* I do."

Thinking that it was not *all* she did either, Starr began to feel that uncomfortable rush again. The sooner she got Evelyn out of her room, the sooner she would be comfortable again. "Just what is it you want?"

"I told you. I want to know what's wrong?"

"And I told you . . . nothing."

"Well, I don't believe you. Everyone's noticed."

It was as though Evelyn had butted her in her middle. "Noticed what?" She tried to sound unconcerned.

"How you're acting."

"Like what?"

"Oh, Starr! Like this. You act like . . . I don't know what." Evelyn sounded quite defeated.

Starr was almost sure now that Evelyn didn't know anything. It had been silly of her to feel nervous. After all, she knew very well she'd been withdrawn lately. "Then, if you don't know, why pursue it?"

Evelyn slumped against the bedpost, not knowing what to say.

Starr ran a finger over the binding of her book and waited. After several moments, when it was clear Evelyn was not going to say anything, Starr began to whistle.

Evelyn stared at her.

Then Starr sang. *"Now is the hour when we must say goodbye."*

"Is that a hint?" Evelyn asked.

Starr shrugged and continued humming the tune.

"I just don't understand you, Starr. I thought we were best friends."

The humming continued.

"Did I *do* something? Is that it? Did I do something? *Answer* me, Starr?"

"Soon you'll be sailing far across the sea," she sang.

"I thought you cared about friendship . . . I thought friendship was the most important thing to you. What about friendship being Love without his wings and all that?"

Still humming, Starr reached for a copybook on her night table and tossed it toward Evelyn.

The agitated girl looked down and saw the favorite quotation had been obliterated by black ink. Starr had crossed it out just as she was crossing out Evelyn now. Evelyn began to cry. "Oh, Starr, please tell me what's happened."

Starr hummed louder as if the sound could screen her from Evelyn's tears. But it didn't. Starr was moved by Evelyn's obvious misery. Just as she was about to reach out, to touch her friend, Evelyn said:

"What is it, Starr? Is it some secret or something you're afraid to tell me?"

Those words resolved Starr's conflict. "You really are a do-do, Evelyn." She spat out the words. "Don't you understand anything? I'm not interested in your friendship anymore. Yours or Mary's or anyone else's in this infantile school. You're all a bunch of dopes as far as I'm concerned and I don't want anything more to do with you."

Evelyn could not accept this. "Why? Why now . . . I mean what's changed?"

"I've changed, if you must know. My eyes have been opened. I now see that I've wasted my time with you and Mary. You're nothing but children."

"I can change," Evelyn said softly.

Starr jumped off the bed and walked toward the door. "You just don't understand, do you?"

"Understand *what?*" Evelyn sobbed.

Holding open the door, she answered angrily. "I don't like you anymore, Evelyn. Is that plain enough?"

Evelyn swallowed noisily. Starr was motioning her out of the room with a sweeping gesture. Coming abreast of Starr, her eyes red and nose running, Evelyn cried out: "Oh, Starr!" Then she let out a deep sob and ran from the room.

Starr slammed the door and stumbled back to the bed. After a few moments, she plumped up her pillows, settled into them and picked up her book. The words blurred as the book moved in her shaking hands. She began to hum softly and then, gaining more strength, she started to sing.

"While you're a-way—O, then re-mem-ber me—When you re-turn, you'll find me wait-ing here."

As the words on the page began to focus, have meaning, her singing fell to humming and finally stopped.

Faithfull Girl's Burial Halted By New Clews
—Herald Tribune, June 12, 1931

June 5, 1931
New York, New York

"You certainly are putting it away," Stanley said.

She forced a smile, then finished the last of her eggs.

In her room she very carefully chose her clothes. After all, when found, she wanted to look her best. The dress would be her favorite. It was a black and white foulard with red, white and green sleeves. Black pumps, a black straw hat, black bag, tan stockings held up by a girdle. She would definitely not wear any underpants.

Five

When he closed his eyes he could still see the whites of *her* eyes. He remembered pulling back the lids. Only the white showed. It was too awful. Think of something else, he told himself. Cathy.

Cathy had been his friend once. She adored him. Everyone said so. They also made jokes. Like: "When Cathy gets married Orr's going to go along on the honeymoon and sleep in the middle!" Then there was Dr. Tobin. "You've got to give that child some room. If you don't, you'll pay for it later." And Fran. "You're going to ruin that girl. She has to have some freedom."

But he couldn't help it. He had to make sure nothing would happen to her. Who knew better what kind of accidents could happen to a pretty girl? *Accidents.* Anyway, she loved him . . . then.

Even later in her early years in New York she still cared for him. Then what happened? It was when she was in the hospital.

The doctor said: "It's best if you don't see Cathy for awhile. She needs some breathing room."

Never the same after that. That was part of the reason he hated those psychiatrists. They ruined everything.

55

And certainly none of them had ever helped him. Two breakdowns, four doctors. Nothing. Well, of course, he hadn't told them about *her*. How could he?

———————

August 5, 1918
Brookline, Massachusetts

It was another wheatless Monday. It was also Elisabeth Tucker Wyman's seventh birthday and Helen was adamant about the child having a cake . . . war or no war! After all, this wheatless thing was voluntary and surely even·President Wilson wouldn't want a little girl denied her birthday cake!

Helen knew that having the party was a little risky. She'd kept the girls isolated nearly the entire summer and now she was going to expose them to possible infection from the influenza epidemic, still raging along the eastern seaboard. However, the children she'd invited to Tucker's party had been carefully chosen. They too had been kept isolated.

As she sifted the flour for the chocolate cake, Tucker's favorite, Helen wondered, as she did every day, how long the war would go on and how long it would be before Frank came home? She also wondered what it would be like when he *did* come home. He'd been gone almost a year and she didn't miss him in the least.

She wrote to him, like a good wife, two or three times a week, but it was getting harder and harder to think of things to say. At least tomorrow she would be able to stretch this party into a few pages. Frank wrote much less than she did, and his letters were short and said little. All she really knew was that he was in France, the director of Foyer Du Soldat which had something to do with the Y.M.C.A. He wasn't in any real danger so Helen did not have to worry and for that she was grateful.

The fact that she'd been alone for almost a year, raising her two daughters by herself, pleased rather than pained her. Helen liked being the one and only authority in the house. She also enjoyed not having to answer to anyone for her time or thoughts. Not that she'd like to be thought of as a Suff, those women who were trying to get the vote. Not that she wanted to be like a man. She firmly believed, as a matter of fact, that the man should wear the trousers and be head of the house. But if he wasn't around—well, what choice did a woman have?

As for missing Frank as a husband, a companion, a lover—well, the truth was they hadn't been close companions the last few years anyway. And being lovers had never been terribly interesting to her. So what was there to miss? She supposed having an absent father was hard on the girls yet neither of them ever asked for him. Perhaps, in Starr's case, it was because Andrew had been such a wonderful substitute.

Helen wiped her hands on a small towel and removed the eggs from the wooden icebox. Consulting the *Boston Cooking School Cookbook,* she discovered she would need six. She patted her brown hair checking the two buns on either side of her face which the children referred to as "cootie garages."

Yes, Andrew certainly had done his best to be a father to Starr. He'd tried with Tucker too but she just didn't seem to take to him. He always let the girls dig in his pockets for fifty-cent pieces. Andrew would say he had a surprise and then they'd dig around in his pocket until they found the fifty-cent piece. Helen supposed his interest in the girls was because he only had sons. Starr, in particular, was the daughter he didn't have. He went often to her school, taking her out to dinner or driving in the country. This past summer he'd visited frequently, sometimes taking all of them out, sometimes requesting he be alone with his "little sunshine." It was important, he explained to Helen, that a girl Starr's age have a male influence and that she occasionally have him all to herself. Helen supposed that was quite true and was grateful to Andrew for assuming the role.

Anyway, Andrew Peters was a good person to have on her side. After all he was the Mayor of Boston. He was also rich and times weren't easy now. Often he pressed a folded bill into Helen's hand, suggesting Starr might need new shoes or a new dress. Helen protested but he would insist. And the bill was always far more than was needed. Yes, Andrew was definitely a man to have around.

Helen stirred the batter. She wondered if the change in Starr had to do with Andrew or the beginning of menstruation, or the fact that her father wasn't around, or something else. She'd spent the whole summer in her room reading, writing in her diary. The only time she participated in anything resembling conversation was when Andrew visited.

Once Helen and Starr had been friends. Now they just didn't connect. Helen supposed it was a stage that mothers and daughters went through. Why else would Starr change so? Not that she'd ever been your ordinary child. There was always something special about her. And not just her startling beauty. She was so bright. And not only in school. Starr's curiosity, awareness, her thought processes struck Helen as precocious. She'd mentioned it once to Frank but he'd said she was just trying to be special, as usual. But Helen still believed it. And watching Tucker grow, going through the same phases, convinced her even more. As intelligent as Starr was though, there'd been nothing odd or peculiar about her. And she was loving. Oh, so loving. Frank, being the undemonstrative man he was, did not encourage this but Helen had always returned Starr's affection.

Since last fall, however, she could count on one hand the number of times Starr had kissed her. She appeared often to be brooding over something. And then there was that strange incident at the beginning of the summer. They'd gone to the beach and Starr had refused to wear a proper bathing suit, bathing instead in a pair of old knickers. She wouldn't give Helen an explanation and sulked the whole day.

Helen contemplated talking with her daughter. Perhaps Starr would confide in her. Perhaps she'd discover she'd been worrying for no good reason.

She poured the batter into the pans. A talk was definitely in order. Tomorrow. She would take her dear, sweet child aside and have a real old-fashioned heart-to-heart.

The pans were in the oven, clock checked. Helen washed her dishes, cleaned the counter and headed upstairs to make the beds. A talk tomorrow. Absolutely.

*   *   *

Starr was reading *The Innocents*, a novel by Sinclair Lewis. She understood only about 50 per cent of it, partly because it was beyond her, partly because she was distracted. She didn't want to attend her sister's birthday party. The children were much younger and she knew she would be bored. But her mother insisted Starr be there. She could not, her mother said, stay locked in her room all afternoon. When Starr asked her why not, her mother just shook her head and walked away. Why was it grown-ups never gave you answers to anything? They said a thing was so and you had to believe it. Or they said you must do something and that was that. Starr couldn't wait to be grown up enough to do what she wanted and not have to give reasons or explanations to anyone. Now, when her mother asked her something, Starr just stared at her until she went away. Her father was a little harder to get around. Just staring didn't work. She had to make up lies for him. Of course, there hadn't been that much to lie about when he'd been around. But it was different now—different since Andrew.

She snapped shut the book and turned over on her back staring at the ceiling. Everything was different since Andrew. That was the way she thought of her life now. B.A. (Before Andrew) and S.A. (Since Andrew). In her mind, there was as clear a line between November 2nd, 1917, and November 3rd, 1917, as if it had been drawn in India ink on a huge calendar.

It had been exceptionally cold November 3rd. When Miss Parker sent for her she hoped whatever the woman wanted wouldn't involve going outside. Entering Miss Parker's office, she was shocked to see her cousin Andrew Peters. She was also afraid though she didn't understand why. He'd come to the house twice the previous summer and he'd always been nice. She didn't know why she was feeling all pincushiony now. Of course, there was something scary about those eyebrows, so big and hairy, sticking out the way they did. And then there was the way he looked at her. It made her feel like she was wrapped in a wet towel.

Soon she was sitting beside this big man in his maroon car. She'd never been in a closed car before and she liked it. Miss Parker had said something about going home. Starr hadn't been paying attention so now she asked Andrew.

"Cousin Andrew, where are we going?"

"Just call me Andrew, Starr dear."

"All right."

"We'll have some dinner at a place I know in Lynn."

"Lynn? I thought Miss Parker said you were taking me home?"

Andrew patted her knees. "Home is where the heart is." He chuckled.

She felt she shouldn't question him further and sat back in the plush leather seat, feeling like a princess in a chariot. Andrew began talking about his campaign for Mayor. She tried to make appropriate comments, mostly in the form of positive and negative sounds.

During dinner he told her he had a surprise for her later. He asked if she liked to read. She said she did. He said he had a book she would love but he would only let her read it if she was a very good girl.

"I *am* a good girl," she said, smiling.

"But are you a *very* good girl?"

She wondered why he was pushing his knee against hers. "What do you mean by a *very* good girl?"

"Ahhh! That's a good question, isn't it?"

"Is it?" Now she felt his hand on her skirt and she experienced a sensation that was like being afraid of a noise in the dark.

"Well, a *very* good girl is a girl who does what she's told."

"I guess I'm not a *very* good girl then." She felt his hand searching for the outline of her thigh. It made her breathe in a different way.

"You mean you don't do what you're told?"

"Sometimes. Sometimes I do." She cocked her head to one side, looking at him from under long, long lashes. "It depends on what it is I'm told to do."

His hand was running up and down the inside of her thigh, its touch somewhat dulled through her skirt and petticoat, but still distinct.

"I think," he said, his speech thickening, slowing down, "that you would be a *very* good girl for me, wouldn't you?"

She shrugged. "It would depend on what you asked me to do." His fingers danced on her thigh.

"Suppose I asked you to read to me?"

"I would do that. I like to read."

"Good." He called for the check.

Starr felt a mixture of relief and disappointment

when he removed his hand. But what in the world was he talking about? Did he really want her to read to him? If so, she hoped it would at least be a good adventure story and not some soppy romance.

When they left the dining room he guided her in the direction of the stairway. She turned and looked up at him, questioning.

"Be a *very* good girl, starting now," he said, applying pressure to the back of her neck with his large hand.

He told her number five was her room and number seven was his. Inside, she found her small suitcase which she'd left in the car.

"Why are we staying here? Aren't you taking me to Brookline?"

"Tomorrow," he said. "It's too late tonight. I thought you would enjoy a nice meal and that it would be fun for you to stay in an inn and sleep in a big bed." He looked hurt.

"Oh, it is," she said quickly, hating to see the sad look on his face. "I just wondered, that's all."

This seemed to cheer him up and he showed her the door connecting their rooms. "Shall we read in your room or mine?" he asked.

"Mine," she answered.

"All right."

He lit the fire which was laid in the marble fireplace and pulled a green wingback chair closer to it. Then he moved a small table with a kerosene lamp next to the chair.

"Would you like to undress for bed?" he asked.

"No," she answered quickly. She felt frightened.

He shrugged. "I'll be right back." He went into his room through the connecting door.

Starr stood in the middle of her room. A kind of dread was building up within her, and yet, a part of her felt like she did right before she belly-flopped on a steep hill.

When Andrew returned he was carrying a book. He went directly to the green chair and motioned her to come with him.

"Sit," he commanded.

He was occupying the only chair. "There?" she asked, pointing to his ample thighs.

"Of course," he said.

She sat. Andrew put an arm around her shoulders and she settled back, feeling oddly comfortable. He handed her the book. She read the title. *The Psychology of Sex*. The author's name was Havelock Ellis.

"I'll show you where to start," he said. He quickly flipped through and stopped at a dog-eared page. "Here, at the top."

Starr began to read, stumbling over some of the words. He told her not to worry and to read slowly. She read without any comprehension, her mind and body totally focused elsewhere. Andrew's breathing had become heavy and very loud. His hand, which had worked its way under both her skirt and petticoat, was inching its way beneath her cotton panties.

Caught between fear and pleasure, Starr decided to continue reading and let Andrew do what he wanted. After all, who was she to question a man who was probably going to be the Mayor of Boston?

Now, many months later, she lay on her bed, rubbing herself the way Andrew had that night. In a few minutes she experienced that wonderful shivery feeling but it was a minor version of what she felt when Andrew made it happen. In that orgasmic moment, she desperately longed for the older man. An instant later she thought of him with unqualified loathing.

Later, when the children and their parents began arriving, she felt even more rooted to her room. Particularly when she heard the voice of Mr. Considene. He was always pinching her cheeks and saying how pretty she was and Starr detested him. She'd hoped he would go to France with her father but he had flat feet and stayed home. If only he didn't look at her *that* way. He made her feel like she was covered with mud from the Charles River.

When Starr finally made an appearance, Helen almost fainted.

"What . . . what is the meaning of this?" she gasped.

Starr was wearing one of her father's suits, much too large for her, and had pulled her hair back into a bun. She looked at her mother and said nothing.

When Helen demanded she go to her room, she left

willingly and peacefully, noting the very sour look on Mr. Considene's face.

That night when Helen pushed for an explanation Starr simply stared until her mother went away. It was never mentioned again. Nor was there ever an old-fashioned heart-to-heart.

Another day of depression. Blue Monday. What can I expect? Dawn will soon be here. God damn it.

—From Starr's diary, 1928

June 5, 1931
New York, New York

Starr emerged from her room looking ravishing.

"Will you be back for lunch, dear?" Helen asked.

"I doubt it."

"Will you be back *after* lunch?"

"I don't think so. I'll probably have dinner out."

"I think you ought to come back before going to dinner."

Starr wondered why. She said, "Oh, I'll be all right, Mother. If I find I can't return I'll send you a telegram." She smiled.

"I'm sure," Helen said, glumly.

Before opening the door she turned once more to look at them both sitting on the bed. They looked sad, old, worn. She would never see them again. That was fine.

Six

August 6, 1977
Orange, New Jersey

The nurse changed the bottle that dripped life into his arm.

He thought of Fran. If she'd lived she'd be here now. She'd be talking away, not caring if he understood or not. Just like his sister. His last remaining sister. Always talking, talking. What did they find to talk about? When they had lived with his parents the women were always talking.

Living with his parents. That, perhaps, had been the worst thing he'd done to Fran. How she loved that house in Allwood. He'd recovered from the breakdown and they'd been happy there. The house was small but adequate for the three of them. Fran loved the friends she made on the street. She urged him to buy the house; renting, she said, was a waste of money. He could never bring himself to do it, kept putting it off.

Then in 1941, two months before Pearl Harbor, the truth about Papa's finances came out. He was dead broke. The children would have to help.

Silvio had a new baby, a new job and no extra money. Nina was in Canada with five children and could only contribute a little. Toni and Max were already living with Mama and Papa, helping all they could. He could not afford to keep the house in Allwood and help support the one on Van Ness Place. He told Fran they'd have to give up the Allwood house and live with his parents. She cried desperately. She said she would go to work but he forbade it. In November, right before Fran's fortieth birthday, they moved to Van Ness.

They stayed for a year. During that time Silvio, Carol and the baby moved in too. Fran developed terrible stomach pains. The doctor said she must move out. They found a house in South Orange and, once again, they rented.

But Fran never liked the house as much as the one in Allwood and, true or not, he felt she never forgave him for making her leave there.

When she was in the hospital the second time he wrote her a letter. Cathy insisted. He dictated and Cathy typed.

"Tell her I'm sorry about the Allwood house," he rasped.

"You can't say that. She'll know something's very wrong if you say that. No apologies for anything. It's too late for that."

Too late. Always too late. It had been too late when he realized he should have gone home that day instead of driving out to Long Beach with that strange, beautiful girl. Always . . . always . . . too late.

November 11, 1918
Malden, Massachusetts

Starr was dreaming. It was a pleasant dream. She was flying. Not horizontally, with her arms flapping. But perpendicular, three or four feet above the ground. She glided down the street passing amazed citizens to whom she shouted greetings. When the school bell reached her consciousness she was annoyed to be awakened.

It was still dark out when she opened her eyes. Barely awake, she heard, over the ringing of bells and other unidentifiable noises, her roommate, Winifred Davis.

"What, in heaven's name, is that? Starr? Are you awake? Do you hear that? What, for Lord's sake, is going on? What time is it? Starr? Starr? Are you awake?"

"No." She inched herself up in the bed, propping her pillow against the bedstead.

"I thought you were dead, for mercy's sake. Do you think it's the Armistice?"

"Again?"

"I mean the real one."

Four days earlier the girls had participated, along with the rest of the country, in a celebration which turned out to be a false alarm.

"Well, what else could it be?" Winifred asked. "Prissy Parker wouldn't be ringing bells in the middle of the night for nothing, Lord knows."

"Then I guess it's the Armistice." She stretched.

"Well, for heaven's sake, Starr, I should think you'd have a little more enthusiasm. Don't you care?"

"No." But she did. It meant her father would be coming home. It meant changes—changes that would affect her on weekends and holidays and during the summer.

"But your daddy will be coming home."

"Yes, I know."

"Well, don't you think that's just wonderful? For Lord's sake, Starr, I just can't wait until I see my daddy again."

"Good for you."

"Oh, honestly."

There was a knock on the door.

"Entré," Winifred said.

The round face of Mary Gray poked into their room. "C'mon you two . . . get up . . . it's the Armistice . . . really. We're all meeting in the chapel. Hurry."

"Should we dress?" Winifred asked.

"Nah . . . just put on your robe. Hurry, Freddy."

Starr yawned. "What time is it?"

"Oh, Starr," Mary said and slammed the door.

Starr stared at the closed door wondering what she'd said to evoke that response. What was wrong with asking the time? Oh, well, what difference did it make what Mary Gray thought? Or anyone else.

From the floor under her bed, Winifred said: "Aren't you coming?"

Starr looked at the raised behind of her roommate and asked what she was doing.

"Looking for my slippers."

The last time Starr had seen them they were near Winifred's bureau.

"Aren't you coming?" Winifred asked again.

Starr had no interest in joining the others. As far as she was concerned, she had nothing to celebrate. But if she didn't go Miss Parker would be nosing around in no time. Better to go than stay and create a lot of attention. She swung her legs over the side of the bed.

"Oh, for mercy's sake," Winifred sputtered, "I can't find the dopey things." She came out from under the bed and stood, hands on hips, looking around the room. "Have you seen them, Starr?"

"No." She put on her own slippers and scuffed across the room to the wardrobe, passing Winifred's bureau on the way. Her roommate's slippers were sticking out from underneath. Starr gave them a push with her toe, hiding them completely.

"Well, I just can't go in bare feet," Winifred whined.

Starr thought the girl might cry. She put on her robe.

"I'm going to miss everything."

"What's *everything?*"

"Well, who knows? I'll just have to go in bare feet and hope that Parker doesn't notice."

"You'll catch a cold," Starr said.

"I don't care. I'm not going to miss it just because I can't find my old slippers, for Lord's sake." She went for her robe.

Starr listened to the sound of the girls in the hall. Why was she being so mean to Winifred? True, she didn't like her, but what was the point of this? Often lately she did mean little things and didn't know why. Sometimes she was surreptitious, other times openly hostile. The other girls stayed away from her more and more. Wasn't that what she wanted? She didn't need all this bosom-buddy stuff. Who needed a lot of prying questions?

Winifred was jumping from one foot to the other. "Oh, it's cold. Let's go, for heaven's sake, before my feet fall off."

It occurred to Starr then that if Winifred *did* get a cold she would be stuck in bed which meant Starr would never have the room to herself.

"C'mon," Winifred said, opening the door.

"Your slippers are under your bureau." She stepped past her roommate.

"What?" Winifred squealed.

"You heard me." Starr started down the hall.

"Well, for heaven's sake, Starr. Honestly!"

In the chapel Starr sat by herself. Miss Monroe was at the organ, her auburn hair hastily done up so that long strands flew around her face as she energetically kept time with her head. The girls were singing "I Didn't Raise My Boy to Be a Soldier." They'd already been through "Smiles," "Pack Up Your Troubles" and "There's A Long, Long Trail."

Winifred entered and joined a group of girls two rows in front of Starr. Starr watched her predictably whispering to her friends who then all turned to look at Starr. She gave them her haughtiest stare.

Miss Parker held up her hands for silence and the girls finished the song.

"Girls, as you know by now, the Armistice has been signed. I think we should take this opportunity to thank God for ending this dreadful war. Let us bow our heads for a minute of silence in remembrance of those doughboys who won't be coming home." She bent her head.

Softly, Miss Monroe began to play "Abide With Me." "Abigail . . . no," Miss Parker whispered angrily. The organ stopped.

Starr smiled as she watched this scene between the two women. Miss Monroe's face flushed and huge tears filled her eyes, as they always did at the slightest provocation. Starr surveyed the small sea of bent heads in front of her on either side of the aisle. What saps they all were! What good would a minute of silence do the dead doughboys in Europe? That was for the birds! And she certainly wasn't going to be a party to it. Crossing her arms and stretching out her legs, she stared straight ahead, anger growing inside her.

"Now girls, I think it would be in order to declare the rest of November eleventh a holiday," Miss Parker said when the minute of silence ended.

A cheer went up.

"We'll get dressed, have breakfast and then meet back here at nine when we'll plan our demonstration for the village. Dismissed."

As the girls pushed and bobbed against each other, Miss Monroe played "Smiles" for their exit. Starr, arms still crossed, eyes still straight ahead, waited for the others to leave. Now the anger felt like a huge prickly ball in her stomach.

When Evelyn Henry, Winifred's best friend, passed Starr's row, she said: "You are hideously demented, Starr Wyman."

Mary Gray added: "Some people!"

Starr did not look at them; she blocked out any further epithets. The ball was working its way up into her chest. When the last girl had passed her she stood up, ignoring the eyes of Miss Parker. She made her way to the aisle. The sun had begun to penetrate the chapel windows. In her throat, Starr felt the ball pressing against her windpipe, then moving upward until it was right behind her eyes. As she headed for the door, it exploded behind her eyeballs and silently she began to cry.

November 11, 1918
Newark, New Jersey

Orlando sat in the abandoned tool shed with Ruth Shiffenhauser. The afternoon light peeked through a small window, casting strange shadows across Ruth's brooding profile.

"What's wrong?" Orlando asked.

She shrugged.

He knew Ruth was not one of the most talkative girls (that was one of the things he liked about her) but usually she opened up with him. Especially in their *castle*, where they were today.

"This is supposed to be a happy day." He wasn't happy or unhappy. The end of the war had nothing to do with him. But it did mean a holiday from school.

"I don't care what it's supposed to be."

He looked deep into her large, dark eyes. No message there. "Are you upset about something?"

There was a twitch at the corner of her full lips. She shook her head, looking at him as though he were a poor unfortunate. "You don't understand anything, do you?"

"I understand that I love you," he said.

"Oh, Orlando, don't. Not today."

"But why? What don't I understand, Ruthie?" Did she really know so much more just because she was eleven months older?

"Have you forgotten about Ivan?"

Her brother had been killed in the war. He had not forgotten; he just hadn't connected it with today. "I'm sorry."

"You don't understand."

"What? What don't I understand?"

She poked at the dirt with a broken trowel. "Ivan was treated rotten. By his own company. Because he was a Jew. And he died defending this stinking country."

Orlando was shocked. He had been taught to love his country. The land of opportunity and justice. "Don't say that," he whispered.

"Why not? Are you afraid of the truth?"

"No."

"Well, that's the truth. The soldiers picked on him, called him terrible names and made him eat alone. He wrote us. That's why Mother's the way she is."

Sylvia Shiffenhauser hadn't left her room since word of Ivan's death, eight months before.

"Why didn't you tell me?"

"What do you care? You don't know what it's like to be Jewish."

"I don't have to be Jewish to understand when something's unfair, wrong," he said indignantly.

"Orlando, let me ask you a question."

"Sure."

"Why do you want to keep us a secret?"

Something inside him tightened. "What do you mean?"

"Have you suddenly gone deaf? Or maybe you don't know the English language anymore, huh?" Ruth dropped the trowel and leveled her gaze at the boy sitting cross-legged in front of her.

"I . . . I know what you said. I mean . . . look, Ruthie, I love you and . . ."

"Answer my question, Orlando."

His black hair fell over one eyebrow and he pushed it back. "I just thought it would be fun . . . more romantic." He looked away, toward the door.

"At first I tried to tell myself it was 'cause you didn't want anyone to know you had a girlfriend . . . maybe your friends would make fun of you . . . but then when I realized that they all had girlfriends, too . . . well?"

"I don't see what . . ."

"How long have we lived across the street from you?"

"I don't know . . . about three years, I guess."

"Do you know that in all that time your mother has never called on mine?"

"Mama doesn't call on anyone, Ruthie."

"They sent flowers when Ivan died, though. I'll say that for them."

"Why hasn't *your* mother called on mine?"

Ruth smiled, laughed—short, derisive. "You see, you *don't* understand anything. We were the new neighbors. It was *your* mother's place."

"She just doesn't do that and . . ."

"And your father? He could have called on mine. Only your sister Connie has ever been in our house. You know why? Because she doesn't care."

"Care about what?" He wished they were kissing as they usually did and wondered if he could get things around to that.

"Care that we're Jewish."

"I don't either," he said, adamant.

"Yes you do."

"I don't."

"Then why are we a secret?"

"I told you."

"I don't believe you."

"I can't help that," he said sulkily.

"All right, Orlando." She stood up, wiping the dirt from her skirt. "Let's go over to your house and tell your mother and father. Come on." She held out her hands to him.

"Tell them what?"

"That we're boyfriend and girlfriend."

"Oh, Ruthie, I can't do that." The thought of confronting his parents with that information was humiliating. "I mean, how could I say that?"

"You said you wanted to marry me."

"Well, not today."

"I know that, dummy. But why can't we tell them that we're going to be married *some*day?"

Slowly, he rose. She was being unfair. He couldn't say that to his parents no matter who the girl was. He told her that.

"All right then, I want you to take me to the Thanksgiving dance. I'm tired of not going anywhere with you. If I don't go with you I'll have to go with Harold Bachrach and he always steps on my feet."

Orlando was taking Giullieta Mondini. He could tell Ruth he'd take her. It might at least save this day. But then it would be worse than ever when he told her the truth. He explained.

"Break the date," she said.

"I can't do that."

"Why don't you admit the truth. You're not taking me because I'm Jewish. Why don't you just admit it."

He could not admit it. It was true but he simply could not admit it.

They stared at one another.

"I'm good enough to kiss . . . and touch," she whispered, though there was no one else to hear. "But I'm not good enough to take to a dumb school dance. You stink, Orlando Antolini. You really stink." She started toward the door.

Orlando grabbed her arm. "Ruth, now *you* don't understand. Papa would kill me." It slipped out.

She looked at him, her face hard, taut, eyes cold. "It's always been this way. It always will be. I shouldn't have expected you to be any different. Goodbye, Orlando."

And then she was gone.

He wanted to call her back, tell her he would break his date, tell his parents, become engaged to her if she wanted, anything. But he did not call or move. He had never loved a girl before Ruth and was sure he would never love another.

He sat back down in the dirt and cried.

November 11, 1918
New York, New York

Stanley Faithfull was in New York on the day the Armistice was signed. Awakened at five in the morning by sirens and bells he was for a moment frightened and confused. Not only was he in a strange room but he was alone.

He called down to the desk and they informed him the war was over . . . definitely, this time. Lighting a Lucky Strike, he walked to the window, forgetting that he overlooked nothing but a cement court. He wasn't able to afford a room with a view.

Sitting in the dark on his bed, smoking his cigarette, listening to the noise outside, Stanley realized how peaceful it was to be alone. His body felt light and he opened and closed his legs, making an arc with his heels. It didn't even matter that the room was dingy. He couldn't see it anyway. The only thing that mattered was that he was alone. For the first time in twelve years! He smiled. The world was free of war and he was free of Margaret—at least for another thirty-six hours.

At a newsstand on the corner of Broadway and Forty-fifth, Stanley put down his two cents and bought a *New York Times*. Standing there, he read the headline.

ARMISTICE SIGNED, END OF THE WAR!
BERLIN SEIZED BY REVOLUTIONISTS;
NEW CHANCELLOR BEGS FOR ORDER;
OUSTED KAISER FLEES TO HOLLAND

He folded the paper and put it under his arm. The day was fair so he decided to walk to Fifth Avenue and see what was going on. With his business appointment postponed until the next day because of the Armistice, he was free to do what he pleased. As he walked, people smiled at him and nodded greetings. He supposed the occasion had put smiles on the people's faces.

Having little money to spend on lunch, he stopped at a street vendor for a sweet potato. It was hot and he juggled it from hand to hand. When it cooled he bit into it carefully, the warm pulpy flesh soothing, sliding around on his tongue.

By the time he reached Fifth Avenue the potato was devoured. As he turned the corner onto Fifth Avenue, going uptown, he could see throngs of people milling about in the street. Some were shouting and singing. Others carried signs: *We KO'd the Kaiser,/We Won, We Won,/We Beat the Hun,/Kick the Kraut in the Snout.* People pounded him on the back, shook his hand and, for the first time in years, Stanley Faithfull felt really alive. He began to smile and then to grin.

Farther along, going up the Avenue, a group of men carried a fake coffin made of old soapboxes. They shouted that the Kaiser was inside, resting in *pieces!* This made Stanley laugh. He'd have to remember that to tell the men in his office.

He kept walking, greeting people, occasionally stopping to talk with a stranger. At Fifty-ninth Street he crossed back to Broadway where he headed uptown again.

More of the same was going on there. At Seventieth Street, a crowd had gathered in a circle, their heads bowed. As he got closer he heard shouts: "Kill the Kaiser!" "Rub him out!" "Give him one for me!" He inched his way through the crowd and soon was peering into the circle's center. A young blond boy was drawing on the pavement with chalk. It was a picture of the Kaiser. When he finished people surged forward, trampling on the drawing, the shouts accompanying their frenzied rub-out. When the picture was just bits and pieces of chalk line, the boy started a new drawing.

Absorbed by the people dancing on the Kaiser's face, it took Stanley a moment to become cognizant of the soft body leaning against the side of his arm and along his leg. Later, when he thought about it, he wasn't sure if it was her body pressure he noticed first or the sweet scent she wore. Lilacs. Soon he felt her breath on his neck. When he turned he found his face almost touching hers, his chin against her nose. He pulled back and looked down at her. Immediately, he noticed the red cheeks and painted lips. No one he knew personally used paint.

She smiled, showing deep dimples in each cheek. Shyly, Stanley smiled back.

"Hello," she said.

"Hello."

"Ain't this exciting?"

"Yes. Yes, very." Did she mean the day or something else? Well, he could play the game. After all, it wasn't as though he were a hick! "It makes the blood race," he said, trying to be suggestive.

"Yeah. You're not from New York." It was a statement.

"How do you know?"

"Your accent. What is it?"

She couldn't mean an English accent—that was too long ago. She must mean Boston. "I live in Brookline, Massachusetts. That's near Boston."

"Yeah, I guess that's it. Boston. Are you a Mainliner?"

"That's Philadelphia."

"Oh. Yeah, sure."

He realized then that they were shouting at each other over the noisy crowd. "Shall we move on?" he suggested.

She shrugged. "Okay."

They pushed their way back onto the sidewalk and started walking downtown. With a little distance between them he was able to get a better look at her. She was pretty, even with the paint.

"It's a great day, huh?"

"Yes. Have you been over to Fifth Avenue?"

"Nope."

"It's really something." He decided to try it out on her. "Ah, there were some men over there carrying a coffin . . . ah . . . not a real one, of course, a hastily put together one made of wooden crates or something. . . . Anyhoo, they were carrying it up the Avenue and shouting that the Kaiser was inside resting in *pieces!*" He began to laugh and in a second she joined him, raucously. Thrilled that she'd responded, feeling a sense of power, he pressed his advantage and cupped her elbow in his hand as they crossed the street. On the other side, he slipped his arm through hers. She did not object. It had been a long time since he'd been with a strange woman but the moves came back to him as though it were yesterday.

"I suppose I should introduce myself. My name is Stanley E. Faithfull."

"I'm Viola Grosselfinger. Don't laugh. I thought about changing it but unless I change it altogether it wouldn't be much better, you know? I mean, what's nice about Viola Gross? Or Viola Finger? So if I change it I'll have to change it completely and I can't think of a name I like. What'd you say your name is?"

"Stanley."

"Your last name?"

"Oh. Faithfull."

"Hmmm. Viola Faithfull. Hey, I like that." She giggled.

He joined in her laughter but felt uneasy. She couldn't be serious, could she? She wouldn't.

"Yeah, that's nice. Would you mind?"

"Mind what?"

"If I took it, honey?"

Honey. "Of course not." He was sure she wouldn't. It was just talk. "I'd be honored," he added magnanimously.

She smiled. "That's real nice of you, Stanley." She squeezed his arm with hers. "How about a drink?"

"Absolutely." He hoped his shock didn't show. He'd never known a woman who drank.

"I know a place where they don't mind serving ladies."

"Fine," he said, inwardly laughing at her use of the word "ladies."

When they reached Forty-ninth and Sixth, she steered him into a place called Hurley's. Inside there was sawdust on the floor, an ordinary bar and a few tables on the side. Viola went to one of the tables. Stanley started to sit across from her but she patted the chair beside hers. He sat there.

A waiter, dirty white apron tied around his middle, stood above them.

"What will you have, Viola?" Stanley wanted the waiter to know that he *knew* his companion.

"Beer," she said.

"One beer and a Bronx." When he looked back at her she was taking a cigarette from a pack of Camels. Another first. Quickly, he fumbled for his box of matches.

"Thanks," she said, as he lit her cigarette. "Don't you smoke?"

"Yes, I do. I was just going to get one." Again he reached into his pocket and brought out the almost empty green and red Lucky pack. He lit a cigarette for himself.

The drinks came and they toasted.

"To the doughboys," she said.

"To the doughboys." They clinked their glasses together.

"Hiya, Johnny," she called to a big man who was taking off his jacket.

"Hiya, Viola."

To Stanley she said: "That's John Hurley, one of the owners. He and his brother own this place with Pat Daley. They're all good guys."

"You come here often?" Stanley tried desperately to eliminate any sound of disapproval from his tone.

"You might say it's my home away from home." She took a deep drag on her cigarette and Stanley noticed the greasy red lipmark on its end when she removed it from her mouth.

"And where's that? Your real home?"

"Oh, I got a place over on Eighth Avenue."

"Do you live alone?"

"Well, I sure don't live with my mother." She laughed, a kind of cackle.

Stanley joined her, letting his hand fall casually on her knee. She didn't react at all. He signaled to the waiter to bring another round.

"You're cute, you know that?"

He did not know and he certainly didn't know what to say to that. No one had ever called him cute. And since he'd had to start wearing glasses, he thought he looked peculiar.

"How old are you, Stanley?"

"Forty-six. Why?"

"I just wondered. You married?"

He wasn't sure how to answer. He decided the truth was best. "Yes."

"Kids?"

"No."

"Why not?"

"I . . . we married late. She didn't want any."

"Too bad. Me, I'm gonna have a whole bunch. Five, maybe six or seven."

Could he have read this whole thing wrong?

"When I get married I'm gonna make sure the guy likes kids. I can't see the point of getting married unless you have kids. At least not for me." She patted his hand which was still on her knee.

Stanley was amazed. She actually expected to get married. And be a mother! Was he completely wrong about her? He couldn't be. She wore paint and drank and smoked and he was sitting here, right this moment, in public, with his hand on her knee. And—and her hand was on his thigh! He was definitely not wrong. He moved over closing the small gap between them and her fingertips touched his penis. He realized she was still talking.

". . . and then I'll move out of this burg to some nice quiet place, you know, and me an him will . . . Jesus!"

"What's wrong?" he asked, startled. She had just locked her hand around his erection.

"You've got the biggest sausage I ever felt!"

"I do?" It had never occurred to him that there was anything unusual about his size. Feeling proud, he asked if they might go somewhere else and she said sure. Why not her place?

* * *

"Say, what the hell do you think you're doing?" Viola said.

Since Stanley was just about to enter her, he was not only shocked by her question but almost frightened. What did she think he was about to do? The Castlewalk?

"Look, Stan, with a cucumber like that you gotta do it right."

"Huh?"

She gave him a push and, at the same time, slid out from under him. "Lie down. On your back. You and me has got to have a talk."

He did what he was told, his erection beginning to collapse.

Viola lit a cigarette. "Ya want one, honey?"

He shook his head.

"Have one." She stuck one of her Camels in his mouth and lit it. "Now," she said, propping up a pillow against the iron headrest, "how old did you say you was?"

"Forty-six." He felt like a child.

"Forty-six. And you've been pumping for years, huh?"

"Pumping?"

"Yeah, you know." She made a circle with her left hand and drew the forefinger of her right hand in and out of the circle.

"Oh, yes . . . yes, years." What in the world was she leading up to?

"So you got a knockwurst to beat the band about and all you do is shove the bastard in. I mean, that's all you care about, right?"

"Well, I don't know, I . . ."

"Yeah, well I *do* know. I'm gonna teach you something, Stanley. Don't ask me why. I ain't sure, except this is a holiday. Maybe I'm just feeling patriotic. I don't have no heart of gold or any of that. So why should I do a dummy like you a favor? Maybe I'm thinking of your wife . . . I'll really be doin' her the favor. But don't get the wrong idea . . . don't think I ain't gonna charge ya. In fact, this'll cost you double." She squashed out her cigarette.

Stanley had no idea what she was talking about but he decided he'd do whatever Viola Grosselfinger told him to.

"Now, you see these grapefruits I got here? They're very nice. Good size. Not too big, not too small. Just right. And what do you do? You pass over them like they're two dried-up prunes. Here." She took his hand and put it on her breast. "Rub it. Hey, easy. I'm real sensitive there. Je-sus. Why do all you mugs think it feels good to a girl when ya pinch, huh?"

"Doesn't it?"

"No. It don't. It hurts. How would ya like it if I pinched the end of your carrot?"

Stanley nodded, imagining the pain.

"Okay. Now rub it. Real slow. That's it."

"It's getting hard," Stanley said, excited.

"Sure. Okay. Now put it in your mouth."

He stared at her.

"What's wrong?"

"Nothing."

"So go ahead. That's right. Now lick it real soft. Good. Yeah, that's right, suck . . . soft . . . soft."

As he sucked one of Viola's breasts he softly rubbed the other, the nipple hard between his thumb and forefinger. His penis was stiffening again.

"Now rub my body with your hand. Take your fingers and stroke me lightly . . . the inside of my arms, my sides, belly, the inside of my thighs . . . keep doin' it . . . everywhere but *there*. Yeah, that's good."

As she gave him directions she began to stroke *him*. He had never felt anything like it. His entire body was alive, every centimeter of his skin at attention.

"Okay, Stan," she said, her voice lower than before, "now start kissing me all over and when you get down there, lick inside my thighs . . . then I'll spread and you can lick me there."

It was as though he were a balloon and she'd pricked him. He felt himself go soft. In a moment, his hand stopped stroking her, his tongue came to a standstill.

"What's wrong?"

He didn't know what to say. How could he tell her that the thought of putting his mouth, his tongue in that dark, wet place revolted him?

"Ya afraid to go into my clam? Ya never done that, huh? Yeah, well, I can see where it might be spooky. But listen, Stan, I'm clean. And I guarantee ya, you'll like it. If ya don't ya can stop, okay?"

"Okay." Clean or not it was impossible for him to believe that it wouldn't smell and taste like . . . well, he didn't exactly know what. But he knew it would be awful. Still, he had a kind of obligation to Viola. He could at least try. Slowly, he began to kiss her, rubbing his lips over her skin. He made a zig-zag path down her body. Although he was apprehensive, he found himself enjoying the softness of her pink flesh, the sweet, salty taste. As his chin hit the soft tangle of hair, his belly lurched. Immediately, he noticed the difference between the texture of Viola's hair and the texture of Margaret's. Margaret's was much more wiry.

Sliding down a little farther, licking the inside of Viola's thighs, he realized he was holding his breath. He also realized this was ridiculous. There was no way he would be able to do what she wanted and hold his breath. At least not the entire time. Anyway, she'd promised he could stop if he hated it.

He felt Viola move and he opened his eyes. She was holding herself open, a hand on either side. His eyes took in the pinkness, the many parts, smooth and wet. Tentatively, he touched a smooth, shiny place with the tip of his tongue, quickly drawing it back, tasting. Slightly salty. He realized then he had been breathing and what he smelled was not unpleasant. He tried it again, this time his tongue stayed longer, exploring. It was not just salty. It was—he couldn't identify the taste. But it was pleasant. He liked it. He wanted more.

"Easy, Stan, easy. Real soft. And slow. Lick it slow."

He did what he was told.

"Mmmmm, good," she said. Then: "Turn around."

He heard the words but didn't know what she meant.

"Mmmm, yeah, you got it. Now turn around. I wanna suck your banana."

No one had ever done this to him. He surprised himself by getting into position with a minimum of clumsiness. The first touch of her tongue thrilled him.

He didn't want it to end, yet he knew how near climax he was. Then her mouth closed around him and he thought he must fly over the edge. She slid him in and out of her wet, warm mouth as he gently sucked and stroked her. Just when he thought he wouldn't last another second she stopped and pushed his head away from her.

"Let's have a cigarette," she said.

Was she crazy? He began to protest.

"Just do what I tell ya."

He did.

They smoked a cigarette and, when it was done, they began all over again. This time Stanley needed no instructions. And when the end finally came, it was the most ecstatic moment of his life, the most extraordinary feeling he had ever experienced. He lay back against the pillow, tears of joy in his eyes. Whatever price she asked, he'd double it.

"You're okay, Stan," Viola said.

"You, too." How inadequate, he thought. I should be showering her with diamonds. "I think you're wonderful."

"Ahhh!" She waved a hand at him.

"You know what?" He knew the perfect token of his gratitude. "I think Viola Faithfull is the right name for you."

"Yeah? No kidding?"

"No kidding," he said.

"Ya wouldn't mind?"

"Mind? I'd be honored. I insist. As soon as possible, I want you to change it legally and whatever it costs I'll pay for it. I'll give you my office address and you send me the bill."

"Really?"

"Really."

And she did. And he did.

She was a narcissist. Three-quarters of her waking hours were occupied with thoughts of her physical appearance.
—Anonymous, *New York Times*, June 13, 1931

June 5, 1931
New York, New York

When she reached the sidewalk it was nine-thirty in the morning. She stood for a moment staring back at the yellow building. It had been her home for six months. But she felt nothing for it. She started down the street, slowing in front of number six. Nothing happened and she kept walking.

Her black coat was slung over her arm. Later it might get cool. No need to hide today. She didn't give a damn who saw what.

On West Eighth Street she entered her favorite bookshop. New books were displayed on one of the tables. Starr picked up *The Bell Street Murders* by S. Fowler Wright. It was two dollars. She thought of buying the book, then realized she wouldn't have time to read it. And what for anyway? Why had she read all those books? What for? She put the book back on the table.

Suddenly, she hated the store. Hated the smell, the colors, hated all those books she would never read.

She left, slamming the door behind her.

Seven

August 6, 1977
Orange, New Jersey

Nina, Renato, Connie, Max, Mama, Papa, the first Silvio, Fran, all dead. His sister Nina had only been dead six months. When had he last seen her? What a beautiful woman she was. And Connie. Not so beautiful but a saint. If only he'd driven her . . . no, no, no.

If he had the strength, ability to move, he'd pull the plug from his arm. Living with memories like his was hell on earth. He wasn't afraid to die. He desired it. Toni would take care of the dog. Cathy had her own life. The house would be hers. He'd finally bought it in 1962. Worth maybe forty thousand now. But Cathy had her own money. She did all right. It amazed him. He never thought she'd be anything. Always wanted to be a writer . . . like Daddy. Like Daddy. What a laugh! He'd never thought she was very good but then she sold. So much for what he knew. He was wrong about everything, wasn't he? God knows he was wrong about the girl being . . . no, don't think about it. No.

83

September 8, 1919
Boston, Massachusetts

Andrew sat at his desk in City Hall staring at his nails. Because of all this madness he had missed his manicure and his half moons were not in proper shape. He glanced up at the square New Haven clock hanging on the wall nearest his desk. There was at least half an hour before he should leave for his dinner with Governor Coolidge at the Union Club. Had he known he'd have this free time he would have scheduled a manicure.

He rubbed his eyes. Tired. The last few days had been a mess. Damn the Police Commissioner. Obviously the police must get more money and what was the difference if they wanted a union? Unions were coming in everywhere. It would happen sooner or later so why not go along with it? Of course idiots like Lodge thought it was Red-inspired but he didn't know the Boston Police like Andrew did. Most of the men were Irish Catholic and if they struck it was because they wanted a living wage, not because they were Bolsheviks. And deep down Police Commissioner Curtis knew that too. The problem was that he *had* to be right. If he had just let it alone when the boys applied to the AFL. Oh, no. He had to institute his rule 35. "No members of the force shall join or belong to any organization, club or body outside the department." So then he was forced to suspend the leaders when they were given a charter. Who cared?

Goddammit, I don't, he thought. But he was forced to care. The Mayor had to care. Or had to act like he cared. The truth was he would rather play golf or go yachting any day. Jesus, why had he gotten into this mayor thing? It wasn't as if he wanted to go any further in politics. His mother wanted him to and Martha had *her* plans but his ambitions had never matched theirs. Even if he'd wanted a higher office he'd made that impossible in 1917. Any opponent could have discovered the truth about him with a minimum of digging. When he thought about it like that, a shiver of something like embarrassment began at his center and spread into his extremities.

Naturally, no one would understand his relationship with Starr. How could anyone understand a union between a forty-seven-year-old man and a thirteen-year-old girl? It would be considered depraved. Perverted. Abnormal. Monstrous. And he would be called a degenerate. A deviate. People always had to label what they didn't understand. He removed his handkerchief from his breast pocket and wiped his domelike forehead. Who would understand his need for, his wanting of, Starr? His mother? Martha? Governor Calvin Coolidge? The bastard.

If Coolidge had gotten off his bony ass no one would be in this mess. He didn't have to let things go to the brink this way. Now Andrew had to waste a night having dinner with the dunce, begging him to take some action. Boston couldn't afford a police strike. Curtis, of course, didn't believe the men would really go through with it. Andrew was convinced they would. If only Curtis had accepted the Citizens' Committee Compromise Plan. But no, not Curtis. "I refuse to accept anything which might be construed as a pardon of the men on trial." That's what he'd said instead. Wasn't the important thing to keep peace? Keep the streets safe? If the men went out on strike and the Governor didn't call out the State Guard, it could go on for days and Andrew would be stuck in Boston for the weekend. He couldn't tolerate that. It had been almost four weeks since he'd last seen Starr.

The telephone rang. It was Jesse Stevens, the Adjutant General of the State Guard. The fifth time they'd spoken that day. Andrew planned to ask Coolidge either to override Curtis and accept the Compromise Plan or call out the State Guard. He and Stevens had decided to mobilize, quietly, some of the mounted troops at the Commonwealth Armory. Stevens called to say that was accomplished. Andrew urged him to keep the action as quiet as possible.

In the bathroom he adjusted his tie and combed his thinning, red-tinged hair. As much as he hated the responsibility, and longed to walk away from this whole thing, he wished he had a little more authority. He would have accepted the compromise and, that failing, called the State Guard out hours ago. However, he was powerless. He put on his hat, pinching the high crown and snapping the wide brim into place. He would do his best with the damned Governor but, after all, a man could only be expected to do so much!

*   *   *

In a private room of the Union Club, Andrew and banker James J. Storrow sat in plush leather chairs facing the Governor. Several members of the Citizens' Committee waited in another room for these three to join them for dinner.

Storrow, head of the committee, passed a meaty hand over his sparse gray hair and made a scraping noise in his throat.

"Governor, Mayor Peters and I requested this time with you tonight to explain the Citizens' Committee Compromise Plan."

Coolidge stared at them, his thin tight mouth almost disappearing. He said nothing.

"We feel, sir, that if you were to sponsor this plan we could avert the strike."

Coolidge said nothing.

Storrow took a quick sideways glance at Andrew.

Andrew pretended he didn't notice. He supposed he should join in and help but it was all he could do to *look* at the little man opposite him, let alone speak to him.

"I would like to outline the points of the plan," Storrow went on.

Andrew stared at the gold chain looping over Coolidge's middle, and wondered what time it was.

Storrow was making scraping noises again.

Coolidge said nothing.

"First, the plan allows for an unaffiliated union." Storrow waited a moment for this to sink in.

Coolidge stared at them through narrow eyes.

Good Christ, Andrew thought, can't the man say anything? There was no way to read his hatchet face. If there was a strike, Andrew would miss his time with Starr. For that he could easily have wrung the scrawny Republican neck encased in that very stiff collar.

"Second, if the men call off the strike there will be no disciplinary action taken against the leaders."

Silence.

"And then," Storrow continued, his voice wavering slightly, "their other grievances would be submitted to an impartial board."

Silence.

Now Andrew was forced to speak. "Governor, we know that if you accept this plan, and urge Commissioner

Curtis to do the same, the men will agree and we can avoid a disastrous strike." You ass, he added to himself.

There was silence for several moments, then Coolidge fingered the second button of his vest as he spoke. "Wal, I think not," he said, nasally.

Andrew and Storrow looked at one another.

"But Governor," Storrow started, "if you . . ."

"Dinner," Coolidge said, rising.

"Just a moment, Governor." Andrew felt desperate. Coolidge slightly raised one meager eyebrow. Andrew knew this was a warning signal but, obsessed, he pressed further.

"Governor Coolidge," he said, his normally high voice pitching still higher, "will you at least mobilize the State Guard?"

"We will have riots and crime in the streets if you don't," Storrow pointed out.

"Will you do it, Governor?" Andrew pleaded.

The three men faced each other over a small table. Storrow was motionless. Andrew tried desperately not to grind his teeth. Coolidge, his grim expression unchanging, finally spoke.

"No," he said.

"But why not?" Andrew sputtered. "Don't you realize that . . ."

"All is safe in the Commissioner's hands."

And that was that. Coolidge walked stiffly to the door, opened it and went down the hall.

Storrow and Andrew stared after him, the set of their bodies reflecting his decision.

"The fool," Andrew said. "If only I had some power."

"We must hope for the best. Now we'd better go into dinner."

"I'll be there in a moment."

Storrow nodded and left the room.

So this was the way it was going to be! No plan. No Guard. Chaos. And the Mayor would be held responsible. The thought made his knees feel crumbly. All he wanted to do was run—get his maroon Pierce-Arrow and drive straight to Miss Parker's School where he'd pick up Starr. Then to New Hampshire or Maine or any place where they didn't know him.

And what would everyone think? His mother? Martha? His sons? The public? Thoughts of fleeing were childish, he knew. Closing the one button of his jacket, Andrew headed for the door.

As he walked toward the noisy private dining room, he thought only of the bastard Coolidge and trying to remain calm. He had completely forgotten Jesse Stevens and the mounted squadron of the State Guard who awaited orders at the Commonwealth Armory.

*   *   *

Martha Peters opened her eyes at the first sound of the ringing telephone. She watched as Andrew fumbled with the long black earpiece, trying to pick it up without knocking the whole thing over.

"Peters here."

Martha studied his face as he turned on a light. She could tell by his eyes he hadn't been asleep. But of course neither had she.

"What? Now? How long ago? All right. I'll leave immediately." He clanked the earpiece back in its home. Then he rang the servants' quarters and asked for his driver and car.

Martha knew there was no point in asking what it was all about. Her eyes followed him as he began picking up the clothes he'd strewn about the room when he'd undressed. She knew the police were threatening to strike but not until the next afternoon at five. It certainly wouldn't be happening at—she reached for Andrew's pocket watch which lay on the marble-topped night table—eleven forty-five.

She felt bereft. Martha longed for a husband she could share things with. Before their marriage Andrew had confided in her, trusted her, used her as a sounding board for his ideas.

"Where's my other stocking?"

Sitting up in bed she spied it beneath the rocker next to the fireplace. She said nothing. He didn't want her advice or help. Let him find his own stocking.

In the last two years he'd become even more distant. She supposed it had to do with his becoming Mayor. Before that he had paid her a modicum of attention and occasionally had intercourse with her. By the time he took office he had five sons. The one time since that they'd had intercourse she became pregnant again, giving him what she hoped would be his last child. She supposed she should be glad he no longer made sexual advances toward her because she didn't think she could possibly endure another pregnancy.

Andrew grunted, throwing off the one stocking, going to his bureau for another pair.

Still, the fact that he hadn't touched her for over a year must mean something. She wondered if he had a mistress. It seemed unlikely. Although she was certainly not an expert in these matters, she sensed that Andrew was not a particularly sexual man. There was something about the way he touched her.

Martha watched as he wrestled with his tie. She supposed if she were a *good* wife she would have gotten out of bed and helped him. Well, she didn't feel like being a good wife. If he wasn't going to tell her what was happening, she wasn't going to make things expedient for him. Of course, she hadn't asked him. But she knew. To prove her point to herself she spoke.

"What is it, Andrew? What's going on?"

"Nothing. Never mind."

She almost smiled, leaning back into the pillows.

Andrew went to the door and pulled it open. "Don't wait up. This may take some time." He left. The door didn't quite close and Martha was annoyed as she crossed the cold room to shut it.

At the door she heard her mother-in-law's voice down the hall. "Where are you going, Rew? What's the matter?"

"It's all right, Mother. Don't worry. I have to go out. Go back to bed and I'll tell you all about it in the morning."

Envious, bitter, Martha closed the door, knowing that indeed he would tell his mother everything at the first opportunity.

*   *   *

The Pierce-Arrow was waiting as he came down the stairs of the house on South Street. Settling into the back seat he couldn't be sure what made him angriest: his own stupidity in forgetting the mounted Guard, that Coolidge was on his way to the Armory to disband them or that he saw his time with Starr receding farther and farther into the distance. A fury began building inside Andrew, making his heart drum and his hands shake in his lap.

O'Donlon came to a squealing stop in front of the Armory. Andrew did not wait for his chauffeur to open the door.

"Where's Stevens?" Andrew squawked at one of the troopers inside the Armory.

"Sir?"

"Stevens . . . Stevens. Never mind. Is the Governor here?"

"Yes sir. He went up to the orderly room with Major Gallup and . . ."

Andrew didn't listen to the rest but headed straight for the stairs.

As he reached them, he looked up. Coming down toward him were Coolidge, Curtis and Gallup. Andrew gripped the knob of the iron balustrade, watching the trio descend. Curtis was pale, his puffy face almost obliterating his contemptuous eyes. Major Dana Gallup looked bewildered. Coolidge, leading the triumvirate, kept his eyes on his patent-leather shoes, attempting to ignore the Mayor.

"How dare you do this?" Andrew yelled.

Coolidge didn't raise his eyes until he passed the last step. Then he faced the shaking, nearly apoplectic Andrew, his small eyes narrowing further as he stared at him.

Andrew, unnerved by Coolidge's coldness, began to sputter. "You can't . . . I insist . . . I demand that you . . . why . . ."

Without any inflection the Governor said: "You have no business here!"

The sound of that dry, nasal voice fractured something inside Andrew and he leapt across the three feet separating him from the Governor and began to swing. Even in the confusion Coolidge's cleft chin cried out to Andrew as the perfect target. Drawing back his fist he propelled it toward the cleft with the force of a lifetime's anger. He felt it connect, but not with the chin. He had, instead, landed his punch directly in the middle of the Governor's left eye. As Coolidge grabbed for the balustrade with one hand and his eye with the other, Andrew was seized from behind.

Two troopers, one on each arm, pulled him away as Curtis and Gallup closed in around Coolidge and quickly led him from the Armory.

Andrew's shaking body slumped slightly against his captors. Then he caught his breath and, realizing his position, tried to free himself.

"Let go of me," he ordered.

The troopers, commanderless for the moment, were unable to decide what to do. Then Gallup reentered the Armory.

"Let him go," he commanded.

Andrew brushed at his clothes, looked around for his hat. A trooper found it and handed it to him.

Placing the hat on his head, Andrew left, looking neither right nor left, knowing he had accomplished nothing, yet experiencing a sensation of total and absolute satisfaction.

* * *

At five minutes to four on Tuesday afternoon Andrew left City Hall to walk the two hundred yards to the State House where he would once again meet with Coolidge. The elation of the night before had vanished. Now he was apprehensive and embarrassed.

How was he going to look the man in the eye? He chuckled, realizing he'd made something of a joke. Then the joke turned sour in his stomach. Andrew had never been given to violence. He felt, in fact, that fisticuffs of any sort were vulgar. His behavior at the Armory was a mystery to him. He couldn't imagine how, or why, it had happened.

He entered the State House. No matter what he felt personally he knew he must put it aside and make one last effort to force the Governor to see the dangers of a strike. Of course, after what had happened, it wasn't likely that Coolidge would listen to anything he had to say. Entering the Governor's reception room, the futility of the meeting began to weigh him down.

At one minute after four he entered the Governor's office. Curtis was already there. It would be even more humiliating to have to apologize in front of this antagonist. Clipped greetings were exchanged and Andrew was seated. Coolidge, ever-present cigar in hand, sat silent behind the huge desk, waiting.

Andrew stared at his thinness. Everything about Coolidge was thin, he thought. His sandy hair, his pale skin, his fingers, his body. And surely his mind was thin. Andrew felt anger spurting up inside him. He searched the pinched features for something positive. There was nothing. Time was ticking away. You must speak, he told himself. You must apologize. That thought caused him to look directly at the Governor's left eye. It was almost shut. The skin around it went from shades of gray to shades of black, here and there tinged by blue and purple. Did he really do that? A mixed feeling of revulsion and pride coursed through him. He must do away with the pride before he spoke. He concentrated on the horror of the eye and the uncontrollable violence that caused it. He was ready.

"Governor, before we discuss what we are here for I'd like to apologize for . . . for my behavior last night."

Coolidge puffed on his cigar and said nothing.

Andrew waited for some kind of acceptance but none was forthcoming. Within a few seconds he realized that none would be. The man had the manners of a pig. Andrew simply must overlook that and go on. Once again he made a case for calling out the Guard. When he finished Coolidge took a long puff on his cigar, blew the smoke into the room and said:

"Mr. Peters, why don't *you* call out the Guard?"

Andrew's tufted brows came together. "I would if I had the power."

"You do," he said dryly. "Perhaps if you were more familiar with your office . . ."

"I don't understand."

"In an emergency the Mayor has the right to call out the units of the State Guard stationed within the Boston area." Coolidge clamped his tight lips around the cigar and settled back farther in his chair.

Andrew felt as though he were falling.

Immediately, Curtis piped up. "I don't need the State Guard. I'm ready for anything."

"I believe that concludes this meeting," Coolidge said, shifting some papers on his desk.

There was movement around him, Andrew knew, but no way on earth he could move himself. It was as though his veins had been opened and all his blood poured out of him, leaving his tissue-paper body glued to the leather chair. How could it be true? How could he have not known? He did know the Governor wouldn't have said it if it weren't true. All this time . . .

"Mayor," Curtis was saying, "the meeting's over."

"Yes, yes." On spindly legs, which seemed to belong to someone else, he rose, his eyes on Coolidge's face. And though it seemed impossible, just before he turned away Andrew was sure that a very small, but definite, smile flashed back at him.

*   *   *

An hour after 1,117 of Boston's 1,544 police had struck, Andrew sent for his car. He'd been informed that small knots of people were gathering on the Common and that mud had been thrown against some of the police stations. He also knew that those small groups, harmless at the moment, could and would meld together, forming a crowd. And he knew that the crowd could be triggered by almost anything. What started out in innocence could turn to violence and death.

Now aware of his power, he was unable to use it. All he had to do to avert possible bloodshed was to pick up the telephone. Time after time, in the last hour, he'd reached for the phone; time after time, his hand had frozen in mid-air. If he called out the local Guard, he would go against both the Commissioner and the Governor. The responsibility of that was simply too great.

He had never felt so alone. There was no one in his administration to discuss this with. He couldn't go home and face Martha and his mother. Particularly not his mother. But to be alone on this night would be intolerable.

Stepping into the driver's seat after dismissing O'Donlon, he could hear the hum of the people on the streets. Nothing had really happened yet but if it did, he didn't want to be in the vicinity. For all he knew they might rush City Hall and—it was too horrible to contemplate. Why should he jeopardize himself? He would be needed later. Feeling somewhat justified, with only a small doubt gnawing at him, Andrew put his car in gear and started toward Miss Parker's School.

Returning to City Hall Wednesday morning, he learned that the night before windows had been smashed and stores looted around Scollay Square. There had been a few holdups and several women had been molested. Mattresses blocked streetcar lines and some of the empty police stations were stoned. As far as he was concerned, nothing serious had happened.

Feeling like a new man, not giving a damn about the Commissioner or the Governor, wanting his weekend with Starr more than ever, late in the morning he called out the Guard. Then he issued a statement to the press.

"During this crisis I have received no cooperation from the Police Commissioner and no help or practical suggestions from the Governor."

After that, he removed Curtis from office and began to call up volunteers. Taking this firm command of the situation, he figured no one dared ask him where he'd been the night before.

On Wednesday evening the crowds gathered again, some of them armed. Employees of banks and large stores stood ready with guns inside their buildings. And in Scollay Square, where the mob was ugliest, the Guardsmen, steel helmets in place and bayonets fixed, waited for the first overturned vehicle or scream or sound of shattered glass. When it happened, bricks and bottles were hurled at the Guardsmen. They opened fire, killing three. There were attempted lynchings and a sailor was killed during a skirmish on the Common. In South Boston two more men were killed.

By Thursday morning things were calmer, more orderly. Now Coolidge acted. He called out the State Guard and ordered Curtis back into his office.

When Samuel Gompers of the AFL demanded reinstatement of the strikers, Coolidge answered: "There is no right to strike against the public safety by anybody, anywhere, any time." The *Boston Herald* called him "the pilot that weathered the storm."

By Friday the Boston police voted to return to work

but were repulsed by Curtis who began to recruit a new force. Coolidge had become a national hero, his picture in newspapers all across the country, a congratulatory note from President Wilson on his desk. And Andrew J. Peters, a case of champagne on the back floor of the Pierce-Arrow, began his weekend with one hand on the wheel and the other between the legs of thirteen-year-old Starr Wyman.

Yesterday I swear I was completely overcome by depression.

—From a letter by Starr Faithfull

June 5, 1931
New York, New York

At Sixth Avenue and Ninth Street, Starr stood for a moment, watching cars go by.

Mr. Lieberman, the proprietor of the newsstand there, watched her. She was something to look at. A regular beauty. A shiksa but still a beauty. Nice clothing, too. Expensive.

"The *Times*, please," she said, coming over to his stand.

"Sorry, dahlink, I'm out. It's 'leven-thoity. Ya want a *News*?"

"All right."

They made the exchange of money and paper.

"Bee-oo-tiful day, ain't it?"

"Yes, I guess."

"Ya guess? A bee-oo-tiful dolly like you is only guessing? Every day should be bee-oo-tiful to a dahlink like you!"

She stared at him a moment, tucked the paper under her arm, snapped shut her purse. "What the hell do you know about it?"

Lieberman's mouth fell slack as he watched the retreating figure of the beautiful girl. It takes all kinds, he thought.

Eight

August 6, 1977
Orange, New Jersey

Pulse. Blood pressure. Heart. The doctor wrote on his chart, left.

Orlando's mind whirred. Back, back, back. August, 1954. Cathy. Sitting in the living room. A Sunday. Fran was drinking, as usual. They had both been frantic since ten that morning when they'd discovered Cathy hadn't spent the night at her friend Tina's.

At noon Cathy walked in. All smiles. Not knowing they knew. Then she saw their stricken faces.

"What is it?"

"Where have you been?"

"Tina's."

"Don't lie to us. We spoke to her father."

Screaming: "Why are you always checking up on me?"

His guts churning. Some boy. Some terrible boy she'd spent the night with. Now the time he'd dreaded had really come. The reason he hadn't wanted her at all. You were always reading about these nice quiet boys who murdered girls.

"Who is he?"

"Who's who?" Cathy asked.

"The boy."

"What boy?" Sullen, snippy.

"The boy you spent the night with?"

A turn of her head, eyes closing, explosive laughter.

He and Fran looked at each other. What? What was so funny?

"Oh, God. I think I'd better tell you. I . . . I . . ."

He'd kill the boy if he'd hurt her.

"I don't know how to say this. Well . . . I was in New York. I like the bars there . . . oh, hell . . . I'm gay."

"What?"

"Gay?"

"I'm a homosexual."

He watched her face flush.

Now, in 1977, everyone was telling everyone they were homosexual. He saw them on television, talking, marching. But then, way back then . . . it had been very brave of her then. And he hadn't cared. In fact, he'd been glad. Ecstatic. It kept her out of harm's way.

October 3, 1919
Newark, New Jersey

In two days he would be fifteen. Orlando wondered if he would feel any different. It wasn't a very important or interesting birthday. Turning thirteen or sixteen meant something. Anyway, all he really cared about was getting to be eighteen so he could go away to college.

He crossed his short legs at the ankles and stared at the history book in front of him. The Reconstruction. He would read it at home tonight. The smell from outside was wonderful and distracting. It was unseasonably warm, eighty-seven, someone had said. He wished he were outside, walking, lying on the grass, kicking leaves—no! Oh, why did he have to think of that today? Damn! Remembering it always ruined his day. But it wasn't his fault; he had nothing to do with it; everyone said so. Still. Logical. I must be logical. The familiar litany began in his brain. *If I had hidden in the leaves with Warren the car would have driven over both of us and we both would have been killed and how would that have helped anyone?* Still.

"C'mon, Orr, hide here with me. They'll never think to look in this big pile."

"I got a better place."

Thinking about it now, he got cold, then extremely warm. It was always the same. Why? Why didn't he hide in the leaves with Warren? What was so good about his place? *At least I didn't get killed.* Had he known? How could he?

"C'mon, Orr, hide here with me."

"I got a better place."

What was so good about hiding on the back steps to the cellar? Everyone always looked there. It wasn't as if he'd suddenly discovered some new hiding place. Hiding in the leaves *was* a new place. No one had ever done it. The day before they'd raked the leaves from four lawns and put them in one huge pile in front of Warren's house. They were planning to burn them that night and cook potatoes in the leaves. Potatoes were great that way. So why didn't he hide with Warren? There was enough room for *three* boys!

Now he heard Horace Allen's voice, as always. "*How come, Orr, you didn't hide with Warren? I heard him ask ya.*" And the look in Horace's eyes. Accusing. Knowing. Knowing what? There was nothing to know. How could he have known Warren's brother would come along with his girlfriend in his Locomobile and think it was great fun to ride through the leaves?

Down in the dark on the cellar steps, the wooden door closed above him, he couldn't hear the horrible scream, described by the other boys, when the tires went over Warren. In fact he heard nothing. And finally, after a long time passed, he came out. There was a big crowd in front of Warren's house and even where he stood he could hear Warren's mother sobbing and screaming and he knew. Almost as if someone had told him the exact details. That confused him, making him think he *had* known beforehand. Like déjà vu.

"*How come, Orr, you didn't hide with Warren?*"

Everyone, suddenly, looking at *him*. Accusing? Why hadn't he hidden with his friend, they wondered? Why hadn't he died too? That was what they really asked. *Orr was supposed to hide with Warren but he didn't. I wonder why Orr hid in the cellar.* As if his hiding in the leaves would have kept his friend alive. He began to believe it. But then Connie talked to him and she never asked why he hadn't hidden in the leaves because what did that have to do with anything anyway? Then Mama, too, said how happy she was that he had *not* gone into the leaves. And Nina. And others. Still . . . something nagged.

"C'mon, Orr, hide here with me."

He had to try and think of something else. He thought about the chords for the new song "Tishamingo Blues." He was glad he was learning the banjo. He would have preferred the piano but there was the terrible, inevitable comparison. Orlando liked music, he had an ear for it, but he was no genius. He hoped sometime he might play in the band at school dances. Of course, then he couldn't *go* to the dances. But so what? He could see girls other times. Girls seemed to like his looks even though he was short. Five feet six inches. It was his damn legs. They were the short part. His torso was long, his shoulders broad, ready for at least two to four more inches. But the legs said no. He'd been five-six for almost two years. And no matter what anyone told him he knew it was rotten to be short. Particularly when two of your three sisters were taller. But the worst was his little brother, the second Silvio. He was eight years old and already five feet tall. They said eventually he'd probably be over six feet.

"C'mon, Orr, hide here with me."

It wasn't going away. He tried to read the page in front of him but it was no good. He stared down at his nails. They were perfectly shaped and white. He was disgusted by filthy, ragged nails. Just because you were male didn't mean you had to have them black and unmanicured. But a lot of boys thought you had to be rough and dirty so that no one would call you a sissy. There was nothing wrong with wanting to be clean.

"C'mon, Orr, hide here with me."

Ice pick in the heart! The truth was snaking toward the surface of his brain. He could almost see it. So simple. So awful. Who would understand? It was his hair. He had beautiful black wavy hair. Everyone said so. If he hid in the leaves bits and pieces would get in his hair, in his ears. He would get dirty. He did not want to be covered by leaves, some of them wet, moldy, smelly.

"I got a better place."

Dark but clean. That was why he'd turned down Warren's invitation. Had he known that before now? In a way. It had always been there, lying in wait, a witness against him. And now it was unclothed, free, betraying him to himself.

Orlando felt his cheeks heat up and a tremor in his legs. The game was over. Should he tell someone? Connie? What would he say? I didn't want to get dirty; that's why I didn't hide in the leaves. I don't like sticky, icky things on me. I am a clean boy. No one would understand. They would say he was crazy, a liar, a sissy. Better to let it go. No one talked about it anymore, anyway. It had been years. Put it out of his mind. Yet he knew it would never go completely. The words would, from time to time, beat on his brain like pelting stones, leaving a lasting, painful imprint. And he accepted that as his punishment for living. A fair exchange.

August 14/15, 1920
*Atlantic Ocean and
Brookline, Massachusetts*

They were, with the exception of the crew, alone on Andrew's yacht, the *Malabar VII*. It was late and quiet.

He lay on his bunk in his blue-striped silk robe and white silk pajamas. There was a timid knock on the door.

"Come in."

The door opened and Starr, her long dark curls framing her luscious face, entered the cabin.

"Hello, my dear," he said.

"Hello." She closed the door behind her and went to the one chair in the room, a few feet away from him.

He watched as Starr's eyes flitted from surface to surface. "What are you looking for?" he asked although he knew.

"Nothing." She dropped her head, the long lashes making her eyes appear closed.

"Shall I guess?"

She shrugged, almost imperceptibly.

"Let's see now. Would it be cookies?" He rose from the bunk and went to the small table where a bottle of champagne and two glasses were set. "Is that it, Starr? Cookies?"

She giggled and shook her head.

"Could it be raisins?" A favorite of Starr's.

"Oh, no." She crinkled her nose.

Andrew poured the wine into the fine crystal glasses.

Starr took a glass from him, easily swallowing the bubbly liquid. She had been drinking with Andrew for at least two years.

"I know," he said, "you're looking for a toy."

"Oh Andrew, a toy!" she said, disdainfully. "Really."

"Well, there are toys and there are toys." He touched his glass to hers. "One man's toy is another man's poison." He chuckled.

She looked quizzical.

"Never mind. Let's get back to what you were looking for so frantically."

"It wasn't frantic," she said quickly. "*I* wasn't frantic."

He knew she didn't want him to know how eager she was. He sat down on the bunk, patted a place next to him and she slowly came across the room. He took her hand, kissed the palm, tickled it with the tip of his tongue. She pulled away. As usual, she would give nothing until he gave her what she wanted.

He put down his glass and reached into his robe pocket. Her eyes fastened on his hand, the prize concealed inside. Starr bit her upper lip.

Holding up his fist, he said, "I wonder, could this be what you were looking for?"

A tiny smile played at the corners of her full pink mouth. "Maybe." She tried to sound nonchalant, forcing herself to look away, sipping her wine.

He smiled, knowing and appreciating the game she was playing. "I guess I must have been wrong. I'll just put it away."

"No," she blurted out. "I mean, how can I know if it is or isn't until I see what you have there?"

"Hmmm. I suppose you have a point." Slowly, one at a time, he uncurled his thick fingers revealing bit by bit the small green container. He watched her face as it became softer, pinker, the skin taking on a glow at the sight of the ether bottle. Soon she would be all supple in his hands, his mouth. Her hand reached up, taking his hand-kerchief from his breast pocket. She held it out to him.

Andrew unscrewed the top of the bottle, quickly pouring the sweet-smelling liquid into the handkerchief. He capped the bottle, put one hand behind Starr's head and, with the other, held the soaked cloth to her nose.

"Mmmmm, oohhh, yes . . . God . . . ohhhh." She lay back on the bed, her eyes closed, her arms spread up near her head.

Andrew removed his robe, folding it neatly.

Later, they lay close together in the bunk.

"What's troubling you, my pet?" He stroked her hair.

"Nothing."

"Something. I can always tell, you know."

"It's nothing you'd care about," she said, wanting to be coaxed.

"How can you say that? If it has to do with you, why then of course I'd care about it. Tell me."

Starr had graduated from Miss Parker's School in June, thrilled to be getting out of grammar school, terri-fied at the prospect of starting public high school. There were two reasons she hated the thought of Brookline High. One was that she'd be living at home with her fa-ther. The other was that Brookline High was coeduca-tional. Even the *thought* of going to school with boys frightened her.

Starr wanted desperately to go to Rogers Hall School in Lowell but her father said he couldn't afford another private school. He also said it would be good for Starr to get away from such a rarefied atmosphere. Both she and Helen tried to impress upon Frank that all the young women in Helen's family, all the young women of any *good* family, went to Rogers Hall. He didn't care. It was either Brookline High or nothing.

Andrew took for granted that Starr would be going to Rogers Hall in September. She'd never said otherwise. But now she realized how dumb she'd been. Andrew would be as upset by the news as she was. It would be much harder for him to see her if she went to Brookline High. This would be an incentive for him to talk to her father. Why hadn't she thought of it before?

"It's about school," she said.

"What *about* school? I thought you were looking forward to Rogers Hall?"

She explained the situation.

"That school . . . Brookline High . . . is it a girls' school?" he asked when she was through.

"No. Boys go there too."

"I see. And you would, of course, be living at home."

"Of course," she answered. And just to make sure Andrew got the point, she added a little something from her imagination. "And you know what else?"

"What?"

"My father says he'll expect me to stay home on weekends studying. He says now that I'll be living at home he'll be watching over me very carefully."

"Is that so?"

"Absolutely," she said.

"I'll see what I can do," he said after a long silence, running his thumb along the slight indentation in her chin which was not quite deep enough to be considered a cleft.

"Thank you, Andrew."

The next day they headed back to port and by late afternoon were driving toward Brookline. When they arrived at six, her mother and father were entertaining two people introduced as Stanley and Margaret Faithfull. Starr hoped they wouldn't stay too long. She wanted Andrew to have the opportunity to talk to her father.

On her way into her room, just before closing the door, she heard Mr. Faithfull say, "Your daughter is simply lovely. Breathtakingly beautiful."

"She'll do," Frank said.

Starr shut the door.

*   *   *

"Well," Stanley Faithfull said, slapping his two bony knees with the palms of his hands.

"Yes indeed," said Helen, nervously.

Andrew, sitting in a straight chair, stared at Faithfull and his unbelievably ugly wife. Was he going to have to outsit this peculiar couple?

Frank pulled at his narrow trousers as he crossed and uncrossed his legs. Andrew J. Peters always made him feel slightly uncomfortable. The man looked at him as though he were smelling a three-day-old fish.

Margaret Faithfull, one brown eye looking at Andrew, the other turned in toward her large nose, said, "And how do you feel, Mr. Mayor, about the nomination of Mr. Harding and Mr. Coolidge?"

Immediately, at the mention of Coolidge's name, Andrew felt the usual twist in his stomach. He also felt a kind of shock that a woman would broach the subject of politics. She was probably a suffragette. Certainly mannish enough to be one, he thought, eyeing the dark hair above her lip. Before he could answer, Stanley Faithfull broke in.

"Well now, Margaret, I'm sure the Mayor has had enough politics for one day."

Grateful as he was for the interruption, Andrew couldn't help wondering what this odd-looking fellow meant.

"Really?" Margaret said, not to be stopped. "On a Sunday?"

"Would you like another drink, Andrew?" Frank asked.

"Yes, thank you."

"That's very good stuff," Stanley said. "I'm a chemist, you know, so I can tell."

"I didn't know," said Andrew.

"Yes. I work for the Avery Chemical Company."

"I thought," Margaret said, "the nomination of Mr. Harding was very surprising. Mr. Coolidge, on the other hand, was no surprise. And I think it's lovely to have a man from our state on the ticket, don't you? Even if he is a Republican and not exactly one's favorite. I mean," she said, pulling at her suit jacket, "we *really* know him here, don't we?"

Andrew was becoming interested. This woman had a head on her shoulders. He was about to answer when, again, her husband spoke up.

"Have you heard the latest Ford joke?" He clapped his hands together.

"What?" Andrew said.

Frank handed him his scotch.

"Oh, do tell it," Helen said, wiggling in her chair.

"The latest Ford joke."

"Oh." Andrew had always hated these though he hadn't heard one for ages. They'd been out of fashion for at least a year. Now this fool was going to insist he listen to an idiotic joke about an idiotic car.

"Well," Stanley said, "it goes like this. One fella says to the other: I named my Ford after my wife. The second fella says: That's odd, how come? First fella says: No it isn't. After I got it, I found I couldn't control it!"

Helen and Stanley shrieked with laughter. Frank sipped at his drink. Margaret stared contemptuously at her husband. Andrew tried to smile. When Stanley stopped laughing he looked to Andrew for approval.

"I haven't heard one of those for a long time," Andrew said.

Low, but audibly enough, Margaret said, "No one has!"

"Oh, tell another one," Helen begged.

Stanley was delighted. "Really?"

"Go on. I just love those Ford jokes."

"You do?" With thumb and forefinger he began to stroke his small mustache. "Well, let's see? Oh yes, here's one. One fella says to another fella: I hear they're going to magnetize the rear axle of the Ford. The second fella says: Oh yeah, what for? The first fella says: So it will pick up the parts that drop off!"

Helen practically doubled over with laughter and Stanley joined her.

Frank stared at his wife as if he'd never seen her before.

Margaret cut through the piercing laughter. "Have you read G. K. Chesterton's latest story in *The Saturday Evening Post*, Mr. Mayor?"

"I'm afraid not," Andrew said. Chesterton was a Catholic and Andrew made it a point never to read him. He decided he wouldn't mention this to Mrs. Faithfull.

Frank, still staring at Helen, said, "I told you that joke last year and you said you didn't get it."

"Oh," she said, wiping the tears from her eyes, "did you?"

"Yes."

"Well, I don't know why I would have said that. There's nothing to get."

"That's what *I* said at the time."

"Perhaps, Mr. Wyman," Margaret said, "it was the way you told it. Perhaps you don't have a joke teller's . . . mmmm, how shall I put it? A joke teller's mentality?" She smiled, first at him and then at Stanley, who looked back at her with open hostility.

"That's probably right," Helen said. "You just don't know how to tell a good joke. Mr. Faithfull, on the other hand, is a born story teller."

"Thank you, Mrs. Wyman." Stanley wiped his round glasses with a white handkerchief.

Andrew thought he might go mad. For a moment he considered leaving. Then he thought of Starr and knew he had to stay.

Margaret Faithfull rose and smoothed out her gray skirt. "I think we should be leaving," she said.

"Oh, so soon?" Helen asked.

Stanley glared at his wife.

"We don't want to outstay our welcome. Do we, dear?"

Reluctantly, he stood. "No, of course not."

"But you're not. We're having a marvelous time. Aren't we, Frank?"

Frank mumbled something and got to his feet. Helen followed suit. They walked their guests to the door.

Andrew paced the living room as he waited for the Wymans to return. How could he suggest to Wyman that he would pay for Starr's education without insulting the man? He was sure Helen would be on his side but she wouldn't have anything to say about the decision. The trouble was he really didn't know Wyman. He didn't know what methods to use.

"Well, that was fun," Helen said, coming back into the living room.

Andrew smiled at her.

Frank looked sullen and Andrew felt even more apprehensive. This probably wasn't a good time to raise the subject but if he waited Rogers Hall might not have room. As it was, it was quite late. School started in less than a month.

"Sit down, sit down, Andrew." Helen was extremely flattered that Andrew was visiting with them. Usually, when he brought Starr home, he stayed no more than a minute or two. She was particularly pleased that they'd had guests who could see how well they knew the Mayor. It would certainly give that awful Mrs. Faithfull something to think about!

Frank refilled Andrew's glass. "Sorry about those two," he mumbled. "We hardly know them. In fact, this was only the second time we've seen them . . . and the last, I'll tell you."

"They *were* a bit . . . odd, weren't they?"

Helen wanted to say that *Mr.* Faithfull seemed quite nice but decided since Andrew thought they were odd she'd better say nothing. "Did you have a nice weekend, Andrew?" she asked instead. "How are Martha and the boys?"

"Fine, fine."

"Martha must enjoy having a little girl around once in a while."

"Yes, she does." He didn't like this topic one bit. "How's business, Frank?" he asked abruptly.

"Oh, it's all right. I enjoy my work at the Y."

"I suppose it's very rewarding."

"Yes, it's that."

"But not, I would guess, very rewarding, ah, financially." He hoped this wasn't too impertinent and tried to temper it with a kindly smile.

"No . . . the rewards don't lie in that direction." He took a large swallow of his drink.

"Look, Frank," Andrew said, trying out his best-buddy sound, "I know this is none of my business and I hope you won't be insulted but . . ."

"You can say anything you like to us. Can't he, Frank?" Was Andrew going to offer Frank a job?

"Well, yes. Sure." Frank wished Andrew's voice weren't so high. He found it distracting.

"As I was saying, I don't want to insult you but . . . well, it's about Starr."

"Starr?" Frank was surprised.

"She told me she'll be going to Brookline High this fall."

"That's right."

"Well, I always assumed she'd be going to Rogers Hall like the other girls in the family."

"I always assumed that too, Andrew," said Helen sulkily.

"We can't always have everything we want," Frank snapped.

"But we can try." Ignoring the angry look on Frank's face, Andrew went on. "She wants very much to go to Rogers Hall, you know."

"Did she put you up to this? That little . . . I thought we settled all this ages ago. That girl has no sense of decency." He slammed down his glass and stood up.

"Don't blame her," Andrew said quickly. "She simply told me about it. It was my idea to talk with you."

"There's nothing to talk about. I've made a decision and that's that."

"Of course. I understand."

Helen's momentary exaltation ebbed away and she sank back into the couch.

Andrew's instinct was to let the matter drop. Then he thought of years of not seeing Starr at his convenience. They stretched before him like arid plains. "I've found in politics sometimes when I've made a decision that I think is final, I find a reason to change that decision. Or some-one else gives me a reason to change it."

Frank said nothing.

"I guess the best way to put this is very bluntly. Why don't you let *me* send Starr to Rogers Hall? You know, I think of her as my own little . . ."

"You mean, *pay* for it?"

Andrew nodded.

"I'll be damned."

"Frank!" Helen said.

"What do you think I am?"

"I don't know what you mean. I see nothing wrong with . . ."

"Well, I do! You think we take charity here?"

"Oh, really. It's hardly that. Think of me as Starr's sponsor or patron. It's done all the time."

"Well, it's not done by me." Frank unclipped his bow tie and opened the button of his stiff collar.

Helen sat quietly, looking from one man to the other. She had never hated Frank more than she did at that moment.

"Look, I know you're the Mayor but I'm going to run my family the way I want to and if you don't like it you don't have to come around here anymore."

Andrew felt as though he'd been punched in the face. He couldn't press the issue or he'd lose everything. "There's no need for this, Frank. I told you I didn't want to insult you . . . please."

"Well, you did!"

He swallowed. "I'm sorry." If the only way to continue seeing Starr was to lick the man's shoes, Andrew knew he would do it.

"Let me tell you something," said Frank. "If I *had* the money, which I admit I don't, that girl would not be going to Rogers Hall. She's gotten too big for her britches as it is. Her nose is too high up in the air. It's time she came down to earth. Between you and Helen that girl thinks she's the queen of the world."

The fear of separation clutched at him again. "I didn't know you felt this way, Frank. I've only tried to . . . I guess it's because I only have sons that I spoil her a little."

"Yeah . . . well."

"I'm sorry." He knew his only chance now was a gamble. "If you'd rather I didn't see the child . . ."

"Oh, no," Helen cried, getting to her feet. "Frank doesn't mean that. Do you, Frank?"

"I didn't say that," he grumbled.

It was all right. He hadn't won the Rogers Hall battle but at least he hadn't lost her completely. "I think I'd better be going. Please forgive me if I've insulted you in any way." He offered his hand.

Taking it, Frank said, "Sorry I got so hot under the collar."

"Oh, that's better," Helen said. "I'll see you to the door, Andrew."

Handing him his hat, she apologized for her husband.

"Think nothing of it. I understand."

"I'm so glad you do. And I want you to know how much I appreciate your offer, Andrew. And how much I appreciate everything you've done for Starr."

He couldn't help smiling. "It's nothing."

"Well, I know better. Please, feel free to visit any time and I hope you continue to think of Starr as your own dear child."

"I will," he said. "I certainly will."

When he reached his car he turned and waved at

her. He would find a way to see Starr when he wanted and Helen Wyman would help.

* * *

Helen lay in her bed wondering when Frank would come upstairs. After Andrew left, he'd slammed out of the house and hadn't come back until everyone was in bed. Now he had been downstairs for almost an hour. She wondered if he'd gone to a speakeasy. Lately he'd taken to doing that at least once a week. Not that she cared whether he drank or didn't or came home or didn't or anything else! But if he was drunk he might start a fight when he came up. She stared at the cover of *Collier's* which lay across her knees. If she didn't want a scene she'd better turn out the light and pretend she was asleep. She tossed the magazine aside.

Why, she wondered, had Stanley Faithfull married such an ugly woman. Of course, look at her own situation! She had married a handsome man and was miserable. Looks had nothing to do with anything. And, by most people's standards, Stanley Faithfull probably wouldn't be considered good-looking. But he was cute. There was just something about him. And he was funny. And interesting. And full of life. Not like Frank who was always grumpy and sullen.

Ever since he'd come home from France her life had been hellish. It was hard to adjust to someone else giving the orders. Hard on her; hard on the girls. Especially Starr, who had a strong will. But it had been most difficult to adjust to sex. It was bad enough before the war but after sixteen months without it—after sixteen months of peace, of being able to get into bed without the specter of *that* hanging over you—well, it was just terribly difficult to adjust.

Helen often wondered if other women felt the same way. She wished she could ask some of her friends but that wasn't something you talked about with your girlfriends, or anyone else for that matter. And what was there to say, after all? Could she say she hated the weight of her husband's body on hers? Could she say that when he put his hands on her breasts, pinching her nipples, she felt nothing but pain? And who would understand that she experienced only a kind of ache when he entered her? Then a burning irritation as he pumped in and out. Surely no one would sympathize with her feeling of revulsion at the sticky fluid on her thigh when he had finished and withdrawn. A normal woman was supposed to like all that. Or was she? She remembered her mother telling her sister, on the eve of her marriage, that she shouldn't expect to like her marriage bed—it was her duty. Something like that. But her mother had said nothing to her before she married Frank. She hadn't been prepared for what she experienced as a brutal act. But what bothered her even more than the brutality was the boredom of it all! Perhaps it was something only meant for men to enjoy. Yet she never sensed any joy in Frank. He puffed a lot and made a few strange noises before collapsing but there was never any indication that he actually *enjoyed* what he was doing.

Involuntarily, she hunched into an embryo position as she heard his heavy tread on the stairs. She faked deep breathing. The door opened and he switched on a light.

"You asleep?"

If she had been asleep, he would have awakened her. That was annoying. She didn't answer.

"Helen?" He approached the bed and hunched over her.

She could smell the alcohol. Now she felt apprehensive.

"Helen? Are you awake. Wake up. I want to talk."

It was useless to pretend. He would not stop, she knew. "What is it?" she asked, sleepily.

"I want to talk." He pushed at her, indicating she should move.

She opened her eyes. His beard was already coming in and he looked grimy.

"Move over."

She did and he sat down on the edge of the bed, lighting a Chesterfield.

Helen looked up into his eyes. They were only half open. "It's late," she said.

"I want you to unnerstand somethin'. I don't want that pansy paying for anythin'."

"What pansy? What are you talking about?"

"Peters, for God's sake." He blew a large puff of smoke toward her.

She waved it aside, moving farther away from him. "Please don't blow smoke in my face, Frank."

"Sorry. Anyway, I don't want the pansy payin'."

"Andrew J. Peters is certainly not a pansy. Don't be ridiculous. He has six sons."

"I don't care if he has *sixty* sons. Did you ever hear a voice like that on anybody but a pansy?"

"I don't know any pansies. Besides, the man can't help his voice. That's something you're born with . . . oh, this is ridiculous. I want to go to sleep." She started to turn away but he grabbed her.

"Don't. Okay, maybe he's not a pansy but there's somethin' wrong with him." He nodded his head, as if for punctuation.

"There's nothing wrong with *him*. There's something wrong with *you*."

"What's that supposed to mean?"

"It means that you're drunk and you don't know what you're saying."

"I know what I'm saying . . . don't fool yourself, kiddo. I know what I'm saying better than ever. There's something wrong with him."

"I refuse to have this conversation. Andrew has been perfectly wonderful to us. When I think of all he's done for Starr . . ."

"Tha's just what I'm talking about." The end of his cigarette was soaked and began to shred, leaving pieces of tobacco on his bottom lip.

"What's what you're talking about?"

"What he's done for Starr."

"Well?"

"Something smells in Denmark." He flicked at the tobacco with his tongue.

"The only thing that smells is you. You reek of alcohol and old cigarettes."

"Tha's just too damn bad. I'm tellin' you he's queer."

Now she was infuriated. It was enraging to have to listen to these lies. "Frank, I am not going to listen to this. It's late, I'm tired, you're drunk and . . ."

"You'll lissen," he said, grabbing her arm and squeezing.

"You're hurting me."

He eased up but held on. "You'll lissen."

"You're not making any sense."

"I'm telling you that . . . that . . ."

"That what?" she said automatically.

He stared at her. A strange kind of glazed look came over his eyes and she knew in an instant that he'd forgotten what he'd been saying. It had happened before when he was drunk. She could remind him but she had no intention of doing so.

"That what?" she asked again, hoping to make him squirm.

"Hmmmm?"

"That what?" she repeated, knowing the words would make absolutely no sense to him at all.

"Accch," he growled, giving her arm a push as he let go and stood up.

Helen watched him fumbling around the room looking for an ashtray, unsteadily finding his way to the door. Flinging it open, he mumbled something she couldn't understand, then slammed it behind him. She listened as he made his way down the stairs, haltingly. He would sleep on the couch in the sun parlor. He'd done that when he'd been drunk other times.

While she smoothed out the bed Helen wondered exactly what had gotten into Frank? Besides alcohol. Why in the world was he so crazy on the topic of Andrew? Implying this and implying that! Well, who knew what he was even getting at. None of it made any sense and she intended to put it out of her mind this second!

After she turned out the light and found a comfortable spot right in the middle she reflected on how perfectly wonderful it was to have a big bed all to one's self. There was nothing like it.

———

MISSING HEIRESS DIES IN MYSTERY *Sea Casts Up Body*

—*New York Daily News*, June 9, 1931

June 5, 1931
New York, New York

The noise of Grand Central Station hurt her ears. It was a mystery why she was there. It was as though someone else, something else, had guided her. Two days in a row. Strange. Perhaps she was meant to throw herself in front of a train. But how stupid. Trains were slower here than anywhere else. Was she meant to get *on* a train?

Then she saw it. Rumaker's Beauty Salon. She had noticed it yesterday. That was probably why she'd thought about a permanent that morning.

Inside a young woman, marcelled red hair, nails to match, approached Starr. "C'n I help ya?"

"I'd like an appointment," she found herself saying.

"For what? Wash and set? Perm? Nails?" The red nails touched a narrow, plucked eyebrow.

"A permanent." This was insane but she couldn't stop now.

"When for, dearie?"

"Now?"

"Oh, I ain't got room now, honey. Later though. How about two this after?"

"Fine." She turned to leave.

"Hey?"

"Yes?"

"What's yer name?"

"Starr Faithfull."

"Huh?"

"Starr Faithfull. That's my name."

"Yer kiddin' me."

The usual irritation when someone questioned her name was absent. "No, I'm not. That's it."

The woman shook her head. "That's some moniker. Now me, I got the commonest name in the book. Mary. That's me." She pointed to the window where it said: Mary Rumaker—Prop.

Starr could think of nothing to say so she just smiled and backed a few paces toward the door.

"Well, Miss Faithfull," Mary said, as Starr opened the door, "I hope you're faithful about keeping yer appointment!" She hooted, the laughter pursing her lips like a blowfish.

Nodding, smiling dumbly, Starr closed the door and gave a half wave to Mary Rumaker who was wiping tears of laughter from her squinty eyes.

As she walked through the station she wondered what in the world that had been all about. She had no intention of having her hair done. Even if she weren't planning to be dead by this time tomorrow, she had no money for permanents. Things were getting away from her. She must pull herself together. Figure things out. Food. She needed food and coffee and a quiet place to sit.

Nine

August 6, 1977
Orange, New Jersey

One of the newspapers said she'd been an alcoholic. Others said she didn't drink at all. They called her an heiress, goodtime girl, rich girl. Later, John O'Hara called her Gloria Wandrous. Orlando, when he thought of her, called her Rose.

September 18, 1920
Brookline, Massachusetts

It was ten minutes until the first bell. Starr stood by herself, her eyes trained on an open history book. She was not really reading. She was listening to a group of boys and girls nearby who were still talking about the big explosion in New York City two days before.

"Wall Street was three inches high with blood," a boy said eagerly.

"Oh, Harry."

"It's true. And worse than that, the carcass of this horse was all over the place. The guts were hanging over the hood of a car and there was a leg here and a leg there. The eyes had flown right out of their sockets and one eye sailed right into the mouth of a lady."

The others screamed and groaned.

"Did she swallow it?" a boy asked.

"Oh, Bill, don't!"

"Yeah, she swallowed it."

More screams of protest.

The description made Starr feel a little sick but she found she couldn't move away. She'd read about the bomb in the paper but there hadn't been all these details. The paper said the bomb had gone off at a few minutes before noon at Broad and Wall streets and that thirty people had been killed and hundreds injured. She wondered where the boy had gotten all his information.

"What else?" another boy asked.

"Weeell . . . when the bomb went off there was this huge cloud of greenish and yellowish smoke that went up at least ten feet high."

"Really?"

"And?"

"Well, nobody could see and people kept stepping on dead bodies and steel came flying into people's flesh and one man put out his hand to help him find his way and he felt something all wet and sticky and then this cloud of smoke cleared a little, you know, and he saw that he had his hand right in the middle of another man's open belly."

"Oh, no!"

"Stop!"

"That's disgusting."

"How do you know all this, Harry?"

"My uncle," he answered quickly. "He was there. He told me."

"Was he hurt?"

"Nah, not really. Just a few scratches."

"Tell us more."

Starr couldn't decide whether she wanted Harry to tell more or not. A voice interrupted her thoughts.

"He's making it up, you know."

She looked up from her book into the face of Edmond Chalmers, star quarterback of the Brookline football team. He had never spoken to her before and she was terrified.

"He's making it all up. You *were* listening, weren't you? I know you were. I've been watching you."

She could think of nothing to say. Since school had

started two weeks ago, she had spoken to no one, except her teachers. A few girls had tried to engage her in conversation but she'd put them off with monosyllabic answers. When she walked through the halls she kept her eyes on her feet and hugged her books to her chest. No boy had tried to speak to her and for this she was grateful. Now Edmond Chalmers was standing right in front of her waiting for her to answer. He was not only a football hero but also school president. A senior. She'd heard people talking about him. She couldn't understand why he was talking to *her*, a lowly freshman.

"Cat got your tongue?" He smiled and his blue eyes almost closed.

Unless she just walked away she had to say something. "Are you addressing me?" she said, stupidly.

He began to laugh, not raucously so that others would hear and turn, but softly. "I don't see anyone behind you, do you?"

She felt like an idiot. Either she was going to talk to him or she was not. Well, there was no harm in talking, she decided. "What is it you want?"

He smiled and shook his head. "You *are* strange. Oh well. My name is Edmond Chalmers."

She stared at him.

"Well, aren't you going to tell me *your* name? Never mind. I already know your name. If I can believe it, that is. I've been told that it's Starr, with two r's. Is it really?"

"Yes," she answered defensively.

"It's a beautiful name."

"Thank you." She wished the bell would ring and then she wished it wouldn't.

"Do you foxtrot, Starr?"

"I beg your pardon?"

"Foxtrot? Do you know how to foxtrot? It's all the rage, you know."

"Yes, of course," she said.

"Yes, of course, you know it's all the rage or yes, of course, you foxtrot?"

She knew it was the new dance craze but she certainly didn't know how to do it. Who would have taught her? Tucker? And who would she have danced it with? Andrew? How could she answer this handsome boy, standing there smiling at her? She felt panicky.

"I can teach you," he said.

"I'm not interested in things like that." She adjusted her books in her arms, looking past him.

"Oh? What *are* you interested in then?"

"I'm interested in improving my mind."

"Well, so am I, but that doesn't mean I don't like to have fun. Don't tell me you don't like to have fun?"

Fun. An odd word. A word Starr had never connected to herself. She'd never thought of anything she did with Andrew as *fun*. What was fun? Had she ever had any? Maybe long ago—long ago, B.A.

"Well, do you?" Edmond asked, his head cocked to one side, waiting.

"Do I what?" She stalled.

"Do you like to have fun? My God, you *are* a queer one."

She almost laughed. If he only knew *how* queer. "Doesn't everyone?" she answered quickly, surprising herself.

He smiled, relieved. "Yes, exactly my point."

"I'm afraid," she said, on guard again, "I've missed your point."

Edmond was beginning to lose a bit of his aplomb. He shuffled his feet and pulled at his tie. Still, he was not about to retreat. Not with eyes like that to look into. And that mouth. "Look, Starr, I guess I am being a bit obtuse but what I'm driving at is this. The first dance of the season is next week and I wondered if you'd like to come with me?"

She was genuinely startled. He was asking her for a date! That had never happened before. What should she say? What would Andrew say? He had warned her about boys like Edmond, warned her that—

"Well?"

She must say something.

"Do you have another date?"

As if dazed, she shook her head.

He grinned at her. "Then you'll go with me." Edmond Chalmers was not used to being refused.

She began to protest, the thought of Andrew looming like a huge bobbing balloon, but the bell cut her off.

As everyone pushed toward the entrance, Edmond gently took Starr's elbow and, with propriety, guided her through the crowd. "The dance is a week from Saturday," he said. "I won't be able to teach you in the afternoons because I have football practice, but early evenings will be just . . ."

"I know how to dance," she said firmly.

"Oh, I thought . . ."

"You thought wrong."

"Sorry." He grinned.

In spite of herself she smiled, eyes softening.

He walked her to her homeroom.

"Well, I'll be seeing you soon, Starr."

She nodded curtly and left him staring after her, looking puzzled.

All day she alternately cursed herself for allowing her silence to be interpreted as acceptance of his invitation and churned with fear at the thought of Andrew's reaction. Only near the end of the school day did she realize she didn't have to tell Andrew. As things stood now, they had no plans to see each other until the first weekend in October. Andrew wouldn't have to know.

Half her problem, therefore, was solved. But why in the world had she told Edmond she could dance? Of course, she could always break the date. But she didn't want to. Frightening as the thought of going was, it intrigued and tickled some untapped part of her. But what would she do about dancing?

Starr went over and over the problem, finding no answers. By the time her mother came in from an afternoon tea, Starr was feeling desperate.

"Oh, that woman," Helen exclaimed, plunking herself down at the table opposite Starr.

"Who?"

"Margaret Faithfull. She really is dreadful."

"Then why do you see her?" Starr didn't really care.

"One has one's duty."

Starr didn't want to pursue it.

"One can barely look at her over tea and cakes. Takes away the appetite."

"Mmmmm." In books, daughters were always going to their mothers for advice, help, comfort. Starr, of course, had shied away from this, fearful of too many probing questions. But she wondered now if Helen could help her. After all, wasn't this a *normal* problem?

"And her conversation," Helen went on, "honestly. She goes on and on about politics and such. It's all a person can do to . . ."

"I'm going to a dance," Starr blurted out. She had counted to ten and then said it.

Helen's mouth remained in the shape of an o for seconds after Starr spoke. "A dance? What dance? With whom?"

"A school dance. With Edmond Chalmers." She smiled. "He's the star of the football team and the school president." She felt absolutely wonderful. A regular girl talking to her *mom*. Right out of her books.

"Chalmers, Chalmers . . . mmmm, is he the son of Preston Chalmers?"

"I don't know." A bit annoyed, fantasy fading.

"I think he must be. A fine family, Starr. You say he asked you to the dance?"

"Well, I certainly didn't ask him."

"You say he's the school president?"

She nodded, proud.

"He must be seventeen, eighteen then. I hope your father won't think he's too old for you."

Unable to help herself, Starr burst out laughing. A rarity.

"What's so funny?"

"Nothing. Never mind."

"Tell me."

Her laughter subsided. "It's nothing . . . I mean, all the freshmen go out with seniors."

"Yes, I know, but your father's very old-fashioned."

"I don't care," she said defiantly. "I'm going."

"Well, don't take that attitude when you ask him. You catch more flies with honey, you know."

"What do you mean, ask him? Why do I have to ask him?"

"He's your father. The head of the house. Of course you have to ask him. You can't do any old thing you please, you know."

"He makes me sick."

"Starr! Don't say that. Don't ever say that."

"Why not? You do. I've heard you."

Helen rose from the table, glaring at Starr. "Go to your room."

How could it all have fallen apart this way? Nothing ever ended the way it started. No. She wouldn't have it. Rising, she came around the table and, bowing her head slightly, touching her mother's hand with her fingertips, she apologized.

Helen said nothing for a moment, surprised at this strange behavior. What was Starr up to now?

"I want to go to the dance. He's a nice boy." The thought of not being *allowed* by Frank to go made her determined. It overshadowed her inability to dance and eclipsed her fear of Edmond Chalmers.

"Well," Helen said, forgetting their harsh words, "we'll ask him nice. We girls will stick together, hmmm?"

Helen had lost on the school issue but Starr was sure she wouldn't lose on this one. She was wrong.

When Frank came home that evening they both prepared him in the customary way. Helen made him a drink; Starr brought him his slippers.

"All right, what do you want? It better not have anything to do with Rogers Hall."

"Oh, it doesn't," Starr said, thinking ahead to the dance lessons her mother had promised. Right after dinner, she'd said. They would put on the records of "Japanese Sandman" and "Whispering" and Helen would teach her.

"What is it then?"

Helen encouraged Starr to ask. She did.

"President of the school? How old is he?"

Helen knew Frank well. She crossed her fingers behind her back.

"I didn't ask him," Starr said, trying to keep the edge out of her voice.

"Well, if he's president he must be a senior . . . so he's seventeen, eighteen, right?"

"I guess."

"How old are you? Fourteen?"

She nodded.

"Well, I don't think so, Starr. You'd better go with someone your own age." He picked up his newspaper.

"Well, how am I supposed to do that? I mean, Edmond Chalmers asked me, not some dumb person my own age. Just how can I go with someone my own age when Edmond asked me? Huh?"

"Someone else will ask you. You'll see." He opened the paper and folded it over to the spot he wanted. "These older boys get funny ideas."

She wanted to wrench the paper from his hands and tear it into tiny bits. "You mean I can't go?" Her voice was without emotion.

"Not with a boy three four years older, no."

Oh, how she wanted to scream out about Andrew. Scream out what he did to her, what she did to him. Shove the words down Frank's throat, dangle pictures in front of his eyes. But she didn't. She controlled her rage, gave her mother a withering look and went to her room.

All that night, tossing about with sleeplessness, she heard her parents fighting. Good. She was glad she'd given them yet another thing to fight over. Maybe this would be the thing that would drive her father from the house forever.

During the night Edmond assumed the guise of savior. *If* she went to the dance with him, he would fall in love with her. *If* he fell in love with her, she could tell him anything. She would tell him about Andrew and he would understand. Somehow he would get rid of Andrew and they would marry. But of course, because of Frank, that was not going to happen. Because of Frank, she was destined to suffer Andrew's desires. Because of Frank, her life was ruined. And what would she tell Edmond? Certainly she couldn't tell him the truth. He'd think she was a baby.

By morning, fatigue showing in her face, she still hadn't solved the problem of what to say to Edmond Chalmers. Her mother gave her an out.

"Don't worry, Starr, I'll keep working on him."

She would say nothing to Edmond. Not yet.

For the rest of that week and all of the following, Edmond Chalmers walked her to and from most of her classes. Other students stared at them jealously and Starr loved it. Each morning she questioned Helen as to her progress with Frank; each morning the answer was negative.

By Friday of the second week, the day before the dance, he still hadn't relented. All hope was gone. Now

Starr would have to tell Edmond. After all, she couldn't just let him show up at the house, could she?

Edmond was waiting for her outside her last class of the day. As usual, they walked together to her locker.

"Well," he said, "I guess you'd better tell me your address." He was smiling, eyes bright.

There were several things she could say. She chose the easiest for her, perhaps the hardest for him. "What for?" she asked, taking books from her locker, not looking at him.

He laughed uncomfortably, sensing, somewhere always knowing, this was no ordinary girl. "How can I pick you up if I don't know where you live?"

"Pick me up?" She swung around and looked directly at him.

He was confused. "For the dance," he said quietly.

Starr weighed her next words carefully. She couldn't ask what dance. There were posters everywhere announcing it. And he had mentioned it many times. But his references had been general. He'd never said "when *we* go to the dance" or anything like that.

"I think we must have crossed wires," she said, so sweetly.

"Crossed wires?"

"Hey, Chalmers," a teammate yelled as he passed them, "you're gonna be late for practice."

"Be there," Edmond called back. To Starr he said, "Please tell me what you're saying. I don't understand."

"I'm afraid you'll have to tell me what *you're* saying." She felt terrible, hating to see the tremor around his lips.

"What *I'm* saying? Well, what I'm saying is that I have to know your address so I can pick you up and take you to the dance tomorrow night. That's what I'm saying." His voice shook slightly.

"I'm really sorry, Edmond, that you seem to have gotten the impression that we were going to the dance together but I never . . ."

"But you did. I remember it distinctly. It was the first day I met you. I asked you to the dance and you said you'd go." He sounded desperate.

"Yes, you did ask me but I never said I'd go." The truth.

"But . . ."

"I think, Edmond, you made an assumption." She pushed past him and began walking down the hall.

After a stunned moment he followed and grabbed her arm, stopping her. "I asked you if you had another date and you said no."

"That's right. But I never said I'd go with you. Please let go of my arm."

He did. She began to walk again.

"I don't understand, I don't understand," he said, walking alongside her.

Her eyes straight ahead, she said, "There's very little to understand. You assumed something, that's all. Never assume with females, Edmond. Oh well, you'll learn." So worldly-wise.

He stopped.

She didn't turn around but she heard him just the same.

"Now I'll have to go stag. I never go stag. What will everyone think?"

The words stung her. Was that all he cared about? His image? Didn't he care that he wasn't going with *her*? She kept walking, widening the distance between them. She was glad the hall was empty so no one else heard.

"That's a rotten thing to do, Starr Wyman. You're nothing but a vamp!"

She smiled to herself, liking that idea immensely. Edmond was still shouting as she opened and shut the door to the street.

Walking home, she decided she was well rid of him. Imagine thinking he would protect her from Andrew! Edmond Chalmers was obviously a spineless, conceited egomaniac. Still, she could not forget those blue eyes, clear, large, kind. And the touch of his hand on her elbow when they walked through the halls. And the gentle, sweet things he'd said to her from time to time. She couldn't forget the good clean young smell of him or the firm line of his chin. Surely he had yelled those things at her only because he was hurt. Anyone would have done the same.

By the time she reached Park Street he had once again become her savior, her secret lover. This time, however, she knew it would never be a reality. The only secret lover she had was Andrew J. Peters and certainly he would never be her savior. Anything but. And he would continue making her life a nightmare and an ecstasy. He would continue governing her with threats, as he did when he found out about Edmond.

October 6, 1920
Brookline, Massachusetts

When Andrew arrived to pick up Starr the Edmond Chalmers incident was still fresh in Helen's mind. She complained to Andrew about it. Frank was impossible! And she was so grateful Andrew was taking Starr to a party where she might meet some young people.

On the way to the inn where they would be staying alone for the weekend, Andrew showed his anger.

"How dare you accept an invitation from some boy? Have you forgotten everything I told you about boys that age? Have you forgotten your loyalty to me?"

"Well, I didn't go, Andrew."

"But you would have if your father had let you."

There was no way to deny this after what her mother had said.

"Yes, of course you would. You're a sly girl, Starr."

And what was he, she wondered. Still, his tone, the look in his eyes, made her feel guilty.

"I'm sorry," she said.

"And if Frank had let you go is that what you'd be saying now? I'm sorry?"

She did not think it wise to say she would never have mentioned it. "I . . . I just didn't think there was anything wrong with it."

"But you promised," he said. "And right away, right in the first few weeks of school, you break the promise. Or you would have. Same thing."

"It was just a dance."

"Do you think he would have stopped there, this Chalpers?"

She started to correct him, then decided she didn't want him to know Edmond's name. "What do you mean, stopped there?" she said instead.

"Stopped at one dance? There would have been other invitations, and you would have gotten to know him better and then he would have . . ." The car swerved as he shook his head in horror. "I can't even think about it."

"I'm sorry," she said again, not sorry at all.

"How can I trust you from now on?"

"Well, you know my father won't let me go out with him even if you don't trust *me*."

"There'll be others. Others will ask you . . . others your own age. And then what? He'll let you go with ones your age."

"I won't go," she said. Would there be others?

"How can I believe that?"

"I promise."

"You promised before. No, you need to be punished."

He'd never said that to her before and it was frightening. Would he beat her?

"There will be no little green bottle this weekend."

A beating would have been easier. At the inn he kept his promise and withheld the ether, forcing her to go through the sexual rituals that were the spine of their relationship without it. When she balked he threatened her with exposure. He would tell her parents that she'd made advances toward him. She was sure they would believe him. He was, after all, the Mayor of Boston. So she complied with his demands, hating him, fantasizing throughout about Edmond Chalmers.

Convinced Andrew would find out if she ever went anywhere with a boy, she vowed to herself she would never even consider another invitation. It was a meaningless vow.

Whether it was her aloofness or whether Edmond Chalmers had spread the word, in the two years she spent at Brookline High not one boy ever spoke to her in any social way. And certainly no girl ever tried. She told herself she was glad, that this way she was free. What she was, in fact, was horribly, achingly lonely.

Autopsy revealed traces of Veronal but death was definitely attributed to drowning.
                                    —Outlook Magazine, July 1, 1931

June 5, 1931
New York, New York

She sat in a booth by herself. The black coffee
steamed, the thick blue willow mug solid in her hand.
Real. Nothing else seemed real to her. Even the sound
coming from the static-filled radio behind the counter had
a dreamlike quality to it. She listened carefully trying to
find some reality. An orchestra played "Star Dust." An old
song. Perhaps this wasn't 1931. What day was it? She
looked down at the *News*. June 5, 1931. Friday.

"Here ya go," the waitress said, banging her order
down before her.

Starr studied the food. Turkey, gravy, bread. French
fries. Green beans. She smiled thinking about the gravy
and bread and potatoes. For once she would eat them in
peace.

As she chewed, tasted, savored, she tried to think
what she would do. How to spend the rest of this, her last
day? She really should go to a party. A party was the only
proper way to end. After all, wasn't she considered a party
girl? But she knew of no parties. Then it struck her.

She opened the paper to the news of sailings, running
her finger down the page. There it was. *Mauretania* 5
P.M. *Bahamas Pier* 57. Another whoopee cruise. Unlimited
parties. She could pick and choose.

She ordered apple pie a la mode for dessert and,
when she finished it, ordered another.

Ten

August 6, 1977
Orange, New Jersey

"Oh, Orr, you look just fine. I can't see anything wrong with you. Sure, I know you have difficulty moving but your color is good. That's what I mean. Now when I went to see my neighbor in the hospital, he . . ."

It was Toni. Talking. Always talking. She leaned against the edge of the bed, her little red mouth moving, moving in her round face.

He closed his eyes shutting out her face, her words. Still, he knew, she went on. Always talking. Telling. She had been the one to tell him about Papa. At first he hadn't believed her. Called her a liar. Then she showed him receipts for the money orders she'd found. Twenty-five here, thirty there, fifteen here. All for Natalia Smith. Who the hell was she? It was obvious who she was, Toni said. But he couldn't believe it. All those years of trying to live up to a fraud. It made him feel crazy. How dare he? It was *their* money. Nina's and Toni's and Silvio's and his. Why was he giving their money to Natalia Smith?

Toni said he had to go see this Smith woman. She couldn't tell Papa she'd found the receipts. Couldn't embarrass him. He went. She was a woman in her fifties. She'd been Papa's mistress for a number of years. Now

129

they just played chess, listened to music. She thought Papa was rich. From now on she would return the money order to Toni. Papa would never know. He never did. Natalia said she assumed his sons knew about her . . . and the others before her! The others!

All those years trying to be like a liar. He'd been forty-three when he found out and he felt duped. If only Toni hadn't told him. But, no, she had to tell.

". . . my friend from upstairs, says that depression comes from a lack of interest. Now that's you all over, Orr. You have no interest in anything. When you get out of here you have to get some interest in something. The first thing you should do is . . ."

October 10, 1921
Lancaster, Pennsylvania

When Frances Hess, Jennie Licht and Loretta Braunschweig stepped out into the street from the Capitol Theater there was a line for the second showing of *The Sheik* twice as long as there had been for the first.

Arm in arm, Frances in the middle, perhaps because she was the shortest, they walked in unusual silence down N. Queen Street toward The Crystal, an inexpensive restaurant.

Coats hung up, settled at their table, Jennie was the first to speak.

"You might as well all know it now . . . I'm in love."

"Me too," Loretta said.

Frances smiled and said nothing.

"Well?" Jennie asked her.

"Well, what?"

"Don't you think he's just dreamy?"

"Valentino? He's all right. But I like blonds." Actually, although Frances dated a lot of blond men, she always found dark men far more appealing.

"Not me," Loretta said. "I just could drool over those big brown eyes and . . ."

"What'll you girls have?" the waitress interrupted.

When they went to The Crystal, once a week after

the movies, they always ordered the same thing. Western omelettes and home fries.

"If you're so mad for the Valentino type," Frances said, after the waitress left, "how come you're so thick with Larry Shannon?" He was a redhead.

"Just because we've dated a few times doesn't mean anything. We're not pinned, you know. Anyway, what am I supposed to do? Stay home instead of go out with him? Not everybody has a date with a different boy practically every night, like some people."

Frances knew Loretta meant her. She did date new boys all the time. What was the point of living in a college town if you didn't experiment? There were so many cute boys, why confine yourself to one? If people thought she was fast, it didn't bother her. She knew she wasn't.

"You know, Fran," Loretta went on, "I don't see how you're going to find a boy to marry if you keep jumping from one to another like that. I mean, how are you going to get to know anyone?"

"Who says Fran *wants* to get married?" Jennie asked. She and Frances were closer to each other than they were to Loretta.

"Well, of course she wants to get married. Everybody does."

"That's really dumb, Loretta. Of course everybody *doesn't*. Everybody's not the same, you know."

"Still."

"I'm twenty years old. I've got plenty of time," said Frances. "The thing is I'm having too much fun."

"I don't see what's fun about fighting off those fraternity boys time after time. Sometimes I think each one of them has a dozen hands. Unless you don't bother fighting them off." Loretta leaned her chin in her hand, pinky between her thin lips, and stared at Frances with small blue eyes.

Frances stared back, choosing to say nothing, a tiny smile in the place of a defense. She also hoped her silence might create an air of mystery.

"Here comes our supper," Jennie said, breaking the look between the other two.

When they'd finished and cups of steaming coffee had been set before them, Jennie pulled out a crumpled pack of Chesterfields from her pocketbook.

"What are you doing?" Loretta asked, her voice almost trembling.

"I'm going to have a smoke," Jennie answered coolly.

"Here? In a public place? Are you crazy?"

"Yes, here in a public place. And no, I'm not crazy. All the girls are doing it."

"What girls? Not any girls we know. You talking about those college girls some of the boys bring down here on weekends or what?"

"I dunno . . . just girls. Times are changing, Loretta." She took a cigarette from the pack and a match from a small box.

"I swear, Jennie Licht, if you light that thing I'm leaving."

"What?"

"Frances, talk to her," Loretta said. "Put some sense in that head."

Though Frances didn't smoke herself, because she didn't like it, she didn't care if Jennie smoked or *where* she smoked. She'd be the last one to try and stop her. "Look, Loretta, I think you're being silly. Who cares?"

"*I* care. Okay. Where's my check? Miss? Miss?" she called to the waitress. "Just wait, please, until I leave and then you can take your clothes off if you want. I suppose you want to be flappers, huh? I suppose next you'll be wearing cosmetics and rolling your stockings down below your knees? Well, I've seen this coming for a long time. We're just not cut from the same cloth, that's all. I'm an old-fashioned girl, that's all." She was standing up, wrestling with her coat and trying to take out her money at the same time.

Jennie lit her cigarette.

"You have no feelings, Jennie Licht. You don't care about anyone but yourself . . . couldn't you just wait one second until I paid my check?"

"No, I need my nicotine." Jennie looked across the table at Frances, trying desperately not to laugh.

"I've been thinking," Frances said, touching her long brown hair, "of having my hair bobbed."

Loretta drew in her breath and slammed down her money. "I bet you will, too. Well, it really doesn't matter because you couldn't have a worse reputation than you already have. You can't imagine how many nights I've spent defending you."

"No, I can't," Frances said.

"Well, my mother was right. She said I shouldn't hang around with you . . . that you were heading for trouble and I can see now that she was right all along even though I defended you and argued with her and practically broke her heart going out with you girls and . . ."

"Why don't you go, Loretta?" Jennie blew a puff of smoke in her direction.

"You're headed straight for hell . . . both of you." Loretta turned, making a great deal of noise as she left the restaurant, her long, out-of-style coat flapping behind her.

Frances and Jennie collapsed with laughter. Then collecting herself, Frances said, "I guess we were real mean, huh?"

"She had it coming."

"Well, I feel sorry for her. I mean, you know. She's really a poor thing. That awful family."

"That's no excuse to behave the way she does. I just don't know why we stood it for so long." She stubbed out her cigarette. "Are you really?"

"Hmmm?"

"Are you really gonna have your hair bobbed?"

"Well, I've been thinking about it."

Jennie grinned. "Me too."

"Honest?"

"I have. But not a single girl in Lancaster has done it yet."

"I know. And Papa would kill me if I did it. As it is he keeps hollering about the length of my skirts but he sees a lot of other girls wearing them that way so . . ."

"Why don't we be the first, Fran?"

Frances pressed her full cupid's-bow mouth together as she thought about her friend's suggestion.

"Oh Lord, I can just see the faces on some of the men at the factory," said Jennie, lighting another cigarette. "They'll just die."

"I can see one face in particular," Fran said. "Papa."

"Well, what can he do? He can't make you put it back, after all."

"That's true. He could keep me in though."

Jennie's father was dead and her mother, deep into

bootleg gin, would probably never notice, so she pressed the issue. "Fran, think of it like this. Bobbed hair is coming in . . . I mean, the magazines show it and all the girls in the cities and the movie stars have it and it's just a matter of time until every girl in Lancaster has it. Right?"

"Probably," Frances answered, her fingers feeling the thickness of her hair.

"And somebody is bound to be first. Right? Well, why not let it be us. Think of what a sensation we'll cause."

"I am thinking." The idea definitely appealed to her. Only the vision of her father held her back.

"Let's do it tomorrow. I'll make the appointment on my way to work. For five-fifteen. Okay?"

"I'm really sick to death of my hair like this," Frances said.

Jennie took that remark for consent. "Oh, I love you Fran . . . you're such fun." She reached over and squeezed her friend's hand.

"So are you," said Frances. Now there was no way to say no. If her father killed her, he killed her. A person had to take chances in life or there was no point to living.

*   *   *

Frances, who usually had no trouble, found it impossible to fall asleep that night. Excitement and fear played havoc with her. What *would* her father do? Maybe he'd like it. Never. He never liked anything new—unless it was a new horse he hadn't heard about!

Her hair, completely undone, spread out on the pillow. She ran a hand over it, taking a chunk between her fingers. It was thick. Silky. She sat up, turned on the light and went across the room to her vanity. Slowly she began running her brush through her auburn hair. She'd never been consistent about giving each side one hundred strokes as her mother recommended. She finished a stroke and hunched forward, resting her chin in both hands. She was cute—even pretty. If her nose hadn't been quite so short, so turned-up, she might have been beautiful. Certainly her eyes were beautiful. Hazel. What made them so spectacular were the lashes. Black, thick and long. Very long. Two months ago at a Deke party there was a contest to see which girl had the longest lashes. The trick was to see how many stick matches you could hold on them. She had won with five.

All in all she was a good-looking young woman, she thought. Good features, good skin and gorgeous long hair! Was she crazy? But, of course, Jennie was right. Soon bobbed hair would be commonplace and Frances, always in style, would have it anyway. So why not be first? She picked up a handful of hair, held it out to the side and then slowly let go, watching as it fanned back down to her shoulder.

Well, what was the sense in all this? She'd promised Jennie and that was that.

* * *

By four-thirty in the afternoon Frances was so tense that she literally jumped at the sound of a knock on her office door.

"Come in."

It was Ann Marie Pearl from the packing department. "Frances," she said, poking her long skinny face around the door.

"Come in, Ann Marie."

"I got a message." She strode in, both defiant and fearful, unnerved to be in what she considered the upper echelon of the factory. "It's from Jennie Licht."

She had called off the appointment! The barber shop burned down! A law had been passed forbidding bobbed hair! Frances held her breath, dangling nervously on the tip of relief.

"She got sick." Ann Marie took covert glances around the office where she'd never been before. She felt she should be the one working here, not Frances.

"What do you mean, sick?"

"Sick . . . sick."

"Really? Where?"

"In the wastebasket in the hall."

"That's not what I . . . never mind. Where is she now?"

"She got sent home. That's why I'm here." Ann Marie ran a hand over the copy of *Main Street* Frances had on her desk. "What's that?"

"It's a book."

Ann Marie clucked her tongue. "I know that. I mean what's it doin' there? Is it yours? Do ya read on the job, or what?"

This last question was closer to an accusation. Frances knew many of the girls resented her having what they considered a soft job, this job she found so boring and lonely.

"I read on the way to and from work."

"Oh yeah," Ann Marie said, a suspicious tone in her voice. "What is it, that book?"

"Look, Ann Marie, I'll be glad to talk about books with you some other time but right now I want to know about Jennie." She didn't care if the girl thought she was rude or snobby. She thought about the hair appointment less than forty-five minutes away. "Would you please tell me."

"I told ya. She threw up in the wastebasket in the hall and Pickering sent her home. She told me to tell ya. Oh yeah. She said she was sorry." Ann Marie opened the cover of the book and flipped some pages, staring at the print upside down.

Frances resisted slamming it shut. "That's all? That's all she said?"

"She couldn't get no more out I guess . . . except for the throw-up."

"Okay, okay," Frances said abruptly. "Thank you, Ann Marie."

"Yeah." She slowly walked toward the door where she stopped, turned and, cocking her head to one side, chin in the lead, said, "Is it dirty?"

"Huh?"

"The book. Is it dirty?"

"No."

"I wondered, is all. See ya."

Frances was relieved when the door shut her out. All the anxiety, the sleeplessness, had been for nothing. She was off the hook. Free. So why was she feeling annoyed? Let down? Disappointed? Perhaps because she'd wasted so much energy on the problem. Well, it was over. If Jennie wanted to have her hair bobbed, she could just do it alone when she got better.

After work, Frances decided she'd go to Snell's Barber Shop to break the appointment. After all, there was no reason to be rude about it, to leave the barber waiting.

A bell tinkled as she opened and closed the door feeling somewhat giddy entering this all-male domain. Two men having haircuts almost fell out of their chairs when they saw her. The youngest of the barbers put down his scissors and walked over to her, smiling.

"Can I help you, Miss?"

"Miss Licht made . . ."

"Oh yes." He frowned. "But you're not Miss Licht." He brightened. "You're the other one."

"Yes."

"She said there'd be two of you."

"Yes."

"Well, if you'll just sit down I'll be with you both in a . . ." He frowned again. "Will Miss Licht be late?"

"Yes. I mean, no. I mean, she's not coming. I've just come to . . ."

"Not coming? Why not?" He looked quite disturbed.

"She's sick."

"Oh God. What's wrong with her?" He twisted a small towel in his hands.

"Do you *know* Miss Licht? I mean, personally?"

"We just met yesterday."

"Oh." Why was he behaving as though she'd told him his mother had died?

"Hey, Artie, how about it?" one of the men called to him.

"Yeah, Mr. Schlesinger, in a minute. All right, Miss . . . Miss . . ."

"Hess."

"Miss Hess. If Miss Licht is sick, she's sick, and there's nothing to do about it, is there?"

Frances shook her head completely bewildered.

"So, if you'll just sit down I'll be with you as soon as I finish Mr. Schlesinger." He started to walk away.

"Oh, no." Her arm flew out and touched his shoulder.

"Hmmm? What?"

"I said, no, I can't."

"Can't what?" He began the towel twisting again.

"You see, I . . . well, I just came by to break the appointment."

"Break the appointment?" He dabbed at his face with the towel.

"Yes. I'm not going to do it." She nodded her head to prove that it was final.

"Oh, no . . . oh, no, you can't . . . you mustn't . . ."

"Look, Artie, could you talk to the skirt some other time? I got an appointment."

"I'm coming," he said. "Please Miss, would you just wait until I'm done with this customer so I can talk to you? Please."

"But there's nothing . . ."

"Please."

Frances thought the man might go down on his knees. To avoid any further embarrassment, she agreed. Sitting, waiting, the smells of soaps and pomades assaulted her nostrils. Why did everything men had seem so much more interesting than what women had? This smell, a kind of spiciness, was much more interesting than the smell of sachet in a woman's quarters, for instance.

Mr. Schlesinger was finished. Artie was standing before her, his security towel firmly in hand. "So, Miss, where were we?"

"I was telling you," she said as she stood, "that I came here only to break the appointment. I'm not going to have my hair bobbed."

"But we would be the first, don't you know?"

"We?"

"You the first to have it done, me the first to do it."

"Yes, I know. I've thought about that . . . about *me* being the first . . . not you . . . but, well, there's my father and . . ."

"Miss," he snapped the towel under his left arm and gripped her shoulders with his long thin hands, "do you think Irene Castle thought of her father when she cut her hair?"

"Irene Castle?"

"The dancer."

"Yes, I know who she is but I don't see what she has to do . . ."

"Don't you think she had a lot more to lose than you

when she made that big decision? 'Course she did. The whole world was watching her."

"Well, I don't think she had a choice. I read somewhere that her hair had gotten burned so she had to cut it. Besides, the whole world may not be watching me but all Lancaster will."

He grinned. "Yeah. And me, too. You know, Miss, I'm really surprised at you. You look like the kind of girl who wouldn't care about a lot of wagging tongues."

She was pleased that he could see that. "I *don't* care."

"I would think a girl like you would enjoy a few raised eyebrows from some stuffed shirts."

She smiled. "I would."

"Then how come you want to cancel?"

She couldn't remember. "I don't," she said.

"You don't? You don't? Yeah, yeah, okay, c'mon, we'd better hurry."

"Why, what's the rush?" she asked, as he dragged and pushed her toward the waiting chair.

"Well, ah, it's getting late."

"Oh."

He took her coat and hat, draped a huge white towel around her neck, clicked his scissors open and shut once, and lifted a hank of hair out to the side.

* * *

"There," Artie said, "that should do it."

Staring, she heard the bell tinkle when the door opened and closed, but she couldn't turn away from this person in the mirror who was Frances Hess. The change was extraordinary. Her features were much more defined and, to her eye, they all looked huge and vulgar. Almost in a state of shock, she paid no attention to the whispering behind her. Then, slowly, it began to register and she also became aware that her name was being called. As she turned toward the sound a light blinded her and a terrible smell permeated the room. For a split second, she thought her father had shot her and she was dead. When the smoke lifted and her eyes cleared, she saw the man who had called her name standing behind a camera, smiling.

"Okay, Miss, would you turn this way a little more?"

Artie gave the chair a small push and now Frances faced the photographer head on. "What is . . ."

"Okay," he said, pushing his hat farther back on his head, "say cheese."

"Cheese." She said it like a robot.

Again the light, smoke and terrible smell. Artie must have arranged this. He'd had it all set up in advance. Of course.

"Now," said the reporter, stains of chewing tobacco in the corners of his mouth, "I just want to ask you a few questions."

Well, it was done. The hair was cut, the picture was taken, she might as well cooperate. And it wasn't every day or every year or *ever* that you got your picture in the paper. And it certainly wasn't every*body*.

*   *   *

Her father's reaction was far more horrible than she had anticipated. He cried. She would have preferred his wrath. But it never came. Only the tears, then silence. The anger and hostility she'd expected came from another source entirely.

Her picture appeared in the morning paper along with a two-column, quarter-page story. The caption under the picture said: FRANCES HESS, FIRST GIRL IN LANCASTER TO HAVE BOBBED HAIR.

She kept the paper in her desk drawer and whenever she had a free moment that day she took it out and read the story again.

A few minutes before noon her office door burst open.

"Some friend! Some friend you are, Frances Hess!" It was Jennie, holding the paper folded open to the story.

Frances stared at her. She had never seen Jennie look like this, eyes wide, mouth tight and drained of blood.

"How could you? Just how could you do it?" Her voice squealed the last two words.

"But Jennie . . ." It had never occurred to her that Jennie might be angry. Even now she was bewildered.

"Don't Jennie me, all wide-eyed and innocent. You're a Benedict Arnold."

"Is it my hair? What about it? It was *your* idea."

"That's right. *My* idea. And you stole it."

"But you made the appointment."

"Not for you *alone*, Fran. For both of us. Could I help it if I got sick? You took advantage of my vomiting to gain your own ends, didn't you?"

"What ends?" Frances asked, thinking of the ends of her hair lying on the barber-shop floor.

"This." She held out the paper. "You couldn't wait. You had to get all the glory for yourself, didn't you?"

"I just thought as long as I was there in the first place I might as well . . ."

"What were you *doing* there, anyway?" she screamed.

"I . . . went to break the appointment."

"Ha!"

"Listen, Jennie, you can believe it or not but I didn't know anything about the photographer until after. I don't see what you're so upset about, anyway. We'll go over today and you can have yours done."

"And just what would that make me, Fran? That would make me a follower, that's what. A follower of Frances Hess . . . like you're some big star or something. No thanks."

"It would make you second in Lancaster. That's what it would make you."

"A follower," she hissed.

"Second."

"A follower."

"Second."

It was a stalemate. Jennie left the office as huffily as she'd entered. Frances sat back down at her desk, slammed things around, then cried.

*　　*　　*

Within two months a number of the girls had bobbed their hair. By 1922 almost all of them had. Except Jennie, who never did. And though Frances was remembered for a long time as "the first girl in Lancaster to have bobbed hair," she never really enjoyed the distinction. Whenever she saw Jennie she was always bothered by a small nagging feeling that perhaps Jennie had been right. Perhaps at the moment she decided to go along with Artie the barber, she knew that it would make her really special, really important. So much more special and important than if there had been two. She just didn't know.

Just a year ago today. Happy memories are few.
Oh Hell!
    —From the diary of Starr Faithfull, 1928

June 5, 1931
New York, New York

As the handsome man in the stateroom poured champagne into her glass, she told herself she must drink very, very slowly if she were going to keep her wits about her. She mustn't get pickled and muck it up.

"I'm so glad you're sailing, Miss . . .?"

"Parsons. Olive Parsons." A name from the past.

"Yes, it certainly will make this cruise more interesting. Cheers!"

They touched their sheer glasses, making a tiny pinging sound, and with her eyes Starr smiled over the rim.

Eleven

August 6, 1977
Orange, New Jersey

His mind frayed. Threads. How much longer would
this go on?

HUNT 2 MEN IN GIRL'S MURDER. The words from the
headline so long ago flashed across the back of his eyes.
That had happened often over the years. Out of nowhere,
as they said. He could be at work, at a movie, reading,
eating dinner, mowing the lawn, shaving . . . nothing
was protection. Even with a large group of people talking,
drinking, laughing. Suddenly. WHOOPEE SHIP CLUES LEAD
OFFICIALS TO BOSTON. And whatever he was doing would
be ruined, spoiled, for the day or night.

Even now, lying in a hospital room, those old headlines haunted him. They would, he knew, pop up as long
as he lived, frightening him anew. Another good reason to
die.

November 15, 1922
Lowell, Massachusetts

Starr, on her bed, held a large notebook and inside it
a slightly smaller magazine. THE FLAPPER WIFE, she read,
What Happened to a Girl Who Wanted a Husband, Not a

Home. It was a well-worn copy of *True Story*, the magazine all the girls at Rogers Hall whispered about. Her roommate, Muriel Sinclair, had asked Starr if she wanted to see it but Starr declined, feigning boredom. As soon as Muriel left the room, however, Starr picked it up.

Starr had met Muriel when she came to Rogers Hall two months ago. They were both in the eleventh grade. Muriel had been there since the ninth grade. For a month Starr rejected all Muriel's efforts to teach her about the school, as she rejected everyone else's overtures. Then one day, when Starr was at her desk, Muriel came up behind her, putting both hands firmly on Starr's shoulders.

"Starr," she said, "I truly would like to talk to you." Then before Starr could respond, "And don't be smart and say, so talk, or one of your other clever repartees. I want to have a real talk, face-to-face." She guided her, as though she were blind, to a small settee where they both sat. Still holding Starr's hand, she went on. "I want to know why you act the way you do . . . as though you hated the whole world."

No one had ever been so direct with Starr and she was silenced by the question. Staring at Muriel, looking into those affable, clement brown eyes, Starr's usual hostility, which she carried about like a sack full of rocks, began to dissolve.

"I don't know," she blurted out, committing herself to the conversation, surprised to find she didn't mind.

"Honestly?"

Starr nodded.

"Oh, dear," Muriel said, "it's worse than I thought."

"What do you mean?"

"Well, it'll be a lot harder to exorcise if you don't know why, won't it?"

"I . . . I guess." Muriel let go of her hand and Starr was vaguely aware of wishing she hadn't.

"Well," Muriel said, "I suppose you know that it's just awful . . . the picture you present."

Starr shrugged.

"Mmmm, it's even in your shrug."

Starr looked away, ashamed, another uncharacteristic reaction.

Muriel put her hand under Starr's chin, turning Starr back to face her. "All right, let's settle one thing at a time.

Do you, I mean, are you, aware that you go around this room and the halls of this school as though you were Ebenezer Scrooge? Do you know that?"

Starr almost smiled at the analogy and she could see Muriel too had a slight twitching at the corners of her mouth. "I . . . I've certainly never thought of myself as Ebenezer Scrooge but yes, I know I'm not too pleasant."

"Not too pleasant? You, my dear girl, are hideous. Everyone talks about it, you know. I mean, you're so *pretty* and you make yourself so ugly. I don't think you realize that."

Involuntarily, she shrugged again.

"Oh, stop that silly shrugging," Muriel chided gently.

"I can't help it," said Starr.

"Of course you can. It's just a terrible habit. Now, let's see if we can't figure this thing out together."

"What thing?"

"What makes you act in such a horrible way."

"Look," Starr said, getting a little of her cutting edge back, "if you think I'm so horrible, why are you bothering?"

"I don't think you're so horrible, I think you just *act* horrible. There's a difference. Now, is it because you're afraid?"

"Afraid of what?" she asked, feeling afraid.

"People."

"People?"

"Yes. Are you shy and all jelly inside when you have to talk with people?"

It would be easier to say she feared people than to admit she disliked them. Maybe she should just say yes.

"Let me ask you something else." Muriel interrupted her thought. "Do you smoke?"

Starr stared at her roommate. Was Muriel a spy for the School Council? Was she trying to trap her into getting demerits? No. She wouldn't come right out and ask if she were working undercover. Of course Starr smoked. But only with Andrew, in private. "Why?"

"I thought if you did you might like one, to relax."

"Here?"

"It's been driving me crazy not to be able to smoke these last weeks . . . in the room, I mean. Can I trust you?"

She started to shrug, stopped herself, smiled and nodded. "I smoke."

"Good." Muriel went to a drawer in her desk and took out an ashtray and a package of Camels.

They sat smoking in silence for a few moments and then Muriel began again. "I think, if you're going to trust me . . . you don't, do you? I mean, why should you? Anyway, I think I should tell you some things about me. First of all. I'm not sixteen. I'm twenty."

Starr's mouth opened in surprise.

"I know I don't look twenty but I am. You see, I was very sick for four years and I missed out on my schooling."

"Is that why you don't do sports?"

"Yes."

Starr, who had a passion for swimming, had never understood why Muriel wouldn't even go in the water. "What was your illness?"

"I had consumption."

"Consumption! But you shouldn't be smoking then, should you?" She was genuinely concerned, still another unusual feeling.

"Oh," Muriel said, with a wave of the hand, "I'm all cured. Besides, I don't intend to live my life like an invalid. I'm going to have fun if it kills me! I go along with the sports ban because I don't care that much and it makes everybody think I'm being a *good* girl. Though I *would* like to take a dive in that pool now and then. Anyway, Starr, nobody here, except the teachers, knows how old I am and I'd rather they didn't."

She was suspicious again. "Then why have you told *me* of all people?"

"Because, oddly enough, I like you. No, that's not quite true. I don't like the you you present to the world, I like the you I know is underneath that. But perhaps I'm giving you too much credit. Am I?"

"How can I answer that?"

"I guess it *is* an unfair question." Muriel stubbed out her cigarette, waving the lingering smoke toward the window she'd opened. "At any rate, Starr, I would appreciate your keeping silent on anything I tell you. Can I trust you?"

She thought about it. Who would she tell? She decided she could safely and honestly tell Muriel that she could be trusted.

"Good. Do you have a boyfriend? I've never seen you with one but that doesn't mean . . . well, do you?"

Did Andrew count as a boyfriend? Weighing this, Starr realized she was in the position she'd tried to avoid for years. Someone probing into her life. If she answered one question, she would invariably have to answer others. "I don't like that kind of question," she said, sounding prim.

"You mean you think it's too personal? Well, I suppose it is. But let me explain. One of the reasons I like you, or think I do, is because you don't seem like the other girls."

"I'm not," she said, proud.

Muriel smiled. "What I mean is, you seem older, wiser. More worldly, I guess. Of course that could be a pose. I mean, you do try to be mysterious, don't you?"

Starr had never been aware of trying for that effect.

"Are you with me, Starr?"

A good question. And now was the time to decide. She could either end this whole thing or step across an invisible bridge into something murky and possibly dangerous. Danger had always held an appeal for her.

"I'm with you." Then, remembering the previous question, she answered. "I don't think I try and be mysterious, Muriel. I just . . . well, I just don't want everybody to know everything about me, that's all."

"I understand. Do you think you could let me know *some* things about you?"

"Maybe."

"Well *I'm* going to trust *you*. You see, the reason I asked if you had a boyfriend," she said, lighting new cigarettes for both of them, "was because I *do* have a boyfriend."

"Yes, I know. I've seen him. He's good-looking."

"Isn't he? His name is Ted. He's twenty-two. I know . . . he doesn't look it either, which is all to the good since everyone thinks I'm sixteen. Anyway, believe me, he's *no* sixteen!" She waved her hand back and forth as though she'd burned it.

Starr was intrigued.

"The thing is, I don't want to shock you . . . or

maybe I do! I mean, after all, you *are* sixteen. I'd feel a bit better about it if I knew you had a boyfriend."

Clearly, if Starr was to get any further information she must say yes. "I have a boyfriend," she said, trying to dispel the image of Andrew's weak blue eyes.

"Good. Is he your age?"

"A bit older." She reluctantly recalled the loose rolls of skin around Andrew's middle. "His name is Edmond." The remembrance of Edmond Chalmers pained her slightly.

"A nice name. I thought you might date someone older. Do you . . . no . . . no."

"What?"

"I was going to ask you a *very* personal question. But before I ask you I think I should tell you something first. Now please, Starr, I've never told anyone this and . . ."

"I won't tell."

"We . . . Ted and I . . . pet."

Pet. She almost laughed. Two years ago everyone had been shocked and outraged by *This Side of Paradise*, in which flappers petted in the back seats of flivvers. Even then, she'd been mildly amused at all the uproar over something so silly.

"Do you think I'm just terrible?"

"No."

"The truth is, I don't either. Ted and I love each other and oh, what the hell, everyone's doing it." She looked deeply into Starr's eyes. "Have you and Edmond?"

She was enjoying this. It was fun talking to another girl. She was sure Muriel wanted her to have petted, but not too much. That way Muriel would remain the wiser and more sophisticated of the two. Starr lowered her eyes in a pretense of embarrassment. "A little," she said, almost inaudibly.

"I knew it," Muriel said, with a swift intake of breath. "Oh God, Starr, don't be ashamed. Just thank heaven we have each other to talk to!"

And Starr looked up at her and thanked heaven she did.

As the weeks passed they confided more and more in each other, although Starr still maintained her aloofness with the other girls. She of course never mentioned Andrew. When she went away with him she always came back with tales of mad necking and petting with Edmond.

Her relationship with Andrew, now almost five years old, caused her to experience great swings of emotion. Sometimes she anticipated their meeting with enormous excitement. Sometimes she approached them with deep loathing and fear. Now that she was at Rogers Hall she saw him quite often. Too often. She'd known that Rogers Hall would mean more of Andrew but when her father finally relented Starr was not about to refuse. Helen had worked on him for almost two years.

Frank had become a boarder in his own house. He'd moved his things to the empty bedroom downstairs. Sometimes he appeared at meals but not often. Starr and Tucker rarely saw him and spoke little when they did. Her parents no longer behaved as a couple. The only time they'd left the house together the preceding summer was to attend the funeral of Margaret Faithfull. By then Frank had agreed to let Starr attend Rogers Hall and to let Andrew pay for it.

The copy of *True Story* fell closed. So now she was at Rogers Hall, had a friend, was on the swimming team and saw Andrew frequently. Today, for instance.

She had half an hour before he was due and got out her Memory Book. This was the fifth volume, blue silk with smooth blue pages. Soon after it all started with Andrew, she'd begun to record things. She sat down at her desk, opened her Mem Book, as she called it, to a blank page, dated it and began to write.

> In a little while A.J.P. will arrive to take me away with him for a short weekend (only about twenty-four hours). Will it be too short? Too long? Don't ask me. I never know in advance. When I think of what will probably take place I shudder. And yet, I long for that little green bottle, or rather for what is in it, for what it does, where it takes me. Oh, my. Even now, after all these many times I have spent with him, I cannot be sure of what will happen. Often it is something new. What would Muriel say if I told her about my beloved Ether? And what it does to me and what it makes me do? And what would my father, who doesn't care, say if he

knew? Why, he would say, of course, I don't care!

She put down her pen. The leaves outside the window were red and golden but there were fewer on the trees than on the ground. The sky, this day, was too blue to believe and she looked away, back to the softer blue of her Mem Book. Again, she took up her pen.

I think tonight I will go very mad and dance naked on his chest.

She closed the book, staring at its silk cover while waiting for the knock that would tell her the Mayor of Boston had arrived to take her on holiday.

August 3, 1923
Sea Girt, New Jersey

Orlando sat on the front steps, leaning against a column, staring out at the ocean as he absentmindedly picked at his banjo. The first line of an anonymous poem he'd read in the *New York World* ran through his head. *Mother makes brandy from cherries.* He played a chord and sang it to himself. The rest followed quietly but aloud.

Pop distills whiskey and gin;
Sister sells wine from the grapes on our vine—
Good grief, how the money rolls in.

He smiled. Again, faster, louder.

"Orlando!" It was Nina.

He looked up. She was holding Aldo, her year-old son. Already you could see that he was going to have his father's large nose instead of his mother's straight small one. Everyone said it was good he was a boy because it wouldn't matter.

"What?" he asked.

"What are you singing?"

"Oh, nothing, just a . . ."

"You shouldn't be singing anything." She sat down next to him.

"Why not?" he asked, annoyed. "What do I care about Harding?"

"It's a matter of respect." She leaned down and put Aldo on the sand.

"Well, I don't have any."

"If Papa were here you'd have some."

"He's not here. And he won't be here until the weekend."

"He's coming this afternoon."

As always, Orlando felt afraid at the thought of seeing his father. But it was worse today because of what he had to tell him. "Why is he coming today?"

"Everything is closed because of the President's death. I wonder," she said, rising to retrieve a small stone from Aldo's fist that was headed toward his mouth, "what kind of a President Mr. Coolidge will make?"

"What do you care? You don't care about the States anymore." Nina drove them all crazy with her Canadian chauvinism.

"Of course I care. I'm still a citizen."

"You'd never know it the way you go on about your precious Montreal."

"Oh, Orly, just because I have taste and culture you . . ."

"Please," he said, hitting a minor chord. Taste and culture were Nina's two favorite themes and he was definitely not in the mood.

She picked up Aldo. "For instance, there is nothing cultured about that terrible music you play. It's Negro music and everyone knows it."

"So what? Anyway, Bix Beiderbecke is white."

"Who in the world is Bix Beiderbecke?" She pushed a strand of dark hair from her forehead.

"Forget it."

"You're so uncivilized. You can never have an intelligent conversation. What is the point of going to college if you can't have an intelligent, cultured conversation with your own sister?"

The mention of college made him feel afraid again.

"I suppose you'd rather talk with those jazz girls you see," Nina said.

He laughed. "Jazz babies?"

"Whatever."

"Jeez, Nina, nobody actually *says* jazz babies . . . I mean, it's . . . never mind."

"What? It's what?"

"Do you think I say, 'hello there, jazz baby' or 'you're some jazz baby'? Do you think that's what goes on?"

"I don't know and I don't care. I think it's all disgusting. And when I think of the terrible things you do with those girls." She closed her eyes, shutting out grotesque images.

"What things? What girls?"

"Just because I'm a visitor doesn't mean I don't know what goes on."

"What things, Nina?"

"You tell me," she said, trying to sound very proper.

He almost laughed out loud. Nina was as transparent as always. Propriety, decorum, respectability were worn like a fancy dress to cover dirty underwear. Nina had an insatiable lust for the details of other people's sex lives. Not that she would want anyone to become *too* graphic.

"Well, Nina," he said, "if you know so much about it all, there's no need for me to fill you in on anything. Of course, there's probably *one* thing you don't know about."

"What's that?"

"I wouldn't want to shock you."

"I'm a very big reader and . . ."

"That's true. Well, maybe you *do* know about it so there's no sense in bringing it up."

"What is it," she snapped. Then softer, "Naturally, if it's too raw I certainly wouldn't want to hear about it."

"Exactly," he said. "I'm not sure if it's even proper for us to be talking this way."

"Well, I am older than you . . . What *is* it, Orlando?"

"Ozonization," he whispered.

She gasped and clapped her fingers over her mouth. Slowly the fingers slid away. "What's that?"

"Now hold on. You don't think I'm going to define it for you, too, do you? Look it up in the dictionary." He tightened a string, listened to see if it was in tune.

"It's in the dictionary?"

"Of course. Aldo's crawling toward the water."

Nina ran to the baby, picked him up and hurried back to Orlando. "How do you spell it?"

He told her.

As she walked across the porch to the door, his eyes

were level with her thighs. It was unfortunate, he thought, for his sisters that the brief one-piece bathing suit had come into style. All of them had huge thighs. They were, he suspected, like his mother's, though she always wore a dress on the beach.

He decided to take a walk. If Nina found a dictionary she'd be furious when she discovered that ozonization meant the treatment of a compound with ozone. He put the banjo on the porch swing and headed toward the water.

How was he going to tell his father that he wasn't going back to Princeton? He should have told him at the close of the academic year but his fear was too great. Fear of his father's reaction. He didn't know precisely what it would be. Still, it terrified him.

It was important to his father that he, the oldest son, go to, and graduate from, a superior American college. His father assumed Orlando would go into law, though it didn't interest him at all. He preferred music, perhaps some kind of writing, both professions that would be anathema to his father. Orlando Sr. believed the dead Silvio had held exclusive rights to the music world. Writing, as far as he was concerned, was not something one did for a livelihood.

Orlando knew he would have to study law but where he would do his undergraduate work was now a mystery. Princeton did not want him back. He hadn't done anything major, only a lot of minor infractions adding up over the year. The Dean felt he just wasn't Princeton material. His fear of his father returned, clearer now.

There would be no punishment when Orlando told him the truth about Princeton. Probably not even a word. There would be just penetrating cold. Ice. A biting chill. A frost so cutting he shivered now thinking of it. That was it, had always been it. Intolerable. It was, in the end, the glacial silence that destroyed him.

In the distance, there was a figure coming toward him. He did not want to talk to anyone. He would have to walk the other way. But what if his father was at the house already? He couldn't move.

Soon he could make out the outline of the figure down the beach. A woman. Her gait was long, ungraceful. Familiar? He thought he saw a spark near her head. Not a spark. Sunlight. Reflection in glasses. Immediately, his eyes went to the legs. There they were, the large thighs. It was Concettina, Connie, his sister. She was waving. He began to warm up.

Sitting on the beach with Connie, his favorite sister, he felt better than he had all day. She had a kind of inner peace that always calmed him.

"I never get upset about things that are going to happen because they never happen the way you imagine them," she often said. "There's plenty of time to get upset when they *do* happen."

He wished he could adopt that philosophy and he'd tried. But he could never stop his mind from jumping ahead, imagining the worst, agonizing over it.

Connie was special. No question about that. So why did she waste her attentions on Jack Ward? Nobody could see it. Certainly not Papa, who'd forbidden her to see him. Still, in secret, Connie persisted.

Jack was ten years older, separated from his wife, and unemployed. By trade he was a salesman, although the only thing he was selling currently was himself to Connie. He was unusually handsome but Orlando couldn't believe Connie would be taken in by something so superficial. There was nothing else about Jack Ward that was redeeming. Still, he was the only suitor Connie had ever had and he did seem to care for her and to treat her with respect. Unlike Nina, Connie was not beautiful. Her eyes were nearly hidden by thick glasses which rested on the bridge of her large, hooked nose. Her mouth was small and thin, like her brothers'. She looked like no one else in the immediate family.

Examining her face now, Orlando wondered why people were so shallow. Why couldn't they look beneath her exterior at her gentle, loving personality?

"Why are you staring at me, Orr?"

"Am I? I'm sorry. I thought I was just listening."

"I wasn't saying anything." She smiled.

"Oh." He should have been embarrassed but he wasn't. You couldn't be embarrassed with Connie.

"What are you thinking about?"

He wondered if he should raise the subject of Jack

Ward. He never really had. "If you really want to know, I was thinking about Jack," he said finally.

"Jack? My Jack?"

He nodded.

"What were you thinking about him?" She traced a J in the sand.

"I was wondering why you keep seeing him? Especially when Papa hates him so."

"I love him," she said simply. "And as for Papa hating him, well, he'd hate anyone. You wait until you bring someone home you're really serious about. Actually, maybe it'll be different with you boys. But for the girls, nobody, believe me, nobody is good enough."

"What about Renato?"

"And who picked him for Nina? Papa. That's very different. When he picks, that's different."

"You're not at all afraid of him, are you?"

"No."

"Then why do you see Jack in secret?"

"To keep peace."

"What if Papa finds out? What would you do?" With his foot he accidentally rubbed out the J.

"I'd give Papa a choice. Either I'd go on seeing Jack or move out."

The thought of Connie giving Papa an ultimatum made him feel giddy. "You wouldn't!"

"I would. I'm twenty-three. Most girls my age are married. Who's Papa to tell me what I can do and who I can see?"

"Well, he *does* tell you."

"I know. But I only pretend to obey . . . as I said, to keep peace." She reached out and pushed a strand of his hair from his eyes. "You're afraid of him, aren't you, Orr?"

He looked away, out to sea.

"It's all right. I understand. He can be very frightening." She took his hand.

He turned, looking into her eyes. "It's different with his favorites."

She didn't pretend, as Nina or Toni would have, that Papa loved him dearly. Instead she simply squeezed his hand.

He found himself telling her about Princeton. And then she was reassuring him and soon they were laughing and he was feeling good, unafraid. Connie was his oasis, always would be. He would be lost without her.

There was a crack of thunder and a sudden downpour of rain. Hand in hand, they ran toward the house.

They were shrieking with laughter as they came up the porch steps. Nina stood just inside the door, arms akimbo.

"Ozonization, huh?" she asked through the screen.

"What's that?" Connie asked.

"Ask your darling, precious brother, why don't you?"

Connie looked at him as they pushed past Nina.

"It's just a joke," he said, feeling a bit guilty for not feeling guilty.

"You know what's wrong with you, Orly? You have a really dirty, filthy mind," said Nina.

"*Me?*"

"Yes, you. You're a horrible, demented boy and . . ."

"Nina," Connie broke in, "why don't you set up the Mah-jongg board while Orr and I change?"

In the shower he thought again what a help Connie was. So understanding. Gentle. Intelligent. She was like a shot in the arm!

Looking in the mirror as he dried himself he would have sworn he was taller than he'd been that morning. Even knowing that was an illusion, he was still ready to take on his father whenever he arrived.

————

We don't know any more tonight than we did when Starr Faithfull's body was found a week ago last Monday.

— Elvin Edwards, *New York Daily News,*
June 20, 1931

June 5, 1931
New York, New York

When Starr got into Murray Edelman's cab she was drunk. She couldn't understand how it had happened. She'd promised herself to drink slowly and she thought she had. How many glasses of champagne had there been? Goddamn, goddamn, goddamn.

Edelman asked where she wanted to go.

"I want to go to a speakie," she said automatically. What was the difference now. She'd ruined it. What a chump.

"Which one?"

"I don't care which one . . . just so long as it's wet."

At Tenth Avenue and Fourteenth Street she told Edelman to stop.

"I don't have any money. I just remembered."

Edelman was nice about it and let her out.

She stood on the corner, coat over her arm. It was hot. She was tired and thirsty. She had no plan.

Twelve

August 6, 1977
Orange, New Jersey

What's this? My God, a priest. Last rites? Who sent him? Surely not Cathy. Toni? No. Routine? Well, he didn't want him, need him. That was over with a long time ago.

"How do you feel, Mr. Antolini?"

Jackass! Didn't the fool know he couldn't talk?

"I'm Father Joe. Shall we pray?" He bent his head.

No, we shall not pray, Orlando thought. He wished he could tell him to get the hell out of his room. Instead he closed his eyes. If there was one thing he wasn't going to do it was to go running to the bosom of the Catholic Church at the last minute as his father had done.

"Orlando," the old man had said, head propped up, eyes sunken, skin like wax, "I wish to see a priest."

"A priest, Papa?" He couldn't have been more shocked.

"Do not argue." The tip of his tongue flicked over his dry, cracked lips. "Get me a priest."

Orlando Sr. received communion and the last rites within twenty-four hours. Orlando Jr. stared into his father's milky brown eyes with amazement. Is this what it all came down to in the end? Did everything one believed in give way to fear? What had the old man told the priest?

Had he told him of Natalia Smith and the others, whoever they were? Were the women the reason he was so afraid? It made Orlando want to laugh. Whatever his father's sins, they couldn't possibly be worse than his. For once he had something over the old man.

Orlando opened his eyes as Father Joe was blessing him. Oh, no. He was not going to follow in his father's footsteps. He tried to give the priest a look of disgust.

"I'll come see you tomorrow, my son." Father smiled and removed himself from Orlando's line of vision.

The door opened, shut.

Tomorrow, Orlando thought, I hope I will not be here.

———

Summer of 1923
New England

At the end of May, Frank Wyman, taking his few clothes and some personal papers, moved to the YMCA in Boston. He was content.

Helen was relieved. Her time was occupied, as it had been for almost a year, with the widower Stanley Faithfull.

Tucker was finishing the seventh grade and seemed, for the first time, to be doing quite well.

Starr was about to complete the eleventh grade, her first year at Rogers Hall.

The one cloud on Helen's horizon was Starr's imminent return to the house on Park Street. For one thing, she was sure it would upset Tucker. It was no coincidence that Tucker's improvement in her school work and in her disposition came about after Starr's transfer to Rogers Hall. For another, Helen feared Starr's presence would complicate her relationship with Stanley.

So in June, when Andrew Peters presented Helen with an alternative plan for Starr's summer, she was thrilled.

"Martha and I will be traveling up through Maine and Vermont, then across Canada and we'll probably see where our fancy takes us after that. The two youngest boys will be with us and, of course, Starr would be a big help there."

"It sounds wonderful, Andrew," Helen said.

Starr knew there would be no Martha, no two boys on the trip. It would be just Andrew and her. For eight weeks. Night after night. Surely he wouldn't be able to—not *every* night! But what if he did? She knew when her mother asked if she'd like to go on the trip she would have to say yes. Andrew would kill her if she said anything else. It never dawned on her that her mother would *not* ask her! That was more killing, insulting, humiliating than anything. She was stunned when she heard her mother consent.

"I think that'll be just lovely, Andrew, and we certainly appreciate all the advantages you've given Starr. Of course she can go. I wouldn't dream of standing in her way."

That her mother never even consulted her, that she behaved as though Starr didn't exist, had no thoughts, feelings, wishes of her own, was unforgivable. And for Starr it set the seal of finality on their already tenuous, strained relationship.

❖　　❖　　❖

STARR'S DIARY ENTRIES

July 2　Left with AJP for North Haven in the car.

July 3　Stopped in Portland at the Lafayette Hotel and remained there about two weeks and four days.

July 20　Started for Canada. Stopped at a small inn somewhere around the border.

July 21　Arrived at the Chateau Frontenac in Quebec. Remained two days.

July 24　Stayed at the Newport House in Vermont.

July 25　Bretton Woods in the White Mountains.

July 29　To Marblehead.

August 14　Started for New York. Overnight at Mohican Hotel in New London.

August 15　The Plaza. 5 days.

August 20　Springfield—Hotel Kimball.

August 21　Viewed Smith College stayed at the Bancroft in Worcester.

August 22　Motored to Marblehead.

August 26 Biltmore Hotel, Providence. Oh, Hor-
ror, Horror, Horror!!!
August 27 Barnstable.
August 30 Home. The end.

* * *

At the Biltmore Hotel in Providence on August 26 their rooms were next to each other, as always. This time he had registered as A. J. Peters, Boston, and Mrs. S. Wyman, Boston. Starr wondered who he thought he was fooling. Sometimes, standing in a hotel lobby, she thought of blurting out the whole thing. She knew, of course, that she never would. Still, it gave her pleasure to imagine it from time to time.

She waited in her bed. There were only a few nights when Andrew hadn't joined her. And she prayed for those nights, even though she felt somewhat rejected, slighted, when they occurred.

She was glad the trip was almost over and anxious to get back to school. They'd spent most days sightseeing or on the beach. They spent the nights eating good food, drinking excellent wine and in sexual activities.

Until this summer Starr had been the only one to give oral pleasure. Then in July, at the Lafayette Hotel, Andrew attempted to put his mouth on her. She tried to stop him. The idea embarrassed her, curious though she was. But he persisted and she, weakened by the ether, eventually submitted. She had loved it. For the next few days, insisting they not travel but stay locked in the room, she begged for more.

Now remembering those mad days, she was both embarrassed and lustful. If only she could have been waiting for someone else. Well, what difference? As always, she would close her eyes and pretend Andrew was Edmond.

The door opened. Andrew, dressed in suit and tie, carrying a small brown paper bag, walked to a chair near the bed and began to undress.

Starr turned her head away. She hated to see his fleshy body, the thickish coat of hair covering his arms, chest, back. The less she saw of him naked the easier it was. Lately, Andrew had taken to leaving on a light. Although she kept her eyes closed she knew that he looked at her, at her most private places. And it wasn't just looking. She could tell from his movement, sound, breathing, touch, that he was *inspecting* her. It made her feel unreal, inanimate. She loathed it.

"I have a surprise for you, Starr."

"Really?" She did not look at him.

"That's why I was so long. I had trouble finding what I wanted. I had to get a substitute but it'll work just as well."

She felt the bed sink down as he joined her, heard the rustling of the paper bag.

"Don't you want to see?"

She couldn't keep turned away forever; she'd try not to look at his body. When she turned, he was sitting up, holding the bag out to her.

"Look inside." He sounded mischievous, like a child.

She unfolded the top and looked in. Inside was a small white china container. She pulled it from the bag and removed the lid. "It looks like butter," she said.

"It is."

She looked from the butter to Andrew, her eyes questioning him.

"I was trying to find some vaseline from one of the bellhops but no one seemed to have any. So I got the butter from one of the boys in the kitchen. It cost me five dollars. It better be worth it." He giggled in his high, annoying way.

She looked again at the butter then back to Andrew.

"Well, don't tell me you don't understand," he said.

"I don't," she said, hating to admit it.

"Well, Starr dear, it's very simple. The butter will make my entry easier. That's all."

"Entry?" Saying the word, she began to decipher the meaning.

"Yes, of course. You're seventeen. You have been for some time. I don't know why I've waited for so long. At any rate, it's time. You can't be a virgin forever."

She knew about intercourse. But the fact that Andrew never suggested it hadn't seemed to her odd or surprising. She assumed it was just something he didn't care to do. And she was grateful. The idea of his swollen penis going into her was frightening. She was convinced that it would produce excruciating pain. Some time ago she'd decided that the man she eventually married couldn't be interested in intercourse. That would be a definite prerequisite.

"What for? Why do we have to?"

"Do you want to be a virgin always?"

Was she a virgin just because he'd never entered her? She didn't feel like one. Good God, he'd done everything else to her. "I don't care."

"Well, my pet, I do. I've waited long enough. I'd always planned to do this when you turned seventeen but time just got away from me."

"Why? Why seventeen?"

"Well, I have some sense of propriety, you know. After all."

She stared at him as he huffed, smacking his lips in irritation. He was insulted.

She didn't care. "I'd rather not do that."

He turned his head in surprise.

"Can't we do what we've been doing?"

"We'll do that too. Ahh," he reached out, put a hand under her chin, "is that what you're afraid of, my dear? Afraid we won't be doing the things you savor so?"

Embarrassed by the look in his eyes, annoyed by the presumption of his power over her body, she pulled away.

"Oh, don't be like that, Starr girl. I understand."

She wanted to punch him in his fat stomach.

"I know what my Starr likes." He reached beneath the sheet and stroked her thigh.

If she'd had a knife, she would have plunged it into his heart.

"But let me tell you, you'll like this too. Now give me the butter. I'll just put it here on the night table until we're ready."

"What'll you do with it?"

"I'll rub it on us. It'll feel good."

"I don't want to be all covered in butter," she said, sounding like the child she was.

"You'll change your mind. You'll see."

Andrew took the dish, laid it on the table, and climbed under the sheets. In a few moments he'd opened the ether bottle and Starr was floating as they began their ritual of sex.

By the time she felt the first touch of his tongue on

her she'd forgotten what was going to happen. She fell farther and farther away from reality, Edmond's dark eyes dancing before her. Then as she soared, turned, tumbled, she felt an abrupt change in Andrew's movements. He withdrew his tongue, replacing it with his hard fingers, sliding them round and in. Cool, then warm, slippery. The butter! He was filling her with the butter.

She opened her eyes and pulled back. "No!"

"Stop it," he said, breathlessly.

"I don't want to."

"Quiet." He raised himself up along her body, his belly and chest covering hers.

She felt his penis moving against her vagina. With a buttery hand, he reached down and guided it, first up and down, stroking her as he'd done so often with his tongue. Then quickly, abruptly, it happened.

"No, don't," she cried out.

Her eyes were open and they met his which were hard, cold and menacing, a look she'd never seen before. She was afraid.

"Don't you dare yell," he said.

She pressed her lips together, turned her head to the side and squeezed shut her eyes. There was no Edmond now. There was nothing except horrible, splitting pain. He kept going in farther and farther until she thought it would hit her ribs. Finally he stopped pushing and lay, panting, his elbows on either side of her, his chest dripping sweat onto her breasts. Then he began to move, pulling, pulling, pulling. Then, slam! Back in, higher, harder than before, making her feel the top of her head might fly off. Again the pulling, quicker now, a longer stroke. She was in agony. She wanted to scream out, smash at him, but she was too afraid. Slam. The force caused her to expel her breath in a grunt.

"Good," said Andrew, taking the sound for enjoyment.

She didn't hear. The pain blotted out everything. In her mind she saw bits and pieces of flesh flying each time he rammed into her. Between the whacking sound of his loose belly hitting her firm one, and the constant beating against her insides, Starr thought she might go mad. She couldn't stand the pain. Fear of his reprisal was no longer enough to keep her silent.

Screaming, she beat on his shoulders, neck, back. He pumped faster, harder. She scratched and pinched. He quickened his stroke. The more she pounded and tore at him the harder and faster Andrew drove himself.

Finally, a deep groan mingling with her cries, he shuddered, slowed, stopped. His body collapsed onto hers, his shoulder jutting into her throat, cutting off her wind.

With the strength of fury, she pushed him off, rolling to one side, bringing her knees to her chin. She continued screaming, crying, her face in the pillow.

When Andrew reached out to touch her, she jumped away.

"What is it, Starr girl? Did I stop too soon?"

She screamed with outrage. And kept on screaming.

Andrew finally realized she was hysterical and slapped her hard, twice, across the face. She stopped.

"What is it?" he said, almost inaudible.

"I told you I didn't want to do that, An-drew."

"But . . . but you seemed to . . . like it . . .," he trailed off.

"I hated it!" She was vehement. "I've never hated any-thing so much in my life. It was horrible, hideous." Her voice was shrill.

Andrew blinked as the words assaulted him.

"If you ever do that to me again I will tell everyone I know."

Just the mention of this made him giggle nervously.

"I mean it, Andrew. My mother and father, your wife, everyone."

"All right, all right." He was almost sure she wouldn't. Still. "We won't do that again."

"I'm not sure that we'll do anything again. I'm sick of this, of you."

The words stung him. "Now, now, Starr, you're just overwrought."

"What if I get pregnant?"

"Is that what's bothering you? Don't worry. An ex-mayor has lots of contacts. I know plenty of doctors who'd help you out."

As she lay there Andrew's sperm, mingling with the butter, dripped down her thigh. She felt dirty, disgusting, putrid. "Wipe me off," she commanded. "I have your filthy juice and that horrible butter all over me. Wipe it off."

Chagrined, he took a corner of the sheet and hitched his way down the bed. Her legs were closed. Carefully, he opened them and began wiping away the glistening spots.

"Promise you'll never do that again," she said, as he wiped her legs.

"I promise," he whined.

And for the first time in six years she experienced a sense of power.

October 14, 1925
Lancaster, Pennsylvania

The first time Frances Hess saw Orlando Antolini was at a home football game between Franklin & Marshall and Lehigh. She was with Doc Bayne, a young dentist she was growing rather tired of after three months of sporadic dating. He was constantly jealous and sulking now because Fran had just told him she was going to a party at the Phi Sigma Kappa house that night with Hugh Madden.

Fran, when she wasn't watching the game, tried to get another look at the handsome dark-haired guy three rows below her. She wondered who he was, why she had never seen him before and what house he belonged to. During a time-out he looked up into the stands, smiled and waved at someone. Breathtaking. He looked like a movie star. And he was very dark. Not unlike Rudolph Valentino. He faced forward again, putting his arm around the girl on his right. Fran continued observing him. Wide shoulders. Obviously, a big guy. She liked that.

A roar came up from the crowd which rose to its feet. Fran jumped up and saw the quarterback running for F & M's first touchdown. Doc took the opportunity to hug Fran and after he released her, as she looked back toward the field, her eye again was caught by the handsome guy down front. Like everyone else he was standing, waiting for the conversion. Fran was shocked. He wasn't big at all. He couldn't have been more than two or three inches taller than she was. What a shrimp, she said to herself, and never looked at him again during the game.

*　　　*　　　*

The first time Orlando saw Fran was that night at his fraternity party. He wondered if she were Spanish. He was with Babs Hoey, a date he didn't particularly like. He'd asked her as a favor to Earl Paige, his best friend and roommate. Earl wanted a date with Babs's sister and she wouldn't go unless he got a date for Babs. Orlando volunteered.

Babs, on her third gin, was at his side as he continued to steal looks at the Spanish-looking beauty across the room.

"I think that this party is just the bee's knees. Don't you, Orr?"

"Yeah."

"You know, a lot of my friends won't date you college boys because they think you're all too fast but I think that's applesauce. Don't you?"

"Yeah, sure."

"I mean, if a girl doesn't want to neck and pet she doesn't have to no matter who she's with. I don't care if he's some big cheese or what. Unless you're a Dumb Dora, which I'm not, no lounge lizard is going to make me do something I don't want to do."

"Lounge lizard?" This was one he'd never heard.

"Sure."

"Sure what?" The constant slang was really getting on his nerves.

She blinked and looked at him, her lips clamped around the rim of her glass.

"What the hell is a lounge lizard?"

"You don't know what a lounge lizard is? Honest? I can't believe that. That's just banana oil, if you ask me."

"What I'm asking you," he said, even more testily than before, "is, what is a lounge lizard?"

"Oh, I can't believe you don't know what a lounge lizard is, a hep guy like you? That's just got to be baloney."

"Forget it."

"I mean, listen, kiddo, a jake guy like you, well, I bet there's nothing you don't know. In my book you're the cat's meow."

"Nerts," he said. "Give me your glass. I'll get you another."

At the bar, which was in another room, he ran into Fatty Dickerson. Fatty, as usual, was stag. Orlando asked him to take the drink back to Babs, keep her company, and explain he'd had to make a phone call.

As he was planning the tactics he'd use to meet the Spanish lovely, she and Hugh came through the door and over to the bar. Hugh ordered them each a drink and excused himself. Orlando immediately seized the opportunity.

"Excuse me," he said, "do you know what a lounge lizard is?"

"What?"

"Lounge lizard. Do you know what one is?"

"No. Why?"

"It's a long story." He introduced himself and was surprised to hear her name. "Hess? That's German, isn't it?"

"Yes."

"Ahhh, but your mother's Spanish, right?"

She smiled thinking of her mother. "Heavens no. Why?"

"I thought you were Spanish."

"Me? That's funny. But you, are you Spanish?"

"Italian."

"Yes, I thought it was one or the other."

Now he smiled. "You're drinking a Coke?"

"That's right."

"Why?" he asked, genuinely interested.

"I like it."

"With all this superior hooch around?"

"I don't drink."

"Oh boy," he said, making a big display of hiding his drink behind him.

"I don't care if you drink. I don't think it's bad or anything. And I'm not for prohibition. I just don't like the taste."

He was glad she didn't drink, something rather unusual these days, and wondered how else she was different. "Do you smoke?"

"No."

"You don't drink, you don't smoke, what *do* you do?" he asked, smiling, playing.

"Oh, I find things to keep me busy." She smiled back, flirting.

When Hugh returned, seconds later, they were staring at each other in silence, smiling.

"Oh, hello, Antolini. Where's your date?"

"I don't have one," he answered, his eyes still fastened to Fran's.

"I thought you were with the younger Hoey sister."

"Nope. Where's your date, Madden?"

He gave a snort, then said, "Fran's my date."

"Really?"

"Yeah, really." He moved closer to Fran and put a possessive hand on her bare shoulder.

She was grinning now. Gently, she moved a step away from Hugh so that his hand slipped off her shoulder.

Taking his cue from Fran, Orlando forged ahead. "You know, Hugh, I heard that this past summer you were exposed to leprosy."

"Huh?"

"That's right. Did you know that, Miss Hess? You didn't? Well, Hugh, I don't think that's nice. You could at least warn your dates. Shame on you."

"Hey, what is this?" Hugh said.

"I think," Orlando pressed on, "that I can't permit Miss Hess to remain in your company."

"Look here."

Orlando took Fran's arm and started to walk away with her. Hugh grabbed him, turning him around.

"Where are you going?"

"Oh," Orlando said with mock surprise, "I thought I made that clear. We've leaving."

"Leaving?"

"Yes. Goodnight, Hugh." He pulled out of Madden's grip and started for the stairs leading to the front door.

Hugh yelled after them. "Hey, wait a minute. Fran? Fran?"

"I just can't," Fran said to Orlando. "It's too awful."

"You can and you will. Keep walking."

"No, really, I can't. I'd like to," she added quickly, "but I can't."

"Why not?"

"Well, it's rude."

"Haven't you ever been rude before?"

"I just can't."

He watched as she went with Madden into the other room. Well, she'd said that she'd like to go with him. That was certainly worth something. But he wasn't used to not having his way with women. Maybe he'd just get drunk. Then he remembered something. At parties Madden almost always got drunk and passed out. Orlando smiled. He would *not* get drunk. He would simply wait.

It took nearly two hours. During that time Orlando kept hidden away upstairs, giving Fatty Dickerson ten dollars to make sure Babs Hoey got home all right and another five to let him know when Madden passed out. It was twelve forty-five when Fatty gave him the high sign.

Fran stood off to the side watching and looking disgusted as some of Madden's fraternity brothers lifted him from the floor. Orlando walked up to her.

"You see where good manners get you?"

"This was my first date with him," she said, apologetic.

"And your last?"

She smiled. "And my last."

Settled in his year-old Model T, Orlando was suddenly confronted with the question of where to go. Certainly he didn't want to take her home so early. And you couldn't take a woman who didn't drink to a speakeasy. He would like to have taken her somewhere to make love to her but he knew that was impossible. Frances Hess was not the kind you made love to on the first night. Maybe not ever—unless you married her.

"Well?" She was no longer able to appear busy with the blanket around her legs and looked at him, her long dark lashes apparent even in this dim light.

"I don't know where to take you." He couldn't believe he'd said that! Usually, he was so smooth with women. Frances Hess was definitely unsettling him.

"How about Engelside's?"

Engelside's was a speakeasy. He didn't hide his surprise.

"They have a good band. I love to dance. Do you?"

"Yes, sure." He danced well except for this new one, the Charleston. He still couldn't quite get it.

At Engelside's a number of his fraternity brothers and their dates waved at him to join them. Instead he steered Frances to a table in the back by themselves. He ordered rye and water for himself and Coca-Cola for Fran. When the band played "Yes, Sir, That's My Baby" Fran grabbed his hand and they headed for the dance floor.

She was terrific and they moved extremely well together, dancing three numbers before returning to their table.

They talked about movies, agreeing that their favorites were *The Thief of Bagdad* and *The Gold Rush* with *Phantom of the Opera* running a close third. She especially liked Norma Shearer and John Gilbert. She didn't mention Rudolph Valentino because she didn't want to sound like everyone else. He liked Constance Talmadge and Douglas Fairbanks. He didn't mention Mary Pickford because he didn't want to sound like everyone else.

The band started a Charleston.

"Oh, good," Fran said.

"I don't know how to do it," he said.

"Would you like me to teach you?"

"Sure. Sometime soon."

A fraternity brother appeared at their table and asked Fran to dance. Orlando watched. She was marvelous. Her Charleston made him smile. Then he thought of Kay. She was very different from Kay.

At four A.M. they sat outside her house in his car.

"Don't your parents worry about you being out this late?"

"I'm not a child," she said.

"How old are you?"

She hesitated only a moment. "I'm almost twenty-four." She knew he had to be younger and asked him his age.

He thought about lying, pretending to be older. But something made him tell the truth. "I was just twenty-one." Eager to deflect any comment about his age, he asked why she wasn't married.

"I'm having too good a time," she said, smiling.

"But you want to get married?"

"Oh, someday, I guess. Yes, of course."

"You're not a career girl, then?"

"Oh, heavens no. I'm modern but . . . well, I don't have any special talents."

"You have the talent to make me smile."

"You're a real smoothie, aren't you?"

"I try to be," he said. Then, "I'm only kidding."

"No, you're not."

He didn't like the direction this conversation was taking. "What do you do?"

"I work at Armstrong Linoleum. In the office." She didn't want him to think she worked in the factory.

"Do you like it?"

"It's all right . . . better than working at Watt & Shand's as a salesgirl."

"Did you do that?"

"Only for a few months. I hated it. Before that I was in the office at Bayrick Cigar." She wondered what he'd think if he knew she'd left school at thirteen. Some boys didn't care, others did. "I loved school but my family just couldn't afford to let me go on." He would think that meant college. It wasn't her fault if he misunderstood. "What are you studying?"

"I'm majoring in English Lit but I'm going to be a lawyer."

"You don't sound very happy about it."

That was perceptive, he thought. "Really?"

"Are you going to be a lawyer because your father's a lawyer?"

"I'm the oldest son. He wants me to follow in his footsteps. You know how it is."

"Do you *want* to be a lawyer?"

"Actually, no. It doesn't interest me one whit. But I couldn't disappoint my father. He's counting on it."

"But it's *your* life," she said.

"Yes, but . . . well, we're very close, my father and I, and I wouldn't want to upset that." He always told girls that he and his father were close. He didn't know why.

"It seems to me that if you're so close, well then, he ought to know how you feel about it. My sister Dorothy and I are very close and she always knows how I really feel."

He said nothing.

Sensing his discomfort, Frances changed the subject

slightly. "What would you like to do, if you had your druthers?"

"I would be a writer. Or a musician. Or both. I'd write all day and play all night."

She laughed. "Well, I guess *you* don't want to get married, do you?"

"Sure I do. Why do you say that?"

"Write all day and play all night? When would you see your poor wife?"

"Oh, I'd manage. Of course, she'd have to be understanding and in the beginning we'd have to make certain sacrifices. There would be times when we wouldn't see each other as much as we'd like, but it would all be a means to an end."

"And what would that be?"

"Well, whichever thing I got famous for first. And we'd either have the days together or the nights."

"You mean you'd give up one eventually?"

"Yes."

"Well, personally, I'd hate to have a husband who was out every night."

"Then I'd work harder at my writing." He surprised himself. What the hell kind of talk was this with a girl he'd just met?

They stared at each other in an embarrassed silence. Finally she broke it.

"I think I'd better go in."

Immediately, he jumped out, ran around the front and opened her door. They walked up the path to the porch.

"I had a keen time," she whispered.

"Me too." He wanted very much to kiss her.

"Well," she said.

"Tomorrow night? I mean, tonight. Tonight, Sunday night. *Big Parade* is at the Dreamland."

"All right." She made a mental note to cancel her date with Doc Bayne.

He would kiss her. After all, she'd said she was modern. And when he bent his head, his hands touching her shoulders, she didn't move away. It was a long kiss. Warm, sweet. She noted that the slight difference in their height made kissing easier. Perhaps tall men weren't so wonderful. They whispered good night and he waited to leave the porch until she was safely inside.

Fortunately, Earl was asleep when Orlando got back to the fraternity house. He was in no mood for a harangue about Babs Hoey. He hoped his dumping Babs hadn't ruined Earl's evening but, even if it had, he had no regrets. Lying in bed, arms around his pillow, he thought about Fran.

Why was he having this reaction? He frequently dated new girls and never got serious, except for Kay. Now, after just a few hours, he couldn't get this girl out of his mind. It was ridiculous. Kay had never made him feel this way. His feelings for her were profound but they'd always lacked something. Perhaps this tingling feeling he was experiencing now.

Orlando flipped over to his back, his eyes open, staring at the ceiling. He concentrated on Kay.

Kay Chase was a year younger than he, an inch shorter (she always wore flat shoes), from a wealthy, respectable Presbyterian family, a good drinker (she often put him to bed) and a junior at Smith. She had light brown hair, large blue eyes and a straight nose. Her mouth was full, wide and beautifully shaped. At twenty she looked sophisticated, worldly, mature. She was extremely intelligent. Their letters focused often on who they were reading: Fitzgerald, Dreiser, Lewis. Or on music. They'd had a long debate about Gershwin's *Rhapsody in Blue*. Or perhaps philosophy. It was rare, in a letter, that any passionate language passed between them.

Even in person they weren't exactly romantic. Kay had a cynical edge to her and Orlando followed suit. He never thought of their sexual encounters as making love. It was very good with Kay. Strong and fulfilling. But it was not romantic.

They'd met in Sea Girt at the end of the summer of 1923. Orlando had just told his father about his failure at Princeton. Orlando Sr., who'd received the news as icily as anticipated, nevertheless pulled a few strings and got his son into Rutgers. He'd lasted six weeks. This time he quit. In January he went to Brown. By February he was home. In mid-March he enrolled at New York University. By

June he knew he would not return there. In September he tried Syracuse. At the beginning of 1925 he found Franklin & Marshall. Finally, he was home.

He dated countless girls at his various colleges. But always he wrote to Kay. And always, whenever possible, they spent holidays and vacations together. They'd agreed to stay away from each other's colleges, a modern arrangement, they felt. It had suited Orlando perfectly and now, particularly, he was grateful. He would have Frances Hess in Lancaster, Kay in Newark. As far as he could see, it could go on that way indefinitely.

There has been no controlling her ever since she was a child.
—Helen Faithfull, *New York Times,* June 12, 1931

June 5, 1931
New York, New York

At six o'clock Starr found herself sitting in a pew in Grace Church. She couldn't remember how she'd gotten there but imagined she'd walked. Her black pumps pinched her feet. No matter *why* she was there, she was glad. The church was cool. Her head ached. A hangover was beginning. She could, she decided, live with it or fight it, cure it with a drink. Perspiration ran down the sides of her face. Her stomach turned over. She held her hands in front of her and saw the tremor.

The pew vibrated slightly. Starr turned. A woman sat down next to her, smiling kindly.

"Are you all right, my dear?"

"No," Starr said.

Thirteen

August 6, 1977
Orange, New Jersey

He woke from a short sleep. His bladder was full. It made no difference. The catheter was in place. Humiliating.

If only he'd written it all down some place. Cathy might find it, read it and . . . and what? Well, he hadn't written it down. Too dangerous. He'd just written his one novel. It had taken him twenty-five years. Not that he'd worked on it all that time. For twenty of those years he didn't touch it. Then he retired. Wrote the last one hundred and thirty pages. Sent it out twice. No one had wanted it. He put it in his drawer after that. Twice was enough. Cathy said write a new one. He put his typewriter away and turned on the television.

1923–1926
Massachusetts

After her trip with Andrew, Starr decided she'd tell Muriel about him when she saw her again. Muriel was trustworthy, Starr was sure. And she felt she would understand. Since the trip Starr had become increasingly nervous, plagued by headaches. The pressure of her secret was becoming unbearable. Lying around in her room, avoiding her mother and sister and that fool Stanley Faithfull, she counted the days, the hours, until she would be back at Rogers Hall.

They were to be roommates again. The day she returned to school, Starr unpacked while waiting for Muriel to arrive. Just as she was finishing there was a knock. Miss Parsons, the principal, wished to see her in her office immediately.

Olive S. Parsons stood by her large walnut desk. Although attired in a well-made tailored dress, her hair done, her appearance clean, she was almost completely askew. No matter how tidily Olive Parsons started the day, within a few hours hair came loose, clothing pulled, stockings ran, smudges materialized. This disarray served to emphasize the precise, stilted way she spoke and moved.

Miss Parsons nodded curtly at Starr, a clump of hair springing free of the bun on top of her head.

"Sit, please," she said.

Starr did as she was told.

"I called you here to speak to you about Muriel Sinclair."

Suddenly, Starr felt terrified. What if they weren't going to let them be roommates? She realized Miss Parsons was waiting for some response. "Yes?"

"Muriel is dead." Miss Parsons pressed her lips together and ran a thumb and forefinger down the bridge of her nose, leaving a gray mark on either side.

Seeing this, Starr began to giggle.

"I beg your pardon," Miss Parsons said.

Starr continued to laugh, noting a rip on the cuff of Miss Parsons's sleeve.

"Did you understand me?"

Starr nodded, still laughing.

Miss Parsons, though horrified by this response, was not surprised. She'd always thought the Wyman girl was a bit odd. However, horrified or not, she'd prepared a speech and she was going to give it.

"As you know, Muriel was not well. She had been ill for some time. Her death has not come as a shock to her parents or to the faculty here. We all knew it would happen sooner or later."

Starr forced herself to listen, her laughter internal now.

"Three weeks ago she had a heart attack, as expected."

"Expected?"

"She had suffered from heart trouble for years. She died instantly. As all rooms have been assigned, you will have your room to yourself. Good afternoon." Miss Parsons moved around behind her desk and sat.

Starr thought Miss Parsons looked like a tiny child all ragged and rumpled from play. The massive desk reduced her frail body even further. Why had Muriel said she had tuberculosis? More romantic, Starr supposed. She giggled aloud again.

"Good afternoon," Miss Parsons repeated.

Smiling, Starr rose and walked to the door. Before opening it, she asked Miss Parsons a question. "She died instantly?"

"Instantly. It was no shock to anyone."

"It's a shock to me," Starr said.

"Mmmm."

"But it was no shock to anyone else?"

"No. Not to those closest to her. Parents. Sisters. Brother."

"Oh, I hope that's not true."

"I beg your pardon?" She blinked her eyes rapidly.

"It seems to me that death should always be a shock, no matter what."

"They were prepared." A long strand of hair trailed down the side of her face like a scar.

"Prepared? How? How can you be prepared for death? I don't think anyone is ever prepared. Death is too awful, too ugly."

"You're a morbid girl," Miss Parsons said.

"You're an ass," said Starr.

She was not expelled for this remark, the circumstances mitigating her punishment. She was instead confined to campus for two months and forced to eat all her meals alone.

Eating by herself was no hardship for Starr. She preferred it. And the two months' confinement to campus gave her a much needed break from Andrew. Frequently she damned herself for not having taken Muriel into her confidence last year. Other times she was grateful they hadn't become any closer. Her grief was great enough as it was. In the end, she decided, it was probably better to keep things to yourself.

That winter Starr was named captain of the swimming team, an honor traditionally awarded to the team's most skilled member. She wrote the news to her mother. Two weeks later, Helen wrote back. She mentioned Tucker, Stanley, Peter, the cat, Mr. and Mrs. Andrew J. Peters, her Mah-Jongg group, the new radio Stanley had given her and the clarity on that radio of President Coolidge's message to Congress. But not a word about Starr's honor. Nor was there any mention in the two letters which followed.

During Easter vacation Starr announced that the team was, so far, undefeated. Stanley, joining them for dinner for the third night in a row, said that was splendid. Was she a regular member of the team?

"I'm the captain," she said.

"I told you that," Helen said to him, irritated.

"Did you?" asked Starr.

"Of course. I was so proud. I told everyone."

"Did she ever," Tucker said. "It's all you heard around here for weeks. So tiresome."

"Yes, yes," Stanley said, "now I remember. Your mother takes great pride in you girls. Your achievements mean . . ."

"You never said a word to me about it," Starr interrupted.

"Don't be silly."

"You didn't."

"Of course I did. I wrote back right away and said how proud I was of you."

"No."

"What do you mean, no?"

"I mean, you never, never said anything about it to me. I've gotten three letters from you and none of them said anything about my being captain. I'd show you except I tore them up." She popped a bean in her mouth.

"Oh dear," Helen said, hurt. "I'm sure you must be wrong."

"I'm not."

"Is it possible, Helen," Stanley said, trying to mediate, "that there was so much going on that you *thought* you said something to the child and simply forgot? Or, that having said something about it to so many people, you thought you said it to the child as well? Could that be possible?"

"Well, I don't know. I suppose . . ."

"I'm sure that's what happened. After all, Starr certainly knows what you did and did not say in your letters."

"I suppose," Helen said. She turned toward Starr. "Oh, dear, please forgive me. I think Stanley must be right. I thought I told you. I was so proud, Starr. Honestly. I told everyone else. The butcher, the milkman, all the neighbors . . . surely that must mean something?"

"It does," Starr said.

And it did. But not enough.

In June of 1924 Starr graduated from Rogers Hall. In attendance were Helen, Tucker and Stanley. Frank did not come. Neither did Andrew. When the ceremony was over the girls clutched each other and cried and swore they would keep in touch forever. Starr did not cry and knew that she would never see any of them again.

That summer Andrew took Starr away on occasional weekends but his law practice kept him from taking a long vacation. Starr was relieved. That summer she also developed a crush on Johnny Weismuller, star of the Olympic Games, and decided she didn't want to go to college. She'd had enough of school. Now she was ready for fun. After all, she was eighteen.

The previous spring her mother and Tucker had moved from the Park Street house to a slightly smaller one on Grove. It had a third-floor bedroom for Starr, giving her the privacy she craved. Having fun was another matter. She had no idea how to achieve that. She knew no one in Brookline and began to regret her decision to skip college. At least there she could have met people.

As November approached she found herself wishing Andrew would get in touch. Anything for a break in the monotony. In late November he did. He told Helen he wanted to take Starr to New York to see some theater and meet some young people, friends of a niece who lived there.

They stayed at The Astor, registered as father and daughter, saw *They Knew What They Wanted* and *What Price Glory?*, ate splendid meals and spent the rest of the time in bed.

When she returned Starr told elaborate stories about the charming young men she'd met. Helen was delighted and hoped Starr would be hearing from some of them soon.

On February 7th, in Brookline, Helen Wyman and Stanley Faithfull were married. It was a small wedding. Starr was her mother's maid of honor. When the Faithfulls returned from their week-long honeymoon in New York, Helen was a different woman, bubbly, gay, her eyes constantly fastened on her new husband.

Two weeks after they'd come home, Starr discovered what had turned her mother into a mooning, silly schoolgirl. Feeling hungry late one night, she left her third-floor hideaway and tiptoed down the steps. Reaching the landing, she heard sounds coming from her mother's room. She stopped and listened. Clearly, the sounds were sexual. At first Starr was shocked, then embarrassed, then intrigued. Stepping gingerly, she moved closer. Now she could make out words.

"Oh, Stanley, dear-est, oh . . . yes, yes . . . soogooood, mmmmm."

She stood there for nearly a minute. Then, as the passion grew and the sounds and words became more lavish, she was overcome with embarrassment and fled to the kitchen.

From the refrigerator she took the remains of the roast chicken they'd had for dinner, turnips with cinnamon, cold stuffing and a large piece of black forest cake. She didn't give her constant battle with weight a second thought. Mechanically, she began eating. Bit by bit, as the food went down, the numbing sensation took over. She thought of nothing. It was as though a white screen had been lowered in the center of her mind.

At the end of March Starr Wyman became Starr Faithfull. Stanley first suggested it on January 26, her nineteenth birthday, as they drank martinis made from Stanley's gin. A self-declared chemist, he distilled his own liquor. It was safer, he said, than drinking anyone else's.

"Not bad, if I do say so myself," Stanley said after his first sip.

"When am I going to be old enough?" Tucker held a glass of Coca-Cola.

"When you're eighteen," he answered.

Starr almost laughed. She'd been drinking for seven years. Stanley would faint if he knew that.

"Now I have a proposal to make," he said, after toasting Starr. "I've been thinking about this for awhile now. It concerns both you girls." He cleared his throat, took another sip of his drink, and ran a finger over each side of his mustache. "I propose that when your mother and I are married, I adopt you."

Starr laughed out loud. Tucker just looked at him. And Helen smiled benevolently.

Stanley was undaunted. "I want you girls to have my name."

"Don't you think I'm a bit old to be adopted?" Starr asked.

"Well, technically, I suppose. On the other hand, my bambina, you're not twenty-one yet."

He'd started calling her bambina in the last month or two. She hated it and had often said so. "Can we do without the bambina on my birthday, at least?"

"Sorry." Quickly, he turned toward Tucker. "And what do you think, young lady?"

"I don't know. I guess I think it's stupid."

"Stupid?" Stanley took a healthy swallow of his drink. Things were definitely not going as he'd planned.

"Well, what do I need to be adopted for?"

Starr felt a rush of warmth for her sister.

"Well, I thought since I'll be living with you, since I'll be head of the household . . . well, what I mean is, I'll be your father anyway. Why not make it legal, hmmm?"

"I have a father," Tucker said.

Stanley and Helen exchanged a look.

"Yes, of course you do. But . . . well, Tucker, I hate to say this, but I don't think your father has too much time for you girls."

Seeing the stricken look on Tucker's face, Starr lashed out. "If you *hate* to say it, Stanley, why do you?"

"Hmmmm?"

"Nothing." She poured herself another martini.

"What I mean is, Tucker, I really care for you and I'd like to be your dad. Support you, advise you, generally see to your needs."

"Can't you do that without adopting me?"

Another exchanged look.

"Well, yes, of course. And I will, no matter what. But I thought it would be nice to make it legal."

"I don't know. How does my dad feel about it?"

"He agrees."

"He doesn't want me?" Tucker asked, screwing up her face.

"It's not that, Tucker," Starr said. "It's just that Dad is very busy these days. Honestly, Stanley," she hissed at him.

"That's right. Yes, that's right," Stanley said. "He's very busy and if I adopted you it would relieve some of the burden."

"Oh, Christ," Starr said.

Slamming her glass down on the table she grabbed her sister's hand and dragged her from the room. In the hall she snatched their coats and purses and they were outside and down the street before either Stanley or Helen could make a move.

Out here now with her little sister, she had no idea what to do with her. She knew almost nothing about the child. They rarely spent any time together.

"Do you like movies?" Starr asked.

"Sure."

They went to *He Who Gets Slapped* with Norma Shearer and John Gilbert and, for dinner, consumed a large container of popcorn and two Hersheys.

"If I'm adopted will I have to call him Dad?" Tucker asked, on the way home.

"Absolutely not," Starr assured her.

She supposed her sister probably would take Stanley's name. And the more she thought about it, she began to like the sound of Starr Faithfull. It was far more interesting than Starr Wyman.

So when Stanley raised the issue again Starr agreed

and so did Tucker. He was thrilled, honored, he said, that two such lovely and wonderful girls would carry his name.

On April 21st, three weeks after the legal name change, Starr was admitted to Channing Sanatorium. Stanley registered her as Starr Wyman.

Perhaps it was the nightly forays to the kitchen with a stop in front of her mother and stepfather's door, listening to the sounds. Perhaps it was the incredible boredom she experienced day after day. It may have been Andrew's second attempt at intercourse in early April. This time she defeated him but, nevertheless, it was a strain. Or it may have been a combination of all these things that pushed Starr over the edge. Helen discovered her in a corner of her room, on the floor, knees up against her chest, four fingers of her left hand in her mouth on April 20th. She had not come to meals for a day and a half.

"Starr, what is it? What are you doing on the floor?"

Starr's eyes were wide, staring, and tears ran down her cheeks. She kept the fingers in her mouth and didn't answer.

When Helen got no response she called for Stanley. He called the family doctor who arrived within the hour. Starr hadn't moved. She continued to weep and bite her fingers. The doctor called the consulting psychiatrist at Channing Sanatorium which was located in nearby Wellesley. He suggested Starr be admitted for observation.

During daily consultations with the psychiatrist Starr showed herself to be easily excited, nervous, jumpy. But beyond saying she'd like to move from the house on Grove Street, she told the doctor little.

By the time she was checked out on April 30th, her file marked "improved," she couldn't remember what had brought her to the state she'd been found in ten days earlier. She felt now a kind of numbness, a longing to sleep.

Stanley came to pick her up and take her home. Nearing Brookline, he cleared his throat and broke the silence. "Your mother is making you a welcome-home cake."

"That's nice."

"Otherwise she would have come with me. She's been very worried about you and so have I, my little bamb . . . my little bamby."

Bamby? Why bamby? Well, what did it matter? She didn't care.

For the next few months she cared about very little. She stayed in her room, drank a great deal of liquor to keep herself numbed and ventured out only when Andrew called, which was not often.

Then Stanley learned of his transfer to the office in Newark, New Jersey. Starr was thrilled by the idea of a move and pushed for an apartment in New York. When, in early 1926, they moved to a house on Ridgewood Road in West Orange she accepted her defeat. It was at least close to the city. Now, she knew, she could start a new life. And this time it would be a wonderful one.

April 14, 1926
Lancaster, Pennsylvania

"We've been seeing each other exactly five months tonight," Orlando said.

"Four months."

"Five."

"I don't count the month at Christmas. I don't know what you were up to then." Fran smiled but she was serious.

"It was only three weeks. Besides, I don't know what you were doing either."

"No, you don't." She moved away from him slightly, adjusting her frilled garters.

Christmas vacation flashed through his mind like a flickering film. He saw himself with Kay, laughing, naked, having sex.

"And I won't know what you're doing this summer either and you won't know what I'm doing." She sat with her back against the passenger door.

"Is that why you're way over there?"

She shrugged.

"That's kind of goofy, isn't it?"

She shrugged again.

He knew she was in one of her moods. She withdrew from him as always when they'd been necking. A few minutes ago they'd been entwined, kissing, tongues exploring each other's mouths. When he'd asked her, after Christmas vacation, if she was a virgin, she became indignant. Of course she was! And he knew it was the truth.

"Why are you way over there?" He ran a hand over his hair, hard with Slikum.

"Oh, I don't know. I guess I'm afraid I'll get carried away, you know."

"And what if you did?" He tried to hide the fact that he was somewhat disconcerted. She'd never said anything like this before.

"I wouldn't want to."

"Why not?"

"It's not worth it."

"What do you mean, Fran?"

"The consequences aren't worth ten minutes of pleasure."

He laughed, not meaning to, but unable to stop himself. A look of pain crossed her face. "I'm sorry. It's just that . . . why do you assume it would be *ten minutes* of pleasure?"

"Isn't it?"

"I suppose with some it is but it doesn't have to be if you know what you're doing."

"And you do."

It was a statement, not a question. The conversation was exciting him. "And what would the consequences be?"

"I might get pregnant."

"We're not living in the dark ages, you know."

"You might drop me like a hot potato afterwards."

"Never."

"All men say that."

He felt a stab of jealousy. "You've had this conversation before?"

She laughed, covered her mouth.

"What's funny?"

"You sound so shocked."

"Well, I . . ."

"Do you think you're the first man who's ever wanted to . . . to make love to me?"

"No, of course not." He felt stupid.

She moved closer, put her hand on his. "But you're the first man *I* ever wanted to make love to me." It was true.

"Oh, Fran." He reached for her, easily taking her in

his arms. They kissed, long, passionately. His hand slid from her back around to her breast. She pulled away.

"No."

"I don't understand," he said, breathless.

"I want you to but I won't."

"Why not?"

"Orlando, if you don't know I'm not going to tell you." The last thing she wanted was to trap a man with sexual bait.

"I *don't* know. Tell me, please." He felt desperate.

"Let's just forget it."

"Je-sus! It's so damn easy for you girls to say, let's forget it. Jesus!"

"I'm sorry."

"Do you even know what I'm talking about?"

"I think so." She was embarrassed.

Roughly he grabbed her hand and put it, full palm, between his legs.

She wrenched away, shocked and excited at once.

His anger was replaced with something akin to hope. Her hand had rested on him for a beat before she'd pulled it away. It wasn't much to go on but it was something. He feigned horror at his behavior. "I'm sorry. Forgive me. I don't know what came over me."

She barely heard what he said, thinking only of what she'd felt. She had never before touched a man there.

"Will you forgive me?"

"Yes. I understand." Now she wanted to touch him again but there was no way to do it without appearing cheap.

Then he heard himself saying, "You do know I want to marry you, don't you, Fran?" He'd never said that to any girl before, never had to.

"I . . . what?" She thought she'd misunderstood him.

"I want to marry you." Suddenly, he didn't feel like he was lying.

She hadn't misunderstood. Was it a proposal? Did he expect an answer? Other men had proposed to her but not like this.

"Didn't you hear what I said?"

"Yes."

"Well?"

"Well, what?"

"What do you say?"

"Are you asking me to marry you? It didn't seem like you were asking me."

He realized then that he hadn't actually asked. "I . . . it couldn't be for awhile. I have to finish school." He felt foolish.

"I know. It's all right. I don't want to get married now anyway." She knew, though, that had he *really* asked her, *really* wanted to, right that minute, she would have. It was the first time she allowed herself to know how she truly felt about him. She was in love.

March-June, 1926
West Orange, New Jersey

In the six months the Faithfulls had lived in West Orange, the only *wonderful* thing that had happened to Starr was her discovery of Veronal and Allonal. After the move her insomnia worsened. Alcohol began to have a reverse effect on her. Other people, if they drank too much, passed out; Starr just gained new energy. When she drank in the evening it kept her from sleep. She spent hours pacing about the house, playing the radio or victrola. Sometimes she went outside and walked through the streets.

By the end of March her insomnia was making her desperate. She'd tried all the home remedies but nothing worked. A doctor would ask too many questions. She tried the drugstore instead.

The druggist, William A. Binde, was a balding man in his forties. Many people came to Uncle Bill for help. And he gave advice, a sympathetic ear, and sometimes, drugs. He was careful how he dispensed them, selling help for sleeplessness only a few tablets at a time. He prided himself on being able to read people. He was certain he'd know a potential suicide if one turned up. And he'd only been wrong once. After all, he wasn't God, was he?

"I was wondering, Mr. Binde, if you could recommend anything to help me sleep?" Starr flashed one of her most devastating smiles.

"Why don't you call me Uncle Bill like the rest?"

"All right, Uncle Bill." What a lot of crap, she thought, but she kept smiling.

This beautiful girl wasn't new in his store. She'd come in before for his homemade ice cream or for cosmetics.

"Now what seems to be the trouble, Miss Faithfull?"

"Well, Uncle Bill, I just can't seem to sleep lately. It's just terrible. I've tried everything."

"Something bothering you? Trouble with your boyfriend?" He always tried to explore the emotional side of things first.

Starr, knowing intuitively what Uncle Bill wanted to hear, looked away shyly, her head on a downward angle, eyelids fluttering. "I don't have a boyfriend."

"A pretty girl like you! That's hard to believe. Well," he said, chuckling paternally, "maybe you should have one . . . maybe you'd sleep better then."

"Maybe," she answered softly.

"C'mon over here." He motioned toward the soda fountain. "Sit down and tell me all about it. Want a Coca-Cola? On the house?"

Following him, she wondered if she'd get his help with or without a story. Which would serve her better?

Bill pushed the lever for Coca-Cola syrup, then filled the glass with seltzer, the whooshing sound loud in the empty store. He set the glass in front of her. "Now tell Uncle Bill what the trouble is."

Starr took a sip. She'd feel him out, slowly. "There really isn't anything to tell. I just can't sleep." Her large brown eyes looked directly into his narrow gray ones.

"No problems, huh?"

She sensed disappointment in his tone. "Nothing special."

Bill believed her. It probably wasn't anything special. Probably needed to be laid just like the rest of the women who came in for sleeping tablets. Of course, this one wouldn't have any trouble if she wanted it. Still, there was something innocent in those gorgeous eyes. This one was definitely frustrated but there was nothing she was going to do about it until she found the right boy. Bill liked her for that and wanted to help.

"Just can't sleep, hmmm?"

"That's right. I'm sure it'll pass. I've had this trouble

before and it always passes. It comes in fits and starts, lasts a few weeks, drives me nearly crazy and then I start sleeping on my own again."

Uncle Bill took the bait. "What do you mean on your own?"

"Well, as I think I told you, I just moved here in January. But the druggist . . . oh, what a nice man he was . . . the druggist in Brookline, Massachusetts, where I used to live, gave me something to help me sleep."

"What was that?"

"You mean the name?"

He nodded.

"I don't know the name, I don't think he ever told me. He certainly was kind enough."

"I believe in telling my patients . . . customers, what they're getting."

"I guess I never asked."

"Still."

"Do you think you could give me something, Uncle Bill?"

"That wasn't right of him not to tell you what he was giving you."

"I suppose not." Jesus, she thought, what a flat tire this guy is.

"Was it pills?"

Now she was beginning to feel nervous. She took a guess. "Yes."

"What'd they look like?"

"Oh, Uncle Bill, I don't know. They were just ordinary." Her throat felt constricted and she sipped at the Coke.

"I'll be right back."

She watched as he disappeared through a door at the back of the store. Maybe she should just leave. As she weighed the pros and cons, he returned, two small envelopes in his hand. He dumped first one, then the other, out onto the marble counter.

"Was it either of these?"

Starr bit the inside of her top lip. Was he trying to trick her? Was one the real thing, the other a sugar pill? What if she picked the wrong one? She took a chance. "Both. I mean, sometimes he gave me one, sometimes the other."

"This one is Veronal, this one Allonal. Which one worked better?"

"Either."

He nodded. "He should've told you their names."

"Well, I guess he wasn't as smart as you, Uncle Bill."

"Smartness has got nothing to do with it. Just a matter of consideration. See, if he'd told you we wouldn't a had to go through all this. I'll give you four, two of one and two of the other, seeing as how you've had them before. I don't like to give too many at once."

When he gave her the pills in an envelope, Starr felt as though she'd been handed a million dollars.

They worked beautifully. When the four were gone, she waited two days, slept fitfully, and returned for more. This time he gave her six, three of each. On the fifth night she took one somewhat earlier than usual and noticed that it made her feel dreamy, floating, as she brushed her teeth and walked to her room. She liked the feeling.

The next day, to experiment, she took her last Veronal at three in the afternoon. The effects were similar to ether's. She drifted through the house feeling wonderful, her body light, airy. She was happy.

When she got her next supply from Uncle Bill, eight this time, she decided to use them only to feel good. Sleeping, or not, didn't seem so important. By May she'd found three other drugstores who gave her a month's supply at a time. At two o'clock on a Saturday afternoon in June, Starr took four Veronal. Not long afterwards she collapsed on her bed.

When she woke up, Stanley, her mother and a man she'd never seen stood over her. The man was a doctor.

Later, Stanley explained to her what had happened.

"I came in to get you for dinner and I thought you were dead. It was terrible, Bamby. You looked dead. Your eyes were half open and you didn't seem to be breathing. I took your pulse and it was faint. Helen called the doctor and I kept trying to wake you, but it didn't do any good. All your color was gone . . . even the fingernails were white. I was sure it was all over. It was horrible, Starr."

"Then what happened?" She sipped a drink he'd made her.

"The doctor came. Said it was probably some drug you'd taken. What's the name of that again?"

"Veronal. I use it to sleep."

"In the afternoon, dear?" Helen said.

"What difference does it make?"

"Well, if you want to take a sleeping potion, why don't you take it at night?"

"I do," she lied. "I didn't last night and I didn't sleep. I was very tired today so I took it."

"If you were so tired why did you need it?"

"Oh, Mother! I'm tired but I can't sleep, that's all."

She knew then she would have to be careful. Four Veronal were obviously too many if they made you appear dead. And she hadn't really had a bit of fun. She'd drop down to two again and see what happened. The doctor had said she shouldn't take it at all anymore, that it was dangerous, foolish. She appeared to be unusually susceptible. Well, what did he know? Doctors were stupid. She knew how to handle the stuff. And she was not about to give it up. As far as she was concerned, Veronal was a lifesaver.

In many respects she had the mentality of a twelve-year-old girl.
—Anonymous, *New York Times,* June 13, 1931

June 5, 1931
New York, New York

They sat drinking black coffee in a small shop on MacDougal Street. Starr's eyes were bloodshot from alcohol and tears.

Mrs. Royal W. Leffland patted her hand. "It is simply divine providence that I found you. Something made me go into the church. I cannot say what. I rarely visit church on a weekday, you know."

Starr nodded. She had told Mrs. Leffland everything. Well, almost everything. At least she'd told her that she planned to take her life. Mrs. Leffland was horrified. She would help Starr work things out.

Starr also told her she simply could not go home. It was terrible there.

The kind Mrs. Leffland smiled gently and said Starr should come home with her.

Fourteen

So puzzling, thought Orlando. Still puzzling. The whole business about the missing coat, hat, underwear. The shoes and bag he knew about. But there had been no hat or coat. And the underpants? He didn't know about those. Could they have come off in the water? Or maybe she hadn't worn any. Funny it never occurred to the police that she might not have been wearing underpants.

Once, years later, he asked Fran if she ever went without underpants. She'd looked at him like he was crazy. No, of course not, she'd said. Why? He shrugged, said he thought it might be sexy. One day, a week or so later, he discovered she didn't have them on. She always tried to please. And did.

Starr flipped through *Outlook* magazine as the train crept through the New Jersey marshes toward Hoboken. She was meeting Andrew for dinner and the theater. Helen and Stanley would expect her home afterwards but Andrew, of course, would invent some reason for her to spend the night. And her mother would believe it, as she had for the last nine years.

Starr closed the magazine, put it on the seat beside her and looked at her vague reflection in the window. The shingled hair was a bit too long inching its way out from beneath her peekaboo hat. She turned her face to a slightly different angle, trying to see the line of her chin and neck. Was she developing a double chin or was it just a trick of this surrogate mirror? Lately, she'd begun to lose herself again in food. Why the hell couldn't she be one of those girls who could eat whatever they wanted and not gain an ounce? That was stupid. She just wasn't. Would she forever be playing those games with herself? What if? If only. Anything but the reality of her life.

She turned from the offending window and stared at the back of the man's head in front of her. The reality of her life. It was too awful, too boring. She might as well be dead. How many Veronal would it take to do the trick, she wondered. If only she weren't so afraid. But of what was she afraid? Surely there was no afterlife. Man had to have made that up as some sort of consolation prize! The concepts of heaven and hell were completely alien to her. Her mouth slid into a bitter half smile. But if there *was* a hell, surely she would go there. Oh, it was all too ridiculous, too absurd. And she was too intelligent to believe such nonsense. Then what was so frightening?

She looked down at her hands, fingers twisting, intertwining. The skin. Tight, smooth, soft. She imagined it after death. Decomposing. She'd never seen a decomposed body but she could imagine it. Hell, what difference did it make? She wouldn't know. Then why? Was it nothingness? It was impossible to conceive of nothingness yet fear was inherent in that impossibility. Even so, how could death be worse than this life? She was twenty years old and had never known love or sweet desire. She knew only the touch of a man almost three times her age. And drugs, ether, alcohol. But they were her saviors. She'd be dead without them. So? Around and around.

"Hoboken next," the conductor yelled.

Maybe someday, Starr thought, preparing to leave the train, I will not be afraid of nothingness. Maybe someday nothing will be preferable to something.

* * *

In his room Andrew sipped champagne, waiting for Starr to arrive. The large comfortable chair was by the window overlooking Broadway. But twelve stories up there was nothing much to see. He was bored. Also a bit nervous. He didn't look forward to this meeting. Odd the way things changed. Time. Time was the changer. He remembered when a meeting with Starr was the most important thing in the world to him. Now it just produced anxiety.

He left the window and began pacing the room, touching surfaces as he moved about. Andrew hadn't seen her in more than two months. If she hadn't written him the little note he didn't know how much longer it might have been. Perhaps never. What irony that she'd written him now. One note in nine years and he didn't even care.

DEAR ANDREW,
It has been dreadfully long. I am lonely and bored. I need to see you.

Yours,
STARR

He wondered again if she wanted something specific. Could it really be that she just wanted to see him? The thought produced nothing. No flurried heartbeat, no quickening pulse. If anything, he felt a kind of anger. Why did things always come too late?

His glass was empty. He poured more champagne, waited until it settled, poured more. Of course, he could have ignored the note but sooner or later he'd have to confront her. Why wait? Would he tell her tonight? At dinner? After the theater? What could he say? Would she care? Did it matter? Perhaps he should tell her as soon as she arrived. But then what? Would they carry on with their evening as though nothing had happened? Best to wait. He didn't have to say anything, of course. Simply spend the evening and send her home. Then what if another little note arrived? It had always been his tactic to run, avoid, duck, as though his motto were: never confront anything if possible! Did he really think at age fifty-four he was going to change? Not that fifty-four was old.

But how absurd to think he would handle this any differently than he'd handled the rest of his life. No. They would have dinner, talk, see the play and he'd send her home. Perhaps she would have some pride and understand. Perhaps some kind of dignity would cause her to leave him alone. Was it asking so much to be allowed some peace? Didn't she owe him that much? Enough was enough. She couldn't have expected this to go on forever. Everything comes to an end one way or another. *I am lonely and bored.* Well, he was sorry about that but it wasn't his fault. He couldn't be expected to keep her entertained constantly. He had his wife and family, his law practice, certain social obligations. He wasn't put on this earth exclusively for Starr Wyman or Starr Faithfull or whatever the little bitch wanted to call herself. "I'm a busy man," he said out loud.

Feeling foolish, he looked around furtively, checking to make sure the room was, indeed, empty. Satisfied that it was, he cleared his throat, fussed with his cufflinks, filled his glass again. Then he returned to the window, satisfied with his assessment of the situation. He was a busy man and she was a bored girl. There was no contest.

*   *   *

"What the hell is wrong with you, Andrew?" Starr returned her coffee cup to its saucer.

"Nothing. What do you mean?"

"Don't give me that baloney."

"Do you have to use that awful slang?"

"Yes. Now what's wrong?"

"I don't know what you're talking about."

"Applesauce!"

"Finish your coffee, we'll be late for the theater."

Standing outside, after the play, Andrew said, "I'll get you a cab."

"A cab?"

"You don't want to walk to the ferry, do you?"

"You mean you're sending me home?"

"It's late." He looked beyond the theater crowd into the street.

Starr grabbed hold of his sleeve. "What kind of run-around is this?"

He looked down at her, felt her grip on his arm and knew this wasn't going to work the way he'd planned. Clearly, she was prepared to make a scene on the street. He would have to capitulate, for the moment.

"I'll call your mother," he said through tight lips.

Back in the room at the Hotel Astor, Starr stood, hands on hips, facing Andrew who kept his eyes averted, concentrating on a small spot on the wall. Finally, she let her hands fall, crossing to the chair by the window and dropping into it.

"Give me something to drink," she ordered.

Glad for the diversion, he went to the bureau where bottles of scotch and gin stood. "Gin?"

She nodded.

"There's no ice."

"I don't care."

"I can call room service."

"Never mind."

He poured several inches into a water glass, crossed the room and handed her the drink.

As she took it their eyes met, locked.

"Why are you acting like this, Andrew?"

"Like what?"

"Don't start that again. You barely spoke to me all through dinner. Then you wanted to send me home . . . that's not like you. Something's wrong. Something happened."

"Nothing happened."

"You mean," she said, maintaining a level gaze, "the fact that you're not interested in me sucking your cock is normal behavior?"

He spun around, away from her, as though she'd shoved him.

She smiled. In bed Andrew urged her to say the most obscene things she could think of, things he had taught her. Out of bed it was an entirely different story.

"Well?" she asked.

"I think," he said, his back still to her, "I think we've come to the end of our journey."

The words, simple as they were, sounded to her like a foreign language. "What?"

"You heard me, Starr. Don't be difficult." The pitch of his voice was even higher than usual.

She took a large swallow of gin. Then, slowly, the word "journey" entered into her consciousness. "Journey," she said.

He frowned, turning toward her. She was looking in his direction but appeared not to see him.

"Journey," she said again.

"Are you drunk already?"

She looked up at his face. "No. Not yet." She finished off the drink and held out the empty glass.

He hesitated a moment. Would it be dangerous for her to drink more? Well, there was really no way to stop her. He took the glass and refilled it.

"Now, what were you saying?" It was as though she'd left the room and just now returned.

Taking a deep breath, he tried a new phrase. "We must end our liaison."

This time the words were clear. "Why?" she said simply.

How could he explain? "Because it has come to its natural conclusion."

This made her laugh. The sound frightened him.

"What are you talking about? Natural conclusion. Nothing about it has ever been natural. Why should there be a *natural* conclusion?"

Andrew began to pull at his eyebrows.

Conflicting emotions confused Starr. Anger, fear, relief. Andrew was trying to end the relationship that had tormented her for years and yet she felt frightened at the thought of its demise. Was it because he wasn't telling her the reason? This *natural conclusion* stuff was the bunk. "Tell me the truth, Andrew," she said calmly.

"I am."

"No, you're not."

"I don't know what to say."

"Don't you find me appealing any more?" Did she really want to be appealing to this overweight old man? Had she really *liked* his attention? He was letting her off the hook. Why couldn't she accept it? Be grateful? She'd prayed for this moment a thousand times. Yet she'd written him the note. Asked to see him.

"I don't know what to say," Andrew repeated.

"Say you want me." It was as though there were a ventriloquist in the room and she was his dummy.

Andrew lowered himself to the edge of the bed like a man much older than his years. "Starr," he said almost inaudibly.

She turned in the chair and opened her legs directly in his line of vision. Now it was a puppeteer who manipulated her, as well as the ventriloquist. Quickly she closed her legs, deftly pulled down her panties, letting them hang from one ankle as she made a V of her legs again.

Andrew looked down at his knees.

"Look at it," she commanded.

He complied.

She was touching herself.

"Don't," he cried, putting his hands to his face.

She stopped, shocked at herself. What the hell was going on? What was she doing? She didn't want him. She didn't want him to want her. But she didn't want *him* making the decision either. How dare he? She grabbed at her panties and put them on again. Andrew was still slumped on the bed, head in his hands, elbows propped up by his knees.

Starr drank, staring at him. How dare this pathetic creature tell her she was no longer appealing! She with the beautiful eyes and creamy skin. He with his bald head and those disgusting thick lips. Who was he to tell her? She lit a Chesterfield, walked to the bureau and poured another gin. Then she planted herself in front of him. Seconds passed before he looked up.

"You are a piece of filth." She blew smoke down at him.

"I wish I could make you understand, Starr girl."

"I understand," she said. "You're too old to cut the mustard."

"Hmmmm?"

"Too old," she yelled. "Too old and too ugly."

"Too old?" He smiled strangely, then began his high-pitched cackle.

She wanted to smash him across the face. The look she gave him cut his laugh abruptly.

"What's so fucking funny?"

He winced at the words, started to reprimand her, then thought better of it.

"Is it funny that you're too old to get it up? Is it funny that you're too old for me?"

He began the irritating laugh again, his shoulders shaking, belly wobbling.

Starr threw her drink in his face.

He gasped and jumped to his feet, gin dripping from his chin. "You . . . you . . ." he stammered. "It's you . . . *you're* too old."

For a moment she didn't understand. Then it was clear. She was a woman now, no longer an innocent-looking little girl. And it was the look that counted, the idea of childhood, the age. *She* was too old for Andrew J. Peters. "Oh, my God," she said.

They stared at one another like two boxers, each waiting for the other to make the first move. Then simply, quietly, Starr spoke.

"I'm going to tell."

"No, you won't."

"I will." It was a fact. She really didn't want him but she was damned if she'd be tossed aside this way without making him suffer, without making him feel fear.

"Who will you tell?"

"Everyone."

"No one will believe you."

"Oh, yes they will."

"They'll blame you. They always blame the girl."

"A child?"

"You're not a child now."

She smiled. "No, I'm not. I'll tell them about that, too."

His cheeks began to tremble. He believed she'd do it. "Sit down, Starr, we must talk."

The rest of the night they went over and over the same ground. He insisted she must keep quiet. He offered money, clothes, whatever she wanted. She reiterated her intention to tell. By nine in the morning when she left, exhausted, sick from too many cigarettes and too much liquor, Andrew was convinced she would talk. Almost sure that Helen wouldn't believe her, he couldn't be positive. He called Helen and asked if she would meet him for lunch. She agreed.

When Starr arrived at home, ready to tell everything, there was no one there.

June 22, 1926
West Orange, New Jersey

On the last leg of her walk from the train to home, Helen Faithfull realized she was afraid. Afraid for Starr. Afraid for herself. Clearly, she had two choices. She could tell Stanley or not. If she told him, he might do something drastic. If she didn't and he somehow got wind of it, Stanley would never forgive her for withholding the information from him. The last thing in this world Helen wanted was to anger or disappoint her husband. Life with him was a perpetual honeymoon. She felt sick at the thought of anything spoiling this.

Stanley, she knew, loved Starr as if she were his own. But this—well, she couldn't imagine what he might do. It was an awful problem. Perhaps it was best to say nothing. She didn't want to embarrass Starr. After all, she was almost a woman. But suppose she behaved that way with other men? Suppose she went after Stanley!

Helen stopped walking. Children played in the street and a ball bounced past her but she didn't notice. An incredible thought! Surely Stanley would resist. Wouldn't he? Starr *was* lovely. And Stanley was a very sensual man. But he loved *her*. Still.

She resumed walking, her pace accelerating. Of course she would have to tell him. And whatever Stanley decided to do, she would abide by. Perhaps a return to Channing Sanatorium.

"Good God!" Stanley said. "Of all people."

"I know, I know." Helen gripped her husband's hand.

"He's been such a help, so kind. Lord! She must have had bad gin, that's the only reason I can think of."

"Bad gin? With Andrew?"

"No, I suppose not. Well, we're got to talk to her. Let's go up."

Stanley put an arm around his wife and guided her toward the stairs.

"Thank God, Tucker is away at school," she said. "Thank God."

Starr had been waiting all day for her mother to come to her room. She welcomed the knock.

Stanley and Helen entered, and sat on opposite ends of Starr's bed. She leaned against the head of it.

"Do you want to talk?" Stanley asked.

"Oh, God. Yes," she wailed, a flood of tears beginning.

"It's best," he said.

She stopped, leaned forward. "Do you know?"

"Yes, dear," Helen said.

"How?"

"Your mother saw Andrew today."

"I don't understand."

"He called me."

"Andrew called you?"

"Yes, dear. Would you like to go back to Channing?"

"Helen!"

"I just thought . . ."

"Let's not jump the gun."

"I'm sorry."

"Wait a minute, let me get this straight." Starr lit a cigarette and passed one to Stanley. "You saw Andrew today and he told you?"

Helen nodded, ashamed.

"Everything?"

She nodded again.

"I don't believe it. Everything? From the beginning?"

"I don't think," said Stanley, "that he went into all the details, Starr. Just an outline. The man has some sense of decorum and wouldn't want to embarrass you or Helen."

"Embarrass *me*?"

"Naturally. I don't think he would have told your mother anything except for the fact that he thought you might need . . . well, help."

"Wait, wait, wait." Starr's voice rose. "What did he say?"

"Why don't you just tell us what happened?"

"When?"

"Why, last night, of course."

"Is that what he told you about, Mother? Last night?"

"Yes, dear. Now don't get upset or afraid. We're not angry. We want to help."

"TELL ME."

Stanley reached out for Starr's hand but she pulled away. "Bamby, don't. It's not such a terrible thing. This *is* the roaring twenties, and girls today . . . well, Peters isn't used to . . . to flappers, I guess."

Helen was horrified that Stanley was trying to minimize the situation but said nothing.

Calmly, coolly, Starr spoke. "I want to know exactly what Andrew told you. Please."

"Well," Stanley said, adjusting his round glasses, "this is third-hand of course, but, to the best of my understanding, Andrew told your mother that you . . . made advances toward him."

Starr screamed. It was pure rage.

Helen jumped and Stanley dropped his cigarette.

"SON-OF-A-BITCHING-BASTARD!"

"Oh, Starr," Helen said.

Stanley retrieved his cigarette.

"FUCKING HOG."

Helen went to the open window and shut it.

Stanley blinked, embarrassed. "Bamby, Bamby."

"YOU-DON'T-KNOW."

"All right, all right. Calm down, just calm down."

"Please don't scream like that, Starr," Helen said.

"It was bad gin, wasn't it, Bamby? That's what made you do it. Right?"

Again, she screamed.

"Stanley," Helen said, "should we call someone?"

"NO! Don't you call anyone, except maybe the police. SIT DOWN," she ordered. "I'll tell you . . . I'll tell you everything."

During Starr's recitation of the ugly nine-year story Helen, unconsciously, kept shaking her head. She was horrified, not because Starr was accusing Andrew of unspeakable acts (he'd warned her Starr might say anything to protect herself) but because her daughter knew of such things. Where had she learned all this?

Stanley was fascinated. There were moments when he wanted to stop her but could not. It was like watching an accident.

When she was through, Starr fell back against her pillows.

Helen looked at her husband. What were they to do next? Surely this outburst of filth and fantasy would convince Stanley that the girl needed to be hospitalized again.

"Well," Starr said, "what are you going to do?"

Stanley and Helen exchanged glances.

"What would you like us to do, Bamby?"

"Put him away forever."

"You mean have him arrested?"

"Yes."

"Oh, Starr." Helen felt great waves of sympathy for her demented daughter.

"Well, why not?"

Stanley touched the middle of his mustache with his tongue. "Well, for one thing we have no proof."

Helen was stunned. "Proof?"

"Why, yes."

"You mean you believe this story?"

"Mother!"

"Please, Starr. Andrew warned me you might try something like this. We're not fools, you know."

"Every word was the truth."

"You're just making things worse."

"Helen, I don't think this is necessary. Starr is upset today. It's natural that . . ."

"GET OUT OF MY ROOM!"

"Please."

"I HATE YOUR GUTS."

"Bamby . . ."

"GET OUT, YOU FUCKING SHITS!"

"I will not take this abuse." Helen slammed out of the room.

"Bamby, listen . . ."

"OUT!"

At the kitchen table Helen cried, as upset with Stanley as she was with Starr. He tried to console her.

"How can you believe any of that dreadful story?" she asked.

He didn't know. He wasn't sure. But something about it rang true to him.

"Andrew warned me that she might try and put the blame on him. He said she probably would turn things around . . . oh, Stanley, can't you see what sense that makes?"

"Yes, I can, Helen. But think about this. If what Starr says is true, it would be very smart for Andrew to warn you in that manner. Do you see what I mean?"

She didn't want to. It was too awful. If it was true, she'd been a party to it all those years. It just couldn't be true. Certainly, a mother would have known, suspected. But something like that would never have entered her mind. She just didn't think that way. Who would? She couldn't be blamed. Blamed? Blamed for what? It wasn't true. It couldn't be. She could not endure it.

"It is not true, Stanley."

"I don't know."

"I think she should go back to Channing."

"I disagree. We can't be sure."

"I'm sure."

"How?"

"I know Andrew. Think about it. Would a man in his position take such chances?"

"I suppose not. But why would she . . .?"

"Because she's bad. I've always known it. I never wanted to admit it but she's always been bad." Always? When was it that Starr changed? She couldn't think about it.

"Helen, don't say that. Perhaps she's disturbed. But bad?"

"I can't talk about it anymore."

"We'll have to do something."

"A trip. We'll send her on a trip. A nice boat trip."

"If you think that's best, dear."

"I do."

"All right."

Stanley kissed her forehead, patted her shoulder and put some water on for tea. He would do what Helen wanted. Perhaps she was right. It would be good for Starr to get away. And certainly he didn't want Helen upset. What could they do anyway, even if the story were true? It was Starr's word against a prominent, respected man. Who would believe her? Even her own mother didn't. If he could just talk to Peters. Maybe one of these days he'd get in touch with him. But not now. Now he wanted to do nothing that would upset his wife further. Now he had to make peace. Protect his wife. Protect his Bamby. But what if he was protecting Peters? If only there were proof. Then they wouldn't have to make it public. They could go to Peters privately and demand—what? An apology? What? Money. Proof. Eventually, alone, he would talk to Starr again. There was plenty of time. After the trip. Proof. Money. He smiled.

January 20, 1927
Lancaster, Pennsylvania

When Orlando returned to school after Christmas vacation, having enjoyed the usual sexual activity with Kay, he was determined to make Fran see their relationship must change. That changed involved sex. He loved her, she loved him. It was the right thing to do. Expression of love was everything. To hell with the puritans!

They sat in Crystal's eating their lunch of hamburgers and home fries. Fran sipped on a lemon Coke. Orlando wondered how to broach the subject.

"Fran," he said finally, "you know I love you, don't you?"

She nodded, smiled, took a bite of the potatoes.

"And you know I'd never do anything to hurt you?"

She nodded. A bite of hamburger.

"And you know that I respect you?"

Again, the nod as she took another bite.

"Fran, do you think you could stop eating for a minute?" He'd never seen anyone eat the way she did.

"Why?"

"So I can talk to you."

"You *are* talking."

"Well, I'd like some response."

"I can respond and eat at the same time." A forkful of home fries zipped past his eyes.

He took a deep breath. No good if he got mad. And no reason she couldn't eat if she wanted. Try again. "Fran, do you love me? I mean *really* love me?"

"You know I do. I'd like some dessert."

He hailed the waitress. "What do you want?"

"Lemon Meringue."

"Why don't you get fat?"

"I don't know. I just don't."

He shook his head, smiled at her. The waitress came and he gave the order. "Now, as I was saying . . ."

"What are you leading up to, Orr?"

Why not just say it? "Sex."

"Sex?"

He nodded.

"What about it?" Her pie arrived and she immediately dug in.

"I want it. I mean, I want you. I can't go on like this anymore, Fran. I can't study."

She sipped at her coffee, ate more pie.

"You don't know what it's like."

"Don't I?"

"Hmmm?"

"You said I don't know what it's like. I said don't I?" A cut of pie disappeared.

"But what did you mean?"

"Well, I suppose I shouldn't say this, I mean I know girls aren't supposed to say these things, but it isn't easy on me either, you know."

"What isn't?"

She looked at him a moment, considered. "Never mind. Forget it. Forget I said anything."

"No, wait. I'm sorry, I was just . . . surprised. You mean you . . ." He couldn't express it.

"I have feelings, too. *Those* kinds of feelings. You boys think you're the only ones. Well, you're not. Now I suppose you think I'm awful. Well, I don't care."

"Good God, no. I'm . . . I'm overwhelmed."

"You'll never want to see me again."

"Fran, darling, don't say that." He put his hand on hers.

"Oh, it's all so unfair. Who made up the rules anyway?"

"What rules?"

"The sex rules. They stink."

"Let's get out of here, okay?"

"In a minute," she said and went back to her pie.

The fraternity house was almost empty. Earl was at Cedar Crest College visiting Mary Fearing for the weekend. The room was theirs.

Fran sat primly on the edge of his desk chair. He sat on the edge of the bed.

"Have you changed your mind?" he asked.

She shook her head. "I just wish it were night."

"Do you want to wait?"

"No, let's get it over with."

He winced.

"I didn't mean it that way."

"I know."

"I don't know what to do."

"Why don't you come over here and sit next to me?"

She didn't move.

He held out a hand to her. They weren't very far apart.

She remained motionless.

"What is it?"

"I can't move."

"Why not?"

"I don't know. I just can't. Orr, what will my father say?"

"He won't know. Jesus, you're not going to tell him, are you?"

She shook her head. "Maybe he'll know just by looking at me."

"He won't." Orlando stood in front of her, touched her cheek, hair. "Come on, darling."

She looked up at him, long lashes blinking. "You'll still love me?"

"More than ever. It's *because* I love you, Fran."

She rose.

He guided her to the bed. Expertly, he pulled her down and they lay together, his arm under her, around her shoulders. "See, isn't this nice?"

"Yes. But this isn't *it*."

"Trust me."

"I do or I wouldn't be here. I trust you, I love you and, dammit, I want you."

He kissed her, a long, warm kiss, their tongues intermingling. Slowly, he began to undress her. He was pleased when she helped him, more pleased when she began to unbutton his shirt.

When they were both naked and under the sheet, facing each other, they pressed their bodies together. The heat was extraordinary. He felt they were melting, one into the other.

Carefully, he touched her breast, his fingers circling the small pink nipple. He watched it grow erect. He felt Fran move, grip his shoulder. He kissed her throat, his fingers dancing over her nipple. Then his mouth was on her breast. She moaned as he fluttered his tongue over its center.

He took a long time, touching her everywhere, feeling her soft skin, exploring. He loved every inch of her.

When he entered her, she was ready. He was careful not to hurt her. Bit by bit, slowly, he made his way inside her. Once she cried out. He stopped, looked at her. Her eyes were open.

"I'm sorry."

"I know. It's all right. It'll be all right now."

And it was. When he was all the way in they held each other, kissing. Then smoothly he began to pull back. Her nails dug into his back. He liked it. She liked it.

As he moved, back and forth, slowly, rhythmically, he knew he had never experienced anything as wonderful. Fran wasn't doing anything special. She *was* special. Love, he decided, made all the difference.

His eyes squeezed shut as he climaxed. He lay quietly for a moment, gently withdrew, rolled over and removed the condom, placing it in a handkerchief to be dealt with later. Then he turned back to Fran.

"It didn't happen for you, did it?"

"No. But I don't care. It will."

"Are you all right? I mean, did it hurt?"

"Not as much as I thought it would. Was it . . . I mean, are you all right?"

He smiled, kissed her. "Yes. It was wonderful. I love you. I can try and make it happen for you if you give me a little time."

"It's all right. I don't think I could. It's too much for one day, if you know what I mean."

"It'll work out, you know," he said.

"I know. I could tell that. We just fit so perfectly. I mean our bodies . . . all of us."

"Yes." It was true.

"I love you terribly. I wouldn't have done it if I didn't."

"I know that."

"You're sure?"

"Yes. I love you terribly, too."

They kissed, sweetly.

"Fran, do you . . . do you feel any different?"

"Not really."

"Well, how *do* you feel?"

"You really want to know?"

"Of course."

"Hungry," she said.

They laughed and held each other very close.

June, 1927
Atlantic Ocean

It was four in the afternoon and Starr was drunk in her cabin. She'd had a long leisurely lunch with two young men from Montreal, both good drinkers who'd kept up with her drink for drink. Not everybody could do that. Drinks before lunch, wine with the meal, drinks after lunch. She was to meet them back in the bar at six.

She lay down on her bunk. This was her second cruise. The first had been less than a year ago on the S.S. *California*. After her revelation about Andrew, her mother and Stanley offered the cruise like some sort of consolation prize. She'd accepted. She didn't have anywhere else to go. And it was fun. She'd met a young officer and begun a shipboard romance, immediately fantasizing that they'd marry and she'd leave the house in West Orange. When the cruise ended she discovered he was already married.

After she returned, Stanley took every possible chance to question her about her relationship with Andrew. When she finally revealed that Peters had often signed hotel registers as Mr. and Mrs., he seemed especially pleased and left soon after on a trip. He came back armed with copies of many of those signatures. When Starr asked what he planned to do with them, he simply smiled and said she'd see.

Helen begged for Starr's forgiveness and she gave it, grudgingly, after making her mother squirm.

What Stanley did with the evidence was to take it to

Charles Rowley of Peabody, Brown, Rowley & Story. Rowley went to Peters and began negotiations. The deal they struck was for twenty-five thousand dollars. This was to cover the expenses—doctors, hospitals, etc.—of Starr's recovery. At the end of June Starr would sign a release exonerating Peters from any and all responsibility regarding her future mental health and making it impossible for the Faithfulls to obtain any further monies from him.

At first, Starr was against the deal. Money be damned! She wanted to issue a warrant for Andrew's arrest. But Stanley convinced her that a monetary settlement would, in the end, be far more gratifying. If they were going to take money, she then argued, they should ask for a lot more. Rowley advised that Peters couldn't afford more and, if pushed, he might decide to take his life or his chances and they'd gain nothing. So, finally, Starr agreed.

Now it was just a matter of a few months until she would feel rich. At last, it seemed, some dreams were going to come true. However, aboard the *Aurania* sailing from Montreal to Glasgow—at this moment—she was bored. She pushed her buzzer for a steward.

It seemed that hours passed as she paced the small cabin. Eventually there was a knock at the door. She flung herself down on the bed.

"Come in," she said weakly.

The steward opened the door, stepping just inside. "May I help you, Miss?"

She stared at him. He was only a boy, red-cheeked and blond. Not for her.

"Miss?"

"Please send me the ship's doctor." She surprised herself. She hadn't planned that.

"Yes, Miss."

When he'd gone Starr undressed, putting on a low-cut silk nightgown. She threw off the cover and lay down beneath the thin sheet. She wanted a cigarette but knew that wouldn't fit the image of sickness. So she waited impatiently, drumming her fingers on the mattress.

*　　*　　*

By the time the doctor arrived Starr was feeling very testy. He'd taken his good sweet time about it! But up close, he was even better-looking than she'd thought when she'd seen him across the dining room. She held her tongue about his delay.

"I'm Dr. Jameson-Carr," he said, removing his cap. "What seems to be the trouble?"

She looked up at him, her eyes wide, innocent, trying hard for a pained, but brave, look. "I'm not sure, Doctor. I have a lot of pains."

"Oh? Where?" He sat gingerly on the edge of the bunk.

Starr pulled the sheet down to her waist and carefully touched herself below her breasts. "Here."

He leaned over, gently feeling where she had indicated.

"No." She pushed his hand up to the base of her breasts. "Here."

Jameson-Carr deftly, subtly, moved his hand away, his eyes riveted on hers. "What did you eat for lunch?"

"The same as you. What's your name?"

"Dr. Jameson-Carr. I told you."

"Your first name."

"George."

"Ugh. George. I hate that name. I'll call you Bill."

"Bill. Why?"

"Just for the hell of it. I've never known a Bill."

He found it hard to believe she didn't know a man by every name in the book. "Look, Miss Faithfull . . ."

"You know my name?" He told her he'd looked it up in the passenger log, as he always did before seeing a patient. "Miss Faithfull, I think . . ."

"Please call me Starr."

He nodded and continued, calling her nothing. "I think you've had too much to drink."

She sat up. "How dare you!"

He stood.

"What kind of a doctor *are* you?"

"An honest one."

"Are you saying that I'm lying about the pains in my stomach?"

"Why, of course not, Miss Faithfull. I'm simply saying that you might be imagining them and if you'd take a little nap you'd feel better."

She sank slowly back against her pillows. "I can't sleep." Her full pink lower lip jutted out.

"Oh?"

"I have a terrible time, Doctor. At home I always take Allonal or Veronal but I forgot them. I can't believe I was so stupid."

"I hope you don't take them all the time. They can be habit-forming."

"Of course not. Just when I'm having a really bad time sleeping."

Jameson-Carr opened his bag. "I have some Allonal here."

Starr held her smile.

"I'll give you two. I wouldn't take one now if you want to make dinner and after dinner you should go to bed early. And don't drink anything alcoholic if you're going to take these, Miss Faithfull."

"Starr. No, of course I won't. I guess I did have a little too much to drink. It was the excitement of the first day and I'm not used to spirits."

"Understandable. Well, be sure to call me if you need me."

"Thanks, I will. And thanks for the medicine."

He picked up his cap, nodded.

"See you later, Doc."

Starr wondered, adding the two Allonal to the thirty she had with her, if the doctor was married. Chances were, considering his age and his looks, he was. She was sick to death of falling for married men. Still, married or not, she was determined to have Jameson-Carr. In fact, she was sure she would fall in love with him. That was the way it happened for her. Immediate, or not at all. Jameson-Carr was certainly her type. Mature. Of course, it would take a little work—not much but a little. He was interested even though he tried to pretend he wasn't. She'd seen how he looked at her breasts. But after all he *was* a doctor. He was used to seeing breasts. Perhaps his look was impersonal. She turned face down on the bunk, arms hugging her pillow. Perhaps he wasn't the least bit interested. The hell with it! She'd make him interested. He was a man, wasn't he?

After dinner that night Starr danced with half the men aboard. She spaced her drinks, careful not to get too drunk. She wanted to be ready for Dr. Jameson-Carr. She'd learned that he was unmarried, in his forties and considered quite a ladies man. Women, apparently, were always falling head over heels for him. When he finally asked her to dance she was actually weak with shyness. The few drinks she'd had were no help. His grip was strong, reassuring, but not overpowering like so many men's. She felt secure.

"I thought I told you to go to bed early, Miss Faithfull." He smiled, the creases in his cheeks deepening.

"I, I . . ." She could think of nothing to say. There wasn't an excuse in the world that she believed would wash with him and the only other alternative was the truth: she wanted to see him.

"How do you feel?"

"Much, much better."

"Good."

When the dance was over and he started to walk her back to her table she stopped midway.

"Doctor, I wonder . . . could . . . could we talk?" She had no idea what she would say. She knew only that she didn't want her time with him this evening to end.

"What about?" There was a desperate look to this girl. He would be gentle. "Are you in some sort of trouble?"

"Yes." She would think of something.

Jameson-Carr was apprehensive. He wanted to help but he didn't want to get into something messy. Well, talking wouldn't hurt. "Let's take a walk."

The evening was cool, clear. Walking along the deck Starr kept her lace stole wrapped around her shoulders. Her mind raced with stories she might tell the doctor. None of them were suitable. She knew he was waiting for her to speak.

As they approached the stern of the promenade deck Jameson-Carr felt he must give the girl some encouragement.

"You know, I'm a doctor. There's not much that could shock me."

Starr stopped and looked up into his kind face. She

knew what he said was true. By the time they'd circled the deck Starr had told him about Andrew, about the other men in her life, her addiction to pills and ether and he'd added that she was probably drinking too much as well.

As promised, he was not shocked. He'd heard worse. But he was moved. The beautiful young woman who stood next to him looking out over the sea had been terribly wounded, perhaps beyond repair . . . perhaps not. She'd had absolutely no proper guidance in her life. Maybe he could help. These trips always bored him—rich women with too much time on their hands eager for a little romance or a chance to get even with philandering husbands. Maybe now, this time, he could do something worthwhile.

Lately he'd been disgusted with himself, feeling his existence added up to zero. Jameson-Carr was not a religious man but he was a bit superstitious. Starr Faithfull's appearance in his life at this moment was no accident, he decided. He must help her if he could.

As though she'd read his mind she said, "I feel so helpless. I just don't know what to do anymore."

"I'll help you," he said, having no idea what he'd do. "You will?"

He sandwiched her hands between his large ones, patting them gently. "I'll try." Soft, smooth, safe.

"Oh, thank God."

*　　*　　*

The first thing Dr. Jameson-Carr did was to make certain Starr dumped her cache of pills overboard. Together they watched them fall to a watery grave. The second thing was to ban drinking altogether. Until she was better, he told her. Then he listened. At times he felt a bit guilty hearing this girl's innermost thoughts, secrets. After all he wasn't a priest or a proper alienist. But, he rationalized, confession to someone was better than no confession at all. And she did seem better. Less agitated. Softer. At times she even expressed happiness. For the first time in years Jameson-Carr felt his life had some real meaning.

Starr wondered when Dr. George Jameson-Carr would get around to kissing her. It made her laugh that she was thinking in such schoolgirl terms. But her "Bill" was different. He really cared about her. The real her, not just her body. Still, she would have liked more physical contact than just holding hands as they did when they strolled the deck.

When he'd first outlined his "recovery program" she had been horrified. No pills. No liquor. The future seemed bleaker than ever. But she wanted to please him and since nothing was working her way, why not give it a try? After almost two weeks of his conventlike regime she was surprised to realize how well she felt.

As they danced at the final party the night before docking it was easy for her to promise she'd continue her abstinence. She would have promised him anything. Not since Edmond Chalmers had she felt anything like this. And this was even more real, mature. She knew she was truly in love for the first time.

Now, in front of her cabin saying goodnight, goodbye, she was terribly nervous. Surely something physical would happen. It was clear they wouldn't be sleeping together. She'd decided that he couldn't do that aboard ship. But a kiss?

"Will you write?" she asked.

"Of course."

"And when you're in New York next you'll come and see me?"

"As soon as I can, Starr. In the meantime you'll be a good girl?"

"I will." She meant it.

"And when you get the money you'll start seeing a doctor?"

"Yes. But I'll see you before that, won't I, Doc?"

"I hope so." He smiled, his blue eyes benevolent.

As he leaned down toward her she thought she might faint. She closed her eyes and was shocked to feel his lips touch her cheek. Opening her eyes, she stared at his wonderful face dumbfounded.

"Goodbye, dear girl. Take good care of yourself. I'll see you soon."

Lying in her bunk she wondered how Bill managed such control. Surely he was the most wonderful, mature, decent man she'd ever met. Visions of the various dreadful men she'd given herself to since Andrew momentarily marred her thoughts. She pushed them aside. They were in the past. Dr. George Jameson-Carr was the only man in her life now. And if he wanted their relationship to be on a different plane until they were married that was all right with her. Once they were married sex would be perfect. She wouldn't have the trouble with him she'd had with other men. Intercourse would be pleasurable instead of almost intolerable. He would be gentle yet commanding, leading her, guiding her. George Jameson-Carr would obliterate the damage that Andrew had done. She could hardly wait and fell asleep with the craggy image of his face on the pillow beside her.

At the end of June he called her and she went into New York to have dinner with him. It was a wonderful evening but again it was chaste.

She managed to continue to stay sober, having only an occasional drink, living on his letters and fantasies of the future. As far as she was concerned she and Jameson-Carr were having a deep and meaningful love affair.

———

Miss Faithfull took exception to descriptions of her dead sister as a wild, gin-drinking habitué of speakeasies, attributing all her escapades to "artistic temperament."
—*New York Times*, June 13, 1931

June 5, 1931
New York, New York

The duplex on MacDougal Alley was elegant, tasteful, luxurious.

Royal Leffland was as handsome as his wife Diana was beautiful. They were both in their mid-forties, had been married for eighteen years, and were childless.

For Starr, the place, the people, were a dream come true. She could be very happy in a place like this. Perhaps she would be the daughter the Lefflands never had. Perhaps her whole life would change.

Royal poured himself a martini and one for Diana. Starr was given tomato juice.

"When you get healthier you'll be able to have a cocktail with us, my dear. Of course, we never have more than two," Diana said.

Two would be perfect, Starr thought.

Fifteen

Fran, Fran, Fran, Fran. How sweet, innocent, gentle she'd been. At first. Later she changed. After Allwood. After Van Ness. When was it she'd started to drink? Was it before Cathy was born? FAITHFULL GIRL'S BURIAL HALTED BY NEW CLEWS. Like flashing neon lights. Ignore. When was it Fran started to drink? During the Depression years? Yes. But much worse later. Later, in the South Orange house. It was sherry during the war years. She'd be pie-eyed by the time he came home from work. Then she gave up the sherry.

Cocktail hour. Drinking whiskey. If only she'd waited for him. But she always had a head start. A buzz on, as Fran said. And even though he watched *his* drinks before dinner, he couldn't watch hers. How many nights had she fallen in her food?

So mean. Fran got mean when she was drunk. Said awful things. Threatened to leave time and time again. He hated Cathy seeing that, hearing.

Then Dr. Kramer said No more, Mrs. Antolini. Bad liver. And just like that, she stopped. Everyone said it was the German in her that made it possible to quit that way. Much nicer those last years. Four of them before he had

219

the stroke. Good times, then. Almost. Said she felt wonderful. Wished she'd done it years before. Wished she'd never started. Why *had* she started?

Summer, 1927
Sea Girt, New Jersey

Kay Chase rested her head on Orlando's shoulder, watching the end of *Sunrise* with Janet Gaynor and George O'Brien. Afterwards, they drove to their favorite speakeasy, Little Joe's. Kay knew chances were they'd get very drunk, drive to the beach, take a blanket and have sex on the sand, as near the water as possible. Orr liked it that way. He said the natural rhythm of the ocean was exciting. Kay suspected that, for him, their own rhythms just weren't enough. But she didn't say so. There were other things she suspected as well. She'd always known Orr wasn't in love with her but his feeling for her, his enjoyment of her, had some intensity. Now he was distracted. She was almost certain that he'd fallen in love with someone else.

She, on the other hand, was in love with him as she had been for years, although he didn't know it. But now she'd graduated from college and would begin teaching in September. She was twenty-two years old, no longer a carefree girl. Soon she would have to think about marriage, a family. She would have to break a key rule and ask Orlando if there was someone else. It was a risk. If he said yes she'd have to stop seeing him. She really didn't want to do that. If he said no and she tried to push him into a commitment he might become annoyed and stop seeing her. But the threat of passing time, of ending up an old maid, was stronger than the threat of losing him. She decided tonight she would ask.

Little Joe's was only half full, the bulk of the regular crowd never arriving until after eleven. Orlando and Kay took a table for six, knowing some of their friends would wander in. They both ordered gin. Orlando, tapping his foot to the rhythm of "My Blue Heaven," wished he were part of the band. For the first time in his life he looked forward to getting back to school. This year the band would be *his*. That, unfortunately, had one drawback. He would see less of Fran. He'd gotten used to seeing her daily during the year and he'd missed her this summer, writing every other day *(as I turn the leaves of the book I read they whisper Frances, Frances, Frances)*, calling her once a week.

He looked at Kay. Definitely a good-looking girl. But she wasn't Fran. Of course, there'd been times with Fran when he'd wished he were with Kay. She certainly gave him more feedback. They might spend hours discussing the meaning of one line of a Yeats poem. Sometimes, though, Kay's challenges were irritating, her questions unanswerable. With Fran he was always right. And if it was less exciting, it was a lot more comforting.

Kay turned, feeling his gaze. She smiled, blue eyes soft. "What's the matter?"

"Nothing. Why?"

"You were staring at me."

"Because you're beautiful."

She dismissed the remark with a wave of her hand.

Fran would have lowered her eyes, moved closer to him. She was much more feminine, he supposed. "You are, you know," he went on.

Kay had never known how to accept compliments. Particularly when they weren't accurate. And there was no way she could see herself as beautiful. Three tables away, surrounded by four men, there was, in Kay's opinion, a truly beautiful girl. Her brown hair was naturally curly, framing her heart-shaped face. Her brown eyes were large, luminous. When she laughed, the men laughed with her, clearly entranced by her beauty.

"Where are you?" Orlando asked.

"I'm here," she said. "How about another drink?"

Orlando held up two fingers to their waiter.

When Pete Congdon and Virginia Bittner joined them, Virginia immediately asked Kay to accompany her to the ladies room. Touching up her face, Kay noticed in the mirror that the beautiful brown-haired girl had entered. In a few moments she emerged from a stall and sat in front of the mirror next to Kay's. On closer inspection, Kay decided, she wasn't as beautiful as she'd seemed. The features were right but there was something in the eyes. They were hard, cold, perhaps even bitter. It spoiled her looks.

Suddenly, the girl's eyes shifted and locked with Kay's. Embarrassed, Kay smiled. The girl didn't smile back. Her stare, in fact, was almost menacing. Kay looked away, concentrating on applying her lipstick. Then, unable to control herself, she looked back. The girl was still staring. Again, Kay tried a timid smile but none came in return.

"What are you looking at?" the girl asked.

Kay was startled. "Nothing. I'm sorry."

"What was that all about?" Virginia asked on the way back to the table.

"I thought I knew her," Kay lied. "I guess she was annoyed by my staring at her."

"She certainly is a beauty," Virginia said.

"Who is?" Orlando rose as the two women approached.

"Oh, some girl who . . ."

Kay cut her off. "Let's go to Dante's. This place is giving me the heebie jeebies."

"Good idea," said Pete.

As they were filing out, the girl emerged from the ladies room and walked past Orlando. Kay was pleased to see that neither one noticed the other. And she hoped the girl wasn't going to be a permanent fixture around Sea Girt.

The girl, arriving back at her table, ordered another gin and wondered why the blue-eyed woman in the bathroom had been staring at her. Her speculation was interrupted by Claude, the man on her left.

"Penny for your thoughts, Starr."

"Cheapskate," she said.

The men laughed.

* * *

Knowing that by August they would receive twenty-five thousand dollars, Starr had convinced Stanley to take them all on a holiday. She'd chosen the Jersey Shore. Sea Girt. Shadow Lawn, President Wilson's summer place, had been there so it must be nice. And it *was*. She adored swimming in the ocean, feeling the waves breaking over her head.

On the beach men swarmed around her. She joked

with them, played games, dated them. Usually more than one at a time. There was, she felt, safety in numbers. At the end of each evening the men arranged among themselves for one of their number to take her home. Occasionally she had a real struggle but most of the men accepted that she was "not that kind of girl."

Starr had never enjoyed intercourse and she'd never had any kind of sex without liquor or pills. Since she was barely drinking the thought of sex with anyone but Jameson-Carr was impossible. She was determined to remain pure for Bill even though she sometimes thought how nice it would feel to be held, even kissed.

Often it was hard to pass up the drinks the men pressed on her, but she conjured up Jameson-Carr's face to help her resist. She desperately wanted to fulfill his expectations and, for once in her life, do something good. Fearful she would fail, she actually got down on her knees at night and prayed for help to a God she didn't really believe in. She prayed to be able to last until fall when she would book passage on Jameson-Carr's ship.

But tonight was tonight and she was determined to have fun.

"Let's go for a midnight swim," she said.

The men cheered and they all readied to leave.

She knew what each expected and, unlike the old days, she knew what each would get. A midnight swim!

*　　　*　　　*

When they left Dante's, eight of them now, they were all very drunk. In three cars they zigzagged down the main street and out to the exclusive golf club where none of them was a member. The club was dark. Pete, in the lead car, swung around the back of the clubhouse and drove straight out across the course. The others whooped and hollered, following close behind. Somewhere in the middle of the course, Pete stopped and the others followed suit. He jumped from his car, flask in hand, spread his arms straight out, and ran around a green, yelling.

"I'm Lucky Lindy, the Flying Fool!"

The others tumbled and fell from their cars, running behind Pete, imitating him. Orlando stopped, took a swig from his flask and shouted, "Up on your toes!"

Within seconds they were lined up, doing the Varsity Drag. Halfway through, Virginia noticed a distant light. It was in the clubhouse. They scrambled into their cars and raced back over the course to the exit. When they passed the clubhouse, an old man holding a lantern shouted at them but they gave him the Bronx cheer and sped by.

Out on the street they separated. Orlando drove to the beach. As he reached into the back seat for the blanket, Kay grabbed his wrist.

"I want to talk to you," she said.

"So?"

"I want to talk here."

"Why here?"

"I just do."

He dropped the blanket, reached for his flask, took a long swig, and held it out to Kay. She shook her head.

"She doesn't drink, she doesn't pet, she hasn't been to college yet." His voice was singsong.

"That's so stupid."

"He may have been a ham, but his sugar cured him."

"Will you stop?"

"She was so dumb she wondered how electric light poles grew in a straight line." He roared with drunken laughter.

Kay, who was sobering up, lit a cigarette, waiting until he stopped the nonsense.

"You know why whiskey kills more people than bullets? Because bullets don't drink." He giggled stupidly, then sucked again at his flask. "C'mon, Kay, let's go down to the beach."

"No. I want to talk to you." She knew how drunk he was, knew that it was probably a bad time. But maybe, drunk as he was, he might tell the truth.

"We call her Marigold because that's what she's trying to do!"

"Oh, Christ." She turned her body away slightly and crossed her legs, the silk of her culottes swishing.

"Okay, okay, Kaysie. What do you want to talk about?"

"You're too drunk," she said, challenging him.

"The hell I am." He straightened up. "Okay, what is it? I'm all ears."

Kay suddenly realized she didn't know how to begin.

Should she just ask him straight out? Her thoughts were interrupted as he reached for her hand. "No."

"What's wrong?" This time he grabbed her hand in a firm grip.

"No," she repeated. How could she ask him if they were holding hands? "Let me go."

"C'mon, Kaysie." He tried to pull her closer.

"I want to talk."

"Later." She felt his breath against her cheek.

Perhaps, she thought, later would be better.

They kissed, tongues slick and hot in each other's mouths, then tracing each other's lips. He drew his mouth away, kissed her cheek, neck, etched the outline of her ear with his lips, breathing heavily into it, filling the opening with his tongue, whispering. "I want you."

She moaned, feeling her nipples harden. He slid her way and she opened the door, reaching out a leg, feeling the road beneath her foot. They had to let go of each other. She ran across the boardwalk, jumping the three feet to the sand, undoing her culottes, pulling them and her underwear down and off. When Orlando landed beside her she was already waiting. He started to take off his pants.

"No," she said. Sometimes she found his body clothed more exciting than when it was naked.

"It'll hurt."

"I don't care."

He knelt between her legs, then lowered himself, entering, filling her.

Orlando came first but then, always the considerate lover, he lowered his head between her legs and brought her to climax too.

Back in the car, fully clothed, Kay could feel her skin smarting where his pants and the sand had rubbed against her. She didn't complain. They both smoked cigarettes. Orlando was still drunk, but not silly.

"Jesus, that was good," he said, his arm around her shoulder.

"Mmmm."

"You're the best."

The implication was that there were others. She didn't care.

"Am I the best?" he asked.

"The only," she said.

He smiled, satisfied. "What did you want to talk about?"

"Nothing," she said. "It doesn't matter."

"Good."

"Good," she repeated, knowing she was stupid and foolish and not giving a damn.

*   *   *

When Orlando awoke the next morning, he had a headache. Lying quietly, listening to see if anyone was in the hall, he had no idea what time it was. When he heard nothing, he carefully tiptoed down the hall to the bathroom. The door was open.

While he was relieving himself, there was a knock.

"Just a minute," he called, silently swearing. He was in no mood to talk.

His mouth felt like he'd been drinking lye. He rinsed it out and opened the door. It was Connie.

"Hello, darling."

He smiled. He could bear seeing her.

"What time is it?"

"Eleven. You got in late."

He didn't mind Connie knowing when he'd gotten in.

"I have something to tell you. Can I come into your room?"

"Sure."

Orlando lay on his bed. Connie sat at the end.

"Jack is coming down today," she said.

He tried to hide his disapproval. "Swell. Where's he going to stay?"

"He's taken a room in a boarding house in Manasquan."

"Has he got a car?" Manasquan was next to Sea Girt but one needed a car to get around.

"Yes."

"Is he working? Is this his vacation?" He knew Ward hadn't had a proper job in years.

"Well, right now he's between jobs. It's hard for Jack," she said quickly, "he's so sensitive. He needs the right kind of a job and they're not easy to come by."

Orlando nodded. He wanted to ask what the *right* job

would be for the sensitive bastard, but he didn't. "What kind of car does he have?"

She looked away. "Oh, it's just a Model T."

"Con," he said, unable to control his curiosity, "where'd he get the money for a car?"

"How should I know?" She started to get up. Orlando stopped her with his foot.

"Hey, Connie, you didn't."

"Oh, Orr, he wanted it so badly and I didn't need the money." She pushed up her glasses which had slipped onto the bridge of her nose. "You should have seen his face, Orr. He's so beautiful."

He was embarrassed to hear his sister talk that way, especially about Ward. "Where'd you get the money?"

"I saved it . . . birthday and Christmas money . . . you know, over the years."

"Jesus." He knew he sounded judgmental now but he couldn't help it.

"What do I need money for? Why shouldn't he have the car? And, in a way, it's my car too."

"Yes, I guess." He forced himself to hold back.

"You disapprove."

"Well, what the heck, Connie . . . I mean, my God."

"Why shouldn't I give the man I love a present?"

He thought a moment. "No reason," he said.

"You don't sound convinced."

"What if Papa should find out?"

"He won't. And what if he did? I'm twenty-seven."

"You're always saying that. I mean, how old you are. I don't think Papa cares how old any of us are as long as we're under his roof. But since you've brought up your age again, what about it? Don't you think it's time you got married?"

"Jack's not divorced yet." She seemed to think that was a satisfactory explanation.

"I know. How long are you going to wait?"

"As long as it takes."

"And what if he never gets a divorce?"

"Then . . . then we'll go on the way we've been."

For the first time Orlando wondered exactly what that meant. Did Connie sleep with Ward? He couldn't bear to think so, yet he couldn't imagine Ward hanging around all these years just to hold hands.

"I was wondering," she said, "if you'd pretend I was going out with you tonight."

"Sure."

"What's wrong? You have such a funny look on your face."

He'd been imagining Connie in a passionate situation, picturing her on the beach with Ward the way he'd been with Kay the night before. It made him feel queasy. "I don't feel too hot. Hangover I guess."

"Oh, Orly, you've got to be careful what you drink. That bootleg stuff can be lethal."

He smiled. The disturbing image vanished as he listened to Connie, his nurse, mother, friend. "Yes, I know."

"You'd better have something to eat. I'll tell Dolce. What would you like?"

As he gave his breakfast order, Silvio shuffled in and dropped onto the bed, sprawling out on his back, his bulky legs spread-eagle, feet touching the floor.

"What do you want, Fatso?"

"Don't," Connie said.

Looking at his big brother upside down, he said, "I got a message."

How could anyone so tall let himself get so fat? "What's the message?"

"What do I get if I give it?" Silvio's round cheeks wobbled as he spoke.

"A kick in the pants."

"Then I'm not giving it."

"Who's it from?"

"Papa."

Orlando felt himself grow taut. "What is it?"

Silvio yawned.

"Sil," Connie said, "if Papa sent you up here with a message I think you'd better deliver it or you'll get what for."

"He wants to see you. Right away. He's waiting for you on the porch."

Orlando guessed he'd get a lecture about his late hours and didn't look forward to it, particularly on an empty stomach. There'd be no time for breakfast now.

Orlando Sr., dressed in a white linen suit, dark tie, high-crowned straw hat, sat stiffly in a wicker chair. On the wicker table beside him was a glass of celery tonic, an ashtray with the butts of three cigarettes, his ivory holder and gold case and the morning mail. He crossed his legs, the spectator shoe making a tapping motion in the air.

Orlando Jr., an artificial smile pasted on his tanned face, joined his father. "Good morning, Papa."

"Good morning."

Orlando looked out over the sea. Small fat white clouds blew across the sky. "It's a beautiful day."

His father said nothing.

"You wanted to see me?"

"Sit down." He motioned to a chair on the other side of the table. He picked up one of the Players cigarettes Nina brought him from Canada, inserted it in his holder and cleared his throat three times, an unconscious signal that what was ahead was not good.

Orlando tried to think of excuses. Flat tire, out of gas, date sick, etc. He wished he were more like Connie and could just explain that a man of twenty-three had a right to stay out as late as he wanted.

"Who is Fran?"

Orlando was jolted. He'd never mentioned Fran to his family, even though they were pinned.

"Fran?"

"Yes. Who is Fran?"

A million lies careened through his brain at once. But why should he lie? He wasn't ashamed of her. He loved her. "She's a girl I see at school."

"What kind of a girl?" Orlando Sr. adjusted his pince-nez and blew a narrow stream of smoke into the air.

"She's a nice girl, Papa." He couldn't bring himself to ask how his father knew about her.

"Are you going to marry her?"

It was a hot day and Orlando wondered how his father kept from sweating when he, in his bathing suit and shirt, felt beads of perspiration rolling down his sides and the back of his legs.

"Did you hear me?"

"Yes, Papa."

"Well?" Angrily, he stubbed out the cigarette and blew a last puff of smoke from the holder.

"I . . . I don't know. There's school."

"Eventually?"

He had to ask. "Why, Papa? Who told you about her?"

The man stared at him, touched his small mustache with his ringed index finger, then reached for the pile of mail on the table, sorting through it and handing a small white envelope to his son, who accepted it as though it were filled with germs.

Orlando saw his name on the front, the familiar handwriting and paper. *Fran.* How dare his father open his mail! He could feel his cheeks burning. He read.

DEAR ORLANDO,

I miss you terribly. It's so dull here without you. I live for the mail. Oh, dear God, Orr, I didn't want to tell you this but I just must. I thought I would make this a newsy kind of letter but I can't go on any longer. I think I am pregnant. I am three weeks overdue. I'm beside myself with fear. What should I do? I will do whatever you want. Believe me, this is not a form of blackmale. I wouldn't have told you but I'm very scared and have no one to talk to. I thought about telling Jennie but what could she do? I promise to do anything you want. I'll wait to hear from you. I love you more than life itself.

Yours,
FRAN

He could barely understand or believe what he was reading. His anger at his father for opening his mail, and his fear of the man's reaction to the letter, kept the words going in and out of focus. He shut his eyes to clear them, then quickly read the letter again. How could it have happened? He'd always taken precautions. However, anger overshadowed these questions and everything else. For the first time in his life he challenged his father. "Why did you open my mail?"

"I thought it was for me."

Orlando turned over the envelope. Fran had forgotten to put Junior after his name.

Looking out to sea Orlando Sr. said, "I am sorry."

His father had never apologized to him for anything. "What are you going to do about this?"

"I'll call her."

"I do not mean that, stupido," he said through clenched teeth. "I mean what are you going to do about the situation?"

"I guess we'll get married."

"What about Kay Chase?" Orlando Sr. liked Kay very much and admired her family.

"Kay's a friend."

"Do you love this Fran?"

"Yes."

"She cannot spell."

"I know. I'll call her after dinner. We'll see."

"What about school?"

"What can I do?"

"Are you sure it is your baby?"

"Yes."

"Of course, I want you to do the proper thing. You are a fool, Orlando."

He hung his head.

"What is this Fran's last name?" He lit another Players.

"Hess."

"Hess." Couldn't he ever pick a nice Italian girl? "She is German?"

"Yes."

"And the family? What does the father do?"

"He works in an office."

"What kind of an office?"

"They make cigars." He didn't want to use the word *factory*.

The Chase girl's father was a doctor. "Do you think this girl would take money?"

"Money?"

"Yes, money," he said, angrily. "You know what money is, do you not? You spend enough."

"You mean you want me to pay her off?" He felt his eyes beginning to sting.

"Why not?"

Orlando jumped up, the rocker he'd been sitting in lurching behind him. "I love this woman." He needed only to place his hand over his heart to complete the picture.

"Get out of my sight."

But Orlando stood, unable to move, wanting desperately to say something more to his father though he didn't know what.

"Go!"

He opened his mouth, then closed it. There was nothing to say. He turned and strode across the porch to the door, letting it slam behind him, something his father hated. Standing still for a moment inside he heard his father say: "She cannot even spell."

❋   ❋   ❋

Orlando spent the remainder of the day in his room, nibbling some cheese, picking at a leftover salad limp with garlic dressing. The time crawled by as he waited for five-thirty when Fran would come home from work.

He thought of Fran, alternately with love and with anger. How could she have been so stupid as to leave off the Junior? Who had more beautiful eyes? Was the error deliberate? Was she indeed trying to *blackmale* him? Her sweetness, gentleness, were incomparable.

At some point, it occurred to him that he might, indeed, have to marry Fran. A comforting thought, in a funny way. He would go to classes. Fran would cook, take care of him, perhaps even learn to type his papers. But if he married he would have to give up Kay.

He thought about the night before. It had been quick but exciting, good. With Fran it was sweet but not insane or madly sexy. For one thing Fran didn't drink and her inhibitions remained intact. And, basically, making love before marriage went against the grain for her. If they were married she would probably relax more. And if she gave herself completely to him he wouldn't need Kay or anyone else. He wanted to be like his father, a man who respected his marriage vows. One woman and one woman only. He felt depressed.

He gave the operator Fran's number. Unfortunately, the phone was in the living room and most of his family were on the porch, just beyond the living room windows.

Fran's mother answered. "Who?"

"Orlando Antolini, Mrs. Hess."

"Mrs. Hess? I'm Mrs. Hess. Which Mrs. Hess are you?"

"No, no, this is Orlando . . . you know, Orlando, Fran's friend."

"Oh, Orlando. Yes. How are you?"

"Fine, thank you. And you?" It wouldn't be easy for Fran to talk either. Her phone was in the kitchen and it was dinner time.

"I'm fine. How's the weather there?"

"Fine. How's it there?"

"Hot. You could fry an egg on the sidewalk."

He agreed that in Sea Girt you could do the same.

Finally, she said, "You want Fran?"

"Yes, please."

"Just a minute. Nice talking to you, Orlando."

"You too."

It seemed hours passed before he heard Fran's voice.

"Hello."

"It's Orlando."

"I know. How are you?"

"I got your letter." He imagined his father's face.

"Oh. I just wrote you another."

"How did you address it?"

"What?"

"I said, how did you address it?"

"I don't know what you mean. The same as always."

"You forgot to put Junior on the last one," he whispered.

"What? I can't hear you."

He repeated it, a bit louder, certain everyone on the porch had heard.

"I don't know what you mean," she said.

"Junior. Junior."

"Junior?"

"How are you, Fran?"

"It's hot. Is it hot there?"

"You could fry an egg on the sidewalk." He tried to keep the anger out of his voice.

"Here, too."

"Can you talk?"

"I am talking."

"You know what I mean."

There was silence.

"Is your mother there?"

"You just talked to her."

"I mean, is she right there, listening?"

"Well, yes, I guess."

"Can you answer yes or no?"

"Yes."

"Good." He had no idea how to ask what he wanted to know. He wasn't even sure what it was he wanted to know.

"Orlando? Are you there?"

"Yes."

"Oh."

"Fran, about the letter, you said I should call you."

"I did?"

Actually, she'd said she'd wait to hear from him. "Well, you said you wanted to hear from me."

"I did. I do. Look, forget about that letter. I wrote you another one."

"Forget about it? You mean everything's okay?"

"Yes."

"You mean," he whispered, "you're not."

"What?"

"You're not?" he said louder.

"That's right."

He felt like killing her. "Swell."

"Yes. I'm sorry if you were upset."

"Well, sure I was."

"I know. I'm sorry. I wrote you another letter."

"How did you address it?"

"Why do you keep asking me that?"

"Because," he lowered his voice, "you left the Junior off the last one."

"What?"

"The Junior," he yelled, turning quickly to look toward the porch.

"What Junior?"

He closed his eyes. "Well, listen, Fran, I guess we'd better get off."

"Okay."

"You sure everything is okay?"

"I'm sure. Orr?"

"What?"

"Are you mad at me?"

She was talking about the false pregnancy. He was mad about the faulty name on the letter. But he wasn't going to bring that up again. "No, I'm not mad. I'll write to you."

"I do, you know."

"Yes, me too."

"What?"

"Me, too." Louder. He felt his cheeks warm.

"Good. I'm glad you're not mad."

"I'm glad you're okay. Well, I'll write. Tonight."

"Good."

"Goodbye."

"Bye."

When his anger passed he felt relief. That night, out with Kay, he realized how glad he was there was still time for other women.

For the next few days he made sure he was present when the mailman came around. Fran's letter, when it arrived, had the Junior properly in place. He thought of dropping the whole thing, not mentioning it to her, but decided in the end that it was too risky. She, of course, never left off the Junior again.

*   *   *

On August 27th, Nicola Sacco and Bartolomeo Vanzetti were executed in Massachusetts. Orlando Antolini Sr. and his family, along with thousands of others, were convinced of their innocence and outraged at what they considered a miscarriage of justice. What would have been a day of mourning for the Antolinis, however, was made into a nightmare by their own problems with the law.

Early that morning, John Charles Ward was arrested in Newark and taken to jail. Unaware that Orlando Antolini Sr. was himself behind the arrest, Jack called the house in Sea Girt. Connie, after getting off the phone, begged for the use of the Packard. When her father refused, she broke down and told him why she needed it.

"Oh, Papa," she cried, "Jack is in jail." She hadn't spoken Ward's name to her father in years.

Orlando lit a gold-tipped cigarette. "Good," he said. His daughter had defied him! Clearly, she'd been in touch with Ward all along.

Connie was stunned. "How can you say that?"

"With ease. The man is a criminal." The muscles in his cheeks rippled.

"Don't say that. I know you hate him but he isn't a criminal."

"No? Evidence proves otherwise."

"Evidence? What evidence?" News of Jack's arrest was not a surprise to her father. Connie was horrified. "What do you know about this?"

Orlando shifted uncomfortably in his wicker chair. The paper slipped from his lap to the floor. "Did he tell you why he was arrested?"

"Larceny."

"And forgery? Did he not mention forgery?"

"Papa," she screamed, "what is this? What have you got to do with this?"

"He used my charge at Bamberger's." Orlando had assumed Ward stole the card years before, had it copied, and had begun to use it only recently. How could he have been so naive?

"Bamberger's," she mumbled.

"He charged five hundred dollars' worth of goods."

"Oh, no." Connie slumped, her behind hitting the edge of a chair, resting there.

"He forged my name, the fool."

"Oh, Papa." Tears ran from the corners of her eyes.

"It is obvious that you have been seeing the man, Concettina, but surely he has not been in our house. How did he steal the card?"

"I gave it to him, Papa . . . he needed some . . . some underwear."

She might as well have struck him. He was, for once, speechless.

She rose, as if on a spring. "I must go to him, Papa."

"Are you insane?"

"I don't know. Perhaps. Please give me the keys to the Packard."

Orlando stood, ashes spilling on his white suit. "How dare you?"

They faced one another, silently, each condemning the other to some private hell. Then Connie turned and ran down the steps toward the beach, her flared skirt flapping behind her like a tail.

Orlando watched his daughter go. He'd done the right thing, he was sure of that. He'd done the only thing possible. Justice had to be served, no matter who got hurt. Even if it was his darling Concettina, foolish girl that she was. But he could not remember ever feeling so desolate.

Orlando and Kay lay on a blanket, their eyes toward the sea. The strange wailing noise that frightened and alarmed them was unidentifiable until they turned. Connie ran across the sand, stumbling, falling. In a second Orlando was on his feet, Connie in his arms, her face streaked with tears. He led her to the blanket. The wailing eventually dwindled down to chokes and hiccups.

"Connie, what is it?" Orlando held her. Kay stroked her hair.

Bit by bit she told them the story.

"What can I do?" he asked.

"Take me to Jack," she begged.

Involuntarily, his eyes skidded away from her face to the house in the distance. He was sure he could see the figure of his father on the porch. Slowly he looked back at Connie. She held her glasses in her hands, exposing her small, red-rimmed eyes.

"You want me to drive you to Newark?"

"Yes. Please."

"I don't know."

"What do you mean?"

Again, he glanced in the direction of the house. The mirage of his father loomed larger. "Papa," he murmured.

"Papa?" Connie repeated.

"What would he say? Do?"

"Oh, Orlando, there's no time for that. I must go to Jack now. He needs me."

"He'd kill me." Orlando heard his words as though someone else was speaking.

"I thought you wanted to help me." Connie returned her thick glasses to the bridge of her nose, hooking the metal rims over her ears.

"I do, Connie. I really do. But I can't take you to Newark. Anything else."

"There isn't anything else." She turned to Kay. "Say something."

Kay shrugged, shaking her head, sad.

"Then at least lend me your car." Connie's mouth was tight.

The thought of his father tormented him. "I can't."

"But why?"

"You're not a good driver." He knew it was weak.

"I'll be careful."

"Please, Connie. Try to understand."

Kay handed him a cigarette. "I know it's none of my business," she said, "but do you think you should go? After all, your father *is* a lawyer. What if someone sees you. There might be talk."

"She's right." He was grateful to Kay and touched her hand with his fingertips.

"You don't understand. I must bring him bail money and I don't care who sees me. I don't care what it does to Papa."

Orlando couldn't decide which was more stunning. That she didn't care about Papa or that she was going to put up Jack's bail. What he did know was that she'd make a damn fool of herself if she went through with it. He couldn't be a party to that. As a brother he had a duty, a responsibility, to protect her. By refusing to drive her or to lend his car he'd save her from disgrace. And, incidentally, keep from tangling with his father. "Connie, why not think this thing over?"

She rose to her feet like a newborn colt, her eyes never leaving his face. "I've always depended on you."

This surprised him. He'd always depended on her.

"I guess I've been a fool," she said.

It stung.

"You're a very cowardly person, Orlando." It was a flat statement, without emotion.

He watched her go, unable to speak. Kay touched his arm. "She'll calm down later, Orr. You'll see."

He said nothing, eyes on the diminishing figure of his sister. When she'd become nothing more than a speck, he turned and looked back at the ocean spanking the shoreline.

"She doesn't understand," he said, after a few minutes.

"She's very upset. I can imagine what I'd be like if it were you."

"But it never would be me. What will happen?"

"I guess there'll be a trial. He'll be sentenced."

Guilty until proven innocent, he thought. A fantasy flashed through his mind. He was Jack's lawyer, eloquently defending him. Connie smiling, proud, nodding benevolently. Next to her his father, grim, jaw set, eyes ice. The fantasy shredded. "Let's go for a swim."

He couldn't think about it, about her, anymore.

Forty-five minutes later Orlando and Kay, ready for lunch, walked up the path to the house. Orlando Sr. rose out of his chair, staring at his son as though he'd never seen him before.

"I thought you'd gone," his father said. "Did you give her your car?"

"No, Papa."

"Liar."

Kay stiffened. "Mr. Antolini, forgive me, but he didn't give her the car."

Orlando Sr.'s lips disappeared. The lunch gong sounded. "Change," he commanded.

"But Papa, aren't we going to do anything?"

"Do?" He arched a thin eyebrow.

"The car," he said timidly. "Connie."

"What we shall do is have our lunch." He went into the house.

No one spoke. The clinking of silverware against china was the only sound in the room. Eventually, Aldo, Nina's four-year-old, cleaved the silence with his piercing little voice.

"I hate this." He poked at his zucchini.

"Eat it. It's good for you," Nina said.

"But I hate it."

Renato Jr., two and a half, with no thoughts of his own, said, "I hate this."

"Stop that. Eat."

Instinctively knowing that "Poppy," as he called his grandfather, was his greatest fan, Renato turned toward the man at the head of the table. "Poppy, I hate this." In his small fist he clutched his fork, a round slice of zucchini speared on a tine.

The muscle jumped in Orlando Sr.'s cheek. "Be a good boy," he said softly.

"See now," said Nina, "Poppy wants you to eat it."

"We hate it," Aldo whined.

Orlando Jr., eyes on his plate, forced himself to swallow the food he'd been chewing. He wished his nephews would stop their mewling.

"We hate this," the boys sang in unison.

"If you don't stop," said Nina, "you're going to have to leave the table."

"We don't care." Aldo.

"We don't care." Renato.

"All right, then. Go to your room."

The boys, giggling, scrambled down from their highchairs. At the dining room door Aldo stopped.

"Now we don't have to eat that. Ha, ha." He stuck out his tongue and crossed his eyes.

"Ha, ha," Renato said.

As they ran from the room, the silence resumed.

Orlando glanced across the table at his mother. Her food was untouched. She slid her fork back and forth on the edge of her plate. Next to her, Silvio was stuffing food in his mouth as fast as he could. Toni, as always, winnowed out the select pieces as though her food was in some sort of contest.

When the knock came on the door, Antonia gasped, dropping her fork. The others remained frozen. Orlando Sr. sent his oldest son to see who it was.

Through the screen, Orlando saw the two policemen. His instinct was to turn away, run back to the dining room, or push past the officers and keep on going. He knew he could do neither.

"Yes?"

"Orlando Antolini?"

"Yes." He knew they meant Senior.

"Do you know a Concettina Antolini?"

"Yes."

"May we come in, please?"

He knew then why they were there but his brain rejected it. When they told him it was a brand new shock. He cried out.

The sound brought the others to the hall. Antonia, seeing the policemen with her son, knew immediately. She screamed. The others, including Orlando Sr., began to shout and cry. The policemen retreated until their backs were up against the door. Neither had ever seen anything like it. They had no idea what to do. In the end, it was Kay who went with them to identify the body.

An hour later, when she returned, she found the family seated silently in the living room. All eyes turned to her. She nodded, shattering their small and desperate hope forever. By eleven o'clock that night the Antolinis were back in the house on Van Ness Place and Concettina lay awaiting attendance in the basement of the Corelli Funeral Home three blocks away.

No one bothered to tell Jack Ward.

At four in the morning Orlando, having not slept at all, climbed out of bed and lit a cigarette, breaking a house rule. Well, he rationalized, he wasn't smoking *in* bed. From his chair by the window, he blew smoke into the night, trying to concentrate on the white stream. Thoughts of his dead sister obliterated everything. Again and again he went over the details.

It had happened in Red Bank. An eyewitness said he saw the car coming down the street, looked away, and then heard the crash. A tree. The police said she'd probably lost control. But how do you suddenly lose control? It made no sense to him. Perhaps she'd been crying, vision blurred, didn't see the turn in the road. But the road was straight! And then a thought he'd cut off earlier, too tired to stop it this time. She'd purposefully rammed the tree. But why? Maybe the whole situation with Ward was too overwhelming. But nothing ever overwhelmed Connie. Flipping the butt through the open window, watching the red ash streak to the grass below, he realized he'd never know.

Connie had broken her neck. A clean break, they'd told Kay. Instantaneous. Not a mark on her. Although her glasses had broken there were no cuts. Untouched. He'd pressed Kay for more details. How had she been found? Head back, resting on the open window ledge. Were her eyes, her mouth, open or closed? Kay didn't know.

Now he couldn't get the picture of Connie, head back, eyes open, mouth open, out of his mind. He saw her as clearly as if he'd been there. Then, like switching the pictures in a stereopticon, she had *closed* eyes and mouth. He tried to replace the image with one of Connie alive. He could not. Minutes later, he could not picture her at all. He could see her body, clothes, hair, but the features were missing as though someone had erased them. It had been this way with the first Silvio and with his friend Warren. In time he was able to see their faces but, in the beginning, for days, weeks, he couldn't recreate their features.

He heard a creaking sound in the hall, then the tread of someone moving down the back stairs. He knew it wasn't his father. The step was too light. He felt terribly lonely and started for the stairs himself.

Opening the door into the kitchen at the bottom of the stairwell, he was shocked to see his mother. She'd been sedated in Sea Girt and had slept on the way home.

She turned, startled. Her pure white hair was held in place on either side by a barrette. She had on nightclothes and her feet were bare. Orlando was not used to seeing his mother this way. They stared at each other for a few seconds.

Orlando was the first to speak. "Why are you up, Mama?" It was the only thing he could think of to say.

She couldn't sleep. The sedative had worn off. She asked if he wanted tea and he nodded.

Together they sat at the kitchen table, something, he realized, they had never done before. Orlando Sr. said kitchen tables were for servants. She blew on her tea, another thing she would not have done in front of her husband.

"Is Papa asleep?"

"Si."

They were silent, looking into their cups as if the liquid would give them their next sentence. Neither wished to speak of Connie. Neither could speak of anything else.

"I know she in heaven," Antonia said.

How could his mother believe in such nonsense! Black magic! But this was not the time to debate her beliefs. "Does that make it easier for you?"

"Che còsa?"

"What I mean is . . . if you believe she's in heaven, doesn't that ease the pain somewhat?" For him, Connie was over, finished.

She began to cry.

He put his hand on his mother's arm, unable to stop his own tears. "Mama," he whispered, "don't."

She took a hanky from her sleeve, wiped her eyes, nose, returned the hanky to its hiding place and sipped her tea.

He wiped his eyes on the sleeve of his robe.

"She so good," Antonia said.

He wondered if his mother knew about Jack Ward.

"Always help others."

It was true.

"Where she going, Orlando? Dove?"

He didn't know what to answer. He had to lie. "I don't know."

"Why you give her you car?"

Was she accusing him? He couldn't be sure. He had to make clear what had happened. "She took it."

"Che còsa?"

"Borrowed it. Without permission," he added.

"Perchè?"

"I don't know why." What was the point in telling her now? "I guess she just wanted to go for a ride."

They looked at each other. He knew the lie made no sense. She knew he was lying.

"I wanted Father say Mass," she said.

"Wanted?"

"Papa say no."

Jesus, couldn't the goddamned tyrant let her have that?

"He don't know she baptize."

"Tell him."

"I no can do that . . . no . . . no . . . it upset him too much."

Better, naturally, to upset herself.

"What dress they pick for Concettina?"

"I don't know."

"I hope blue silk. She look so lovely in that."

How could she talk about a dress, as if Connie were going to a dance or something?

"And pearls. She always love pearls from Grandma Antolini."

He nodded, hoping Toni or Nina had remembered them.

"She must been wearing ring. She always wear it."

It had been his father's diamond baby ring and she wore it on her pinky. Papa gave it to her on her twenty-first birthday. Orlando remembered the party and his eyes filled. He wished his mother would stop.

She did as the door opened and Orlando Sr. stepped into the kitchen. He'd never known his father to use the back stairs. Back stairs, Orlando Sr. said, were for servants. What would his father think of them sitting at the kitchen table? He said nothing. Tonight was different.

Antonia rose as though a king had entered. "Why you up?"

"Because I am. Why are you up?"

She shrugged and led him, like an invalid, to the table. He hesitated for a fraction of a second before he sat down. Without asking, she poured him a cup of tea. He lifted it, sniffed, his nose twitching like a rabbit's. Smelling it was too hot, he returned it to the table.

Orlando noticed his father's shoulders were slumped, head slightly forward. An odd posture for him. He wished desperately that he could think of something to say. His mind was a blank. If only he could console his father. If only, what? He'd win the prize?

Slowly, Orlando Sr. raised his head, eyes level with his son's. "Tell me everything."

"Papa?"

"What did she say to you when she came to you on the beach?"

He glanced at his mother, back to his father.

"Go to bed, Antonia," Orlando Sr. said, without looking at her.

Obediently, she rose, put her cup in the sink and padded across the floor to the door. "Buona notte," she said.

They listened as the stairs creaked beneath her bare feet. Then, in the distance, they heard her bedroom door open and close. Orlando Sr. nodded once, a signal for his son to begin.

Painfully, Orlando recalled his sister's plea that he take her to Ward in Newark. Finished, he looked away, sipping his cold tea, waiting. He hadn't told his father Connie's last words, having just remembered them himself. They echoed now in his brain as though she'd said them only moments ago.

"You should have driven her," his father said.

He was convinced he hadn't heard right. "Papa?"

"You should have driven her."

His bottom lip dropped. He stared dumbly at the man across the table.

"You should have driven her. If you had, she would be alive now."

There it was. Out on the table between them like a signal light. For the last fifteen hours he'd skirted, avoided, run from that thought. But he'd never expected to hear it from his father. He'd been sure if anyone agreed with his decision it would be his father! But he did not. Instead he was accusing him. He must defend himself. "But, Papa, what would you have done if I had?"

The man's eyes narrowed. From his mouth came a sound. "Sssssss." That was all. He left the room, taking the main staircase to the second floor.

Orlando stared down at the empty tea cup, its white china stained brown at the bottom. Sssssssss. The sound lingered, boring through him. It was unfair. All of it. Connie's last words to him. His father's accusation. The hiss. He didn't deserve it. He'd done what had been taught him. A dutiful son. And because of that his sister was dead and his father hated him. More than ever. When his father refused Connie the keys to the Packard, it hadn't occurred to him she might take it anyway. Why then, when Orlando refused her *his* keys, should it have occurred to him? Was he supposed to be a goddamned mindreader?

You're a very cowardly person, Orlando. Sssssssss. Again and again. Again and again.

*   *   *

The Antolinis did not return that year to Sea Girt. After the funeral Nina went back to Montreal. Toni continued life at home with her parents, bored, discontent, permission to work still withheld. Silvio entered his senior year in high school that fall and Orlando returned to Franklin & Marshall and Frances Hess. Kay Chase began her first year of teaching, nothing between Orlando and her resolved, vowing to be more open to the right man, if he came along.

Antonia continued to pray privately, to sneak to confession, receiving penance after penance for her non-attendance at Mass, never mind the reason why! Orlando Sr. returned to his law practice and Roslyn Staten, his mistress of two years. Benita had married after all.

On September 20th Jack Ward left jail, all charges having been dropped. He'd read about Connie's death in the newspaper. Immediately upon his release, he returned to his wife and she happily took him back.

I don't see how my name could be connected with this case. I haven't seen Miss Faithfull in five years.
    —From a statement by Andrew James Peters,
                 June 1931

June 5, 1931
New York, New York

Diana Leffland said she was sorry it was the maid's night off. They would have to have a cold supper as she was absolutely no good in the kitchen.

They had roast beef, very rare, sliced tomatoes with dill and basil, and a bean salad. For dessert there were fresh strawberries and whipped cream. Starr would start a diet the next day.

They sipped espresso afterwards.

"Yes," Royal said, "a nice long rest is what you need, my girl."

"Why are you so good to me?" She felt tears gathering under her lids.

"You need someone, my dear," Diana said. "It was obvious from the first moment I saw you. I don't wish to sound arrogant but we have so much. God wants us to share, don't you think?"

All Starr could do was nod. Even the reference to God was acceptable.

Sixteen

He dreamed about shoes. A recurrent dream. The action was often different but the shoes were a constant.

Orlando's eyes clicked open. Panic and fear pervaded him as always. It took him almost a minute to calm down. Those goddamned shoes.

He hadn't noticed them until he was stopped at a light on Clinton Avenue. Then he glanced at the seat on the passenger side where her bag lay. Next the floor. He screamed. His whole body began to shake. Fortunately, the street was empty and no one heard his scream. Remembering a junk yard not far from there, he made a left at the next light.

And all these years later he still dreamed about shoes. Sometimes they were loafers, sometimes oxfords or spectators but, most often, they were black pumps.

***

August 4, 1927
West Orange, New Jersey
Long Beach, New York

Early in the morning Starr wrote in her diary. First the entry for August 2nd:

247

Stanley's tactics went through and we got $20,000 from old AJP. Five to greedy Rowley. Well, so what? We are all so happy.

Then for August 3rd.

Kept my diet yesterday. Felt I exercised a million billion hours. Lost a few hours.

The few lost hours were between eleven P.M. and two A.M.

For eight weeks Starr had been chaste, without pills and sober. She'd had a drink here and there but never more than two in an evening. But the night before, to celebrate acquisition of the money, she'd joined her family for a drink. And one turned into two, three, four . . . who knew how many. She'd lost count. She'd also blacked out.

During the blackout she verbally attacked Helen, accusing her of knowing always about her relationship with Andrew. She might as well have been sold to him outright! Stanley she called a goddamned ass and accused him of stealing her mother away from her father. She threw things, broke several glasses and awakened Tucker to tell her she was a bore and a dullard. Finally exhausted, at two o'clock she went to her room, somehow undressed and fell onto her bed.

Now, writing in her Mem Book that she'd "lost a few hours," she knew only that she'd been terribly drunk and absolutely did not want to know anything more.

Her hangover was colossal. Her guilt supreme.

The family was planning to drive to Long Beach and have lunch at the Hotel Nassau. It was a long trip but Stanley had heard it was a very posh spot and thought they should celebrate their new wealth in an elegant setting. Yesterday, Starr had been in perfect agreement. Today the thought of driving all the way to New York made her feel dizzy.

They were to leave at nine-thirty. It was seven now. Closing her eyes, she thought of Dr. Jameson-Carr.

What would he feel about her drunkenness last night? He'd be disgusted, revolted, disappointed. Shame crept over her. How had it happened? Why? Should she, when she wrote him, tell the truth? She had promised she would no matter what. But why? It wouldn't happen again. No need to worry him. Perhaps later, after they were together again. In a month she would be sailing with him on the *Franconia*. That was time enough to tell. He would be able to see then that she was sober and whole. She would definitely wait. Dreaming of the approaching voyage she fell back to sleep, feeling quite happy.

The Hotel Nassau was everything Stanley had said. The four Faithfulls sat at a corner table by a window overlooking the boardwalk, beach and ocean. Stanley and Helen seemed in good spirits despite the night before. Tucker, as usual, was sulking.

"Well," Stanley said, "this certainly is an occasion. I guess you could say that we're a well-to-do family."

"I thought the money was mine," said Starr.

Tucker was confused. She'd been told the money was from an old lawsuit involving an auto accident of Stanley's. "How come it's yours if it was Stanley's accident?" she asked.

It irritated Starr that her little sister had to be protected. Look at the horror she'd been exposed to at the same age. "Because I . . ."

"Oh, Starr," Helen said. "Please."

"She's not a child, you know."

"She is."

"I'm not. I'm going to be sixteen."

"Well," said Stanley promptly, "you're not sixteen yet. When you are you can be treated differently."

"I'm going to be sixteen tomorrow."

There was silence at the table as each of them stared at the girl. Clearly, all had forgotten.

"Of course you are." Helen tried to cover. "But I, for one, do not agree with Stanley. Sixteen is not old enough."

"Old enough for what?" Tucker asked.

Helen fussed with her napkin, opened and closed her menu. Stanley cleared his throat.

Starr said, "Old enough to know that your big sister had a . . ."

"Can't we have a nice lunch?" Helen begged.

"Oh, all right," Starr said. "Let's order."

"I want to know," Tucker whined.

"I think the sole almondine sounds nice, don't you?" Stanley said.

Starr looked at him. What a fool he was. "Lovely," she said. "I'll have some clams first."

"Yech," Tucker said. "Raw?"

"Of course."

"How can you?"

"Now your age *is* showing, dear."

"What does age have to do with eating raw clams? Ugh."

"Never mind." Starr had felt the same about raw clams until she saw Jameson-Carr eating them on the *Aurania* cruise.

They gave their order to the waiter and enjoyed the view. It was, without doubt, a perfectly beautiful day. The ocean was truly blue and the lighter blue of the sky was totally empty of clouds. People strolled along the boardwalk carrying small, colorful umbrellas to shield them from the strong sun.

Starr wished she were here with Bill. Or out there with him. Perhaps lying on the white sand, their bodies absorbing the sun. Maybe, with her newly acquired funds, she would offer to take him somewhere—the Riviera, perhaps. What was that remark of Stanley's? They were a well-to-do family. It just showed what an ass he was. Twenty thousand was a nice healthy sum but it certainly wasn't a fortune. Twenty thousand for *one* person was quite nice, however. Just what was Stanley up to now that they'd gotten the money?

"I want to know what you meant by the remark that we were now a well-to-do family, Stanley?"

"Please," Helen said.

"Please yourself. What did it mean?"

"It was just an expression. Not now, Starr."

"Now."

Their appetizers arrived and Starr was momentarily deterred. While they waited for their entrees, she started again.

"I thought the money was to be used for my health."

"It shall, it shall."

She lit a cigarette, inhaling deeply, blowing a large amount of smoke in Stanley's direction. "I'm not well, you know. I'm really not."

Stanley waved the smoke away. "Yes, Bamby, we know, dear."

"What's wrong with you?" Tucker asked. "Seems to me that you just drink too much, that's all."

"Tucker!" Helen was shocked that one of her daughters would say such a thing about the other.

"Well, it's true." She slid down in her chair, lower lip jutting out.

It irritated Starr that no one had given her credit for her eight weeks on the wagon.

"Did it ever occur to you, my dear," she said, "that people drink for a reason?"

"Sure. They like it."

"That's not what I mean. You really are a child, aren't you?"

"Shut up!"

"Shut up yourself."

"Girls, girls." Helen put her hands over her ears.

"Here comes our food," said Stanley brightly.

Tucker stuck out her tongue at Starr. Starr responded in kind. Stanley and Helen tried not to see and fussed over the food.

When the waiter left, Stanley leaned toward Starr. "Don't worry, Bamby," he said softly, "I'm looking into things for you."

"What things?"

"Doctors," he whispered.

"Oh."

It had been agreed months ago that any money realized from this action would be used for Starr's mental health. They'd find a first-rate alienist and Starr would see him as often as needed until she was completely well. Now, once again, Stanley was promising to find someone to help her.

But that day at the Hotel Nassau was the last time mention of a doctor was ever made. And no one, including Starr, seemed to notice or care.

September, 1927
Atlantic Ocean

On the third day of the Whoopee Cruise aboard the *Franconia*, Starr decided Jameson-Carr was the world's shyest man and it was time to take matters into her own hands. For the past two nights they had talked, danced, held hands but nothing more. The ambiguity of their relationship made her terribly anxious and, with no chemicals to smooth her out, help her through, she feared she might break down.

At the end of the evening, when Starr invited the doctor into her cabin for a nightcap, he hesitated a moment or two, then agreed.

She sat on the bed, knees crossed, legs on view. He sat near her on the only chair.

She had no idea how to begin. It was as though she'd never been with a man before. Her palms were damp; her heart pounded.

"Well," he said, "it was a nice party, don't you think?"

She couldn't find her voice and nodded. Then, "Bill, I . . ."

"Now why do you call me Bill?" He took a sip of his drink.

"I don't know." She was glad to be distracted from her purpose. "I suppose I call you Bill because no one else does."

"You just can't help wanting to be different, can you?"

"I guess not." She fell silent.

Jameson-Carr finished his drink. "Well, I should be on my way."

"No," she blurted out. "I mean . . ."

"Yes?"

"Oh, Bill, what's wrong?"

"Wrong?"

Nothing was going according to her script. "I mean, don't you . . .? Look, I know you don't want to . . . on your ship . . . after all . . ."

Jameson-Carr pulled at an earlobe. "I'm not following you, Starr."

She was close to tears. There was nothing left but to

be direct about it. "I know you're shy and I know we're on your boat, your place of work, but I really don't think it would hurt anything for you to kiss me at least." Her words exploded in her ears, making her dizzy.

He stared at her, mouth slightly open, a million thoughts careening through his brain. What a horse's ass he'd been! It had never occurred to him. He'd been too drunk with power . . . too busy playing God! He felt sick to his stomach. He would have to be very diplomatic.

"Starr, dear, I think we must talk."

She waited.

"I think there's been a misunderstanding." He cleared his throat, tugged at his tie. "I'm very fond of you, dear . . . like a father."

She laughed, touched her fingers to her lips.

His discomfort grew. "I wanted to help you. Perhaps my zeal blinded me to other things."

"I love you," she said, her voice hoarse.

"I . . . I love you, too, dear girl. As a friend, a surrogate daughter."

"I love you as a man, a lover." She began to cry.

"Oh, no, no, no," he whispered. "I never meant this to happen."

"Well, it has."

"I'm so sorry."

"But why, Doc? Why don't you want me?"

"It never entered my mind."

"Yes, I know. I'm asking why." Tears fell slowly. "Don't you think I'm attractive? Am I too fat?"

"Fat? What do you mean, fat? You're beautiful, Starr. Lovely. But you literally could be my daughter."

"I'm not."

"I'm much too old for you."

"I've told you I like older men."

"Oh, Lord, yes. I should have realized. I was so involved with helping you I didn't see the forest for the trees, if you know what I mean. And maybe you've confused things, Starr. The patient often falls in love with the doctor and it's not real."

"It's real."

He shook his head, held his palms upward in a gesture of despair. "I feel terrible. I should have foreseen . . . well, it'll work out."

"How? Will I die tonight? That's the only way it could work out." She walked to the small table where the gin bottle stood and reached for it.

"Don't." He grabbed her wrist.

"Why the hell not?"

"Because one thing has nothing to do with the other."

"The hell it doesn't." She tried to free her arm.

"You mean," he said, holding tight, "the only reason you stopped drinking, stopped your . . . dissipating, was because you confused your feelings for me?"

"Oh, Christ. Let go."

He did.

She uncorked the bottle and poured a full tumbler. "Here's mud in your eye," she said, raising the glass high.

Jameson-Carr watched as she drank half the liquid. "You're making a terrible mistake."

"No, sir. It seems I already made a terrible mistake. This is the first smart thing I've done since June." She drank again.

"If you go back to your old way of life you'll be dead in no time."

"So what?"

"Starr, don't be a fool."

"I'm not. I was. I wish you'd go now."

"Please, Starr. I can't leave you like this."

She finished her drink, poured another. "Get the hell out."

It was clear there was nothing more he could do tonight. Tomorrow he'd try again. "I'm so sorry."

"Thanks." She turned her back.

When he was gone she finished her second drink and felt drunk almost immediately. It was a good feeling. After her third drink she left her cabin.

The day before the *Franconia* docked Starr barged into Jameson-Carr's cabin. He lay on his bunk, feet hanging over the end.

"What the hell?" He sat up as she slammed open the door.

"You," she said, swaying drunkenly near his bunk.

Though he'd tried they hadn't spoken since the night of her confession. And for days he'd watched her make a fool of herself, watched her pawed by one man after another, listened to the scathing remarks from crew and passengers. It pained him but there was nothing he could do. Looking at her now he felt a kind of revulsion and was ashamed of himself for the feeling.

"You louse." She fell to her knees and began to cry. "I love you, I love you. Please, oh please, Bill, I'll do anything you want."

"I want you to behave," he said gently, helping her up.

"Will you love me then? Will you make love to me, marry me?"

He couldn't lie. "No."

"Doc, please. I may be young chronologically but I'm very mature . . . really."

How could he say it wasn't just her age? How could he tell her she was much too disturbed for a life partner. Not that he wanted a life partner. "I'm not the marrying kind."

"All right. Okay. You don't have to marry me. I don't care what people say, you know that. Just let me be with you."

Perhaps honesty was the best policy. It would be cruel but in the end it might be better, hurt less. "Starr, listen. I hate to say this to you but I feel I must. I cannot, do not want to, be involved with you romantically. It's not only your age. I'm just not interested in you. You don't appeal to me that way. Not now. Not ever. It's no use. I'm sorry."

"I tried so hard."

"Yes, I know. But . . . you're just not for me."

"Give me another chance, Doc."

"It has nothing to do with chances."

She stumbled toward the door. "I'll straighten out. You'll change your mind. Tomorrow. I'll start tomorrow."

The next day, walking down the gangplank, her hangover drumming through her body, Starr swore to herself that somehow, some way, she would make Dr. George Jameson-Carr love her. And no matter what he said or did, Starr pursued her romantic fantasies of him until the end of her life, driving them both nearly mad.

February 16, 1928
Newark, New Jersey

The weekend of February 16, 17, 18 was not particularly special. Except to Frances Hess. To her it was the biggest event of the new year, except perhaps for the execution of Ruth Snyder for the murder of her husband. That had created quite a sensation, the papers printing the photograph of Snyder in the chair. But it wasn't Fran's event. This was definitely hers. She was thrilled. And terrified.

When Orlando first suggested it, her immediate reaction was pure joy. If he was prepared to have her meet his family it meant he was very serious. She'd never before believed he was. Not until he invited her to Van Ness Place. But after her initial excitement she began to droop inside. How in the world would she be able to face Orlando's father knowing that he knew? And it wasn't just that. These were rich, fancy people. Servants. Education. Who was she? What did she know? She didn't voice these particular fears to Orlando, wanting to appear cheerful, excited and grateful, wanting always to be the light in what she perceived as his *dark despair*. He was a brooder. No question. But he was *so* intelligent. And an artist. A writer. A musician. That's the way they were. It was her job to lighten things for him, not to burden him with her stupid problems, her fears. She kept her anxiety about the weekend in New Jersey strictly to herself. Where it belonged.

Now, bouncing along on the road, Fran wished she were anywhere but here. Her stomach churned and jounced. Two weeks before, about to go on stage at the Armstrong Follies, she hadn't been this nervous. She smiled, remembering her success. Everyone said she was absolutely hysterical, as funny as Fanny Brice. Then her smile faded, thinking of the conversation she'd had with Orlando later that night.

"I feel like a queen."

"You mean like a star."

"Yes. Oh, Orr, it was such fun. I loved it. Is that why you like to play in the band?"

"Is what why?"

"The people. The laughter, the applause."

"If they laugh I'm in trouble." He smiled, dimples showing.

"The applause then?"

"No. It's the thing itself. The music."

"I guess it's different. I could do it again and again. Every night of my life." She felt so high she thought she might spin right off the front porch. "You know Burton Howe, the drama teacher at the high school? You met him. Well, he said I have *real* talent. He said I should try it professionally."

"Burton Howe is a fairy."

"So?"

"So plenty."

"I don't see what Burton Howe's being a fairy has to do with his thoughts on my talent."

"You wouldn't." Pouting.

She decided to ignore this, feeling too wonderful to be dragged down by something so stupid. "Anyway, there were others who said how good I was and that I should go to New York."

He laughed. Snorted.

"What's so funny?"

"Bunch of hicks. Look, Fran, you were terrific, really good. You stole the show." He patted her hand. "But Armstrong Follies isn't the Ziegfeld Follies."

"I know that. But maybe if I went to New York I . . ."

"Do you know how many kids go to New York every year? Every day? What would you do for money? Where would you live? Who'd take care of you?"

"I'd take care of myself."

"Fran, you've never been on your own in your life. You live with your parents, for God's sake!"

"That doesn't mean I couldn't try."

"Listen, you don't know what you're talking about. You're a small-town girl and for Lancaster you've got a lot of talent. But not for New York. Take my word for it."

Her high was winding down. "What's wrong with trying?"

"You'd just be disappointed. And hurt. I don't want anything to hurt you. Besides, you're too good, too sweet, for show business. You have to be tough."

"I'm tough," she said lamely.

"Oh yes, very tough." He stroked her hair, kissed her eyes.

The curtain was slowly but definitely closing on her dream. He was probably right. The thought of being alone in New York was scary. And she could imagine how her father would react! It was all too complicated, too impossible.

"You're my little girl," Orlando said, "not some tough Broadway type." He opened his arms and she curled up against his chest. Dream over.

She looked at him now, jaw set, as he skillfully maneuvered the car over the bumpy road. Definitely a *dreamboat*, as the girls at the office called him. Being with him was a lot more important than being an actress. Too bad she couldn't have both but that was out of the question. Still, she loved making people laugh. Burton Howe said it was an art. The idea that she had an *art* of her own simply thrilled her. But it was enough to know that. She didn't have to do anything about it.

"We're almost there," said Orlando.

The lump in her throat seemed to drop to her stomach and ricochet back up.

He glanced sideways. Fran stared straight ahead. She was lovely. He prayed his father wouldn't look too much beyond that. Not that Orlando was ashamed of her. But she wasn't sophisticated like Kay. Nor as educated. His mother would like her. And Toni. Silvio? Well, who cared? And Connie would—Jesus. He was always doing that. Forgetting she was dead. It had been six months already. But the pain was still there. And the guilt. If only, if only, if only. He mustn't start that. The important thing now was to concentrate on Fran and the weekend ahead. If his father liked her he would formally ask her to marry him. And if his father didn't? Would he just give her up? Like that? Of course Orlando Sr. would object to him marrying anyone before he'd graduated from law school. The thought of that, of becoming a lawyer, made him feel sick, as always. He turned into Van Ness Place, the security guards at the corners waving to him.

Fran was astounded. "Why are they there?"

"To guard the street."

"From what?"

"Undesirables."

"Oh." Like me, she thought.

They pulled up in front of the big gray and white house. This was it. No getting out of it now. The house, though impressive, wasn't as big as Fran had imagined it. Nothing could have been. Orlando came around and opened her door. When she stepped out onto the sidewalk, one knee buckled and she started to fall. Orlando caught her.

"Jesus," he said.

They both hoped no one was watching.

"Are you all right?"

"I guess my leg must have fallen asleep. Sorry."

"Watch it."

She could have killed him. *Watch it!* Good God. Instead of snapping at him, she asked who lived in the larger house across the street.

"People by the name of Shiffenhauser." He thought of Ruth. Her inexplicable suicide the year before still haunted him. Poor, dear Ruth. "Are you ready?"

She would never be ready. "Yes."

They sat in the main living room. The one with the piano. The one that had remained closed for two years after the first Silvio's death. Orlando Sr. sat in his large wing chair, Antonia in her smaller one, a table and lamp separating them. Orlando, Fran and Toni occupied the tufted couch. Silvio was on a straight chair, his flesh spilling over the seat.

Fortunately, Orlando was regaling his parents with college stories because Fran felt she had absolutely nothing to say. She also felt Orlando Sr.'s eyes were fastened on her. She hoped and prayed she would never be left alone with Mr. Antolini. He terrified her. Not that he hadn't been nice, polite, charming, in fact. But something about those eyes made her feel strange. Almost cold. Mrs. Antolini seemed nice, warm, though she barely spoke. Toni, the small sister, was another story. Fran was sure the woman hated her. She could feel her now, sitting next to her, their haunches just touching, sending rays of dislike into Fran's body. She probably thought Fran wasn't good enough for baby brother. And speaking of baby brothers, the huge oaf on the straight chair didn't even have the decency to disguise his gawking. He stared at her openly, mouth hanging slack. For the first time in her life Fran wished she drank but knew that this was not the time to start.

Dolce announced dinner. They rose, Orlando Sr. offering his arm to Fran. She took it, smiling up at him. He nodded his head slightly and they led the way into the dining room. She prayed her knees wouldn't buckle.

Fran sat at Orlando Sr.'s right, across from Mrs. Antolini. Silvio was to her right, Toni across from him, and Orlando at the opposite end from his father. A small dish of thin brown things and shiny red things was set before her. She watched the father and, following his cue, popped a brown thing into her mouth. She chewed. Never in her life had she tasted anything so salty. And prickly. Quickly, she washed it down with water.

"Do you like anchovies, Miss Hess?" Orlando Sr. asked.

"I love them," she said, dying of thirst.

"Good."

She tried the shiny red thing, a pimento. It looked like a red pepper but the texture was silkier. She liked it.

"I am delighted that you are a connoisseur of the anchovy, Miss Hess, but one cannot love an inanimate object." Orlando Sr. gave what passed for a smile.

Orr thought, Jesus Christ!

Fran smiled. "One can if one wants to," she said.

"I beg your pardon?"

"That's all right," said Fran and went back to her anchovies.

He stared at the pretty girl for a moment, then glanced up at his son who was grinning. Quickly, the grin faded.

The second course was soup. Orlando had warned Fran there would be a great deal of food and she hadn't eaten anything but a bite of cheese all day. She was ravenous. She recalled reading somewhere, however, that a lady always leaves something on her plate. Well, too late for the first course. She'd devoured it completely. She decided the advice probably did not apply to soup.

"This is delicious," she said.

"Gracia," Mrs. Antolini replied.

"Did you make it?"

"Si."

Fran was surprised. What were the servants for?

"Mama likes to do some of the cooking," Orlando explained.

"Does your mother do the cooking, Miss Hess?"

She smiled. "Most of the time. But sometimes I do."

"And are you proficient at cooking?" Orlando Sr. spooned his soup in short brief movements.

"Very."

"What business is your father engaged in, Miss Hess?"

Out of nowhere. She had wondered when it would come.

Orlando thought, goddamn bastard. He'd already told him.

"My father is in the cigar business. He manages the office in a cigar factory."

"I see."

She gave him her most gorgeous smile, forcing herself to look directly into his eyes.

He did not smile back, interrupted by the arrival of the pasta.

This was the course she dreaded. Orlando had given her lessons on twirling the spaghetti on the fork, using the plate for support. Only Americans and peasants used a spoon, he told her. When she pointed out that she was an American, he still insisted she learn the proper way. She wasn't bad at it but she'd never be an expert. Watching Orlando Sr. twirl and whirl, no ends hanging, her heart sank. Oh well. She dove into the heaping pile of spaghetti, dripping in heavy brownish sauce, and began to twist. Approaching the end, she looked up and saw that the entire family was watching her. There wasn't a sound. Carefully, lifting her fork to her mouth, she saw she'd done it perfectly. The last end was on top. She mustn't hurry though she could see it beginning to slide. Mouth open, fork in. She made it. Everyone returned to their own plates.

Having conquered the pasta, Fran felt she was home free. At least as far as food was concerned. The next course was meat. Veal scallopini, peas, sliced zucchini. The veal was delicious, tender and rich with Marsala. Should she leave a small piece on her plate? As she cut into her veal, worrying this question, her hand slipped. Although she was looking down, she knew exactly where the peas flew as the knife whacked them away like tiny green tennis balls. There was dead silence. She couldn't look up. Then suddenly, from her right, came a great guffaw and she felt young Silvio's bulk rub against her leg as he shook up and down with laughter. Her face was on fire. How long could she keep staring at the veal and the few remaining peas? Eventually, she would have to raise her head. Silvio continued to snort and gasp. She must look up, apologize. She thought she could hear her neck creaking as, bit by painful bit, she turned to the man on her left.

He sat, erect as always, staring straight ahead. On his cheek was a greasy mark left by a buttered pea and from his mustache a tiny bit of pea skin hung precariously over his lip. Another pea nestled at the V of his vest and still more greasy spots dotted his jacket.

Fran opened her mouth but nothing came out. She suppressed her instinct to pluck the pea skin from his mustache, to dab at the marks with her napkin. Silvio tried to stifle his laughter but failed. Fran watched him run from the room. Why didn't Orlando say something? Well, *she* must.

"I'm . . . I'm so sorry," she said.

There was no response. Not even a turn of the head. Mr. Antolini slowly drew his napkin across the grease spot on his face, then delicately wiped at his mustache, removing the pea skin. The pea peeking from his vest remained as he returned to the business of eating his dinner. Fran turned to look at Orlando. He was looking at his plate. She glanced across the table at Mrs. Antolini who was just raising her eyes to meet Fran's. Instantly Mrs. Antolini smiled, warm, consoling. Fran smiled back, though she wanted to die, disappear, evaporate.

Salad, dessert and coffee followed. The conversation went from politics to books to the new cars. Fran did not participate. When dinner was over, and they all headed back toward the living room, Fran excused herself and went to her room.

Flinging herself across the bed, she sobbed. Her life was over. Nothing so horrible had ever happened to her. Orlando Sr. knowing she'd had intercourse with his son was not as humiliating as this. It could, she knew, have happened to anyone but it did not. It had happened to

her. There was no way now that Orlando would marry
her. How could he marry a girl who couldn't even control
her peas?

There was a knock at the door. She stiffened. What
now? The knock came again, soft, timid. She couldn't pretend she didn't hear. She wiped her face with her hands.

"Yes?" Her voice quavered.

"It's Mama."

Mama. Immediately, Fran began to cry again. "Come
in," she croaked.

Mrs. Antolini entered, and Fran, hands covering her
mouth and nose, watched her cross the room to join Fran
on the bed. She said nothing but put both arms around
Fran, gently lowering the young woman's head against her
mammoth breasts. She stroked her short hair, slowly rock-
ing her back and forth.

Fran bawled without restraint. The combination of
her shame and the soft security of her present position
destroyed her defenses. When there were no more tears,
she slowly raised her head.

"You feel better?"

Fran nodded. It *was* better. Not good, but better.

"You not worry."

"Oh, but it was so aw-ful." She thought she might
start all over but managed to control herself.

"Ahhch." Antonia waved her hand. "Not so bad."

"Terrible. Nothing like that has ever happened to me
before."

"These things happen. I tell you story." And she recalled how Orlando Sr. had fallen from his horse in front
of her balcony. When she finished Fran was smiling.

"He must have been so embarrassed."

"You bet." Now *she* smiled.

"But how can I ever face him, Mrs. Antolini? When I
think of that pea skin in his mustache. Oh, God."

Mrs. Antolini's smile spread. Then, from way back in
her throat, came a strange sound which grew to a giggle
and finally became an outright laugh. Fran stared. She
was really laughing now, her eyes squeezed shut, her body
bouncing. Fran began to laugh too.

"Ooooh, ooooh," Mrs. Antolini cried and pointed to a
spot above her lip.

The two women screamed with laughter, poking and

jabbing at each other. When Antonia had nearly regained control she suddenly remembered the pea caught in his vest. Pointing to the center of her chest she began to laugh all over again, Fran with her.

Their howls and shrieks were so loud neither of them heard the knock at the door. But Orlando, outside, heard them. After his third attempt failed to get their attention, he opened the door.

There were his mother and his girl, flat on their backs on the bed, arms flying, feet tapping and rapping as though both were having some sort of convulsion.

"What's going on?" He was nonplussed.

The laughter died as they slowly raised their heads.

"Ooooh, Orlando," Antonia said, catching her breath.

"Ooooh, Orlando," said Fran, feeling wonderful.

"What's so funny?" He felt left out.

The two women glanced at each other, then quickly away, fearful they would start again.

Antonia removed her glasses and wiped her eyes with a white lace handkerchief.

"What's so funny?"

"Niente, niente," his mother said.

"Must be something." Now he felt jealous.

Antonia rose, pulled down her dress which had worked its way up to expose her plump knees, and patted her son on the cheek. "You got nice girl, Orlando. Nice girl." She turned and smiled at Fran before exiting, leaving the door wide open.

Orlando was pleased his mother liked Fran. He knew she'd never taken to Kay.

"What was so funny?"

She would be damned if she'd tell him after all the comfort and help he'd given her! "It doesn't matter."

"Okay. The hell with it." He started to leave.

"Oh, thanks. Thanks a lot." Her embarrassment and horror began to return.

"Well, why can't you tell me what you were laughing at?"

"I can't explain it. Orr," she said, a plaintive sound in her voice, "how am I going to face your father?"

"You look awful. Your eye stuff is all smeared."

Glancing in the mirror above the large chest, she saw

that black marks streaked her face. "Maybe we should go back to Lancaster tonight."

"Don't be dumb. Go fix your face and come downstairs."

"I can't. I can't face him."

Orlando walked over to her, kissed her gently on the mouth. "You can do anything. It'll be all right. He's not a monster, you know."

"What'll I say?"

"Nothing. I mean, just pretend that nothing happened. Trust me."

She knew she had no choice.

"I love you, Fran."

"I love you."

He hugged her. "I'll wait and we'll go down together."

She was surprised and pleased. At last Orlando was behaving like a man. Uncomfortable with the implications of that thought, she quickly put it aside, grabbed her makeup case and went to the bathroom to repair her face.

Only Mr. and Mrs. Antolini were in the living room listening to Caruso sing "Cielo E Mar" from *La Gioconda*. Orlando and Fran seated themselves on the sofa and waited for the record to end.

The music pained Orlando. But Fran liked it. She thought of the Chautauqua so many years ago.

"That was lovely," she said when it ended, not realizing she was beginning a conversation.

"You like the opera, Miss Hess?"

"Well, I don't know much about it. In fact, I don't know anything about it. But I like what I just heard."

"Would you like to hear more?"

"Yes, I would."

As Orlando Sr. was about to rise, his son interrupted his movement.

"I have something to say."

All three turned toward him.

"I . . . Fran and I are going to be married."

Silence.

"Quando?"

"Next year, in the spring."

Fran couldn't believe what she was hearing.

"You are engaged?"

"Well, we will be."

"Quando?"

"Soon." He took Fran's hand.

The senior Antolinis rose and came toward Fran. Orlando jumped to his feet, pulling Fran with him.

First Antonia kissed her on both cheeks and then Orlando Sr. did the same. His mustache tickled her cheek. When he pulled away, Fran could see that his eyes were moist.

Pleased, Orlando watched the scene. Only after they all were seated again, discussing the details of the engagement, did he realize what he'd done. He almost laughed out loud. Clearly, he would go to any length to avoid listening to the opera. He would even get married!

Later that night Orlando and Fran sat alone in the living room. She was too pleased about their marriage plans to be really angry with Orlando for springing it on her that way. But she thought she should mention it. "Why didn't you ask me?"

"Ask you what?"

"To marry you, of course."

"Did you expect me to get down on one knee and all that baloney?"

"No. But you could have *asked* me. How do you know I *want* to marry you?"

"Don't you?"

"That's not the point."

"This is the point." He kissed her. It occurred to him to take her right there, an exciting idea, although impossible.

"You're not taking me seriously, Orr. You just took me for granted. I think you're very conceited." Her annoyance was growing as they talked.

"Conceited because I know you love me?"

"No, because you just assumed I'd marry you."

"Well, you're going to, aren't you? I didn't hear you jumping up and denying it."

"Oh, Orr."

"Oh, Orr," he mimicked, kissing her again, placing his hand on her round full breast.

"No," she said. "I think I should go to bed."

"All right."

Walking up the red-carpeted staircase, his arm around her waist, he whispered, "Aren't you happy about it, Fran? Marrying me?"

"Yes, sure. It just isn't the way I imagined it."

"What isn't?"

"Your lack of proposal."

They stood in front of her door, across the hall from his parents' room.

"You're so conventional," he said.

"I guess."

"This is 1928, not the dark ages."

"It just would have been nice. It was such a shock."

"I thought you were so modern."

"I didn't know announcing your engagement to your parents before asking the girl was being modern."

"Well, it is."

"I guess I'm old-fashioned then."

"I hope to tell you. I'm going to bed."

"Go fly a kite!"

"Nerts!"

The rest of the weekend went smoothly. Everyone was in good spirits. On Saturday Mr. Antolini had even sent Orlando and Fran to his jeweler to pick out an engagement ring.

Now, driving back to Lancaster, Orlando wondered for the first time why his father had been so accepting of his prospective marriage. Why had he said nothing about school? And what about Fran? Had he had no reservations about her? It occurred to him then, also for the first time, that his father simply didn't give a damn what he did.

It was the truth.

March 12, 1928
Newark, New Jersey

DEAR ORLANDO,

This is a very difficult letter for me to write. I should have done it when I first discovered the truth. My anger, I believe, was at its peak then although it has crested each time I've received a letter from you.

You dare to ask my opinion of *John Brown's Body* as though nothing has changed! You wish to discuss the symbolism in *Marco Millions* as if time had stood still! You mention Gershwin, oh so cavalierly! What kind of a monster are you?

On February 20th, I decided to drop in, on my way home from school, to see your family. Only your mother and Toni were at home. After a few minutes of idle chit-chat, your mother made a reference to the fact that you had been home the previous weekend. At first I could not believe that you had been in Newark and had not called me. Then, it all became clear. Toni said that you had brought a girl with you. Frances Hess. Poor Toni! She was clearly embarrassed. Then it came out that you were ENGAGED. How could you? How could you continue to write me in the same old way? How could you let me find out from your sister? Have you any idea how humiliating it was? Even your mother (though I know she's never really liked me) was overwhelmed by embarrassment.

When I got home that afternoon I decided to call you, then changed my mind, deciding to wait for your letter of explanation. It never came. Oh, yes, letters came. Three to be exact. And no mention of Frances Hess in any of them. No mention of an engagement. They were letters designed to make me believe that everything was copacetic. How could you?

What is in your head? What are you planning? I understand that your wedding is not to take place until next spring. Did you plan to keep me in the dark until then?

I know we have never spoken of love. Nor have we made promises to each other. However, I thought (wrongly, I see now) that we were friends. I cannot believe you would treat even a casual acquaintance in such a shoddy fashion.

I don't want you to think that my reaction to the news of your engagement is because of any romantic feelings I have, or had, for you. It definitely is not. I am angry only because I am a human being who has been your friend for many years and feel I deserve better treatment. Even if you have no respect for me, Orlando, I have respect for myself. And that respect leads me to choose friends who care for me and who have consideration for my feelings. You, obviously, do not. Therefore, I see no reason to continue in any type of relationship with you. You are not worthy of my consideration. How I pity Frances Hess! Clearly, she has no idea what an inconsiderate, selfish man she will be marrying.

Your past behavior indicates you have no interest in me but, just for the record, I think I should tell you that I have met a very wonderful man, Blair Martin, who has asked me to marry him. He is kind, considerate and loyal. Three virtues which you lack entirely.

Under separate cover I am returning *Death Comes for the Archbishop* and *Early Autumn*.

Sincerely,
KAY CHASE

Orlando chose to handle Kay's letter by crumpling it up and throwing it into his wastebasket.

On May 10th he received an announcement.

Dr. & Mrs. Wendell Chase
announce the marriage
of their daughter
Kathleen
to
Blair Martin
on
May 1, 1928

This he tore into many pieces. Then he went to take his final exam in Philosophy.

I am satisfied that my former wife, Mrs. Faithfull, and her friends will do everything within their power to discover the cause of my daughter's death. I had not seen her in several years and shall not intrude myself at this time. As any father would do, I have come to New York for her funeral.

—From a statement by
Frank W. Wyman, June 10, 1931

June 5, 1931
New York, New York

After dinner they sat in the living room. The furniture was all black velvet. Starr ran a hand over the arm of her chair, enjoying the touch of the material as she enjoyed the sound of Beethoven emanating from the victrola in the corner.

When the music ended, after asking if there was anything she wanted, Royal suggested she go to bed and get some sleep.

Her room was pink. The bed a four-poster with a pink satin quilt, the curtains pink ruffled chiffon. Inside, her soul felt pink and she knew she would sleep without the aid of her Veronal which was tucked securely away in her bag.

Both Royal and Diana kissed her on the cheek before they left.

She changed into the white satin nightgown Diana had lent her. The material felt cool, comforting against her skin.

She closed her eyes, head on a goosedown pillow. All thoughts of ending her life had vanished.

Seventeen

August 6, 1977
Orange, New Jersey

It suddenly occurred to him that if his mother were alive she'd be over a hundred years old. So odd. From time to time, he still missed her. Then other times he couldn't remember her face, touch, smell. Now, this moment, he saw her as she was in her sixties. Hair white, heavy, wearing those round steel-framed glasses. And he? How old was he? Late twenties. And it was *after*. Of course it was. That's what had been so awful, so frightening about that moment with her.

She had actually asked him if he had a secret! How had she known? Something gnaws at you, chews on you inside, she'd said in Italian. He wanted to run. Then, in the next instant, he almost told her. The closest he'd ever come with anyone. What he had done instead was to cry. But that hadn't alarmed her. She simply stroked his hair and said he was her poor, sad boy and sent him, as always, home to his wife.

———

October 25, 1928
New York, New York

A chicken in every pot, a car in every garage and a hive on every inch of my skin! Orlando slammed his fist into the pillow. The itching was driving him crazy. It started three days ago. This was the third night.

Yesterday he had gone to the infirmary and the doctor had given him some pink liquid stuff to put on them. Hives, he said, could come from an allergy or be psychologically caused but there was no real cure. They would just go away by themselves. Orlando sank into his Morris chair near the window. Taking the pink medicine and some cotton, he began to cover the huge, ugly lumps on his legs. He was naked, unable to stand any clothes touching his body. He capped the bottle, threw the cotton in his basket with the hundreds of other pink balls, and looked around the room. His law books lay scattered about, opened, unopened. Papers were strewn carelessly. He'd missed two days of classes already and if these things didn't clear up he'd miss tomorrow as well. The idea of falling behind terrified him. But there was no way he could concentrate. It took everything he had to keep from scratching.

"Antolini? You in there?" A sharp rapping accompanied the voice.

"What do you want?" He recognized the voice. It was Rogers Blake, a third-year man.

"I want to come in. Open up, kiddo."

Kiddo. Jesus. He scanned the room for his shorts. Not finding them he went to his bureau and got a fresh pair. "Just a minute." He'd never gone in for the nudity thing with the boys. "What is it?" He opened the door a crack.

"I want to come in, kiddo."

"Well, look, Blake, I'm really not feeling too well and . . ."

"Yeah, I know. That's why I want to come in."

"Oh." He opened the door and Blake entered.

"Je-sus Christ," he said, looking Orlando up and down.

"Sorry I couldn't cover up and spare you but I can't take the contact."

"Je-sus Christ," Blake said again.

Orlando wanted to punch the tall blond. Instead, he offered him a seat.

Blake continued to stand and stare. "That is enough to make a person upchuck."

"Thanks very much."

"I mean!" He whistled.

Orlando clenched his teeth, wishing he'd put on his robe. Anything was better than having this jerk staring at him as though he were a freak.

Blake whistled again.

"Listen, Blake, if you don't mind."

"Have you seen the doc?"

"Yes. He gave me that stuff."

"What did he say it was from?"

"He didn't know." Orlando picked up an Old Gold from his desk and lit it. What the hell was Blake after, anyway?

"Listen, Antolini, have you ever heard of Sigmund Freud?" His eyes blinked rapidly as he waited for an answer.

Orlando blew smoke in Blake's direction. "Of course."

"Well, I'll bet you dollars to doughnuts that this condition is psychological."

The second time he'd heard that.

"You see, you're probably repressing something and it's coming out that way." He turned his nose up as though he were smelling something unpleasant. "Probably something to do with your libido. It usually is."

"Really?" He would gladly have strangled him.

"Yes. For instance, is there somebody you want to lay who you shouldn't be wanting to lay?" His smile was supercilious.

Orlando, who'd never had a physical fight in his life, felt himself growing closer to violence every moment.

"Ahh! I've hit on something, haven't I, kiddo?"

"Look, I . . ." He started to scratch.

"Your lips twitched."

"What?"

"Your lips twitched. And you're scratching."

"I itch."

"But why?"

"Why? Because I do. That's what hives do . . . they itch."

"Yes, I know that, kiddo, but why *now*? Why, when I suggested to you that there was someone you wanted to lay that you shouldn't be thinking about laying, did your lips twitch and your hives begin to itch?" Blake raised a thin eyebrow and crossed his arms, chin tilted upward. "Hmmm? Hmmm?"

"My hives always itch, Blake." Would it be possible to get under that pointed, raised chin with one clean punch?

"And your lips? Do they always twitch?" Blake took a pair of tortoise-shell glasses from his breast pocket, shook them open in one motion and slid them on.

Orlando stubbed out his cigarette and fell into his chair. "Just what is it you want?"

"I want to help you." He was shocked that Orlando hadn't realized that.

"I think," said Orlando wearily, "the best way you can help me is to leave me alone." He shouldn't insult Blake. He was quite important at Columbia Law. But right that moment, itching the way he did, he really didn't give a damn.

Blake sat down on the end of the bed, crossing one long leg over the other. "It's a good thing I can understand that your hostility isn't really meant for me, Antolini. Now who is it that you're so angry with? Hmmm?" He removed the glasses and dangled them over his knees as he waited for a reply.

Orlando saw it was hopeless. Blake was not going to leave. "What makes you so knowledgeable?" It was the nicest way he could put it.

Blake leaned forward, reinstated his glasses and, in a low, conspiratorial whisper, said, "I have an alienist of my own."

"What?"

"A doctor. He's a brilliant man. Heinrich."

"You mean you're being psychoanalyzed?"

"Exactly. So you see, Antolini, I know a great deal about the mind. The id. The libido. These hives of yours are the manifestation of some inner conflict. Repression, as I've already suggested. If it's not sexual, then perhaps some other aggression. Hmmm?"

The hives transcended the itching and began to burn. Orlando leapt from his chair and paced. He wanted to scream, tear off his skin, push Blake's head through a wall.

"Just look at how agitated you are."

He whirled toward Blake, hands in front of him in two clenched fists. "Jesus fucking Christ, Blake! Don't you understand? I'm going crazy from this goddamn itching. I don't give a good goddamn about my libido or my id."

"Well, you should. If you could get to the bottom of it, find out what's causing the hives, they'd go away. Like that." He snapped two long bony fingers.

"I don't *know* what's causing them."

"I'm aware of that, Antolini. That's what we're trying to get at," he said coolly.

We're. We're trying to get at! Orlando wanted to kill.

"All right, for the moment let's put aside the sexual possibility. What's your relationship with your mother like?"

"My mother? What the hell does my mother have to do with my goddamn hives?"

"Perhaps everything. Why does it upset you so much when I mention her?" He removed the glasses.

"It's just that I . . . listen, I think you'd better go."

Smiling, head tilted to one side, he said, "And *I* think we're getting somewhere, kiddo."

"Stop calling me kiddo."

Eyebrow arched. "Oh? Does that disturb you? I see. Are you by any chance the baby in your family?"

"No. I want to get some sleep."

"What's your relationship like with your father?"

"I don't have a father. He's dead."

The glasses went back on. "Oh, now that's really interesting, Antolini. I happen to know that you *do* have a father. He's done business with mine. So, it has to do with your father, does it. Very inter-est-ing." Blake rocked back and forth, ecstatic. "Why did you say your father was dead? Hmmm?"

"To get you the hell off my back."

"You didn't say your mother was dead."

"I didn't think of it then. Please. I feel sick. I want to lie down."

"An excellent idea." Blake jumped up from the bed. "You lie down and I'll sit over here, behind you."

"What?"

"Go on, lie down."

"I want to lie down alone."

"I wasn't suggesting that I lie down *with* you, kiddo."

"Would you please get the hell out of my room?"

"Why do you hate your father?"

Orlando threw the punch. Blake ducked, throwing him off balance. He slammed into the wall and slid to the floor. "I'm getting out," he muttered sitting there in a heap.

"Getting out? Out of where?"

"Out of this dump."

"What dump?"

"*This* dump. This school. This goddamn law school." He jumped up, pushed past Blake and grabbed a shirt and pants from his wardrobe.

When he was dressed, shirt hanging out over his pants, he pulled open his door and ran down the hall, leaving Blake, open-mouthed, in his room.

The phone was on the first floor and for once it was unoccupied. After three rings his father answered.

He took a deep breath. "Papa? I'm leaving Columbia."

There was silence on the other end.

"Papa? Did you hear me? I'm leaving Columbia Law. I can't be a lawyer. I hate it. I hate it, Papa. I hate it."

Still more silence.

"Jesus, will you say something?" Sweat dotted his cheeks, forehead. He'd never spoken this way to his father.

"What is it you wish me to say?"

"Something. Anything."

"I am not surprised. When will you be home?"

"Tomorrow. I'm sorry I can't be a lawyer, Papa, but I just can't."

"I never thought you would be."

"Then why did . . .?"

"Goodbye." Click.

Orlando stood, receiver in hand, staring. When his legs began to shake he hung up the phone. Slowly, he climbed the stairs to his room. Blake was gone. He locked the door behind him and dropped onto his bed. His whole body was shaking. He couldn't believe he'd done it, ended it, spoken to his father that way. It was more clear than ever that his father didn't give a damn about him. But the relief of never having to read one of those lousy law books again obliterated that hurt. Anyway, he'd make it up to his father. He'd get a job, get married, write a great novel. When he was famous his father would forgive him, be proud of him.

He lay that way, face down, for a long time. More than an hour passed before he realized that he didn't itch. Sitting up, he held out his arms, pushed up a sleeve. The hives had gone down! He stood, dropped his pants. The hives were small red marks now. He could hardly believe it. He thought of Blake! Christ! Blake had been right. For a moment it made him mad and then he had to smile. If it hadn't been for that son of a bitch—well, what the hell!

In the morning he packed his suitcases, made arrangements to have his trunk sent and left Columbia Law School forever. He felt wonderful. Even the prospect of facing his father couldn't dampen his spirits. Before leaving New York, he stopped at a flower shop and sent a huge bouquet of roses to Rogers Blake. On the card he wrote:

DEAR ROG,
My libido's swell and my id is tops. Thanks.

ORR

He wondered what Blake would make of that.

October 30, 1928
London, England

Before going to sleep in her room at the Hotel Cecil, Starr wrote in her diary.

Oct. 29. I have experienced every sensation life holds, and if L. C. does not meet me soon, I have nothing to live for.

Awakening early in the morning, she lay on her back staring at the carved edges of the ceiling. Her first thought was Lawrence Crawford. He'd been her first thought every day since she met him aboard the S.S. *Tuscania*, three weeks before. Tall, thin, dark with wonderful large eyes, he had a slightly crooked front tooth which she found enchanting. He was, of course, married. They always were. A year before she'd written in her diary: "Met H. M. today. What a man. He hit me right between the eyes. Why is it that every man I meet and like is married?"

Jameson-Carr was the exception but she was trying not to think of him. Her infatuation with Larry Crawford had made that easier than usual. Not that she'd seen him since they'd docked.

Lawrence had promised to meet her in the lobby of the Golden Cross Hotel at one o'clock on the 22nd of October. She arrived at one-ten not wanting to appear too eager. At two she asked the clerk if there was a message for her. There was not. Obviously, he hadn't been able to get away from his wife. She waited a half hour more then left a message for him saying she would return the following day at the same time.

On October 23, at precisely one, Starr was pacing the lobby of the Golden Cross, smoking, trying not to appear too anxious as she watched the door. At one-thirty it occurred to her to ask if Mr. Crawford had picked up her message. He had not. She tore it up and left, returning at three to leave a new message saying he should call her at the Hotel Cecil. She went back to her hotel and waited. There was no call.

The next day, beginning at ten in the morning, she went to the Golden Cross lobby every hour, on the hour, spending about five minutes, then leaving. Between these visits, she walked the streets of London, seeing nothing.

When she'd been in London the first time, she'd loved it, preferring it to New York where she now shared an apartment on East Ninth Street with her family. But this time she was hating the place. There was nothing romantic about the inclement weather. She loathed every accented voice she heard.

Day after day, sometimes as often as twelve times, she appeared in the lobby of the Golden Cross and waited for Larry Crawford. By the time she went to bed on the 29th she was desolate and desperate.

Now, lying between cold sheets, she decided that life was bloody awful. What was the point in it? People were basically rotten.

She made a small, tired sound and slowly got out of bed. Stopping in front of the large mirror set into the closet door, she viewed herself from all possible angles. How ugly she looked. And she'd been eating too much. There was excess flesh on her hips. I will have to trim down, she thought, and then laughed, wondering what for.

On the writing table was a pack of Lucky Strikes. She lit one. In public she always smoked English cigarettes but in the room, alone, she smoked her American ones.

Pacing the room, dropping ashes on the gold rug, she rubbed them into the wool with her toes. Finished with the Lucky, she dropped the butt into the toilet and flushed. Then back to the bed, picking up a book of poetry, *Fiddler's Farewell.* She riffled the pages but could settle nowhere and finally put the book back on the night table.

She looked at the clock. Almost seven. Too early for breakfast. Too early for anything, she thought. Too early to live.

She stood up and walked with great determination to the bathroom. On the sink was the vial of Allonal. She opened the top and dropped two in her hand, turned on the faucet, filled the glass and swallowed the two pills. Then in twos and fours she took the rest until all twenty-four were gone. Setting the empty glass back on the sink, she walked into the room and sat in the armchair, legs tucked under her. For the first time in days she felt strangely peaceful. It occurred to her then that she was naked. Did it matter? No. Uncomfortable, she shifted around, feet touching the floor and crossed at the ankles. Smiling slightly, eyes closed, she waited.

It was the chambermaid, Agatha Porter, who found her and ran through the quiet halls screaming, "Dead woman 'ere, dead woman 'ere," her eyes bulging, strands of light brown hair slipping down over her forehead like a fallen crown.

But a dead woman was not there. When Agatha Porter entered Starr's room it was only nine-thirty, two hours and a half after she had taken the Allonal. A doctor was called, vomiting induced and Starr was put to bed. At one-thirty Inspector Bainbridge sat at her bedside.

"An accident?"

"Yes. I had a blinding headache and thought I was taking aspirin."

"But how many did you take, Miss?"

"I'm not sure . . . six, seven, eight maybe."

"That's a bit of aspirin, isn't it?"

"Is it? I always take that many." She counted on the fact the English thought Americans were eccentric.

"I see. Well, yes. Allonal, hmmm?"

She nodded, weakly. "It was bloody dumb of me."

The Inspector stared at the girl noting that despite her condition she was unusually beautiful. He cleared his throat of imaginary phlegm. "Well, then."

"I'm very tired," she said.

"Yes, yes, indeed. Ah, Miss Faithfull, one question? Are you sure . . . you, ah, were not trying to take your life?"

"Me?" she said, horrified. "Why, Inspector, I have everything to live for." She gave him one of her best, most seductive smiles, faint though she was.

The Inspector flushed slightly. "Yes, yes, I can see that. I mean, I would suspect that . . . imagine it to be true . . . indeed." He rose. "Well, then, you get a good rest, Miss."

"I shall." She huddled down into the bed.

Her wan smile faded as the door closed, her expression turning grim, eyes sad and angry at once, mouth turned down, taut. She reached over to the bedside table, feeling for her cigarettes. She remembered they were on the writing desk. Gingerly, she climbed from the bed. Everything ached. Especially her mid-section, muscles knotted from the long siege of vomiting. She crept toward the desk, hunched over. Halfway there, imagining a cigarette, the taste, smell, her stomach turned over and she went back to the bed.

Safely between the sheets again, she allowed her body to relax. Her mind was more difficult. She was furious. How could she have been so stupid? She must have known the chambermaid would be coming. Had she wanted to be found? But death had seemed so right, so perfect. Like new buds on a bush, the red petals of a tulip, the burgeoning of a butterfly. Miracles all. Godlike perhaps. Death, too, was a miracle, perfect. She had wanted it desperately. And now, now, now.

Her lids kept closing. She fought the tide of sleep as long as possible but eventually succumbed. When she awoke it was four in the morning. She drank a glass of water, dabbed some on her eyes, sat in the chair. The repercussions of her act began to tumble in on her like a cascade of crumbling rock.

First of all, she had been found naked. There was the chambermaid, undoubtedly the desk clerk, the doctor and God knew who else. At least three people had seen her naked. At least three people knew how ugly she was. That she was fat. Saw her fishbelly skin. At least two of those people were still in the hotel. And perhaps there were others. Maids, bellboys, waiters, even other guests, peering into her room, seeing her in her chair, naked. It was all too hideous.

She began to pull things from the closets, the drawers. Her suitcases were dragged out, flung open, clothes tossed in. By six, packed and dressed, she sat in her room waiting for morning light.

At six-thirty she stepped into the hall, leaving her packed suitcases in the largest closet. She hurried through the lobby, looking neither right nor left. Outside she rushed down the street, the click of her pumps piercing the fog-filled morning air. Her chin tucked against her neck, she kept her eyes on the ground.

Finally, she stopped at a small restaurant and took a table near the back. When a young boy came in a few minutes later, she summoned him over and made him an offer. He agreed eagerly. They left the restaurant together, he turning one way, she the other.

She found an empty berth on a ship leaving for America at three that afternoon. The boy appeared with her luggage in plenty of time.

"What did they say?" she asked, as he put down the suitcases.

"Say?"

"When you gave them the envelope. Who'd you give it to?"

"The clark."

"What did he say?"

The boy shrugged. " 'E tole me t' wait."

"And?"

"I did."

"Then?" she asked, exasperated.

"A boy came w' the cases an' I took 'em."

"Did anyone . . . did anyone laugh?"

"Laugh?"

"Yes. Did anyone?"

He looked at her like she was crazy. "No, Miss, nobody laughed."

"Did the clerk *say* anything?"

"Say anythin'?"

"Yes, don't you understand English?" she snapped.

"What d'ya mean, say anythin'?"

She tried to regain some patience. "What I mean is, when the clerk gave you the suitcases did he say anything about them, or me?"

" 'E didn't give 'em t'me. The boy done."

"But the clerk was there, watching?"

"Yes."

"And?"

"And what, Miss?"

"What the hell did he say?"

"The clark?"

"Oh, God, yes. The clerk. What did he say?"

" 'E asked me if the fog was thick enough for me."

"And?"

"And I said yes."

"Then?"

"Then I left, Miss. Could I 'ave me sixpence now, please, Miss?"

"That was all? He didn't say anything else? Nothing about me? No one said anything about me?"

"No, Miss."

"You're sure?"

"Yes, Miss. Could I 'ave me money now?"

She gave him the sixpence and shooed him away, knowing he was lying. They must have been laughing, sniggering. God knows what they'd said to the boy. Well, at least she hadn't had to face them, their leering, the smug, superior looks. She'd outsmarted them. Once again, she had won. She could always come out on top if she tried. Tried? It really didn't take that much effort. She could outwit most people with her hands tied. She smiled, snapped her fingers for a porter and walked toward the gangplank and home.

April, 1929
Newark, New Jersey

"Fool," said Ben, *"this is life. You have been no-where."* Orlando read the line again. Ben Gant speaking to his brother Eugene in *Look Homeward, Angel,* a novel by the new author Thomas Wolfe. Then one more page until he came to the end of the book.

Oh my God, he thought, if only I could write like that. As soon as he was settled, marriage and honeymoon over, he would try to get down to some writing. And even if he wasn't Thomas Wolfe, he'd be better than Sinclair Lewis. Lewis, in Orlando's opinion, had no sense of the English language. Still, he got published. If he could, Orlando could. It was just a matter of time. Time. Just what he lacked at present. He worked at an employment agency in New York during the day and played in the Halsey Miller band at night. Weekend days he had to spend some time with Fran.

Right now he had to get dressed. Tonight was his bachelor party and he had no intention of being late for that. They were always a helluva lot of fun. And usually, at the end, the guys presented the prospective groom with a beautiful girl for the rest of the night. If he knew his best friend Earl Paige, he'd come up with a humdinger! Only one thing nagged at him. Toni's new husband, Max, would be there. He could have done without a brother-in-law tonight. Soaping his face with the pearl-handled brush, he wondered if Earl had arranged for a brunette, a blonde or a redhead?

She was a brunette. Tall, big breasted, gorgeous. Her name was Sally.

"Listen," she was saying, sitting on the edge of the bed in the Essex Hotel, "are we gonna do anything or not? Because if we're not, I'll just get some shuteye, okay?"

"Huh?" Orlando was very drunk.

"Oh, shit." Sally turned off the light and went to sleep.

When he awoke, he was alone, not certain where he was. Little by little it came back. Slowly he sat up, groaned, then feeling very sick, bolted, crashing against furniture, to the bathroom.

He put his head under the tap, letting the cold water run over his neck as well. It helped a little, not much. He dried his head, cautiously found his way through the darkened room and back to the bed where he fell heavily onto the sheets, face down. After a few moments, he carefully turned himself over. Staring at the ceiling, he felt numb, stupid. After a time he heard a noise. His door opened. He grabbed for a sheet, covering himself.

"Oh, I'm sorry, sir," the maid said. "It's after checkout time."

"I'll be right out," he mumbled. "Wasn't feeling well."

"Yes sir." She backed out.

"Food poisoning I think."

"Yes sir." She closed the door.

Why had he felt it necessary to lie to the hotel maid? What the hell did he care what she thought?

He looked around for his clothes which were strewn everywhere. The prospect of having to bend down and pick them up made him moan.

Finally dressed, he reached for his wallet and saw the lipstick-smeared cigarette butts in the ashtray. Silently he cursed himself for missing his last chance as a free agent. In two days he'd be married and faithful. If Papa could do it, so could he.

On April 20th, at The Little Church Around The Corner in New York, Orlando Antolini and Frances Hess were married. Earl and Mary Paige stood up with them. No one else attended. No family from either side.

Orlando wanted to be married close to home so his friends could come to the reception. Fran wanted to do what he wanted. Besides, she couldn't have married in Lancaster and avoided the Catholic Church. The Little Church Around The Corner was nonsectarian, the reason

Fran's family stayed away. And since her family wouldn't come, Orlando had not invited his. Toni and Max, however, along with thirty others came to the reception in Newark at a fancy restaurant called The Oceanview, though the ocean was nowhere in sight.

They'd planned to drive to Montreal after the wedding lunch but the weather was so horrific—torrential rains and gale-force winds—that they went instead to their new apartment on 20th Street in Newark.

Fran had never seen the apartment. Orlando and Toni picked it out. The furniture was a wedding present from his parents. As she crossed the threshold, Fran's heart sank. Everything was dark, dark, dark. The furniture was heavy mahogany which dwarfed the room. The draperies were thick navy velvet. She could have cried.

"It's wonderful," she said.

The bedroom was the same. Dark. Massive furniture. Fran liked maple but no one had asked her.

"Do you want to call them now and thank them or wait until tomorrow?"

She needed time. "I'll wait."

Trying to fight the tears she felt inching up behind her eyes, she smiled. How was she going to live with this stuff? It was so depressing. "Did you help them pick it out?"

"No. Toni and Mama did it."

She wondered if Toni had done it to annoy her or if it was really her taste.

Lying in bed, waiting for Orlando to come out of the bathroom, Fran laughed at herself for feeling so nervous. It wasn't as though she were a virgin. Still, they'd never had a night like this. She'd never been in a silk nightgown before, waiting in bed for her *husband*.

The bathroom door opened and she jumped. He climbed in, his leg touching hers, his arm sliding around her.

"Well," he said.

"Mmmm."

"Here we are. All perfectly legal. How do you feel?"

"Fine."

"Me too."

"Orr? What will our life be like?"

"Wonderful. We're not just ordinary people, you know."

"*You're* not."

"You aren't either." He kissed the top of her head.

"Oh, well."

"You're very special. You married me, didn't you?" He gave her a hug. "We'll probably travel a lot, meet all kinds of interesting people."

"You think so?"

"Sure. We'll probably hang around with Hemingway and Fitzgerald. All of them."

"Will we go to Europe?"

"Of course." He turned toward her, feeling the outline of her body through their bedclothes.

"Will we go to lots of parties?"

"Naturally." He tried to kiss her but she was still talking.

"I don't want our lives to be like my parents', Orr. I want to go everywhere and meet everyone."

"You will, you will." He rolled over onto Fran, his mouth covering hers, his hand tracing her breasts through the silk. *Fool, this is life. You will go nowhere.*

God, how awful. Why had the line come to him then? Whatever the reason, this was a lousy time for it. And he worked hard to dismiss it as he continued to make sweet love to his wife.

Police seek to learn if she fell or was thrown off boat. Autopsy indicates attack.

—*Herald Tribune,* June 9, 1931

June 6, 1931
New York, New York

It was several seconds before Starr remembered where she was. For once her confusion was not from too much liquor but from the normal disorientation of awakening in a strange place.

The pink room made her smile. She felt peaceful, almost happy. Diana and Royal. The thought made her warm. What would life hold for her now? How would the

Lefflands make her better? She never doubted they would.

She put on a matching white satin robe. Diana had forgotten to give her slippers. She would go barefoot.

Silently, she went down the carpeted stairs, crossed the living room, walked down the short hall toward the kitchen. Raising her hand to push through the swinging door, something made her stop. Diana and Royal were talking.

Eighteen

August 6, 1977
Orange, New Jersey

"Mr. Antolini," the doctor said again, "could you possibly give us a signal if you understand?"

Orlando kept his eyes shut until he heard them leave. The closing door cracked across his mind, through his stomach. A familiar sensation. Whenever a headline entered his consciousness he felt it. Now, GIRL'S MURDER LINKED TO ONE MAN.

The most frightening of all the headlines. But it hadn't, of course, been him. There was something about a man named Peters. But he'd been in Boston at the time. Then something about a seduction. Child molester. The man denied everything, then a few weeks later had a stroke. Poor man. Seven years after that Orlando read that he had died. Lucky man.

———

September 7, 1929
Newark, New Jersey

Fran didn't mind Orlando playing in the band on Saturday nights because it gave her a night off from Van Ness Place. During the almost five months they'd been married they had spent all free evenings with the senior

Antolinis. Of course, Orlando wasn't any worse than Toni. She and Max were there every Saturday night and once during the week. Fran was convinced that if Nina and Renato lived nearby, they too would have been at Van Ness twice a week for dinner. She thought the Antolini children were sickening about their parents.

The second day of their so-called honeymoon might have told her what it would be like. It was still raining and blowing and she and Orlando spent a lazy day lying around, listening to the radio, making love, talking, staring at each other. About four o'clock he'd jumped out of bed and headed toward the bathroom.

"We'd better take our baths."

"What?" Did he take a bath every afternoon?

"Our baths. Shall we take one together?"

"All right." She felt a little shy about that, never having fully exposed herself to him.

He ran the bath water and came back to the bed, sitting on its edge. "I love you."

"I love *you*."

"Have you ever had canneloni?"

"No. Why?"

"I think that's what we're having for dinner."

"Think?"

"Mama said she'd try and make it."

"Mama?"

"My God, didn't I tell you we're going there for dinner tonight?"

She shook her head. Inside, a small part of her dipped low.

"Well, we are." He went to the bathroom and turned off the taps. "C'mon, water's nice and hot."

She heard him getting into the tub, calling her. She didn't want to take a bath now but she went into the bathroom and sat on the closed toilet seat, looking down at him. How wormlike his penis looked under the water.

"Get in!" He was smiling, black hair falling over one eye, giving him a rakish look.

"Orr? I thought this was our honeymoon."

"It is. What are you talking about?"

"Then why are we having dinner with your parents?"

"They asked us," he said, explanation enough. Soap covered his neck, chest, upper arms.

"I thought we'd have this time alone."

"Look, Fran, we didn't have them to the reception. It's the least we can do. We won't stay long. C'mon, get in."

"No, I don't feel like it." She went back to the bed where she waited for him to finish his bath so she could take hers so they could hightail it over to Van Ness Place like two dutiful little children.

But it wasn't until the third month of their marriage that she realized what a telltale sign that first command dinner had been. Not having had one entire night with him since their honeymoon, she asked, "Orr, do we have to go to Van Ness tonight? We haven't been alone in months." He answered, "Don't be so selfish."

Because of Orlando's schedule they never saw anyone their own age and, consequently, Fran hadn't made any friends in New Jersey. Of course there was Toni. They got on better than Fran had expected. Toni liked her as well as she would have liked anyone who'd married her brother. But, married almost a year longer than Fran, Toni felt she was an expert in household matters and was constantly giving Fran advice she didn't need or want. And when Fran had rearranged the ugly wedding-present furniture, trying desperately to make the living room look a little less overbearing, Toni immediately insisted on putting things back the way they'd been. One, it was much better that way and, two, her mother would be upset if things were changed around. Fran had started to protest but Orlando had signaled to let it go. Later, when she argued that it was her house, her furniture, he'd asked what difference it made. Was she so selfish that she'd upset an old lady? She left it the way it was.

Besides Toni, the only other friend she had was Mrs. Antolini. Despite her feelings of resentment, she couldn't help liking her mother-in-law. She was a kind person, affectionate and extremely honest.

Thinking it might diminish her loneliness, Fran had mentioned getting a job. Orlando was against it, adamantly. So her days were spent tidying up the three rooms—this took all of an hour a day—and marketing—she went daily instead of once a week, as Toni urged, so that it gave her a reason to go out. She'd tried sitting in the small park a few times but only mothers with children seemed to frequent it and she found they had no interest in her. She hoped soon she would be joining them with her little daughter or son. But so far, nothing.

In the evenings she read or listened to the radio. And Mr. Antolini had given her a few Caruso records she liked to play when Orlando wasn't home. Tonight she was reading *Dodsworth* and enjoying it even though Orlando had told her it was badly written. Just as Dodsworth and Edith Cortright were about to get together someone rang her doorbell. She was startled. It was eleven-thirty. She felt apprehensive. It rang again, more insistent.

She crossed the room and stood near the door. "Who is it?"

"I'm a friend of Orr's." It was a woman's voice.

She was less afraid, but not ready to open up.

"Which friend?" she asked.

"Kay Chase."

The name wasn't familiar. What should she do?

"Open up," Kay said.

"Orr's not here," she answered quickly, apprehensive again.

There was a small laugh. "I know. I came to see you, Frances Hess."

As though someone had drawn her a diagram she suddenly knew what it was all about. Kay Chase was undoubtedly an ex-girlfriend. Oh, well, what did she have to lose? After all, *she* was married to him, wasn't she? She was inside and this Chase girl was outside! She opened the door.

Standing against the door frame was a creature so attractive, so stunning and sophisticated, Fran almost gasped. She was dressed in a gray satin evening gown, cut to a deep V, her breasts slightly exposed. Over her shoulders was a light-colored fur stole. The woman's brown hair was stylishly combed back behind her ears, then falling in soft waves and tucked under at the nape of her long neck. Her beautiful blue eyes, though slightly glassy from too much liquor, focused on Fran. The woman smiled from one side of her mouth.

"Hi," she said. "How about a drink?"

"Come in." Fran was horrified as the beautiful woman looked around. She wanted to tell her why her living room was so ugly, explain that it wasn't her taste.

But there was no way to explain without sounding like an idiot. "What would you like?" She hoped she sounded easier than she felt.

"Scotch."

"Rocks, water, soda?" Fran asked as though making drinks for strangers in the middle of the night were something she did all the time.

"A little water, *one* ice cube. It's a small affectation." She laughed and Fran couldn't help smiling.

"Please, sit down."

"Thanks." Kay draped herself across the couch, kicking off her gray satin evening slippers.

Fran handed her her drink, took her own ginger ale back to her chair and lifted her glass toward Kay. "Cheers."

"Skol," Kay said.

They drank, eyeing each other over the rims of their glasses.

"So you're Frances Hess."

"Frances Antolini," she corrected.

"Yes, of course."

Fran noticed Kay was wearing a wedding band. "I'm not sure I've heard your name before. What was your maiden name?"

"Chase *is* my maiden name. Martin's my married name, or was. I'm in the process of getting a divorce."

"Oh. I'm sorry." And shocked.

"Don't be. I'm thrilled."

"I see."

"Do you?"

"Hmmm?"

"Skip it."

Fran felt foolish. She'd obviously missed something. Slightly angry, she took the initiative. "Why did you come to see me?"

"I wanted to see what you looked like."

"Why?"

"Because you're Orr's wife."

"And you were in love with him?" For a moment she stopped breathing.

A slight pause. "Yes." She laughed. "I wasn't planning to tell you that."

Fran gained confidence. "It wasn't too hard to figure out."

"I suppose not. But Orr never figured it out."

"I don't understand."

"It's too long, too complicated to explain."

"You mean you weren't his girlfriend?" She would have crossed her fingers if her hands hadn't been exposed.

"Oh, no. But we . . . well, it was more of an arrangement." She held out her empty glass, smiling, looking directly into Fran's eyes.

Fran took the glass. "I don't understand."

"It doesn't matter. Are you happy, Frances? I can call you Frances, can't I? I'll be damned if I'll call you Mrs. Antolini."

"Yes, I'm happy. Call me Fran." She handed her a fresh drink. "And your first name again?" She remembered but she needed the edge.

"Kay."

"Kay Chase," she said sitting down. "No, I don't think he ever told me about you. It must have been quite some time ago . . . I mean, that you had your arrangement."

"Yes, I guess."

Fran didn't like that. She tried to sound casual. "How long ago was it?"

Kay wasn't fooled by her tone. "Before he met you." What would be the point, after all?

"Oh." She relaxed, wondering if Orlando had stopped seeing this woman because of her.

"I guess you think it's queer that I wanted to see you when it was all so long ago."

Fran shrugged. She did think it was odd.

"Just curiosity. And you were my rival."

Question answered. "I'm sorry." She didn't understand why she'd said it.

Now Kay shrugged. "I guess I'm a little ossified."

"Where are you coming from?"

"A club dance. Tedious."

"Where's your escort?"

"I went with my parents. I'm living at home again."

How could such a beautiful woman be without an escort? Suddenly, she wondered if Kay and Orlando had ever made love. Well, there was absolutely no way to ask that question. Why hadn't Orr ever mentioned her? But he'd never really mentioned any other women. He said none of them was important, none meant anything until her. Obviously, Kay had just been another one. What did she mean, an arrangement? Maybe she was making up all of it. Maybe she'd gone out with him only once or twice. Maybe she didn't even really know him.

"What's wrong?" Kay asked, lighting a cigarette.

"Nothing. Why?"

"You were squinting at me."

"Was I?"

"Yes. Well, why in hell shouldn't you? I come barging in here saying I want to look at you and . . . well, what are you supposed to think?" She tried putting her feet back into her shoes and, failing, picked them up and stood in her bare feet. She grabbed her stole from the back of the couch. "I'm sorry."

Surprised, Fran rose as Kay walked a bit unsteadily toward the door. There were too many unanswered questions and the prospect of being alone again didn't appeal to her. "Where are you going?" A kind of desperation underlined her words.

Kay turned. "Home, I guess."

"Stay." It was a cross between a command and a plea.

"Why?"

"I don't know." She could've kicked herself for sounding so stupid.

"Do you have any more scotch?"

"Sure." She thought Kay'd had enough but she certainly wasn't going to say so.

Settled again, Kay with a new scotch, Fran with a fresh ginger ale, they found themselves smiling at each other. Kay broke the silence.

"You're very pretty."

Fran was slightly taken aback. No woman had ever said that to her before. "Thank you. You . . . you are, too."

Kay laughed. "This could turn out to be a mutual admiration society. It's funny though, isn't it?"

"What is?"

"Us being so different. Funny he'd pick us both."

Fran knew then whatever Kay had had with Orlando, it hadn't been casual.

"I came here prepared to hate you. In fact, I did hate you. But I can't. You're very nice. I guess this is kind of an unusual situation. Ex-mistress and wife."

Ex-mistress! Well, so what? It was a long time ago. Besides, she'd always known Orlando had slept with lots of women. Why let it bother her? But Kay was right. It was unusual. She wondered if others would come knocking at her door.

"Listen, Fran, do you think we could be friends?"

At first the suggestion shocked her. It seemed improper. And what would Orlando say? But the idea of having a friend, *any* friend, outweighed the improprieties.

"I don't know. I guess so."

"I mean," Kay said, smiling, "we obviously have a lot in common."

"Yes." She couldn't believe she was agreeing. Why wasn't she scandalized by Kay's remark?

"Of course, Orr might not like it, us being friends."

Perhaps Kay was suggesting this so she could be around Orlando. After all, she hardly knew Fran. Why would she want to be friends? Having something in common wasn't enough. "Are you still in love with him?"

"I haven't seen him for a long time."

"How long?"

"Well, I haven't seen him since New Year's Eve, 1928." Realizing her mistake, she quickly added, "We were just friends by then. It was a party." No need to mention she'd been Orlando's date.

Perhaps Kay had been the reason Orlando always insisted on spending his holidays in Newark. But Kay hadn't really answered her question. "Are you still in love with him?"

"I told you . . ."

"No, you didn't. You just said you hadn't seen him in a long time."

Kay took a long swallow of her drink, unintentionally banged the glass down on the table and tried to level her somewhat sodden gaze at Fran. "The truth? The truth is I don't know. I've been married . . . May-December wedding . . . not quite a Peaches Browning affair . . . but bad enough, although I didn't call him Daddy, God knows. Anyway, it was rotten from the beginning. I married the guy on the rebound. See, when Orr met you . . . dropped me like a hot potato. I'd known him for years . . . had this arrangement . . . friends more or less . . . love was never mentioned . . . I agreed to it 'cause it was the only way to keep him. Bastard. Then you." She reached over to get her drink and knocked it on the floor. "Damn. I'm sorry."

"It's all right." Fran ran to the kitchen for a towel. Kay kept mumbling she was sorry. All Fran cared about was the rest of the story. She made Kay another drink, very light this time.

"Where was I? Oh, yeah. When you came into the picture that was the end of me. So I took up with others. I mean, I'd been seeing other men all along but now I . . . I don't know. Anyway, I met Blair and he . . . well, he didn't exactly swept me . . . *sweep* me off my feet but, anyway, I married him."

"And you still loved Orr when you got married?"

"I guess, who knows?"

I do, Fran thought.

"I jus' wanted to see what you looked like. I was bored at the club."

"How did you know Orr wouldn't be here?"

"Oh, we have some mutual friends. I know he's playin' in a band. Not much fun for you, huh?"

"I keep myself busy."

"Not much of a married life."

"I don't mind," she insisted.

"You must be lonely."

Suddenly, she didn't want Kay to know anything about her. They couldn't be friends. It was ridiculous. "I have lots of friends," she said. "It's unusual for me to be home alone. I was rather tired from running here and there."

"I guess."

Fran wondered if *mutual friends* had let this woman know about *her* comings and goings as well. "And then, of course, when we *are* together we make up for lost time." She hated herself for having said that. It was so unnecessary. She wished she could take it back.

Kay smiled. "I'm sure ya do, sure ya do. I gotta go." She struggled with her shoes again.

"Can I help?"

"Huh?"

"With your shoes."

"It's okay."

Fran watched as Kay fumbled with her shoes. Finally, she couldn't stand it anymore. She knelt down in front of her, gently placing each foot in its proper shoe. When she looked up Kay was smiling. Fran felt like a fool and quickly got to her feet.

"Will you be all right?" she asked Kay at the door.

"Fine." Abruptly, she bent her head and kissed Fran full on the lips. Then she was gone.

Fran stood there, shocked. She was not in the habit of kissing anyone but Orlando on the mouth. Not even her family. Certainly not other women. And, aside from being startling, the kiss had been pleasant.

She did not tell Orlando about Kay's visit. Not then or ever. She knew she wouldn't hear from her and that the talk of friendship had been simply that, talk.

Ten years later when Kay Chase married a business associate of Orlando's, and the two women met at a party, they each pretended it was their first meeting. And even when the two couples became friends, spending many evenings together, neither woman ever alluded to that Saturday night in 'twenty-nine.

For the rest of their lives, until Kay's death from alcoholism in 1968, Fran was sure that somewhere Kay still cared for Orlando. But it really didn't matter. They became good friends anyway. And when they met or parted, they carefully kissed each other's cheeks. The way women do.

Fall, 1929
Massachusetts
New York

On October 29, 1929, the stock market crashed.

Herbert Hoover, the twenty-ninth President, had been inaugurated on March 4th, after promising prosperity for all. He had been mistaken.

Frank Wyman, never having cared much for money, never having accumulated any, still employed by the

YMCA, was personally untouched by the crash. It flashed through his mind, once, that the crash' might have affected Faithfull and he wondered if his children were all right. But then something distracted him and he forgot about it.

Andrew J. Peters, who had seconded the nomination of Al Smith at the Democratic convention in Houston, Texas, the year before, was not surprised by the crash. He, like many others, lost in the market but he was certainly not wiped out. And he still had his practice, of course. Oddly enough, the one he knew personally who was affected most severely was his secretary, Alma Stevenson, a widow. Alma had invested everything in the market and had no cash savings. Peters generously offered to support Alma and her beautiful thirteen-year-old daughter, Mavis, until they could get back on their feet.

At 34 East Ninth Street, Stanley Faithfull was concerned about the economy. He wasn't a rich man to begin with and the few stocks he'd had were now gone. He was relieved he hadn't invested Starr's money from Peters, though he'd often considered it. And he wished he could keep Starr from running through it so quickly. His job was safe now but he knew that could change.

Helen was kept in the dark about financial matters and that was fine with her. She only knew that they were all right at the moment but that she mustn't be extravagant.

Tucker, eighteen, languished. She wanted to continue her education but Stanley explained that he couldn't afford it. She'd written Frank, asking if he'd send her to college, but she'd never received an answer. She wasn't willing to work her way through school. Once it occurred to her that perhaps Andrew Peters would be willing to sponsor her. When she suggested it to her mother, Helen immediately burst into tears. Then, the story of Starr and Andrew's relationship was revealed to her. Tucker went to her sister.

"Are you serious?" Starr was appalled.

"Why not?"

"I should pay for you to go to some bloody college?"

"You have plenty of money."

"Yes. For me, dear girl, for me."

"To do what with?"

"That's my bloody business. You can jolly well make your own money."

"The way you did?"

Starr slapped her hard. "Bitch."

So Tucker remained at home.

Starr was not affected at all by the end of the Big Bull market. Her cash was secure though more than half of it had already been spent; her life continued as though nothing had happened. She'd crossed to England several more times since the episode at the Hotel Cecil and always on the *Franconia* so that she could see Dr. Jameson-Carr. Each time she started off with the best intentions, promising herself to behave around him, to show him she was mature, worth loving. But each time something happened. After too many drinks, intentions forgotten, she'd throw herself at him. By the end of her last cruise, when forced to deal with her, he treated her like a pesky child. The rest of the time he studiously avoided her. And when she wasn't on board ship with him she wrote long letters, laboring over them, in which she discussed books, poetry, music, art. Convinced he was an intellectual, she hoped such discussions would appeal to him. He never answered her letters.

He was not, of course, the only man in her life. In New York she spent a great deal of time in speaks, meeting many men, some like Edwin Megargee and Rupert Sayers, who became friends, others whose names she could barely remember from one day to the next. She had no real women friends. Women seemed, to her, the enemy. She never knew what to say to them. But there were times she wished she had one for a friend. She remembered—way back before Andrew—B.A.—back to the days of two little girls named Mary Gray and Evelyn Henry. A feeling of lightness and joy came with that memory but it was quickly replaced by sadness. Instinctively, she stayed at arm's length with women and none of them ever tried to be anything but superficial with her.

So at the end of 1929 very little was changed and Starr continued drinking, dancing, dining with her parade of men. Unhappy as always.

Fall, 1929
Pennsylvania
New Jersey

On October 29, 1929, the stock market crashed.

Orlando Antolini Sr. lost the money he'd invested in stocks and the bottom fell out of his own company, Paradise Land. Only the cash which he kept in his office safe was intact. Benito Rosselli, his partner in Paradise Land, was not so lucky. Everything he had was tied up with the company which owned four hundred acres of beautiful woods and rolling meadows in Suffern County, New Jersey. Now it was Paradise Lost and Rosselli jumped from the window of his tenth-floor office onto Market Street on October 30th. Orlando was disgusted. He had no use for cowards. But that did not affect his concern for the widow. From his safe he took five thousand dollars, put it in a sealed envelope and sent his secretary to the Rosselli house with the gift.

Antolini's style of life changed little. All his children were married, except Silvio who was in his second year at Rutgers. Though many boys had to leave college, Silvio did not. Orlando and Antonia were alone at Van Ness with a new servant, Maria. Dolce had died the year before. They had few expenses and Orlando could comfortably continue to support his mistress. When Max lost his job, it was easy for Orlando Sr. to absorb him and Toni into the household until things picked up.

Fran's parents had not fared so well. Joseph Hess lost his job and his house. There were no savings. Any extra money that came to him he gambled away. He and his wife moved in with their eldest daughter, her husband and two sons.

Orlando Jr.'s daytime job was secure but band dates had dropped off. Now he played only on weekends. Monday and Thursday he and Fran had dinner at Van Ness. Tuesday and Wednesday evenings they had to themselves.

Fran was delighted that Orlando was playing less frequently, even though it meant less money. She knew that someday, when he settled down and started writing, they would be rich and famous. For now it was enough that she had him alone for at least two nights a week. She would have preferred three, canceling one of the two nights a week at Van Ness, but the pull the senior Antolinis had for their son was greater than hers. She remained grateful for what she had.

Orlando enjoyed the time with his wife, even though he missed playing. Fidelity was not as difficult as he'd anticipated. They had a new active social life and friends enjoyed coming to their apartment. Fran always made everyone feel welcome and, besides being a good hostess, she was turning into an excellent cook. They had also acquired an English Bull Terrier, Deirdre, whom they doted on.

But in the summer of 1930 band bookings picked up and Orlando went back to playing five nights a week. That left one night a week to spend with Fran, the other at Van Ness. Having had a taste of her husband being at home in the evenings, Fran was now more dissatisfied than ever.

The most important thing now is to find the fur-collared spring coat, hat, shoes, bag, and underwear.

—From a statement by
Elvin Edwards, June 11, 1931

June 6, 1931
New York, New York

". . . see why not tonight?" Royal said.

"She's too frightened. Too vulnerable. We must gain her trust."

"I'm going to have an erection all day," he said, sulking.

"Just as long as you don't do anything about it, pet."

"God, she's lovely."

"Mmmm. We'll have the whole weekend to win her over. By Monday morning she should be ours for as long as we want her."

"All last night I kept picturing the two of you together."

"Funny, I kept seeing the two of you," Diana said.

"Pass the butter, dear. You know, she reminds me a little of that French one. What the hell was her name?"

"Yvette. Starr is much more beautiful. More coffee?"

"Thanks. You *are* a funny bunny. You always think the present one is more beautiful than any of the others. I remember when . . ."

Nineteen

August 6, 1977
Orange, New Jersey

It was strange, Orlando thought, how his fear of death had turned so completely into a desire for death. Perhaps because the torture of living had gone on too long.

His fear had spilled over everyone connected with him. For forty years he had called Fran three times a day . . . just to say hello, he told her. But really, it was to see if she was all right. And, of course, the fear had almost consumed his daughter. Every step she took was a dangerous one in his eyes.

At the beach it was worst. Always afraid she would drown. Fran did not swim, was afraid of the water and he didn't encourage her to learn. One less thing to worry about. But he couldn't very well keep his child from learning. Always he watched, eaglelike, at the edge of the shore, standing there, keeping guard.

Oh, how could they be so sure? Autopsy. Maybe they were wrong. Somewhere it said something like . . . *the fact that sand was found in lungs and throat indicates she regained consciousness . . . tried to reach shore . . . became fatigued . . . died in shallow water.* Alive. She had still been alive! He would never get over it. Not until death took him, too.

———

"God, I hate this bloody dump." Starr's remark was directed at the walls, ceiling, furniture but Stanley Faithfull, sitting on the corner of the couch, knew where it was truly aimed.

He watched her pacing the small living room, puffing on a cigarette, distractedly fussing with the buttons on her satin lounging outfit.

"You know, Stanley, you said this was a temporary move. That was two bloody years ago."

"I know, I know. But I didn't know what would happen then, Bamby."

She stopped, stood directly in front of him, her legs almost touching his knees. "Please don't give me the Black Tuesday speech. It bores me."

"But I . . ."

"Forget it." She resumed her pacing. "What time is it?"

"Five after one."

"I have to change. Make a batch of martinis," she ordered, starting toward her room.

"Now?"

Turning back, she put her hand on one hip, jutting out the other. "Yes, now. You have objections?"

"It's pretty early. It's only one."

"I know what time it is, Stanley . . . you just told me. I have a friend coming over if you must know. Wait'll she sees this joint."

It was unusual for Starr to bring friends to the house. Stanley was intrigued, pleased. "Which friend is that?"

"Just some girl I met. Jane Douglas. I must have been crazy to ask her here." Her eyes took in the room. "Make the drinks."

"Yes, Bamby."

When she entered the tiny room she shared with Tucker, her sister was lying on her bed reading.

"You lead a thrilling life," Starr said.

Tucker raised her eyes from the book, said nothing. Starr snatched the book from her hands.

"Hey!"

"*Farewell To Arms?* Haven't you read that yet?"

"Obviously not. Starr!" She shielded her breast as the book came flying back. "You're horrible."

"And you're bloody stupid." She began rummaging through her closet.

"And disgusting. Why do you say that?"

"That you're stupid? Because you are."

"Bloody," she said softly. "Why do you have to say that all the time?"

"Because I like it." She held a silk print dress against her body, then threw it in a heap on the floor.

"It's an affectation," Tucker said.

"Oh, shut your trap." A second dress joined the first.

"Hey! I hope you're going to pick that stuff up. This is my room too, you know."

"Well, if you'd help prod that ass out there to move us some place else maybe you could have your own room."

"You're so crude. And why do you pick on him like that? He does what he can."

"It isn't enough." A blue wool suit hit the edge of her bed and crumpled to the floor.

"You'd better pick up those things."

"Or what?"

"Hmmmm?"

"Oh, stuff it." She settled on a green crepe with a scoop neck, then went to the bureau they shared. She had three drawers, Tucker two. She started digging through her lingerie, tossing brassieres and panties out behind her like a dog flinging dirt from a hole.

"Starr!"

"What?" She continued.

"Stop that. I know you're not going to pick those things up. I just know it."

She did not respond. Finally, she found the silk panties and brassiere she'd been searching for. Pink with roses.

"It isn't fair, you know. When two people share a room there has to be consideration and . . ."

"Oh Christ, Tucker, you give me a pain." She slammed the drawer, a piece of underwear still showing.

"I don't care. Do you think I like being in here with all your junk strewn around?"

She kicked her used panties from her ankle to a spot across the room.

"Oh, really! Come on. That's too much. Do I have to lie here with your smelly underwear all over the place?"

"Now who's disgusting?"

"It's not *my* smelly underwear!"

Starr, naked, stared hard at Tucker. Very slowly, she said, "My underwear does not smell."

"I'll bet."

"It doesn't."

"It stinks."

"Really?"

"Really."

Starr strode deliberately toward her sister's bed.

"Starr. Don't, Starr." Tucker headed for the end of the bed but Starr caught her.

"Stop it." Tucker yelled as Starr pushed her back on the bed.

They began to wrestle. After a few moments of strenuous twisting and turning Starr easily pinned her sister, sitting on her thighs, holding down her arms, Starr's breasts swinging near Tucker's face.

"You bloody bitch," Starr hissed.

"Get off."

"Say uncle."

"Leave me alone."

"I said, say uncle."

The contest continued, both shouting at once.

"Say uncle."

"Stop it."

"Uncle."

"I hate you."

"Uncle."

"Never."

Neither heard the bedroom door open. Helen Faithfull stood in the doorway, horrified. From her point of view she could see only the back of Starr's naked body on top of Tucker whose legs were flailing from side to side. She couldn't begin to imagine what to think and stood, speechless, listening to their grunts and growls.

"Girls." It was all she could manage.

Starr twisted her head around.

"What are you doing?" Helen asked, not really wanting to know.

"Mo-ther." Tucker's voice whined from beneath Starr.

Slowly, Starr let go of Tucker's wrists and, taking her time, she climbed off.

"Mother," Tucker cried again.

Defiantly, hands on hips, Starr faced her mother. "What do you want?"

"I . . . your guest is here."

"I'll be out in a minute."

Helen stood, still staring.

Propped up on her elbows, Tucker said, "Moth-er."

"Thanks for the message." Starr's eyes told Helen to leave.

She backed three or four steps out of the room and softly closed the door.

"Moth-er," Tucker yelled.

"Shut up, you bitch," said Starr.

As she hurriedly dressed, she flung at her sister, without stop, epithets of the grossest sort. As a final insult she took a favorite strand of blue beads from Tucker's small jewelry box and put them around her neck.

"You are the scum of the earth," she said to Tucker before closing the door, "and if you know what's good for you you'll have the room cleaned up before I come back."

In the living room, she smiled winningly at both Helen and Stanley, gave Jane a warm greeting and, ever so prim and proper, waited while Stanley poured her a drink.

*　　*　　*

Jane Douglas was overweight, had small eyes and a large nose. She'd been married, divorced and now lived quite comfortably on the alimony she received from her ex-husband, a doctor.

It had never been easy for Jane to make friends. When Rupert Sayers brought Starr to their table at The New Little Club, and Starr had immediately begun a conversation with her, she was amazed, flattered, intrigued. And when Starr invited her by for lunch the following day, Jane accepted eagerly. It would be advantageous, she could tell, to be friends with this girl, odd as she was. Men seemed to flock around her and perhaps Jane would get the leftovers.

Surreptitiously, she glanced at her watch. It was two-fifteen and lunch still hadn't been served. Was it possible she'd misunderstood? She'd purposely skipped breakfast, assuming lunch would be a gala affair. Now she was starving. She didn't drink martinis and her Coca-Cola, almost empty, hadn't filled her up.

Jane was confused. The night before, Starr had impressed her as being quite well-to-do and, although this address on Ninth Street was acceptable enough, the apartment itself betrayed the facade. It was small and dingy. Of course, there were some very fine pieces here and there, like the old writing desk in the corner. Perhaps the Faithfulls had lost their fortune last year along with so many others. That must be it. Mr. Faithfull, peculiar and odd looking though he was, was certainly a gentleman. Jane was sure he'd known better times. And if some of his conversation was foolish—well, losing everything had affected the minds of more than one person she knew. Still, none of that explained the lack of lunch!

Starr, Jane observed, was quite a drinker. Mr. Faithfull had just poured her third martini. Oddly enough, she didn't seem to be affected by the alcohol. Like last night, she was talkative, charming, friendly. Of course, who knew if that was the drinks or if she was always that way. Whatever the case, Jane was glad to know this beauty and hoped she'd bring her some luck.

Oh yes, you bloody ass, Starr thought, just rattle on like the goddamn fool you are. She smiled and nodded at something Stanley said, taking another sip of the cool, delicious gin martini. The only thing Stanley was good for was making his own gin. And obviously, as far as Helen was concerned, he was good for sex. The thought repelled Starr and she quickly shoved it aside. She finished her third drink and, smiling, held out her glass for another.

"You think you should?" Stanley asked.

Still smiling, a lilt to her voice, she answered, "If I didn't think I should, dear, I wouldn't."

"Yes, I guess so." He poured, filling his own glass as well and then returning to the story he had been telling. Starr watched Jane whose gaze was riveted on Stanley.

Why? She asked herself, over and over, why had she

invited this dumpy, unattractive woman home? What was the point? What was the point of inviting *any* woman home? Where did women ever get you? Well, after this drink she would leave, take a run around the speaks, see what was doing. Jane could come or not. She probably wouldn't since she didn't drink, the chump, but if she did it wouldn't make any difference. She was absolutely no competition.

Starr drained her glass and rose. "Jane and I have to be on our way," she said.

"Well," said Stanley, annoyed that she'd interrupted his story, "it's only two-thirty."

"You know, Stanley," Starr said curbing her hostility for Jane's sake, "I think you're developing some kind of clock complex! You're always telling me what time it is."

"Where are you going?" Helen asked.

"Oh, we have our places, don't we, Jane?" She threw an intense look at the dull woman in the wing chair.

"Oh, yes. Yes, of course."

"Will you be home for dinner?"

"Probably not, Mother. I'll phone you at five if I'm coming."

"Phone me? But . . ."

Starr cut her off with an idle remark, not wanting Jane to know they didn't have a phone. Stanley touched his wife's hand for the same reason.

Stanley helped them on with their coats, they adjusted their cloche hats, said their goodbyes. Out on the street Jane turned to Starr, a tight little smile on her thin lips.

"Your parents are very nice, Starr."

"He's a bloody ass. She's all right, I guess."

Starr began walking west on Ninth, toward Fifth Avenue. Jane followed, timidly asking where they were going.

"I thought we'd check out some speaks, see what chaps are around and . . ."

"But it's only two-thirty!"

"What is this, contagious? I know what time it is. So what?"

"I never go to the clubs until at least after five."

"Well, I go when I feel like it and I feel like it now.

If you don't want to come, don't." She quickened her pace and Jane fell behind.

"Where will you be later, Starr?"

"Here or there. Who knows?"

"I'll look for you."

"Sure."

Starr turned down Fifth without looking back, glad to be rid of Jane. She always preferred traveling alone. It was annoying to have to think of someone else's needs. She liked to drink when she wanted, eat when she wanted—oh, no! She remembered then she had invited Jane to lunch. Well, too bad. She hardly cared whether she ever saw Jane Douglas again. And even if Jane told the tale of the forgotten lunch, who the hell would care what that muttonface had to say? Certainly not any of the men around town and they were the ones who interested her, bought her drinks, made her laugh.

She took a right on Third. Barney's would be the first place. It was restful there and sometimes you'd see a celeb or two. And you never could tell. Today, tonight, she thought, will be lucky for me. I'm gonna get pickled and have one helluva time.

It was quarter to three when she ordered her fifth drink of the day, the only drink that day that she'd pay for herself.

*　　　*　　　*

Between three-fifteen and six-thirty Starr hit The Greenwich Village Inn, Mori's, Pirates Den, Lafayette, Barney's again and the Blue Horse. A year or two earlier, she could have hit three times as many places before heading uptown, but most of the speakeasies were gone, bankrupt. Feeling a little drunk she stopped at a luncheonette, ate half a hamburger and drank two cups of coffee. It helped a bit. At least it would enable her to continue drinking which was what she wanted. It was far too early to be out of commission.

About seven-thirty she entered the Lido uptown. Several men at the bar knew her. One, Edwin Megargee, an artist, immediately ordered her a gin. She liked Ed. He was sweet, bought her drinks, complimented her, but never made a pass. It was a well-known secret that he had a passion for colored girls and when he'd fortified himself enough he'd head up to Harlem and Small's, The Drool Inn, or the Nest. Starr liked being with Ed because she could relax, have some laughs, and keep her eyes open for something good at the same time.

Around eight *something good* came in. He was tall and attractive though balding, and probably somewhere in his fifties. Perfect. He stood at the bar, several people away from her, ordered a whiskey, lit a Camel, and stared at the bottles under the huge mirror.

"Got your eye on somebody?" Ed interrupted her stare.

She smiled. "Mmmm. Maybe."

"Let me guess." Without looking in the direction of the man, Ed said, "Tall, good build and *old*."

"Mature," she corrected.

"Sorry. Mature. How mature? Eighty, ninety?"

"Oh, shut up," she said, laughing.

"Anybody I know?"

She shrugged. "I've never seen him before."

"Is it safe to look?"

"Yes. Casually."

"What else? Everything I do is casual. Don't you know that by now, Starr?" Casually, he turned, took in the man down the bar, then he turned back to Starr. "I don't know him but he looks a bit tough. And he's *mature*, all right."

"Oh, come on, Ed. He's not that old a chap. Maybe fifty, maybe less."

"Or maybe more. You want him?"

"Why not?"

"You sure you can handle him?"

"What's that mean?"

"Well, to be honest, you're pretty drunk. I haven't seen you quite like this in a long time."

The accusation angered her. "The hell I am!" She downed the drink in front of her in one long swallow. "Pete," she yelled to the bartender. "Again. I am bloody sober!"

"Sure. Listen, Starr, I'm not your keeper and we're friends. You do what you want. I just wanted to check . . .

I like you, you know that. We're alike, you and I." He smiled, sadly.

Starr understood what he meant. They both had a problem. She, however, didn't like to think that she had one. She was not convinced that the fact that she liked *mature* men *was* a problem. Anyway, now was no time to start arguing that with Ed. She was far more interested in meeting the man in the blue serge suit.

"So, am I going to meet the bloody chap or not?"

At that moment, the people standing between them left the bar for a table.

"The gods are with me," Starr said.

"Or the devil! Well, here goes nothing." Ed cleared his throat, took two steps sideways and said, "Hello, there. I don't think I've seen you in here before."

Slowly, the man turned his head, looking Ed up and down, small gray eyes taking in every detail. Then he settled on Ed's face and said nothing.

Ed tried smiling. "I wondered if I could buy you a drink? What I mean is, would you like to join us?" He stepped away from the bar and with a sweeping gesture indicated Starr. She smiled. The man smiled back.

"Oh . . . yeah, sure. Thanks." He moved, drink, cigarettes, himself, down the bar, never taking his eyes from Starr. Her face, breasts, legs, hips. He went over and over them as if he couldn't really be sure of his good fortune.

The three of them chatted aimlessly for awhile, then Ed excused himself, joining some people at a table. The man, Joseph Collins, closed the gap Ed left.

After two more drinks and a lot of double entendre, Collins, still standing, leaned into Starr's knees as she sat on her stool.

As the outline of his penis pressed into her flesh, she looked deep into his eyes, assenting.

"Finish your drink," he commanded.

She did. While he ordered a bottle to take with them, Starr went into a blackout. Later, trying to remember the night, it was at that point the evening first went blank. After that she could recapture only a flash here and there.

Collins helped her down from the stool, held her coat, guided her toward the door. Near the door Starr saw a man winking at her, making suggestive gestures. She thought about telling her escort but changed her mind, ignored the man and left.

The man was Edwin Megargee.

* * *

"St. Paul Hotel, 40 West 60th Street," Collins told the cab driver.

"Do you live there?" Starr asked.

"Nah, it's just a place I go sometimes."

"When you have a girl, huh?" She wanted another drink but wasn't sure how Collins would feel about sucking on the bottle.

"Yeah. But I'll tell you something . . . I never had a girl like you. You're some babe." He reached over, pulled her toward him, held the back of her head with one large hand while he kissed her, his tongue filling her mouth. With the other hand he reached inside her coat and easily cupped her breast, rotating his hand.

She liked the way he kissed, liked the feel of his big hand on her breast. With her right hand she reached downward, stroking his swelling penis through the blue serge.

He made a small sound of pleasure, then pulled away. "I don't like this kind of Joe College stuff, if you know what I mean."

She didn't. Starr had spent too much time petting in cars with Andrew to think of it as Joe College. "No, what?"

"Look, I'm grown up and you're grown up. What do we need the back seat of a cab for, you know? We can wait. It just makes it better."

That, certainly, she could understand and agree with. "You're bloody right there."

"You're not English, are you?"

"I've spent a lot of time there."

"Oh. I noticed before you said something about *chaps*."

"Well, I've spent a lot of time there."

"Oh."

They were silent for the rest of the ride. Collins paid the driver and checked them in at the desk as Joseph and Marie Collins. The clerk gave him the keys to room 206.

After throwing her coat over the one chair and tossing her hat on the bureau, Starr sat on the edge of the bed, holding out the small water glass as Joseph filled it. Since her trips to England she always drank without ice but the lack of it irritated him.

"I suppose I could call room service. But they always take so damn long."

"I don't care about ice," she said.

"*I* do!"

"Then call."

"They take too damn long."

"You'll get used to it without ice." She took a sip of whiskey, which she didn't much like, moved back on the bed and leaned against the headboard.

"You comfortable?" He took off his jacket and began removing the links from his cuffs.

"Not too."

"How about getting undressed and into the sack."

"How about you getting me that way?"

"Huh?"

"Undressing me."

"Come on!"

"Come on, what?"

"I don't go in for that stuff. Take your clothes off, babe." Direct, commanding, an order.

She felt slightly apprehensive, sipping again at her drink, unmoving in the direction of his command.

When he took off his shirt and hung it in the closet, he turned back to her. "You still dressed?"

She decided to chance it, push just once more. Why shouldn't she get something out of this? "I like to be undressed," she said.

Collins laughed, short, derisive. "I thought you were a hard-boiled babe. What's this crap?"

"I like a chap who takes his time." She finished her drink.

"Yeah? Well, I like a babe who spreads it. Fast."

Starr was surprised. She wasn't used to this. But it was, in its way, exciting.

"Take off your duds or I'll rip 'em off and leave you here to make your own way. Fast!"

The look in his eyes frightened her, killing her excitement. She was convinced he *would* rip them off. Rising, she tried not to let her fear betray her. She held out her glass. "Fill it up, I fancy another." With her free hand she reached around for the clasp on the blue beads and, understanding she would comply, he took the glass.

Beads unfastened and put on the bureau inside her hat, she took off her dress and flung it to the side. This made Collins smile and Starr felt a bit relieved. Her slip followed the dress, then shoes, stockings, girdle. Taking the drink from Joseph, she crossed back to the bed and sat down.

"What about the rest?"

"Surely a big chap like you can handle a bra and panties," she said.

"Don't give me that shit. Take 'em off." He downed half a glass of whiskey.

Collins was looking meaner by the moment. Slowly, Starr undid her brassiere, letting it fall to her waist.

"Nice tits," Collins said.

"Thanks." She tossed the brassiere aside.

"Take off the panties."

She did, kicking them away from her.

"Now lie down. No, no. Across the bed, let your feet touch the floor. Yeah, like that. Okay, close your peepers."

"Why?" She started to sit up.

"Lie down," he shouted. "Now take the pillows and put 'em under your ass. Hurry up. Good. Close the eyes."

She closed them, listening while he removed his shoes, trousers, the rest of his clothes. She heard his glass being set down on the table. A moment of silence, then, between her legs, she felt something hard and dry jabbing at her. She opened her eyes and lifted her head. Collins, still wearing his undershirt, was standing between her legs.

"Hey," she said, "what's the big idea?"

He looked at her quizzically. "Well, what the hell did you think we were gonna do, play bridge?"

"I don't like to do it that way. I mean, don't you want to do anything else?" Sometimes she could endure intercourse if there'd been enough preliminary play, but she never could go directly into the act.

"I wanna fuck. What do you wanna do?"

She tried a little sweet talk, a little reason. "Joe, listen, you have a nice thing there. I mean, I bet it's bloody good. But you have to get me ready for it, you know. You don't want to hurt me with that huge thing, do you?" No need to tell him it was really quite ordinary.

The adjective served its purpose. Collins was flattered. "Well," he said, backing off a bit, "what do you want me to do? Diddle you?"

She had nothing to lose with this guy. Either he'd do what she asked or he wouldn't. "Why don't you kiss me . . . there."

He stepped back as though she'd kicked him. "You want me to eat that? You must be crazy. I don't eat cunt, lady . . . I fuck it. Now spread those legs."

She closed her legs quickly, rolling over on her stomach.

Collins was enraged. "You fucking bitch."

Starr felt his hand smash down on her bare buttocks and she howled with pain as she instinctively flipped back, front up. But the pain she felt on her lips almost caused her to faint. She screamed and his hand crashed down against her cheek.

"Shut the fuck up, you cunt. Just shut up or I'll give you my fist."

Starr clasped her hand over her mouth.

"Open your legs," he roared. "Open your fucking legs before I pull 'em out of their sockets."

This threat made Starr scream again. He smashed her in the jaw with his fist, then grabbed her by the shoulders and threw her on the floor. She screamed again. He kicked her in the ribs.

"Shut up, shut up, shut up," he yelled.

Starr rolled into a fetal position and sobbed softly into her fists. Collins kicked her once more in the behind, poured himself another drink and collapsed into the chair.

The door was opened with a key. It was the desk clerk and two policemen. Collins, his undershirt plastered to his body, his limp penis wet from the drink he'd just spilled, looked up into the face of Patrolman Henry.

"What's goin' on here, buddy?" Henry asked.

"Huh?"

O'Brien, the second patrolman, rolled Starr over on her back, trying to focus on her bruises, her bloody lip, rather than her naked body. It was hard. "Look at this." He pointed to her face.

"You beat that girl up?" Henry asked Collins.

"She's a cock tease," he said.

"Yeah? What's your name?"

"Joseph Collins." He reached for his pants on the floor, took his wallet from a back pocket, extracted a card and handed it to the officer. Then he began pulling on his trousers.

"Who's the girl?"

"Call her Marie. Marie Collins. She's not my wife but that's all right."

"You're a cook on a Clyde Liner?"

"Yeah, right."

"Okay, get the hell out of here."

O'Brien started to protest, then held his tongue. He was new and ten years his partner's junior. "What should we do with her?" he asked.

"Put her in the bed. You," Henry said to the desk clerk, "call an ambulance."

"Hey, Mac, we don't need no more trouble here . . . she don't need no ambulance, huh?"

"I said, call an ambulance. I'm not takin' any chances."

O'Brien lifted Starr from the floor, carried her to the bed and pulled the covers over her.

Looking up into his kind, blue-green eyes, she said, "All I want you to do is suck me. Is that so bloody much to ask?"

O'Brien turned red, grateful his partner had been busy pushing Collins out the door and hadn't heard. He moved out of Starr's line of vision but still faced her when Henry came back into the room and joined him bedside.

"Poor guy probably spent a bundle on this one," said Henry, pointing at Starr. "And then all he gets is blue balls for his trouble. Poor bastard."

"Yeah." O'Brien watched the blood on Starr's upper lip crusting into a black mass. "Poor bastard."

*　　　*　　　*

When Starr was awakened by a toothy nurse at seven in the morning, she did not know where she was. She remembered nothing of the night before. Neither Collins nor the police. Not Dr. Ruggins of Flower Hospital nor the ambulance attendants, particularly Wilbur, short, young, all ears, who helped her dress and tried to make her laugh. She didn't remember the ride to the hospital in the ambulance. Her admittance. The shot she was given to quiet her down. She certainly did not know who Marie Collins was. And she had absolutely no idea that she was in the psychiatric ward of Bellevue Hospital which was attached to Flower.

What she did know, after taking a slow, painful look around her, was that she was in a hospital, had a helluva hangover, a face that felt like it was on fire and was in some kind of terrible trouble. She was very afraid.

Pulling the thin cotton blanket up around her neck, she watched as the nurse went from one bed to another, waking women of all ages. She was in a ward. Starr Faithfull in a ward! Her mother would die of embarrassment. Stanley would be mortified. There had to be some sort of mistake.

"Nurse," she said. A terrible pain shot up through her nose from her lip. She brought her hand to her mouth and touched the place where the pain had begun. It was bandaged. Tape. What had happened? She looked under the coverlet, a quick glance down her body to see if anything else was bandaged. Nothing was.

"See anything ya like?"

Starr dropped the blanket and looked up into the face of the bucktoothed nurse. "Oh, I'm so glad you're here," she said, trying to sit up.

"Yes?"

"I wonder if we could talk about something."

"What's that?" The nurse stared down, head cocked to one side, arms crossed in front of her.

Starr gazed up into her exceptionally large nostrils wondering if she'd put beans in them when she was a child. "Well, I think there's been a mistake."

"You do, huh?"

"I would prefer a private room."

Three nearby women broke into howling laughter. Starr tried to ignore them. "I really don't belong in a ward, you know."

"Is that right?" the nurse said. "Very fascinating."

The women laughed again, this time harder, it seemed to Starr. Something here was out of kilter. Not just that she didn't remember what had happened or why she was here. That would be simple enough to piece together. She'd been drinking and the bandage on her face indicated she'd been in some sort of accident. So why were these women laughing at her? Why did the nurse have that peculiar sound in her voice—like *she* was laughing at her? She realized she'd been staring into the dark recesses of the nostrils and quickly shifted her gaze, meeting the round, unyielding eyes of the nurse. "If I'm not going to be released right away, I'd like to be moved to a private room immediately," Starr said.

Squeals and shrieks of laughter. Even the nurse's mouth twitched momentarily into something akin to a smile.

"Well, we'll just see what we can do for you, Mrs. Rockefeller."

"Mrs. Rockefeller," a woman echoed and others screeched the name throughout the room.

Starr's panic was now full-blown. "Look, what's going on here? Why are you behaving this way? Do you want me to report you?" She started to stand and was quickly, easily, pushed back down by the nurse's fingers.

"Okay, the game's over," the nurse said.

"What game?"

She started to walk away from the bed.

"Wait a minute." Starr yelled, standing now, painfully.

The nurse kept walking.

"Do you know who I am?" Starr demanded.

"Marie Antoinette?" The nurse spoke over her shoulder as she rattled her keys, unlocking the door.

Then Starr realized where she was. Slowly, she sat back down on the cot, withdrawing inside herself from the loud, piercing laughter. The nurse had *locked* the door behind her. Starr was in a psycho ward. Locked in this room with at least thirty other women. Why? What had she done? She tried to remember. Nothing came. She forced her mind back beyond last night. The afternoon. Jane Douglas. The martinis, Stanley, her mother. The speaks. Night. Hamburger. The Lido. Ed. A man. Joseph Connors—Collins. "Let's get out of here." Collins's voice. She saw herself, nodding, smiling. Collins turns to the bartender, says something. What? The bartender, Pete, the fat one, nods. He hands Collins something in a paper bag. A bottle! Yes, Collins ordered a bottle, got it and—that was all. The images ceased. Where had they gone? What had happened?

Starr lay down, facing the tiled wall. Her head ached and something in her jaw throbbed and pulled. Again she tried to force her mind beyond the exchange of money for bottle. There was nothing. She'd had blackouts before but they had never been so frightening. Or important. Suppose, unless she remembered, they wouldn't let her out? Had she tried to kill herself? Kill him? Had he tried to kill her? Any or all were possible. She wanted her mother.

        ❖   ❖   ❖

"You're next," a nurse said to Starr.

She rose from the hard bench and walked to the door where the nurse stood, waiting. Roughly, she took Starr's arm and pushed her through the yawning doorway, closing the door behind her with a crisp snap. Starr pulled the flimsy, ugly hospital robe tightly around her. What had they done with her clothes?

Across from where she stood with her back to the door, a craggy-faced man sat behind an oak desk. His hair, on top and in front, was blue-black. The sides were beginning to turn gray. His hands reminded her of Stanley's. The nails were neat, clean, shaped; the fingers long. At the front of his desk was a triangular wooden sign. Letters painted in thin black print spelled out his name. Herman Kanzow, M.D.

He sat down on the desk the yellow papers he was holding and looked up at her. "Sit down." His voice was gentle.

She sat in a wooden chair with a green leather seat.

"You are Marie Collins?" he asked, skeptical.

Starr had made up her mind to be as truthful as possible while, at the same time, not admitting to her complete lack of knowledge about what had happened. Surely there would be some way around this. There would be clues. Like this one—Marie Collins. Obviously, she hadn't wanted to give her right name because of the circumstances. Oh, God. What circumstances? She must answer. "No," she said.

"No?" He arched dark eyebrows.

"I mean," she said, trying to appear innocent, wishing she were dressed in her own clothes, "that is not my real name." How could she be seductive, winning, in these rags? "I only gave that name because, well, under the circumstances, you know." She smiled.

"*You* did not give the name. You don't remember that?"

She had gone too far, given more information than was necessary. "Well, what I meant was . . ." Say nothing, she told herself. Let *him* give more information. Stories of people being in psycho wards for months, years, for not saying the right thing, shimmered in her foggy memory.

"What is your name?"

"Starr Faithfull."

Again, the arched eyebrows.

"It *is*." She understood his look. "I know it sounds odd but it *is* my name."

"A beautiful name."

"Thank you." She warmed to his compliment and crossed her legs at the knees, exposing her thigh.

"What were you drinking yesterday, Miss Faithfull?" He took a cigarette from a gold box on the desk, then offered her one.

Happily, she accepted it. "I had been drinking gin, as far as I know."

"As far as you know?"

"Well, you can never tell what you get slipped these days."

"Ahhh." He shook his head up and down.

"This is the first time I've drunk anything for six months." She didn't know why she said it.

The ash on his cigarette was growing long. "How many did you have?"

Was there any point in lying about this? Probably they'd done tests, knew how much she'd had. Best to be honest here. She waited for him to drag on the cigarette which he held between his thumb and forefinger, then gave her answer. "I don't know how many I had . . . I don't remember."

"Do you mean, Miss Faithfull, that you had so many that you lost count or that it is a blank to you?"

What was the answer he wanted? She wished she could read the incredibly long ash on his cigarette the way gypsies read tea leaves. Maybe this was a trick question—the one that would keep her here for weeks, months. Before she could decide what to say, he went on.

"Perhaps I should read you the diagnosis of the attending physician, hmmm? Yes." He picked up one of the yellow sheets. "Acute alcoholism."

Acute alcoholism! Did that mean she was an alcoholic? Impossible. She remembered they'd asked about her drinking at Channing. She'd lied, denying that she drank at all. Now she couldn't do that, but she could certainly deny the charge of alcoholism. "That's ridiculous. Do I look like an alcoholic to you?"

Kanzow smiled, sadly, one-sidedly, shook his head slightly. "Miss Faithfull, I didn't say you were an alcoholic. What I said was that Dr. Ruggins diagnosed your condition as acute alcoholism. This, dear lady, comes from the ingestion of too much alcohol." The ash finally fell, making a trail down the brown lapel of his jacket and onto a portion of his white shirt. He brushed it away, succeeding in making a long gray smudge. He returned to the yellow sheet. "It also says that you have contusions of the face, jaw and upper lip. But, of course, you know this."

She nodded. She did not, of course. She hadn't been allowed near a mirror and could only imagine.

"And you know how this came about, naturally?"

"Yes," she said quickly.

There was a pause and then he said, "Well?"

Did he know? Or was it as much a mystery to him as it was to her? She could only guess and pray that her guess was right. "I suppose someone knocked me around a bit." She tried to smile. It hurt.

Kanzow sighed and shook his head again. "And that is it? You will be telling me nothing else?"

She shrugged, not knowing what else to do.

"Naturally. All right, Miss Faithfull. Do you have a family?"

"Yes."

"Are they here in New York?"

"Yes."

"Give me their phone number, please."

"The phone is out of order."

"How do you know it is *still* out of order? Give me the number in case it has been fixed."

This was the most humiliating moment of the interview for her. She fought back tears. "We don't have a phone," she said, very softly, looking at the paper slippers on her feet.

"Then your address, please," Kanzow asked, not losing a beat.

"34 East Ninth Street."

"Thank you. You can go out this other door and wait in that room until your parents come for you. You will be released in their custody. Try to cut down on your intake of alcohol, Miss Faithfull. I fear it is toxic for you."

"Sure. Thanks." She left his office, walked through a small passageway, entered a larger room, sat on a hard oak chair and, while she waited, tried desperately to remember. She failed.

*   *   *

Stanley, Helen and Starr climbed the stairs to their apartment. Inside, Helen helped her daughter with her coat. Starr allowed this without a word. She was exhausted. And hungover. And frightened. She didn't particularly want to talk to them but she was afraid to go to her room, to be cut off. Tucker stood in a corner of the living room near a window, staring at her. Helen guided Starr to the softest chair.

"Can I get you anything, dear?"

Starr shook her head.

"Tea?"

"No."

"Milk?"

"No, nothing. Oh, yes, anybody have a cigarette?"

Stanley offered her a Lucky Strike.

Usually when she had a hangover she couldn't smoke but today she needed it for her nerves, for something to do. She took a long drag and blew it in the direction of her sister, who, sitting now, was still staring.

"I know I look a bloody mess, but do you have to keep staring at me?"

"I'm not staring," Tucker said. "I'm looking. There's a difference."

"Well, haven't you ever seen anyone who's had an accident before?"

Tucker made a scoffing noise and, for once, Starr ignored the provocation. She didn't have the energy to react.

Helen and Stanley sat across from her on the flowered couch. They too stared.

"Well, if everyone's just going to stare at me, I'm leaving." The threat, of course, was idle and they all knew it. There was no way she could have made it back down the stairs.

"I'm sorry, dear." Helen looked down at her lap and began to pick imaginary lint from her skirt.

Stanley cleared his throat. "Well, then, is there anything you want to talk about? Anything you want to tell us? You don't have to, of course. You're free, white and twenty-one!" He giggled as though he'd just made up the line.

There had been no discussion in the taxi coming home. Only strained silence or Helen's voice describing things along the way as though she were a sightseeing guide. At the hospital they'd all had an interview with Doctor Kanzow and Stanley had done his best to protect her.

"Nothing was wrong with her at 2:30 P.M. yesterday. I know of no reason why she was admitted here." This said looking at her bruised and bandaged face. "I did mix one drink for her. Incidentally, it was prewar stuff." As if Kanzow cared what it was. "She never drank outside since she returned from Europe last fall in late October. She has not had one drink outside the house." Starr wondered what good he thought these lies would do but she, naturally, remained silent. "I'll be honest with you, Doctor. We are not Prohibitionists. But I, being a chemist, have warned the girls about bootleg liquor." It had been easy for Starr to see that Kanzow was not impressed. After asking Stanley if he would be responsible for Starr, and Stanley agreeing, Kanzow dismissed her. Now she wondered what had transpired in that interview.

"What went on with you and Kanzow after I left?"

Helen and Stanley exchanged glances. Starr could not read them.

"Nothing much." Stanley stubbed out his cigarette.

It was, she felt, important that she know. Perhaps there would be a clue to what had happened in those blank hours. "Did he say anything?"

"About what, dear?" Helen asked.

"About anything?"

The elder Faithfulls exchanged another indecipherable look.

"Would you please stop looking at each other like that? It's bloody frustrating." A drink might make her feel better, clear her head. "I'd like a drink, Stanley."

Again the look. They caught themselves, embarrassed, each fussed with a bit of clothing. Stanley made no move. Usually when she asked, he was up on his feet in a flash.

"Stanley? Did you hear me?"

"Yes, Bamby." He did not look at her.

Acute alcoholism. Undoubtedly, Kanzow had filled their heads with that rot. Well, she'd make *them* say it. She wasn't about to make it easy for them. "A drink, please."

"Do you have to, dear?"

"No, I don't *have* to. I *want* to."

"How about a nice cup of coffee?" Helen pleaded.

"How about a nice glass of gin?" Starr replied.

"Oh, dear."

Stanley bit his upper lip, blinked his eyes, shook his head. "All right, Bamby."

"Stanley!"

"She's a grown woman, Helen."

"But the doctor said . . ."

Stanley made a sharp movement with his hand, signaling her to stop.

Inside, Starr smiled. It was too painful to risk a real smile. "I suppose," she said, deciding to help the fools out, "he gave you that bloody rot about alcoholism."

"Yes, dear."

"What about alcoholism?" Tucker asked.

Starr ignored her. "Well, that's just what it is you know. Rot. I got some bad gin yesterday, that's all. Stanley's right. We have to be careful of bootleg liquor. It was just bad gin, that's all it was." When she said *gin* she saw *whiskey*. The first flash of the blank hours.

"Well," Tucker said, "I never heard of gin, bad or not, doing *that*." She gestured toward Starr's face.

"Please," Helen said, sensing trouble.

"I'm sure you're right, Starr. Bad gin."

"Yeah," Tucker said, "bad gin sure packs a wallop."

Starr wanted the drink and she wanted more information. Tucker could wait. "What else did that bloody idiot doctor tell you?" she asked, trying to sound casual.

"Oh, we don't want to talk about this, do we?" said Helen. "Let's just forget about it. It's over. Let's go forward. We must always go forward. No point in brooding about the past. Let's think of something cheerful."

There was no way now that Starr could pursue this without appearing desperate. If Stanley and Helen knew anything, it was closed to her. She would have to find out herself. She would have to remember. Stanley handed her a drink. She took a swallow, thinking for a moment she might gag, then almost immediately it began to work, smoothing her out.

After two drinks she went to her room to sleep. She could not. She took two Veronal and while she waited for them to take effect she once more tried to remember. No use.

*   *   *

Starr stayed at home until every trace of her beating had disappeared. Locked inside that way, she was even more unpleasant and harder to get along with than usual. And the fact that she kept trying to remember but could not served to make her disposition all the more sour. Her family tried to avoid her when they were at home but often they went out, leaving her alone in the apartment.

She spent her time drinking, taking Veronal, reading. On the third of May the last mark on her lip faded away. That afternoon she dressed in a tan linen suit, brown pumps, brown hat and bag, and left the apartment. The three remaining Faithfulls breathed a silent sigh of relief.

The afternoon was spent in Lord & Taylor's, Bergdorf's, Saks Fifth Avenue. At six she ate dinner alone at Dinty Moore's. Roast beef, mashed potatoes, broccoli, green salad, rolls, black forest cake and two cups of coffee. By seven-thirty she was seated at a table at Porky Murray's speakeasy on West Fifty-second Street, with three men, one of whom she didn't know but found very attractive. Later in the evening she left Porky's with the new man, hit several more speaks and spent three hours with him in his hotel room. At four in the morning she arrived back at the apartment on Ninth Street where she promptly passed out in her clothes.

Throughout the spring, she tried to remember what had happened on March 30th but the pieces never came together. By June, when she left for Europe with Tucker and Helen, she thought of it less and less. In July, in England, it was a dim, vague memory that came to her only at night when she had difficulty sleeping. August, September and October came and went with only the most fleeting recollections of that night in March. By November, when she returned to America, it was completely gone from her memory.

God help me, that's Starr's dress.
—Stanley Faithfull making positive identification
at Macken's Morgue, Rockville Center,
June 8, 1931

June 6, 1931
New York, New York

Breathless, her back against the pink door, Starr stood momentarily stunned. Quickly, she pulled her thoughts together, tore the robe and nightgown from her body and threw them across the room. She dressed at top speed, then carefully opened the bedroom door. There was no sound.

Carrying her shoes she crept down the steps. At the bottom she stood for a moment wondering where her hat and coat had been taken. Realizing she could not look for them she tiptoed toward the front door. Diana's purse sat on a small table near it. Swiftly, almost in passing, Starr reached inside, extracted several bills from a wallet, threw the wallet back in the purse. Then, slowly turning the brass lock, she opened the door and went out.

The door closed behind her, she stepped into her pumps. The cobblestones were slippery and the sound of her heels crashed in her ears as she ran.

At Fifth Avenue she boarded the uptown bus.

Twenty

August 6, 1977
Orange, New Jersey

The light in the room was growing dim. People had come and gone. He was alone again. A familiar state. Somewhere inside he'd always felt that way but since Fran died he really had been alone.

SLAYING FOLLOWED LOVE TRYST. No, he wouldn't think of it. His voice was all but gone. No explanation for it, the doctor said. He was sure it was connected to the stroke. But it didn't matter what it was from. The point was he couldn't communicate. And now this. Surely this was the end. It was just a matter of time.

What was that? Did his heart skip beats?

———

Fall, 1930
New York, New York

While his wife and stepdaughters were in Europe, Stanley Faithfull arranged a grand surprise for them. Actually, it was more for Starr than anyone. He found a new apartment. On St. Luke's Place. Number 12. St. Luke's was a beautiful block, houses only on the north side of the street, all facing Walker Park with its flourishing flower garden. And, most impressive of all, right down the street, at number 6, was the residence of Mayor Jimmy Walker. Surely, Starr would adore living so near an eminent figure.

Number 12 had its share of interesting and prominent people too. The apartment beneath the top floor, which Stanley had engaged, was occupied by Arlene and Dr. Van Wessup. She was a vice president of Lord & Taylor's. Below them, on the parlor floor, were the landlords, Mr. and Mrs. Duncan Smith. Smith was a fairly well-known muralist and Alice Smith was a designer for Lord & Taylor's. In the ground-floor apartment was a Mr. Burdett Kinne, professor of French at Columbia University.

The rent was modest enough for Stanley to manage and the apartment itself quite wonderful, even though the room Tucker and Starr had to share was small. There were two beautiful large fireplaces, one in the master bedroom, the other in the living room. Stanley had chosen to make the room at the front of the house the living room and the girls' room was directly off this. The kitchen and bathroom were off the master bedroom. The front door opened onto a kind of hall which Stanley decided might serve as a dining area, even though it merged with the master bedroom. They could always do something about that. Perhaps a screen. All in all, he was pleased and couldn't wait for his three girls to come home.

When he met them at the boat he felt somewhat giddy. He'd missed them, of course. Especially Helen. Six months was a long time, long enough, he was sure, to have gone through the last of the Peters money. Stanley hoped the surprise of the new apartment would keep Starr happy for awhile even if funds were low.

As he put them in the taxi he whispered the address to the driver. When the taxi turned off Hudson onto St. Luke's, stopping in front of a yellow house with a high stoop, Starr said, "What's going on?"

"We're home." Stanley grinned, eyes twinkling.

The three women looked at each other.

"I fancy this is some kind of a joke. Right, Stanley old boy?"

"It's no joke, Bamby. It's our new little nest. Come on."

"If you think I'm going to live in that room with *her*, you have another think coming." Starr stood at the doorway to the small bedroom, hands on her hips.

Stanley's face, sagging slightly, betrayed his jovial tone. "But Bamby, dear, where else can you sleep?"

"Why don't you and Mother take this room? After all, you're in closer contact than Tucker and I are." She stared directly at Stanley, her eyes boring into his.

"Really, dear," Helen said. "Have some respect. We *are* older and should have the better room."

"Well, I'm not sharing this tomb and that's all there is to it."

"Good," Tucker said, "I'll have it all to myself."

"I said I wasn't sharing it, Tuck, not that I was *giving* it to you."

"And what do you expect me to do? Sleep in the bathtub?"

Starr shrugged, moving out of the doorway, through the living room and back into the hallway where she stopped and looked around.

The others followed, Tucker imploring her mother to do something.

"Hello," said Starr, the English intonation clear.

"What is it, Bamby?"

"*This* will be my room," she said.

"This?" Stanley whirled around, arms outstretched. "But this isn't a room."

"It will be."

"How?"

"Curtains. Here and here and one there to block off the front door."

"But you won't have any fresh air, dear," Helen said.

"So what? Yes, I like that idea."

"You won't have any light." Stanley didn't at all like the idea of her being so close to him and Helen with only a flimsy curtain separating them.

"Light? You mean daylight? God, who wants daylight?"

"But Starr . . ." Helen stopped as Stanley put a gentle hand on her forearm.

All three watched as Starr paced off the places where she'd hang her curtains, knowing that no matter what they said it was already a fait accompli.

Within a few days Starr had curtained off her room, moved her single bed from Tucker's room, bought a used chest of drawers on Varick Street and appropriated a lamp from the living room. But she spent little time there and her family barely saw her. She was always out, always moving, managing, though she had few funds of her own, to have a very full social life.

The Faithfulls, wanting peace, never asked any questions but from the bits and pieces Starr volunteered her life sounded like one continuous party. And in a way it was. But the party girl, almost every morning of her life, wished she were dead.

November 15, 1930
Newark, New Jersey

"If you don't quit the band I'm leaving." Fran lit a cigarette, a new habit she'd begun that summer out of boredom.

"What do you mean, leaving?"

"What does it sound like? I can't stand it anymore. A person can read just so much, you know." She poured herself a rye and soda. Another new habit. Same reason.

"Where would you go?" Orlando asked.

"What difference does that make?"

"I just wondered."

"I'd go home or maybe to New York, who knows?"

"And go on the stage?" he scoffed.

"Maybe. Anyway, where I'd go isn't the point, Orr."

"What *is* the point?"

She hated it when he did that, knowing perfectly well what she was talking about. "The point is that unless you quit the band I'm going to leave you."

"Oh, come on, Fran." He reached out for her but she pulled away.

"No, I mean it. I hate to say this but you're a selfish man."

"Sweetheart . . ."

"Don't sweetheart me."

He was beginning to feel afraid. "Okay, tell me what's wrong."

"*What's wrong?*" she screeched.

He'd never heard her, seen her, like this.

"Everything is wrong. We have no life. No life *together*. And I have no life. I'm alone all the time. I think I'll go crazy."

"But honey, you have friends."

"Yes, we have friends. But do you think they want an extra woman around? They don't invite me without you."

"You have Deirdre."

"Oh, shit!"

He was stunned. He'd never heard her use such language and it horrified him. He thought it was cheap, vulgar, low-class. Especially for a woman. Especially *that* word. He never even used *that* word himself. What had happened to her? Smoking, drinking, swearing! Jesus! "Don't you ever say that again."

She was embarrassed. She knew how proper he was. Knew he would never tell her a dirty joke or say anything more than damn or hell in front of her. "It just slipped out," she said meekly.

"If it wasn't in your mind to begin with it couldn't slip out." He raised his chin, his distaste evident.

The look made Fran want to kill him but it also intimidated her. She took a swallow of her drink.

He shot her another withering glance before turning toward the bedroom.

"Where are you going?"

"To bed."

She wouldn't be put off. "I want this settled, Orr."

Now he looked at her as though she were crazy. "You want *what* settled?"

She let out a shriek and threw the glass against the wall, crumpling, falling onto the couch, crying.

Orlando stared. This was a new Fran. Was she drunk? What was he supposed to do? The more she cried, the more he found it impossible to move. Not that it didn't touch him. It did. He couldn't stand to see anyone cry. But, nevertheless, he couldn't move. Tears came into his own eyes. It never failed. He knew he must go to her. Still, he was rooted to the spot.

Fran looked up, face stained with mascara, her eyes red and puffy. "Oh, my God," she wailed, "you *are* horrible."

That set him in motion, going toward her, trying to

put his arms around her. But she hit him in the chest and screamed some more. He sat beside her, waiting for her to stop. When she did he tentatively touched her hair. She didn't push him away. Slowly, he put his arm around her. She was tired and allowed it.

"Now," he said, "what's going on here?"

"I'm lonely," she said. "I'm so lonely."

The sound, the words themselves, dug deeply into him. He could have sobbed for her. After all, he loved her. He didn't want her to be lonely, so lonely.

"What can I do?" he asked.

"Please give up the band."

"We'll have less money."

"I don't care. I'd rather have more of you."

What was he to do? He hated to give up his music but he loved his wife. He wanted what he'd had. Both. "Why don't you go up to Montreal for a few weeks and visit Nina and Renato?"

Fran pulled away from his chest and looked at him quizzically.

"I know they'd love to have you," he said.

"Are you crazy?"

"Hmmmm?"

"Don't you understand, Orr? Don't you understand anything?"

"I just thought . . ."

"You just thought you'd have everything. Everything your way. All the time."

"Be fair."

"FAIR? ME? Oh, good God." She jumped up and poured herself another drink.

"You're drinking a lot lately."

"How would you know? You're never here." At that moment she thought this marriage was the worst thing that had ever happened to her. Who was it who had warned her? Someone. She couldn't remember who. A new idea struck her. "Maybe you just don't *want* to be with me."

"Of course I do. I love you." He stayed unmoving, on the couch.

"Then why are you trying to get rid of me?" She searched the table for matches.

"Get rid of you?" He was incredulous. "I was offering

you . . . you said you were lonely . . . I thought . . . I was just trying to think of an answer . . . something to help you not feel so lonely. Do you think I *want* you to be lonely?"

"I don't know what you want. No, that's not true. I do know. You want to play in the band and you want me to be happy with that. I'm not. I won't be. I want something *my* way for once."

"What's that supposed to mean, *for once?*"

She found a match, finally. It had been right in front of her. "Oh, Orr, we've been married for a year and a half and I've done everything your way. And your family's way. I'm tired of it."

"Like what?" He really didn't know what she was talking about.

"Like this furniture, for one thing." She couldn't help herself.

"Hmmm?"

"It's the ugliest stuff I've ever seen."

"I thought you liked it." He sat forward.

"I hate it. And I hate going to Van Ness all the time." She might as well say it all.

"I thought you liked my family."

"I do. I love your mother, but I don't like *having* to go there."

"So you don't like my father then." He lit a cigarette.

"I didn't say that. I said . . ."

"He's been very nice to you, considering."

"Considering what?"

"Nothing." He crossed his legs, angling his body away from her. She planted herself in his line of vision. "Considering what?"

"Forget it." It was a mistake. He wished he hadn't said it.

"No, I won't. I want to know what that means."

"Drop it." He turned away.

She moved in front of him again. "Tell me."

"I've had enough," he said, standing up.

She barred his way.

"Move."

"No."

He'd never hit her, pushed her, made any violent move toward her and he had no intention of starting now.

But when he moved left or right she moved with him, making it impossible for him to get away from the couch which pinned him from behind. It infuriated him that he was in this position.

"Considering what?"

"Considering that you can't spell!" he yelled in frustration.

She stared. After a few seconds, she said softly, "What?"

"Will you let me by, please?"

She moved away, still staring.

He made himself a drink.

"Can't spell?" she asked.

"Never mind." He turned to her. She looked so confused, helpless. Who wouldn't love her? Even his father had seen her innate sweetness, charm. "Oh, Fran."

"Orlando, what do you mean, can't spell?"

He put down his drink and went to her. "Darling, just forget it. It doesn't mean anything."

"Please."

He couldn't resist her sad eyes and told her about the letter. "But what I said . . . you know, *considering* . . . that was stupid. Obviously, Papa loves you and doesn't care about your spelling anymore."

For a moment she looked at him, blank. Then she dropped his hands and took a step backward. "Why are we talking about this? Who cares about my spelling? You always do this. You always twist and shift when I want to talk about something important."

"But you insisted on knowing."

"Never mind. You make me crazy, Orlando. Let's get back to the point." Who was it who'd said marriage with him would be hard?

"What point?" Truly forgotten, already repressed.

"Don't," she warned. "Are you going to quit the band or not?"

Oh, that. "You're asking me to give up something I love."

"I know that, Orr." Gently. "I've thought a lot about it. But you could write instead."

"I'd hardly be with you then."

"You'd be home. It would be different."

"You accuse me of being selfish but what do you think asking me to quit is?"

"Selfish," she said, unashamed. "I can't help it. I need you at home."

He didn't want to lose her. "All right." He promised he'd leave the band as soon as Halsey found another banjo player. He would give his notice the next night. Promise.

She thanked him, crying a little out of gratitude and exhaustion. Things became soft and sweet again between them and that night Fran, before falling asleep, remembered who had sensed possible difficulty in a marriage with Orlando Antolini. She had.

May 29, 1931
New York, New York

Even though the temperature was in the eighties, when she left the apartment Starr carried her dark coat with the fur collar and cuffs over her arm. She might want to cover up. Although she thought she looked rather nice at the moment, she never knew when she might feel fat and unsightly.

As she stepped from her stoop to the sidewalk, before she could turn toward Hudson Street, a passing man smiled, touching the brim of his hat. Small, frail almost, but attractive, he'd gone on by before she realized it was the Mayor, Jimmy Walker. She'd wanted to meet him for months, sometimes walking up and down the block for hours on end, hoping for just such a coincidence. And now it had happened and she hadn't been prepared. She watched him saunter down the block, trying to think of some reason to call him back, some way to get his attention, but her mind was a blank and he was up the stairs and into his house before she'd really recovered. Starr swore softly to herself. Well, perhaps that chance meeting, the smile, was just a beginning. Perhaps next time Walker would speak to her. She really did like the way he looked.

She walked to Hudson where she hailed a taxi and told the driver to go to Pier 56 at the foot of 14th Street. The *Franconia* was sailing for England at five-thirty that afternoon.

Starr hadn't booked passage. In fact, she hadn't been

anywhere since her return from England the previous November but she often went to parties aboard the ships before they sailed. It didn't matter whether or not she knew anyone who was sailing. She could easily insinuate herself into one stateroom party or another. The guests were drunk, and she was lovely to look at, so who cared? It was a great way to cadge drinks and to meet men. It was also a game she played with herself. She loved fooling people, making them think she was a real guest, making them wonder who she was but afraid to ask for fear they'd appear foolish and uninformed. She always gave the impression that she was *someone*.

But today was different. It was not just seeing how many drinks she could get. Or who would make the biggest ass of himself over her. Or who might take her out for the evening afterwards. Today was a day she'd planned for. Dr. George Jameson-Carr was the ship's doctor and Starr was prepared to confront him one more time. The last time she'd seen him had been an accident. Months ago in Barney's. She'd been very drunk and much of what happened was blank. She remembered only joining his party, uninvited, and then Bill walking her back to her own table, telling her this wasn't the time or place but soon they'd be together. Since then she'd written more letters. But again, no replies.

Now she was tired of the unrequited letter writing and ready to have it out with Jameson-Carr. Either something was going to come of this passion or she would have to give it up. He couldn't keep dangling her forever!

As the taxi neared Pier 56, Starr took a surreptitious, but rather long, swig from her flask. The dock beside the *Franconia* was crowded and noisy. On board, at the right of the gangplank, was a young man, Robert Decker, an executive of the Cunard line, someone Starr had met years before. He smiled showing perfect white teeth beneath his trim mustache.

"Hello there." He offered a hand.

She looked at him, cocking her head to one side, trying to remember. He was familiar. Had she slept with him?

Seeing her confusion, he told her who he was and where they had met. She remembered, was relieved. Nothing but a mild flirtation.

"Are you sailing?" He was hopeful, yet suspicious. "I didn't see your name on the passenger list."

"I've just come to see a friend. Dr. Jameson-Carr," she said, almost haughty.

"Oh? Is he expecting you?"

"Of course." Her ring of authority shrank him slightly.

"Of course," he repeated. "I'll take you down."

Halfway there they were stopped by the ship's second officer, who told Decker that he was needed by the captain. Decker turned Starr over to the officer.

"I wonder," said Starr when Decker was out of sight, "I'm feeling a bit weak. I've just come out of a sickbed after two weeks . . . pneumonia . . . I wonder, do you think I could have a bit of brandy?"

The officer flushed, blinked his eyes rapidly, then said if she'd follow him to his cabin he just happened to have some very good stuff. After a third brandy Starr left, assuring the young man that she knew the way and would see him later.

When she got to Jameson-Carr's cabin she listened for a moment. Hearing nothing, she knocked twice.

"Who's there?"

She breathed deeply at the sound of his voice, crossed her fingers, shut her eyes. "It's just little Starr, Doc."

"What do you want?"

She ignored the gruffness in his voice. "Let me in."

"I'm busy."

"Don't be an old dodo."

After a few seconds' silence, Jameson-Carr opened the door, his jaw set. "Well?"

"I want to talk to you, Bill."

"I'm sorry but you can't just now. I'm very busy. You'd better go back to your party."

"To hell with the party." She wouldn't tell him that *he* was her party. "I've got to talk to you. It's something very important."

Jameson-Carr literally sighed. "It's no use, Starr. I'm too busy."

She tried to see beyond him into the cabin. What was keeping him so busy? Was it another woman?

"Who do you have in there?" She tried to sound playful.

"No one."

"I'll bet."

"Really." He opened the door wider, taking a step back to show the empty cabin, and she scurried past him. "Starr!"

"I have to talk to you, Doc." She sat on the edge of his bunk. "I think I fancy a little drink."

He stood just inside the open door. "That's unfortunate because I'm fresh out. I want you to leave, Starr."

"Well, I'm not. Not leaving and not fresh out." She opened her purse, pulled out the flask Stanley had given her and took a long swallow. Then she held it out to Jameson-Carr.

He stared at her, hard, angrily. "I told you that I didn't want to see you again."

The corners of her full mouth twitched. When? When had he told her that? She took another sip to bolster her bravado. "Don't be silly."

"You're the one who's silly. Or crazy. I'm not sure which."

She pretended not to hear. "Bill, I think it's time to settle this thing once and for all."

His heavy dark eyebrows furrowed. "Settle what thing?"

"Why, you and me, of course. I can't go on like this anymore. I must know where we are. Where we stand."

"I think you *are* crazy."

She went on, unhearing, unseeing. "I do have other chaps interested in me, you know. You're not the only fish in the sea."

Jameson-Carr shook his head with disbelief.

"There's no doubt that you *are* a darling, and certainly one of my favorites, but fun's fun and all that and now it's time to settle down, don't you think?"

"Settle down," he repeated, as though in a trance.

"Settle down. I do get tired of all this running about, fun as it is." She'd gone further than she'd meant to but somehow the words had just gotten away from her. She hadn't the power to stop them.

He was silent, staring, unable to comprehend what

had brought her to this. Hadn't he made himself clear enough over the years? And that final time at Barney's when he'd told her he *never, never* wanted to see her again. Was it possible he hadn't been firm enough? He'd said the words: I never want to see you again. Never. Even if his tone hadn't been severe enough surely the words carried themselves. She was mad. Absolutely mad. How did one handle a crazy person? He supposed he could try telling her again.

"Starr, listen to me. I told you last time we met . . . remember . . . at Barney's?"

She nodded, smiling.

"I told you then that I never wanted to see you again and I'm telling you now. I don't want you to come around anymore. I don't want to see you. Do you understand?"

She looked at him, smile stuck.

"Did you hear me?"

"Of course."

"Do you understand what I said?"

She rose slowly from the bunk. "You mean," she said, as though about to recite a lesson just learned, "that all the years I've known you don't mean anything at all? I thought you were my friend."

"I wanted to be. I would have liked that but you made it impossible. You didn't want friendship, Starr."

After a moment she said, "It's odd."

"What is?"

"You're the only man who . . . nothing."

She pushed past him, not looking his way, and walked down the corridor.

When Starr emerged from the ladies room, eyes swollen from crying, she bumped into the Chief Steward, Edward Jones.

"Is something wrong, Miss?"

"Wrong? Oh, yes. It's my coat."

"Your coat?"

"Yes. I wonder. Could I leave it in your cabin for now. It's so cumbersome to carry around."

"Why don't you leave it in your own cabin, if you don't mind my asking?"

"I'm not sailing, dear boy . . . just visiting."

"Oh, I see. Well, then, of course. I'll be glad to put it in my cabin. It's right down the hall. 4D. When you're ready to leave ship just go right in and take it."

"You're very kind. Next time I sail I won't forget you. I'll be sailing this ship next trip."

"Yes, Ma'am."

She smiled, touching his fuzzy blond hand. He swallowed, bowed slightly and took her coat off toward his cabin.

Laughter cut through a silent moment in the cabin and a number of heads turned to see who was having such a good time. It was the beautiful girl in the blue serge suit. Everyone wondered who she was but no one asked.

The man Starr was talking with was tall, distinguished, middle-aged. She'd told him her name was Sylvia Pierpont, that she was, indeed, sailing, and that, on arrival in England, she was to be married to a man she didn't love because he was dying and it was his last wish. She also indicated she would be happy to meet the gentleman later, after they sailed. She'd left her own party because it was boring but now she must get back. After all, how rude could she be?

On B Deck Starr, very drunk, but still looking beautiful, encountered Tommy Ryan, a bellboy. He'd turned sixteen the day before.

"You *are* a darling," Starr said.

Tommy's dimples, one in each round cherry cheek, appeared fully.

"I'm not sailing, you know."

He looked at her, eyes wide.

"I do wish I were . . . very important."

"There's nuttin' left. No berts or nuttin'."

"So I hear. Listen, Tommy, I have an idea. Why don't you stow me away, hmmm?"

Tommy laughed in short ragged chunks, showing his pointed, separated teeth. "Sure, sure. That's a hot one."

"I mean it." She moved closer to him.

He backed against the wall. "You ain't serious?"

"I am. I haven't got any money though."

"Huh?"

"Money for you. But money isn't everything, is it,

Tommy?" She reached forward, touching the fly of his pants.

His brown eyes bulged and a clammy fear slapped at the back of his neck. "I can't," he squeaked.

"Of course you can." She pushed her hand against his trousers. "You know all the places to hide."

"I'll lose my job."

"I'll never tell." She could see he was afraid and unconvinced. She began to feel desperate; her smile faded; she withdrew her hand. Tears gushed.

"Hey, lady."

"Please, please, I'll do anything," she cried.

"You ain't serious?" he said again.

Suddenly, she began to laugh, tears still streaking her face. The laughter was loud, out of control. From down the corridor, to Tommy's relief, came the Chief Stewardess, Elsie David. Starr, still laughing and crying, saw the woman's approach from the corner of her eye.

"Just kidding, just kidding," she mumbled to Tommy.

He broke into a huge smile. "I knew you wuz. I knew it alla time."

Elsie David was shocked by Starr's appearance. "What's wrong? What's happened here, Ryan?"

"Oh, well, she . . ."

"Please," said Starr, snuffling, "I turned my ankle and the boy was helping me."

"Would you like to see the doctor?" Mrs. David asked.

"No." She screamed as though wounded. Then she laughed.

"All right, all right," Mrs. David said gently.

"So sorry. Excuse me, please. I must get back to my party. Thank you, boy."

Starr hurried away, limping slightly, still laughing.

Elsie David shook her head. The eighteenth amendment was ruining the youth of the country and she hoped that the damn thing would soon be revoked.

At the sound of the first gong warning visitors to go ashore, Starr slipped into the ladies lounge on B Deck. She went into a stall, sat down, put her feet up against the inside of the door and waited.

Starr felt a long time had passed since the boat had begun to move. She'd finished the gin in her flask and was dying for a cigarette. She had no idea what would happen to her when she was discovered. Certainly they wouldn't incarcerate her. Perhaps, depending on who was the Captain, she could persuade him to let her have full run of the ship, promising to pay passage later, or promising something else. The only important thing was that she was sailing with Jameson-Carr and now she could make herself clear to him.

Jameson-Carr could not believe his eyes when he opened his cabin door. He didn't bother to ask any questions but immediately reported to the Captain that she was still on board.

The *Franconia* was just beyond the harbor. Starr had completely misjudged. Now, each arm held by a crew member, she waited for the tug that was coming to take her back. She felt sick, drunk, humiliated. Death was the only way out. The only state she desired. Suddenly, she began to thrash about, trying to free herself, planning to jump. The men held tight.

"No," she wailed. "No, let me go. Kill me. Throw me overboard." She sobbed uncontrollably, screamed, shouted and let her knees buckle, body slumping, when she saw the figure of Dr. George Jameson-Carr standing on deck with the Captain, watching.

When the tug arrived she was lowered into it by rope ladder, one crew member holding her around the waist as they climbed down. Still she struggled, almost knocking them both over as she screamed, "My God! Don't put me off! Throw me overboard! But for God's sake, don't put me off!" Her words jammed together, becoming sounds, ugly, mournful, that drifted back to the gallery of laughing onlookers above.

Waiting on Pier 56 were Customs Inspector Hyman and Patrolman Klein.

"Now, now," said Klein, walking her down the dock, "it's not as bad as all that. Ya just made a mistake."

Starr continued to cry, hearing nothing that was said. At Fourteenth Street, Hyman hailed a taxi and both men gently helped her in.

"Where to?" the cabby asked.

"Twelve St. Luke's Place," she said, through snuffles and hiccups.

Klein closed the door and the taxi took off.

"No, no, don't take me there," Starr said, almost immediately. "Take me to number 5 Fifth Avenue." She didn't know why she said it. She knew no one at that address. But she certainly didn't want to go home. Then, as they neared Fifth Avenue, she leaned forward again. "No. I don't want to go there. I want to go back."

"Back?" Martin Gelb looked at his disheveled passenger.

"Back to the pier."

"Don't ya think ya oughta go home, lady?"

"I said, back to the pier." A royal command.

Gelb shrugged and turned his cab around.

When they got back the pier was deserted.

"There's no one here," she said, like a child who's missed the party. "When does the next boat leave for Europe?"

"In about a week."

She sat for a moment, dejected, her hat askew, the white silk of her collar dirty and rumpled. "Take me to St. Luke's. Twelve."

Gelb helped her up the steep stoop. She couldn't find her key and he searched her bag, removing the empty flask, until he found it. He rang the bell, hoping someone would come down to help the drunken girl. But obviously, no one was home. He could have left her inside the door—he'd gone far beyond the call of duty already—but he felt sorry for her. She looked so sad, so broken. Slowly, they climbed the narrow stairs, passing at each landing the indented coffin corners. At the third floor he took the second key and unlocked the door. She stepped inside and turned toward him.

"Thank you. You're very kind."

"It's okay." He wanted to ask her for the fare but he felt she didn't have it and he didn't wish to humiliate her further. It was all right. He'd take it out of his own pocket.

"Would you like to come in?" Her mouth fell into a strange smile.

Gelb was shocked. Could he be reading her look correctly?

"You'd better go to bed," he said.

The smile slipped closer to a leer. "Yes. Want to come in?"

"Girlie, I'm old enough to be your father."

"I know," she said, smiling fully now.

Gelb shook his head, turned and went back down the stairs. Above him the door slammed violently and he felt the floor quiver beneath him.

Within moments of slamming the door, Starr was face down on her bed, out. Peter nuzzled her hair and purred.

May 30th to June 4th, 1931
New York, New York

When Starr awoke the morning after the *Franconia* incident something inside her was different. It was nothing she could have defined, put a label on, but something had happened. Pressed for an explanation, a description of what was different, she might have said that her inner center, always out of focus, was now flat.

Taking her own life was certainly not a new idea to Starr. She had, of course, even tried it. Now, however, without really thinking the words *I am going to kill myself,* she knew that was exactly what she was going to do. She wasn't sure when or how but she knew it would be fairly soon. Knowing this, she experienced a kind of relief, a sigh.

*   *   *

Saturday, May 30th

For once her hangover was not impossible. She'd slept almost twelve hours. Still, she felt slightly shaky, creepy, guilty. Sleep never eradicated those feelings.

Around ten in the morning she walked to Washington Square South and rang the bell of Rupert Sayers's studio. He was in and welcomed her. She needed money. Could she pose for him? He told her to come back Monday morning. He would pay her a dollar an hour. She thanked him and left.

At Ninth Street and Fifth Avenue she caught a bus uptown. Starr liked riding buses when she wasn't going anywhere in particular. She found them soothing. During the ride, thinking of nothing, she stared out the window and tried to count all the men she saw with mustaches.

She got off at Fifty-seventh Street and walked to the Hotel Plaza. In the lobby she looked around as though waiting for someone. Then, suddenly, she wondered what she was doing there. Why had she come? She thought about having lunch but realized she wasn't hungry and, even if she were, she hadn't enough money. That thought made her angry. She raised her chin higher as she walked over to a writing desk and sat down. She dated the upper right-hand corner of a piece of hotel stationery and began, without any salutation.

> I am going (definitely now—I've been thinking of it for a long time) to end my worthless, disorderly bore of an existence—before I ruin anyone else's life as well. I certainly have made a sordid, futureless mess of it all. I am dead, dead sick of it. It is no one's fault but my own. I hate everything so—life is horrible. Being a sane person, you may not understand. I take dope to forget and drink to try and like people, but it is of no use. I am mad and insane over you. I hold my breath to try and stand it—take allonal in the hope of waking happier, but that homesick feeling never leaves me. I have, strangely enough, more of a feeling of peace, or whatever you call it, now that I know it will soon be over. The half hour before I die will, I imagine, be quite blissful.

> You promised to come and see me. I realize absolutely that it will be the one and only time. There is no earthly reason why you should come. If you do it will be what I call an act of marvelous generosity and kindness. What I did yesterday was very horrible, although I don't see how you could lose your job, as it must have been clearly seen what a nuisance you thought me.

If I don't see you again—good-by. Sorry to
so lose all sense of humor, but I am suffering so
that all I want is to have it over with. It's become such a hell as I couldn't have imagined.

If you come to see me when you are in this
time you will be a sport—you are assured by this
letter of no more bother from me.

My dear—
STARR

She read the letter over, ignoring its inconsistencies
and contradictions. Did it matter that it had been years
ago when Jameson-Carr promised to come and see her?
He wouldn't be back for more than a month. Never mind.
It didn't make any difference. She looked at the words, "I
am going to end my worthless, disorderly bore of an existence . . ." and realized that now she'd committed the
thought to paper, the action must come—and soon. This
letter had, in her mind, begun a cycle which must come to
its natural conclusion. Death. It didn't occur to her to
crumple the paper, tear it into tiny pieces, toss it away,
finish the cycle now before it was really begun. No. One
thing must follow the other in a natural order, whatever
that might be. All would unfold as it should.

She carefully placed the letter in an envelope, addressing it to Jameson-Carr care of Cunard in Liverpool.
Placing on it one of the stamps she always carried, she
rose and walked through the lobby to the brass mail slot
where she dropped it in. The beginning.

At two o'clock she returned home, telling her mother
she'd been to the movies. *City Lights* at the Plaza. It was
quite good and Chaplin was terrific. She went to her
cubicle-room, lay on her bed, her mind floating, no tangi-
ble thoughts. Petting Peter, she saw his fur was separating, no longer silky, and wondered when he would die. He
was seventeen years old. Which of them would die first?
Definitely her. She slept on and off, ate dinner with her
family, joined in their conversation hardly at all.

That night she didn't go out. Stanley, in the living
room, cleaned a pair of gloves with ether. Walking
through the room Starr stopped, sniffed.

"Oh," she said, "I love that."

Stanley looked at her, questioning.

She shook her head and went into her room. There was a night with some man. She couldn't remember his name and brought out her diary, found the page. The initials were D. B. Donald Brautigan, she remembered. Brautigan bought a bottle of ether for her and they'd had quite a night. She read the short entry in her Mem Book.

I am a very weary woman from that stuff. Lord, how I loathe it. Lord, how I love it.

She smiled, closed the book, put it away. She would never sniff ether again. The thought made her sad, then happy. She changed into her nightgown and got into bed, feeling peaceful, quiet. And for the first time she could remember she went immediately to sleep.

* * *

Sunday, May 31st

At ten in the morning Starr left the house. She walked around the Village, watching people going to and from church. What would it be like to believe in God? That made her feel sad and she went into the park, sat for awhile, watched the squirrels and birds and tried to forget about believing or not believing. This was no time to start wondering if there were a God.

Later she went uptown to the Roxy. *Daddy Long Legs*. It was about the romance of an older man and a young girl. She thought of Andrew and she wept throughout. The stage show was a modern Cinderella story, quite spectacular and she liked it.

Back home by three in the afternoon, she spent several hours in her room reading Robert Frost.

That evening she put on a pair of light blue silk lounging pajamas and sat in the living room with her family, chatting and laughing. Stanley and Helen were quite pleased. Starr had refused a cocktail before dinner and this was the second night in a row she'd been at home. It was a radical change and one they liked. Tucker wondered when the ax would fall!

Starr went to bed early, falling, once again, right to sleep.

*   *   *

She arrived at Sayers's studio at ten-fifteen, posing for two hours, making two dollars.

At one o'clock she went home for lunch, left again about three and took a ride uptown on the top of the Fifth Avenue bus. It was a warm, beautiful day and she loved the feeling of looking down at the people in the streets.

By six o'clock she was home again, refused a drink, had dinner with Stanley and Helen and again went to bed early.

*   *   *

Awakening, she immediately felt the deep depression. She lay on her back staring at the ceiling, the walls of her stomach feeling paper thin, her skin aching, even the slightest movement paining her. The touch of the sheet against her skin was almost unbearable. She couldn't get up. She wondered if she would ever get up again. If only she could end it now. Right this moment. But there was no point trying in the house. She would be discovered, saved.

She thought about the different ways it might be accomplished. Could one overdose on ether? Probably not a sure thing. Out. Jumping from a window. Suppose all she did was break her back, paralyzing herself for the rest of her life? She saw Stanley feeding her, emptying her slops jar. Too hideous. A dive from a bridge might not work either. There was always someone lurking about, spotting the potential jumper, calling for help. There'd be a scene, policemen, photographers, newspapermen. No. But the thought of water was appealing. If only she weren't such a good swimmer. Would her instinct, at the last moment, be to swim? Risky. And pills were unreliable. Allonal, Veronal. How many did it really take? She must find the perfect way. Realizing today was not the day, her depression deepened, engulfed her, pushed her body over onto her stomach. She lay inert.

Later, she found herself thinking of gin. It made her feel somewhat better. What was the point of being on the wagon? She couldn't even remember having decided to do it, or why. Well, whatever the reason, whenever conceived, it had been a bloody stupid idea!

Forcing herself to get up, wash and dress, she left the house at eleven-thirty. When she found herself at Fourteenth and Fifth she decided to go to Edwin Megargee's studio at Union Square.

Primarily a painter of dogs, Megargee was finishing a portrait of two Yorkshire terriers, but didn't mind being interrupted. He put down his brush, offering Starr a chair and a drink. She took both. After her second drink she told Ed what had happened on the *Franconia*. She was afraid the spectacle she'd made of herself might cause Jameson-Carr to lose his job because of her. If that happened he'd never want to see her again. Ed suggested she write him a formal letter, stating he'd had nothing to do with her behavior on the ship. If necessary, he could show it to his superiors. Starr thought it a great idea and asked for a third drink.

She told him she was going abroad in a week. He agreed that she needed a vacation.

Halfway through her fifth gin, she began to cry. "I'm no good," she said. "I can't keep sober."

Ed held her, patted her hair, told her she was fine. What was the point of anyone keeping sober in such a hellish world? He suggested she nap on the couch while he finished his painting and then they'd go out somewhere.

An hour later she woke up. Her mouth felt chalky, her head ached. Megargee wasn't there but she heard sounds coming from the bathroom. Not feeling like talking, Starr slipped on her pumps and quietly left the studio. She had a hangover and needed something to smooth herself out. Not wanting to go to a speakeasy, she went home.

No one was there. She poured herself a large gin, got out some Pennsylvania Hotel stationery she'd lifted

months ago and sat down to compose her letter to
Jameson-Carr.

*　　　*　　　*

June 2, 1931

Dr. Jameson-Carr
c/o Cunard Co.
Liverpool, England

DEAR DR. JAMESON-CARR:
　I want to apologize and to tell you how
deeply I regret my conduct on the *Franconia*
last Friday. I had come down hoping to renew
our acquaintance, but I fear I only made a fool
of myself and that it was very disagreeable for
you. I had brought some drinks on the boat with
me and drank them too fast. I become intensely
irrational when I drink and I want you to know
how deeply sorry I am for the embarrassment I
must have caused you.

Very sincerely,
STARR FAITHFULL

She folded the letter into the envelope and put it beneath the handkerchiefs in her top drawer. The rest of the
afternoon she slept.

After dinner with the family she took the letter out to
mail, came back, and sat on the edge of her bed, staring.

At ten o'clock, not answering her mother's questions
as to where she was going, she left the apartment.

A number of men bought her drinks at Barney's but
she saw no one she knew. The gin didn't work the way she
wished it would. At two-thirty she left alone, promising
the man next to her that she'd see him the next night.
Saying no had never been her strong suit but she was
weary, very down. All she wanted was to sleep.

At home she took three Allonal and was asleep by
three-thirty.

*　　　*　　　*

Wednesday, June 3rd

Starr spent the day in bed. She ate nothing, drank nothing. Most of the day she tried to think of the perfect way to end her life. Late in the afternoon she remembered Megargee had told her Bennett Cerf was giving a cocktail party for Miriam Hopkins. The actress was going back to Hollywood after playing on Broadway in *Lysistrata*. Ed said if Starr used his name she'd be able to get in. She dressed and left the house.

Getting off the bus at Fifty-seventh and Fifth she remembered that the party was the next day. She wanted to cry. Instead, she walked to a speakeasy she knew on Fifty-sixth.

Two men bought her drinks. At eight-thirty she told them she had to go home. Her parents were expecting her for dinner but she'd sneak away about eleven and they would all have a wonderful time. She even winked.

Arriving home, quite drunk, she told Stanley and Helen she'd gone to a party for Mariam Hopkins with two men, Bruce Winston and Jack Greenaway, whom she'd met on board the *Franconia* last Friday. She'd had a perfectly wonderful time and was seeing them both again the next day.

She went to bed, passing out.

      ✿   ✿   ✿

Thursday, June 4th

Starr still didn't know how she would kill herself but she now knew when. It would be Friday, the 5th. Very late, perhaps midnight, so that her last day and evening would be full. Knowing this made her feel good. It seemed, finally, that her life had a purpose. Her body felt light, almost weightless. She wondered if death would be anything like sex. Would there be a trembling at the end, a spasm like a climax? Would she shudder, eyes closed? She forgot she'd almost died once and there had been nothing.

So what should she do on her second-to-last day on this bloody, rotten earth? She dressed carefully, cognizant of every motion. About noon she left the house, walking slowly past Jimmy Walker's, crossed Seventh Avenue and went up to Bleecker, looking into the pushcarts as she passed them. The vendors smiled, tipped their worn felt hats, offered their wares. She bought nothing.

It was another beautiful day, warm, bright, clear. At one she entered Lord & Taylor's, having no idea why she was there. She didn't plan to buy anything. But perhaps it would be fun to buy a dress to be buried in. She could charge it. Then she remembered she'd told Stanley she wanted to be cremated. It didn't seem likely they dressed you up before burning you!

She went to the second floor. Perhaps she should look up her landlady, Alice Smith. But what would she say to her? What would be the point? She walked around the store, ending up in the writing room, seating herself at a small desk. On a Lord & Taylor letterhead she began to write.

HELLO, BILL, OLD THING:

It's all up with me now. This is something I am going to put through. The only thing that bothers me about it—the only thing I dread—is being outwitted and prevented from doing this, which is the only possible thing for me to do. If one wants to get away with murder one has to jolly well keep one's wits about one. It's the same way with suicide. If I don't watch out I will wake up in a psychopathic ward, but I intend to watch out and accomplish my end this time. No ether, allonal, or window jumping. I don't want to be maimed. I want oblivion. If there is an after life it would be a dirty trick—but I am sure fifty million priests are wrong. That is one of those things one knows.

Nothing makes any difference now. I love to eat and can have one delicious meal with no worry over gaining. I adore music and am going to hear some good music. I believe I love music more than anything. I am going to drink slowly, keeping aware every second. Also I am going to enjoy my last cigarettes. I won't worry because men flirt with me in the streets—I shall encourage them—I don't care who they are. I wish I got more pleasure out of sleeping with men but I'm afraid I've always been a rotten "sleeper"; it's the preliminaries that count with me. It doesn't matter, though.

It's a great life when one has twenty-four hours to live. I can be rude to people. I can tell them they are too fat or that I don't like their clothes, and I don't have to dread being a lonely old woman, or poverty, obscurity, or boredom. I don't have to dread living on without ever seeing you, or hearing rumors such as "the women all fall for him" and "he entertains charmingly." Why in hell shouldn't you! But it's more than I can cope with—this feeling I have for you. I have tried to pose as clever and intellectual, thereby to attract you, but it was not successful, and I couldn't go on writing those long, studied letters. I don't have to worry, because there are no words in which to describe this feeling I have for you.

The words love, adore, worship have become meaningless. There is nothing I can do but what I am going to do. I shall never see you again. That is extraordinary. Although I can't comprehend it any more than I can comprehend the words "always" or "time." They produce merciful numbness.

STARR

Licking the edge of the envelope, she wondered if he would feel sorry when she was dead. It sounded as though she was going to kill herself because of him but even though that was only a small part of it, she saw no reason to correct the impression.

When she left Lord & Taylor's she headed down Fifth, no destination in mind, the envelope addressed to Jameson-Carr clutched in her left hand. On the street, as usual, men did flirt with her. Ordinarily, unless drunk, she looked away. Today she smiled back but kept walking. Soon she found herself at Grand Central Station. She would get on a train and ride out of her life! That made no sense. In the station she posted the letter.

At Thirty-seventh and Second Avenue she went into a speakeasy. It was three o'clock. By seven when she arrived home she was dead drunk. She staggered, knocking against the walls, telling her mother that she'd been with Robert Decker, whom she'd bumped into at the Savoy Plaza. That night she was meeting him at nine-thirty to go to a party. Both Helen and Tucker said she was too drunk to go anywhere. She grabbed her mother's arm, pinching it, leaving a bruise. She told Tucker to shut up. Stanley was out.

Trying to eat her dinner, she kept dropping her fork. Tucker fed her. Starr allowed this briefly, then batted Tucker's hand away, sending mashed potatoes flying against the wall. Tucker threw water at Starr and ducked when Starr tried to hit her. She also kept setting back the clock, trying to dissuade Starr from going out.

Starr, however, was determined. Somehow she changed her clothes, pushed her mother and sister out of her path and left the house at nine-fifteen saying she was meeting Decker at "the club." She didn't say which one.

Out on the street she managed to pull herself together a bit. She took long deep breaths, walking slowly, heading in the direction of Barney's.

She never got there. At Seventh Avenue and Bleecker two men in a Buick pulled up beside her. Did she want a ride? Yes. How about a ride in the country? She agreed. One man let her sip from his flask.

Gradually, the smells and sounds of the city vanished. Now there were trees and country air. The car pulled off the big road onto a smaller one. It was bumpy and she laughed. The men laughed, too.

The car stopped. The men opened the doors. One man helped her out. When she asked where they were going, no one answered. The other man carried a blanket. When she asked what the blanket was for, no one answered.

They walked away from the car toward a clump of black trees, the men on each side of her, holding her arms, guiding her. One man spread the blanket, told her to lie down. She laughed and said she wasn't tired. The men laughed, then pulled her down with them. They were all on the blanket together. She felt her panties being removed and tried to tell them not to but no words came out.

The form of one appeared over her and she quickly

crossed her legs. He said something. He sounded angry. She hoped he wouldn't hit her. She said she'd suck him if he wanted. He knelt over her, legs straddling her face. The other man placed his penis in her hand. She sucked one, pulled on the other and wondered where she was and who these men were.

When both were satisfied they buttoned up, lifted her from the blanket, straightened out her clothes, folded the blanket and walked back to the car.

They dropped her where they found her, Seventh and Bleecker. It was ten after midnight. She hated the taste in her mouth and wanted a drink. At Barney's she had two, then went home.

Helen, waiting up, was relieved to see that her daughter seemed less drunk than when she'd left the house. Starr told her mother she'd had a wonderful evening. Decker had taken her to a speakeasy in Times Square where she bumped into Winston and Greenaway, and they took her for a ride in the country via the Fordham Road. She said it was jolly good to get out of the city even for an hour or two and smell some nice clean air. Then she went to her room.

When she undressed she realized her underpants were missing. They'd been left behind in the woods. Another time this might have depressed her. Now she only laughed. None of it mattered anymore. Not in the grander scheme of things.

Starr never drank and had never been in a speakeasy. She is not the type to kill herself.
—From a statement by Stanley Faithfull,
June 1931

June 6, 1931
New York, New York

It took a number of trips up and down Fifth Avenue before she allowed herself to think. How could she have been so fooled by the Lefflands?

Depression enveloped her as though she were an embryo in a sack. How stupid, how bloody stupid, she'd been. When would she learn how rotten people were?

What the hell would it take? She vowed to trust absolutely no one ever again. Suddenly hungry, she got off the bus at Forty-seventh Street and walked to a small Italian restaurant where she ordered spaghetti with red clam sauce.

From now on she would make no plans. What was the point? No matter what she decided, what she planned, things just happened to her anyway. It was obvious she had no control over her life, her destiny. Whatever happened would happen. Who the bloody hell cared?

Riding down Fifth Avenue again, she wondered if Stanley and Helen were worried about her. She could send a telegram. Did she mind if they worried? She decided she didn't.

At the end of the line she got off and entered Washington Square Park. She had no idea what would happen next and she didn't care. It was easy when you felt nothing.

Twenty-one

August 6, 1977
Orange, New Jersey

If he'd been able to move he would have sat straight up. Cutting through his sleep like a machete were the words in big black print: HUNT 2 MYSTERY MEN IN STARR DEATH.

He could feel the sweat on his face and body. After all this time. So powerful. It was dark in his room except for the small night light. He wished the nurse would check on him, wipe his face.

He lay listening to his heart beating quickly. Remembered. The mystery men turned out to be no one. Two guys named Bruce and Jack. They never turned up. The point was they weren't hunting him but he didn't know that when he first read the headline.

Right before the story faded from the papers, he decided he'd done her a favor. On the last day of June he read: STARR'S SUICIDE NOTES FOUND GENUINE. She'd wanted to die. It said so in the letters the papers printed. There was nothing to fret over. He'd helped her.

It never worked. Not even now.

June 6, 1931
Newark, New Jersey
New York, New York

Orlando dreamed of Connie again. She begged him to take her somewhere. He refused. Then, suddenly, he was in the funeral parlor, staring down at her in her coffin. Her eyes opened and she looked at him. She raised her hand, pointing a finger in his direction. He woke up. Always, after these dreams, which came about once a month, he was in a terrible mood even though he had no memory of them.

It was a beautiful day, unusually warm for early June. Fran suggested they take a picnic lunch and drive to Bear Mountain. Orlando rejected the idea.

"What's wrong?" Fran asked. "Are you in one of your depressions?"

He shrugged.

That meant yes. He never talked to Fran about them so she had no idea what they were from or how to help him. He just said he had depressions. They seemed to come more often since he'd quit the band. She wished he would start writing. He said he needed inspiration.

He sat in his chair, Deirdre on his lap, staring at nothing in particular, a darkness around his eyes. He looked to Fran as though there were, literally, a terrible black cloud hanging over him. She could almost see it.

"Would you like to go to a movie this afternoon? *Svengali* is at the Hawthorne."

He shook his head.

"You love Marian Marsh."

"I don't love anybody."

She knew he didn't mean her.

"What would you like to do?"

"Nothing."

"You can't just sit there all day."

"Why not?"

"Because." It was the only reply she had.

He didn't bother to look at her.

"It's such a nice day. Can't we do something?"

"You do something if you want to."

"I want to do it with you."

"Well, I don't."

"Is it your job?" Recently he'd gone to work for Park & Tilford in the personnel department. Maybe the change of jobs had something to do with his more frequent depressions. "Don't you like your job?"

He shrugged.

"You're lucky to have a job, you know."

"Yes, I know. I know."

"Can't you tell me what's bothering you?"

"Nothing. Jesus, can't I just sit here without being nagged?"

"I'm not nagging. I just want to help."

"Well, you're not. Leave me alone."

She went into the kitchen and did the breakfast dishes. When she was finished she came back into the living room.

"Is it me? Did I do anything?" She couldn't help herself.

"No."

How could someone suddenly get this way? When she felt bad about things, she always knew what it was and either she did something about it or put it out of her mind. She knew, from reading an article in *The Ladies' Home Journal,* that he'd feel one hundred per cent better if he told her. "You'll feel better if you talk about it."

"Talk about what?"

"What's bothering you."

"Nothing is bothering me except you. Will you leave me alone?"

"I want to help," she said again.

"Then shut the hell up."

"Don't talk to me like that, Orr."

"Oh, God." He jumped up and slammed out of the house.

*   *   *

He didn't want to be out in the sun. The day before had been very hot. He hoped the temperature wouldn't go that high again. His Nash was parked a block from the house. Why couldn't Fran understand he really didn't know what was wrong? Could she possibly believe he enjoyed feeling this way?

He got in the car, not knowing where to go. After a few moments, he decided to visit his mother.

At the house on Van Ness Place he sat across from her on the screened-in portion of the porch. She was peeling carrots. These days she did most of the cooking as Maria wasn't very good at it.

"Chè torto?"

"Niente."

"Bugiardo."

"I'm not lying."

"Chè Fran?"

"Home."

"You fight?"

He shrugged.

"Oh, Orlando." She did not like her children to fight with their mates. "Perchè?"

"She nags me."

Antonia knew Fran wasn't the nagging type. "She don't."

"Were you there, Mama?"

"I know her."

"And I don't?" He wanted sympathy, not an argument.

"What she nag you about?"

"I don't know. Everything."

"You do something bad?"

"No, of course not."

"Not nice to fight. Go home. Not good to leave her alone all day."

"Mama . . . I . . . my God."

"Go home to her."

He wished he could curl up on his mother's lap, head against her heavy bosom. But that was over, would never be again. Where had it gone? Time. Way back, he remembered his mother taking his side. Now she sided against him with this stranger. His wife.

"You always think I'm in the wrong."

"Frances good woman."

"I know that. Don't you think I'm a good man?"

"Si, si."

"Well?"

"Men the cold ones, Orlando."

"What do you mean?" Did she mean his father?

"Niente. Go. Make up. Nice." She waved her hand as though she were brushing something away.

He knew from experience he would get no more from her. He could stay as long as he wanted but she would talk of other things, giving him no solace. He kissed her goodbye.

"Be good."

At the corner of Clinton Avenue he turned right. Away from home, driving down the avenue. Later, approaching the Holland Tunnel, he pulled off to the side. What in hell was he doing? He worked in the city every day of the week. It held no appeal for him. It was hardly an escape. But here he was heading for the yawning mouth of the new tunnel. There was still time to turn back. Back where? If he went home, it would just start all over. Questions he couldn't answer, suggestions he couldn't accept. But New York? Well, why the hell not? It was a Saturday, a holiday. He could do whatever he damn well pleased. He could go to a movie, a speak, maybe even pick up a girl! A small stab of guilt stung him. He hated himself for feeling it—hated Fran for making him feel it. So he couldn't be like his father. So what? He never had been, never would be, not in any area. Why should he try in that one. If a girl came his way, crossed his path, he'd damn well let nature take its course! Pulling the car back into traffic, heading for the tunnel, he already felt slightly less depressed.

He ate lunch in a small Italian restaurant, walking afterwards to the Paramount in Times Square where he bought a ticket, feeling only a slight twinge when he thought how much Fran would enjoy this. *Vice Squad* with Paul Lukas and Kay Francis. And, on stage, Gilda Gray in *Shakin' the Blues* and Rudy Vallee and The Big Show. Vallee was a particular favorite of Fran's. Orlando thought he was a sap but was anxious to see Gilda Gray. The movie was only so-so and, sitting so high up, he couldn't catch Gilda's full flavor. He left the theater feeling disappointed, cheated, still depressed.

Seated again in his car he toyed with the idea of going home, rejected it and decided to make a tour of

Greenwich Village, something he'd never done. Lots of writers lived there. Maybe he'd soak up some atmosphere, get some inspiration. Perhaps even meet a writer and they could talk. So what if he hadn't written a word since college? There was, after all, such a thing as writer's block. Any writer would understand that.

He parked the car on Grove Street, looking up at the Federal frame house and noting that the number was 17, just in case he got lost. He walked east on Grove to Bleecker, turning right there, hearing the peddlers hawking vegetables, fish, meats, clothes, everything imaginable.

At a small street called Jones he made a left. The excitement of not knowing where he was, or where he was going, was exhilarating, an unusual feeling for him. Although it was quite warm he kept on his jacket, hating the look of men in shirtsleeves. But the heat didn't bother him as he walked the strange, twisting streets.

Eventually, he came to the corner of MacDougal and Waverly Place, the edge of Washington Square Park. The arch, a replica of the Arc de Triomphe, showed through the trees. Entering the park he sat on a bench, lit a cigarette and watched the people strolling by.

"Do you have a light?" A young woman sat down next to him.

She was startlingly beautiful. Orlando couldn't help gawking a bit.

"I say, old chap, did you hear?"

He smiled, tipped his straw hat, and reached for his matches. "Are you English?" he asked, lighting her cigarette.

There was a pause as she blew out the match with a puff of smoke. "I've spent a great deal of time there. Ever been?"

"No. Not yet."

"It's heaven there. It's made me just hate America."

He was intrigued. "What's so special about England?"

"Everything." She smiled, long lashes flickering. "Do you live around here?"

"No." He wished he did. Wished he'd lied.

"No one ever does. I do. I'm a native New Yorker. Where are you from?"

"New Jersey."

"Ahhh."

He didn't know what that meant, didn't dare ask. She really was lovely. Perhaps a little tired looking, small smudges under her eyes, but very, very lovely.

"What do you do with your life?"

"I'm a musician." He didn't hesitate a moment. "I play in a band. We're off tonight."

"And what instrument do you play?"

"Banjo."

"Nice. Are you married?"

"No." A slight twinge. Practically unnoticeable.

"I fancy you wouldn't tell me if you were." Her brown eyes looked directly into his.

"I have no reason to lie." Actually, he didn't. This was an isolated experience and he felt sure this girl wouldn't care if he was married or not. "And you?" he asked, gaining confidence. "Do you do anything besides looking lovely?"

"I'm a model. An artist's model."

"Do you pose in the nude?" Risky, but he was almost sure of the answer.

"Sometimes. Say, by any chance do you have a car?"

"Yes, I do."

"Here in the city?"

"Yes."

"Oh, that's bloody wonderful." She cocked her head down and to one side. "At least I hope it is. What I mean is, I'd like to go somewhere."

"Where?"

"Anywhere."

He'd hoped she might show him the Village. "I was sort of planning an evening here."

"Oh." She ground her cigarette beneath her shoe and picked up her bag as though she were going to leave.

He didn't want to lose her. "I could change my plans."

"Good. Where's your car?"

"Over on Grove." He hoped he sounded as though he knew the Village intimately.

"Oh."

"What's the matter?"

"I'd rather not go over to that part of town."

"You don't have to. I'll get the car." He was about to have a date with this gorgeous girl!

"Would you?" She touched his arm lightly, smiled, face lighting up. "Guy Lombardo is at the Hollywood Gardens on Pelham Parkway. We could have a lovely shore dinner. That is, if you want to buy me dinner?"

Fortunately, he'd left the house with quite a bit of money. "Of course. I'd be delighted."

They both stood up.

"Oh," she said, "you're rather short."

If only his shoulders weren't so broad, girls would know what to expect. This one was slightly taller than he.

"It doesn't matter," she said quickly. "It's so awkward trying to dance with a tall man."

They walked back toward MacDougal and Waverly.

"I'll wait right inside the park for you. What kind of car do you have?"

"A yellow Nash. You'll be here when I get back?"

"Of course. I think we can have a bloody good time."

He tipped his hat, started out of the park, then called back to her. "By the way, what's your name?"

"Rose Damion," she said.

"See you soon, Rose."

Giving the operator his number, he realized Rose hadn't bothered to ask him *his* name. Fran picked it up on the first ring.

"Well, where are you?"

"It doesn't matter where I am. I just didn't want you to worry."

"Well I *am* worried."

"No need. I'm fine. I just need some time."

"It's almost five. Will you be home for dinner?"

"I . . . no . . . I don't think so. I need some time alone."

Silence.

"Fran? Fran?"

"Yes."

He thought perhaps she was crying but didn't want to ask. "I know you'll understand. Won't you, honey?"

"Sure. Yes. Orr? When . . . when do you think you'll be home?"

"I don't know. Later."

"Orr? Are you alone?"

"Sure I'm alone. Didn't I just tell you I needed some time alone?" He was irritated.

"I just wondered. Well . . ."

"I love you, Fran. Please understand." He had to get off.

"I do understand. I love you, Orr."

"See you later."

"Orr?"

"Yes?"

"What should I tell your mother?"

"My mother?"

"We're expected for dinner . . . as usual."

"Oh, Christ." He'd completely forgotten. For an instant he thought of junking his plans with Rose and going home. "Tell her . . . I don't know . . . you'll think of something."

"Should I tell her the truth?"

What truth? "What do you mean?"

"That you're off somewhere."

"Better not. Say a friend of ours got sick and we have to go there."

"She won't believe it."

"Say it anyway." He'd deal with his mother later. "I'm hanging up now." He had to get off before the operator revealed the distance by asking for more money. "See you later. Bye."

He didn't wait for her goodbye. Well, things were certainly in a mess but he'd straighten everything out the next day. He could handle Fran and his mother. Could he handle Rose Damion? She was odd, all right. And it had been awhile. He hoped he hadn't lost his touch.

Starting up the Nash, he pulled out into the street. Beginning right now he was putting everything out of his mind except Rose Damion. Come hell or high water he was going to have a wonderful time!

June 6, 1931
New York, New York
Long Beach, New York

By the time Orlando returned, Starr had decided she had no desire to listen to Guy Lombardo. She suggested

the Hotel Pierre instead. It was the highest dining room in
New York and she felt like looking out at the city. But
first they went for a drink to a speakeasy on 50th near
Eighth Avenue. Once there she discovered she had no desire to drink.

"Oh, come on, Rose, have a little something."

"I'm not in the mood right now." Why had she told
him her name was Rose? She hated it. Too late.

It made Orlando nervous that she wasn't drinking.
He'd have to be careful. Otherwise she'd get an edge on
him.

After two rounds, they headed to Sixty-first and
Fifth. In the Pierre dining room they sat by a window,
watching the lights of the city come to life in the growing
darkness. Across the room, Maurice and the Continentals
played softly.

"You're very quiet," Orlando said. He wished they
served liquor here.

"I'm a quiet girl," she said. "Shy really."

"That I don't believe." At the speakeasy she'd told
him all about her life. He felt sorry for her. Being an or-
phan must be tough. And getting through the Depression
on your own was even tougher. He had to admire her.
Would she be insulted if he offered her money later?

Starr looked at the man across from her. Terribly
good-looking, if you liked the type. Tucker would have
gone mad for him. But for Starr he was too sculptured.
The appeal of those straight smooth lines eluded her. And,
of course, he was too young. She did enjoy his dimples.
Too bad about his height.

"Would you like to dance?" The band had just begun
"Sweet Lorraine."

"All right."

Once on the dance floor he was sorry he'd asked.
With those damn pumps she was at least an inch taller.
After all these years with Fran he wasn't used to that.
When the number was over he guided her back to the
table.

"Are you hungry?" he asked.

"Unfortunately, I'm always hungry."

"Why unfortunately?"

"A girl has to watch her weight, you know."

"Not you."

"Oh, yes." She was flattered in spite of herself.

"Well, not tonight."

"Tonight. I'll have the steak and two vegetables. No potato."

He nodded, hailed the waiter.

After dinner, back in the car, he said, "Where to? Another speak?" He hoped she'd have a drink or two now.

"Would you mind taking a bit of a drive?"

"Love to."

"I just thought of a place I'd like to go. It's very elegant."

He calculated quickly what he had in his wallet and blessed the fact that he hadn't gotten to the bank yesterday. "Where is it?"

"Long Beach. The Hotel Nassau."

"Your wish is my command, Rose." He started the car.

What a chump, she thought.

When they pulled up to the Hotel Nassau it was totally dark. Clearly, it hadn't opened yet for the season. In fact, nothing was open. All the houses along the beach were still shuttered. In the car, Starr sulked.

"What a bloody bore." Now she felt like a drink. "You don't have any booze with you, do you?"

His flask was at home. "No, I'm sorry. Should we turn back?" He didn't really want to.

"Yes, I guess so. It's awfully nice here but suddenly I feel like getting pickled."

That was enough for him. His chances would be much better with this one if she were a little sloshed. He turned the key.

"No, wait a minute." She rummaged through her bag.

In the silence the image of his father pressed itself against the inside of his eyes. There was a plunging sensation in his stomach. Damn, he thought. He felt his sexual excitement waning.

"Here they are." She sounded almost merry.

She held a small vial in her hand but in the vague light from the moon, it was hard to tell what it was.

"What have you got there?"

"Magic," she said, unscrewing the bottle.

"What kind of magic?"

"Pill magic. The best there is."

He watched as she popped something into her mouth and swallowed.

"You can do that with nothing to drink?"

"You saw it."

He felt stupid.

"Here." She offered the bottle to him.

"What is it?"

"Veronal. It'll make you feel wonderful. Dreamy and all glidey. Take some. Two, if you've never had it before."

He thought of his one experience with marijuana. It had made him vomit after scaring the hell out of him. He didn't like things like that. Booze was one thing, drugs another. "No thanks."

"Oh, don't be a chump."

"I can't swallow pills without water."

"It's easy. You just make a lot of saliva in your mouth and swallow."

"I can't."

She shrugged. "Suit yourself." She made a swishing sound in her mouth and popped in some more pills. "Let's walk down to the beach."

"Okay." Would the pills make her more sexual? Could he rid himself of the picture of his father long enough to be able to perform?

Near the edge of the water Starr plunked herself down on the sand. "Do you still have your shoes on? My God."

He sat down next to her untying his shoes like a good little boy. Then he took off his socks, leaving his garters dangling against his legs, and tucked them into his shoes.

Starr lay back resting on her elbows. "Mmmm. Beautiful night."

It was. The moon was quite bright, the stars like bits of polished silver. The water, at low tide, was calm. Waves broke and fell softly. Orlando and Starr were quiet.

"Look." She broke the silence.

He followed the direction of her gaze as she rose, a bit unsteadily, and walked toward a small overturned rowboat.

"Let's go out in it," she said.

She couldn't be serious. "We don't know anything about it," he said approaching the boat.

Her laugh sounded crazy. "Oh, really? Like what? Its age and where it went to school and who its parents were?" Again, the manic laugh.

He wished he were home. Fran never made him feel like an ass. "I meant," he said primly, "that we don't know if it's seaworthy or not."

"Oh, who cares."

"I do. Do you want to drown?"

"Don't be such a scaredy-cat. I'm an excellent swimmer. How about you?"

"I'm a very good swimmer."

"So then les' take it out."

He noticed she was beginning to sound drunk. Maybe it was the pills she'd taken.

Together, they turned the boat over and found the oars underneath.

"You'll get wet," he said, "your dress and everything."

"I don't give a damn. Oh, God, I feel good."

They dragged the boat into the water and stood, watching to see if it leaked. So far so good. He'd taken off his trousers and jacket and the water was cool on his legs.

"It's watertight," she said. "Les' not take all night."

Orlando held it steady while she climbed in. Then he hoisted himself aboard. They faced each other.

"Where to?" Years ago at the Jersey shore he and Kay had taken moonlight rides like this.

"Just row," she commanded.

Her tone was irritating but he put the oars in their locks and did it, moving east, parallel to the shore.

"Row out," she said.

"I'll do it my way."

"You're a chump."

If she said one more nasty thing he'd take her immediately back to shore. But she didn't. She said nothing.

Orlando rowed, his shoulders, unused to this, aching slightly. Then he stopped, letting the boat drift.

"Is it leaking?" he asked, noticing her eyes fixed on the boat's bottom.

She did not answer.

"Rose?"

Nothing.

"Hey, Rose, are you deef?"

No response and he noticed now that her head bobbed peculiarly on her neck. "Rose! Answer me!" He wasn't kidding any longer.

Starr's shoulders sagged, bent, fell forward.

What? Just what, what what? He pulled in the oars and carefully made his way to the silent young woman. Kneeling in front of her he put his hand under her chin and lifted her head. There was a sharp intake of breath. His.

"My God," he said aloud.

Her eyelids were half open and, even in this light, he could tell that her skin was a ghostly white. He lifted her limp wrist, searching for her pulse. He couldn't find one. Her fingernails too had lost their color. He slapped her across the face and her head wobbled loosely. He pulled back her lids. Only the white showed.

"Rose? Rose, please answer."

There was no answer.

Putting his arms around her waist, he felt with his ear for her heartbeat. Here. There. He kept moving his ear around, trying for a sound. There was none.

"Jesus Christ."

He didn't know how or why but he knew she was dead. Whimpering, he backed away from her, falling on his behind, his legs splaying out in front, tipping the boat slightly.

He stayed there staring at the slumped figure before him. Then, all in a rush, one thought after another, cascading, knocking together, toppling, senseless. He tried to sort them out. He was off the coast of Long Beach in a stolen boat with a dead girl he really didn't know. How could he explain? What would Fran say? What would Papa say? Papa! Jesus God! But who knew where he was now? No one. Who knew that he knew Rose Damion? No one. The speakeasy had been dark. Only the waiter at the Hotel Pierre had spoken to them. Risky, perhaps. Still, no other choice. He could not be found with this dead body! How did she die? An overdose. Good God! Drug scandal as well. Lord no. Dead already. What's the difference?

Carefully, he got up from the bottom of the boat, back onto his knees. Centering himself as much as possible, he reached for her middle and pushed to the left.

With great effort he fed her body over the side of the boat.

When she disappeared into the water, he quickly found his place between the oars. Rowing. Watching the shoreline for the big structure of the hotel, his signpost showing where they'd gone into the water. Rowing. His body shook. Cold. Skin salty from spray. Rowing. The hotel loomed up like a long lost icon. Everything in him picked up speed.

When the boat was back in place, his trousers, jacket, socks and shoes back on his body, he felt slightly more whole. Still, his mind was like powder. He flung open the car door, turning the key before he'd closed the door. He drove faster than he'd ever driven in his life, his only purpose to put as much space, as quickly as possible, between him and the drowned body of Rose Damion. He had to fight the tears that were straining to flush down his cheeks. Later, he told himself. Later I will have time to cry. Racing along, he didn't notice her black purse on the seat or her black pumps on the floor.

As Starr hit the water she came to but it was several seconds before she actually knew she was in water, several more before she came up, breaking the surface. What water, why she was in it, were mysteries. Never had she felt so tired. So confused. Perhaps she was in the center of a dream. Her arms moved so slowly. She heard the sound of lapping water. A boat. A boat was coming to save her. It must be a dream. Whose dream? She tried to call. No sound came out. Her mouth opened but no voice came through it. The boat. It wasn't coming toward her. It was going away! Alarm seized her. The moon on the water showed her she was some distance from shore. Well, she was a bloody good swimmer. She'd swim.

It was not so easy. Though the current wasn't strong neither was Starr. She was exhausted. Sleepy. Then she remembered the Veronal. Must fight the Veronal. One arm, then the next. Kick. Kick. After making a tiny bit of headway, she lay on her back, floating. Within a second she went under. She'd fallen asleep. Floating was no good. Again she began to swim. It felt like she was swimming in taffy. Taffy from the boardwalk at Asbury Park. That was it. She was in Asbury, swimming through taffy, and it was in Andrew's dream.

Between the first and second times she went under, her mind came sharply into focus. I am drowning, she thought, and this is not the way I planned it. Then her mind blurred. Andrew Carr. Stanley-Daddy-Evelyn. Boston.

Coming up, after the second time, she thought she felt the bottom. Then she knew she did. It was shallow here. She wasn't going to drown, after all. Swim, fight, kick. Arms, legs, breath, must have breath. Eyes open. They would not. Tired, so tired. Help me. Please. Vomit. Help. Sleep. Help. No. Not now. Kick.

She died.

Twenty-two

August 20, 1977
Orange, New Jersey

Cathy and Toni looked down at him.

"You look good, Orr," Toni said.

He closed his eyes. They knew now he understood. A few days ago he'd made the mistake of reacting to the suggestion of a nursing home. A sound burst out of his throat, his eyes filled with tears. They all said it was a great breakthrough. He knew it was his downfall.

"Are you ready, Daddy?"

He opened his eyes. It was a stupid remark and Cathy knew it. He could see that.

"The hospital bed's installed and we've moved the television into your room. I'll take good care of you, Orr."

Two orderlies came into the room.

"We're ready to move him now."

"All right, fine."

Carefully, they lifted his frail body onto the ambulance stretcher and began to wheel.

His eyes followed the ceiling as they moved along.

"Did Cathy tell you about the last set of tests, Orr?"

Did she expect an answer? Tests. Tests. That's all they'd been doing, day after day. Who cared about tests? Wasn't it bad enough that he was still here? Going home?

They didn't let people die in hospitals anymore. He'd heard that on television. Now they sent you home to die. Some nonsense about being with family and in your own surroundings.

". . . so everything seems perfectly normal. I mean as much as could be expected," Toni went on. "But the wonderful thing, Orr, the wonderful thing is that the doctor said you could last for years. Isn't that wonderful?"

He closed his eyes. If only he could close his ears. Years? Could she be right? Was she just saying it to make him feel better? No. He knew what Toni said was true.

He was lifted up into the ambulance.

"I'll take the car home, Orr. Cathy will ride with you."

The sound of the slamming doors jarred loose an image and sent it scuttling through his brain. BODY OF MISSING GIRL FOUND AT LONG BEACH.

So it would continue. He would lie there, day after day, year after year, everything paralyzed but his eyes, his mind, his guts.

The engine turned over and the ambulance, siren going, began to move.

He lived.

ABOUT THE AUTHOR

SANDRA SCOPPETTONE, a novelist, screenwriter and playwright, has had her work produced on television and film, as well as on the stage. In 1972 she received a Eugene O'Neill Memorial Theatre Award and the following year was given a grant by the Ludwig Vogelstein Foundation. Her novel *Trying Hard to Hear You* was selected by the American Library Association as one of the best young adult books of 1974. She lives alternately in Greenport, New York and New York City with author Linda Crawford.

RELAX!
SIT DOWN
and Catch Up On Your Reading!

Bantam Book Catalog

Here's your up-to-the-minute listing of every book currently available from Bantam.

This easy-to-use catalog is divided into categories and contains over 1400 titles by your favorite authors.

So don't delay—take advantage of this special opportunity to increase your reading pleasure.

Just send us your name and address and 25¢ (to help defray postage and handling costs).